Deadly DARLING

ACACIA LOCKWOOD

12. Chapter Twelve — 123

13. Chapter Thirteen — 133

14. Chapter Fourteen — 141

15. Chapter Fifteen — 149

16. Chapter Sixteen — 157

17. Chapter Seventeen — 165

18. Chapter Eighteen — 175

19. Chapter Nineteen — 183

20. Chapter Twenty — 191

21. Chapter Twenty-One — 199

22. Chapter Twenty-Two — 207

23. Chapter Twenty-Three — 215

24. Chapter Twenty-Four — 225

25. Chapter Twenty-Five — 233

26. Chapter Twenty-Six — 241

27. Chapter Twenty-Seven — 249

28. Chapter Twenty-Eight — 257

29. Chapter Twenty-Nine — 267

30. Chapter Thirty — 277

31. Chapter Thirty-One — 285

Dedication   VII

Content & Trigger Warnings   IX

Prologue I   3

Prologue II   9

1. Chapter One   15

2. Chapter Two   25

3. Chapter Three   35

4. Chapter Four   45

5. Chapter Five   53

6. Chapter Six   63

7. Chapter Seven   73

8. Chapter Eight   85

9. Chapter Nine   95

10. Chapter Ten   103

11. Chapter Eleven   113

32. Chapter Thirty-Two   293

33. Chapter Thirty-Three   303

34. Chapter Thirty-Four   311

35. Chapter Thirty-Five   321

36. Chapter Thirty-Six   331

37. Chapter Thirty-Seven   339

38. Chapter Thirty-Eight   347

39. Chapter Thirty-Nine   357

40. Chapter Forty   365

41. Chapter Forty-One   375

42. Chapter Forty-Two   385

43. Chapter Forty-Three   395

44. Chapter Forty-Four   403

Epilogue I   415

Epilogue II   421

Epilogue III   427

Acknowledgements   435

About Acacia Lockwood   437

To Mankind's Bad Habit.

Content & Trigger Warnings

Within the Relationship:

Graphic consensual violence

Torture used as foreplay

Knife play

Blood play

Sadomasochistic sexual content

Threats/intimidation in a sexual context

Toxic codependency

Muzzling

Collaring

Restraint

Degradation

- Light pet play

- Obsession and possession

- Light dubious consent

- Blood used as lubricant

- Characters who kill without remorse

- Male Pregnancy

Outside the Relationship:

- Graphic violence

- Blood and gore

- Explicit on-page torture

- Child endangerment themes

- Discussions of sexual assault

- Brief flashbacks of sexual assault

- Past abuse

- Past incestual abuse

- Manipulation/toxic dynamics

- Characters who kill without remorse

- Mentions of human trafficking

- Past rape

- Threats of rape

- Transphobic language

- Brief forced feminization

- Degradation

- Humiliation

- Dehumanization

- Forced imprisonment

- Mind break

- Nonconsensual drugging

- Forced pregnancy

- Forced birth

- Medical abuse

- Threats of child murder

- Threats of forced abortion

Graphic Violence Contains:

- Dismemberment

- Disembowelment

- Mutilation

- Eye gouging

- Skull crushing

- Throat crushing

- Chest crushing

- Bone breaking

- Teeth ripping through flesh

- Violent fantasies

- Character death

The alpha filled the doorway with his broad shoulders, his stench of damp and rotting wood snaking through the breeding center's bleach and disinfectant like a creeping fog.

Sidian Vey pressed his back into the corner of the room, never taking his eyes off of the predator who stalked into what little space he considered his own. If he smashed himself hard enough into the walls, maybe they would split along the seams and swallow him into the waiting blackness. If it meant falling into shadows accompanied by the desperate need clenching his gut and the echo of his heartbeat in his clit, he would choose it without a second thought. If it meant being choked by silence, he would answer the call of the void. At that point, he was certain he could sustain himself even in the face of utter madness with nothing more than the handful of positive memories he'd clawed free from a life of utter misery and pain.

Anything was better than the alpha who sauntered toward him, stinking of the water damage back in the trailer that Sidian grew up in. Better than the half dozen alphas who spilled into the room behind their pack lead like pus gushing from a lanced, infected wound, each one more nauseating than the last. It took what little strength Sidian still possessed to avoid gagging on the spot.

But he would show no weakness. Not in the faces of those men who had come to take what little he had left.

The leader studied him with crimson eyes that burned beneath the shock of his coiffed white hair. "The good doctor told us you were beautiful. I must confess that I thought he told us what we wanted to hear, little omega."

Sidian's lips twisted back from his teeth in a silent snarl as he weighed his options, pressing his palms flat to the walls on either side of him. He could make a run for the door and pray that none of the towering, powerful alphas chased him down and caught him. If they did, he wasn't certain they would have the decency to bring him back to his room. They might rip down the thin white cotton pants he wore and break him then and there, uncaring of whoever might walk by.

It wouldn't be the first time someone entertained themselves with his violation.

"Not a talker?" The alpha's bloodstained eyes raked over his body like hands forcing unwanted caresses. "That's fine with me. We'll have days to unearth every beautiful sound I think that pretty little mouth can make. What do you think, boys?"

Leering, lecherous gazes and greasy smiles answered the words, along with low, rumbling laughs that made Sidian's stomach ache. If the alphas themselves didn't catch him, the staff would, and he knew about what they might inject him with to keep him docile during his heat. Would that be better or worse? Would he feel more or less broken if he fought back and lost, or if he was forced to lay back and accept whatever abuse they would visit upon him?

He didn't know, given he'd always fought back. He didn't want to find out.

"Do you know who I am?" The alpha's low, purring voice caught a sharp edge, nails dragging along Sidian's spine.

The hair on the nape of his neck prickled, and he swallowed back a mouthful of bile before he found his voice. "No."

"That's interesting." The smile melted from the alpha's face as he stepped closer. Positioned in front of the dim lamp on the bedside table, he cast a dark shadow across the floor that edged ever closer to Sidian's socked feet. "I've always been told I look so much like my father. Does the name Dax Kincaid ring a bell at all?"

Dax didn't; being from the wrong side of a small town meant that Sidian barely knew the handful of alphas he attended high school with, much less someone visibly older than him. But *Kincaid* rang a bell, though he couldn't remember where he heard the name before or what significance it held. He wished he knew why a Kincaid would be present in the breeding center, slowly advancing on him, taking in the sweat dampening his hairline and the pants clinging to his thighs as slick wet the fabric with an expression of pure hunger.

His voice came in a faint, husky croak. "If you touch me, I'm going to fucking *kill* you."

The calm shattered in an instant. Dax Kincaid lunged, and Sidian dodged past his grasping hands, darting for the doorway and whatever freedom might lie on the other side of it. Maybe the alphas wouldn't catch him. Maybe he would slip through the staff's hands. Maybe he could hit the treeline and disappear into the woods, die of exposure while panting like the bitch in heat he was. That would be a better fate than whatever this pack had in store for him.

A boot slammed into his shin so hard it surprised him something didn't crack in response. His legs flew out from under him at the exact moment someone seized him by the back of the shirt, the grip keeping his flailing body in the air as he snarled and swore.

Dax Kincaid swept a hand through his tousled hair as he approached. Without a word, he drove one powerful fist into Sidian's gut, and Sidian crumpled with a choked gasp.

The pain from the impact entangled itself with the pain from his heat; the pitiful whimper that slipped from his lips drew noises of interest from the rest of the pack. The sickly, musky scents of their arousal gagged him like a noose, ripping what little clean air was still in the room from his lungs.

"I'm not above putting a bitch in his place when the need arises," Dax informed him, his gaze cold despite the blazing intensity. "Just like they're going to euthanize that mutt of yours for that little display he put on for the whole town to gossip over. I wanted to stay behind and watch it happen, maybe take a little recording to show you, but it would have been such a waste of your heat to show up late."

Roman. Sidian squeezed his eyes shut at the news—because of course, of *course* Roman wouldn't survive—before he jerked his head back and spit in Dax's face.

Fuck him. Fuck him and the men who'd come to take him away, and fuck every single alpha who thought they owned the body of any omega they set their eyes on. The pack would hurt him, would make him wish for death, but Sidian refused to bend for them, to break for them. They could kill him, fuck him to literal death if they wanted to, but he would make them do it. He would make them do it before he lost a single shred of what made him who he was.

And for dishonoring Roman's memory, he'd make them pay for it.

Dax stared at him for a beat before wiping away the spit on his cheek. "Set him down, Axel."

The alpha suspending him from the floor dropped Sidian abruptly, the impact jarring him slightly as he cast a glance toward the door. *Run.* It didn't matter how far he got or what humiliation he faced for running. If he made it, then he made it. And if not—

"*Kneel.*"

Sidian's knees crumpled beneath him, thudding onto the cold tile of the floor while several of the alphas surrounding him cackled with glee. The command laced itself through his mind like razor wire, cutting through his own thoughts until the weight of it sank into his very bones. Only when a finger curled beneath his chin and tilted his head back did he realize just how fucked he was.

An omega could not ignore an alpha command, after all.

"The good doctor was right about you after all. Obedient little bitch, even when you don't want to be. I think we'll use that over the next few days." A thumb rubbed itself over Sidian's bottom lip, pulling his mouth apart for just a moment. "Starting with this mouth of yours. *Open.*"

The clench in his jaw loosened until his chin fell, his hands clenching into helpless fists on his thighs. He hated alphas, fucking hated them, and the minute he got the chance, he would make this one pay for the sins of the entire goddamned designation.

Dax reached for his belt with slow, unhurried movements, the sound of his buckle clicking like a countdown to the end of the line. "I'm going to show you what that mouth of yours is good for, and then I'm going to fuck your needy little cunt while you're still coherent enough to remember what it feels like to bleed on my knot. Watch and learn, boys. This omega needs proper training."

Sidian sank away into one of the last good memories he had and prayed they could do nothing to rip it from him.

Prologue II

The muted thudding sound of footsteps stirred Roman Kane from his thoughts, his head jerking upright toward the wall of iron bars that separated him from any hope of freedom.

A wry smile touched the corner of his mouth as he pressed the back of his head against the stone wall behind him, sucking in a deep breath of air as he prepared for the inevitable. Why the proceedings had taken so long was beyond him; he knew very little about the legal system and assumed most of what he'd read in books or seen on television was little more than fictional entertainment for the masses. He had no legal counsel to vouch for him and asked for none when pressed, accepting that there was nothing he could do to fight the death sentence dangling over his head like a sword.

No alpha killed two upstanding members of society and walked free.

So be it. He couldn't bring himself to regret the decision as he waited for the executioner, wondering what death would feel like. There had been so many descriptions of it in all the horror books he'd spent his teen years consuming instead of spending any time with people his age, though most of them were tinged with dread. He couldn't bring himself to feel anything but sweet relief.

If he couldn't stand at Sidian's side, he had no reason to draw another breath.

You failed him. The words echoed through his mind, bouncing off the walls of his skull as he watched a shadow appear on the concrete floor. *You failed him. The least you can do is die for it.*

A voice spoke up, uncertain and nervous. "Are you sure about this, Sir? Not that I doubt you know what's best, but just the same—"

"You have the money. I do not see why I owe you any further explanation."

The quality of the voice that spoke was unusual enough that Roman's spine snapped straight, eyes narrowing as a growl rumbled in his chest. Whether it was wise to make such a noise did not matter to him; there was nothing more they could do to him. They took Sidian away from him when he did everything in his power to ensure his mate would be taken care of, so why did it matter how he acted now? What more could they do? There was nothing else left to take.

Nothing but his life. Without his omega, that held no value for him.

The person who stepped into his line of sight was not what Roman envisioned when he thought of what his executioner might look like. He'd imagined a bespoke suit, or perhaps a white coat, something basic and inconspicuous. A middle-aged man who had things to do and places to be and for whom administering a lethal injection was just another part of the messy job.

But the man who pivoted to face Roman when he reached the center of the barred wall would have stood out no matter what crowd surrounded him. "Roman Kane?"

Before Roman could decide whether to answer, every muscle in his body drew taut, and a snarl ripped its way out of his chest like a living creature desperate to escape.

The man studied him for a moment before a strange chuckling noise escaped him, his head tilting from side to side like he was considering an animal at the zoo he might like to gain for his own personal collection. "Let me in to see him. He's harmless."

Harmless? "Who the fuck are you?"

The man didn't answer. Instead, he waited while a guard that Roman recognized but had never learned the name of fumbled with the lock before the door swung inward, permitting the man the entrance he requested. His black boots thudded with every footstep, the leather gleaming as if he regularly polished them before making stops at small-town jails. His entire outfit was black-on-black, a button-down tucked into nice pants with a matching vest on top and a knotted tie. It stood in sharp contrast to the gas mask affixed to the lower half of his face, which distorted every sound and word, and which only seemed to highlight the blood red of his eyes.

A feral, dressed nicer than Roman had ever seen before, but a feral.

Something's wrong with him. It wasn't just the eyes, though they weren't nothing on their own. Some other quality about the man had Roman's hackles up on sight, his teeth bared and his hands clenched as he debated which bone he would snap first.

"I wouldn't," the man said, tapping the side of the mask. "If you give me one reason, I will take this off, and in one breath, you'll be dead. I can't tell you how painful it will be because based on last time, I doubt I'll remember much of it."

"You're a—" Roman started, but the man raised one hand, encased in black leather.

"I know what I am." The amused lilt to his voice provoked another growl, though he seemed far too nonchalant about it for comfort. Even with the security of what he could become should he need to, no one should have been at ease in the presence of someone still stained in days-old blood. "And I know what you did. Very impressive for such a young alpha. How old are you, Roman?"

"Nineteen." Still a child in the eyes of many, but a killer in the eyes of all.

In the end, that would matter more. Roman's age would be used against him, proof that hormonal young alphas going through puberty should be sequestered away from omegas who might tempt them into bloodshed and violence. Easier to blame him, easier to blame Sidian, than to confront the world that propped up everything that led to that one gruesome moment.

Because change would mean admitting their biases and stereotypes were wrong.

"Nineteen. How nostalgic." The man's glove was cold as it slipped beneath Roman's chin, tilting his head back just. "You have two options laid out before you. You can choose to rot in this cell until the needle comes, or you can accept the offer I'm generous enough to give and walk out of this jail a free man. Are you open to hearing me out?"

Roman's mouth dried at the thought. Freedom. What would it look like without Sidian waiting for him? What would it feel like to live in a world without his omega? "I want him back."

"Him." The man tilted his head from one side to the other, as if considering. "The omega?"

Roman's eyes narrowed. "*My* omega."

"We can make arrangements for such a thing, I assume, provided you accept the offer I extend." The man dropped his hand, and Roman waited, watching as he seemed to gather himself. "My name is Lorcan Devereaux, and I own the Viper mercenary squad. We've lost a member in the recent past, and

I've had a difficult time finding a suitable replacement. You just might fill that slot."

Viper? Mercenary squad? How had one of the richest men in the country found his way into Roman's cell to offer such a thing? "You're with Ouroboros?"

"That I am." Lorcan slipped his hands into the pockets of his pants like he had all the time in the world to wait, but why wouldn't he? If he had time to stop in a Podunk little town like Roman's, then he must not have been a busy man. This was just a business meeting for him. "I will have you trained to my standards as quickly as possible in order to ensure you will not be a burden during our missions. If you cannot live up to my expectations, I'll put a bullet in the back of your skull, and I will ensure that no one will find your corpse. How does that sound?"

Better than the inside of a cell. Better than death at the hands of the system that demanded the violence. Roman was more than happy to give them to keep his mate safe. "And Sidian?"

"As I said, I can make arrangements for such a thing." Lorcan arched one dark brow, silent meaning clear.

There was no reason to sit in that cell and wait for daybreak, wait for death, wait to be made nothing but a useless corpse to be tossed into an incinerator since no living member of Roman's family would want anything to do with his body. He would have been satisfied to die if it meant atoning for failing Sidian, but if he had a chance to survive, a chance to be reunited with his omega…

Then it would be a failure not to accept it. "I'll join."

"Good boy." Lorcan turned, snapping his fingers, the sound echoing through the empty cell. "Follow me. We have a long drive ahead of us."

Chapter One

"All right, Mr. Vey." The heavy steel door of the room slammed shut as Dr. Richard Barnes stepped into the room, the impact ruffling the bottom of his long white lab coat as he offered Sidian a thin, unimpressed smile. "Let's go over this once again, shall we?"

Sidian said nothing. He watched the doctor approach the side of his bed from where he curled in the center of the wafer-thin mattress, his arms coiled around the swell of his stomach. "You've got this entire facility to run, and you still make time to come see me in person? I'm flattered, Doc."

Dr. Richard Barnes sank into his usual seat at Sidian's bedside, folding one leg over the other so he could prop the expected manila folder against it as he flipped it open. A middle-aged male beta with thinning brown hair streaked with silver combed over the bald spot in the center of his scalp and sharp blue eyes, he'd become the person Sidian hated most in the world. He didn't think there was anyone he could hate more than he hated Pack Kincaid, but Barnes gave everyone Sidian had ever known a run for their money with ease.

To his credit, Sidian tried to give the beta as little attention as possible. Laying hands on any of the *patients* at the Bell Breeding Center was off the table; leaving the omegas incarcerated in that hellhole bruised and ugly made them unattractive to potential clients. The last thing a beta like Barnes wanted on his hands was a pissed-off pack all riled up over the fact that their usual canvas wasn't blank for them to ruin as they saw fit. They paid a premium for the privilege of getting away with vicious treatment that would have had them all sitting behind bars somewhere.

The thought made Sidian's stomach twist. After his last heat, the staff dropped Sidian off back in his room splotched with black and purple and blue, his skin scrubbed clean but still bearing the phantom itch of blood drying tacky on the insides of his thighs. After the first heat spent beneath Pack Kincaid, he knew it would be bad. He just didn't know it could be worse.

Barnes heaved a put-upon sigh like the weight of the world rested on his sagging shoulders. "You bit one nurse during your gland examination."

"Shouldn't bring those cards around me right now." Sidian's arms curled a little tighter around his stomach, the instinct to shield the most vulnerable part of himself running high in the presence of someone who had been nothing other than an enemy to him.

"Your glands have been sensitive since your admittance into our program almost two years ago." Barnes clicked his tongue, scribbling notes in the file that Sidian knew he would never be given the privilege of reading. "I would have expected you to have grown used to it by now. Perhaps further examination is necessary, though we'll save that for after the birth."

Sidian's fingers splayed over the bump, and the baby gave a slight flutter against his palm as if reassuring him he wasn't alone in this. "You come at my neck, and I'll fucking kill you."

"I'm sure you'd like to believe you will, but you've yet to do much more than cause me mild irritation." Barnes chuckled, the ground grating on Sidian's already-frazzled nerves. "Cataloging your changing scent is an important part of monitoring your pregnancy, as you well know."

"I'm aware of it. Doesn't mean I like it." And it didn't mean Sidian was going to comply with every single test they wanted to run on him just because they could.

"I don't care about your personal feelings on the matter." Barnes wrote something else down, pen scratching over the paper in quick, jagged movements. More notes on how difficult a patient Sidian was? Plans to drug him up through the pregnancy so he couldn't give the staff more headaches? The possibilities were endless with that sociopathic piece of shit. "You know, it's rather impressive you bred so well. Pack Kincaid seems so brutal when they visit you."

Sidian's mouth dried at the mention of the pack responsible for his current predicament, the pack responsible for—No. He didn't want to think about that, think about *her,* right now. "Fuck off."

"Let's see, let's see…" Barnes murmured before clearing his throat. "Bruising around the throat, upper arms, wrists, hips, thighs, ankles, and even ribcage. You know, we thought they might have broken one of your ribs with how deep the mottling was."

"Stop it." Sidian's body curled inward, his arms cinching tight around his stomach as the memories of his last heat assailed him.

Hands gripping him. Pinning him down. Twisting him into any position Pack Kincaid could think of. Fingers digging into his skin, his chest aching with every breath, his throat sore from just how much the pack choked him and how roughly they used him.

Barnes continued on, unconcerned about the impact of his words. "Lacerations on the shoulders, hips, thighs, and breasts reminiscent of the shape of teeth marks—"

"Shut the *fuck* up," Sidian hissed, ducking his head. Covering his ears would mean uncovering his stomach, and he couldn't do that. Every instinct demanded he protect his belly.

"I would have thought they were trying to mark you, but even brutes like that know when an omega is not worth more than the holes he offers them." Barnes never took his eyes off the file. Not once, not even as every word shaved off slivers of Sidian's soul. "Internal damage, of course, though at this point we expect the vaginal and anal lacerations."

Fury blazed through Sidian's veins as bile burned up his throat, his eyes squeezing shut to dam the tears that threatened to fall. His mind split open, refusing to cloak the memories any longer. Memories of Pack Kincaid laughing and joking as they visited brutality onto his body the likes of which he'd never known before. Breaking him down until the facade cracked open, and he begged and sobbed and wept for it to end.

Days of heat-induced lust, alpha pheromones keeping him slick and wanting even as he cringed away from every touch and sensation.

Hoarse shouts and screams as Pack Kincaid seemed determined to see just how much he could *fit* until he tore.

Barnes was quiet. Sidian could feel the doctor's eyes boring into him, watching him shudder and quake on the bed as he fought to regain control of himself. It was fine. Almost twenty weeks. He had so much more time left before they could plan for his next heat, so much more time before Pack Kincaid returned. And he'd be ready next time. Next time, he'd have what it took to fight back. To run.

Finally, Barnes spoke. "I trust we won't have any more tantrums today, Mr. Vey. Get some rest."

The door slammed shut behind him as he left, and Sidian swallowed back another pointless omega whine as he slumped against the mattress.

Roe, where are you?

The common room of the Bell Breeding Center hosted a variety of plush couches, loveseats, and chairs, the upholstery stiff and scratchy against Sidian's skin. Still, he dragged a chair over to the barred window on the farthest side of the room as he did every single day and sank into it, willing his stiff muscles to relax and his tired body to rest. Was pregnancy supposed to take so much out of him? He didn't know. The only pregnancies he'd ever endured were within Bell's walls, and they weren't the conditions an omega was supposed to be pregnant in.

He should have a nest, big and soft and cozy, with all the blankets and pillows he could ask for. Somewhere dark and safe and secure, where the rest of the world was kept at bay and someone stood between him and all possible danger. An alpha, strong and fierce and beautiful, willing to do anything to keep him safe no matter what the risks were.

For one brief, shining moment, he'd had one. The fractured pieces of his life snapped together into a stunning reality of what the future might hold for him. Wrapped in blood-soaked arms, sticky hands cradling his face, he knew peace for once in his miserable existence.

Now, all of that was gone. And he'd never get it back.

His hand dropped to his stomach for the thousandth time today, fingers tracing over the bump that signaled to the world that his last heat was, by the center's standards, a "success." The occasional shifts beneath his skin and kicks against his hand, private and precious, confirmed for him once again that his baby was healthy and more than big enough to make their presence known to him.

It was something he had to himself just the same, though. Something to ground himself with. The center wanted nothing more than to rip him apart until he was docile, submissive, and sweet, but Pack Kincaid might want to keep him then, and he couldn't risk that.

He would never let the spineless, cold-hearted bastards who ran the center take more from him than they already had.

His safety, his innocence, his freedom, his autonomy... Nothing more. Not his soul, black as it may be.

"We'll get out of here," he whispered to his belly, to his baby, though he did not know how to make good on the promise. Even at the peak of his physical health, he'd been able to do nothing more than languish within those walls.

Classical music issued from the television mounted on the wall, its screen depicting a bookstore while rain pattered down on the streets surrounding it. Restless, Sidian turned his attention to the outdoors, to the trees jutting straight up into the sky, the gray clouds overhead promising a thunderstorm on the horizon. Only the true sound of rain brought him any real comfort or rest.

He hadn't been sleeping well for the past few days. Soon there would be talks of sedating him before bed to ensure he received the proper amount of rest for the baby's development. He'd been so agitated during his third trimester last year they'd kept him doped up for weeks on end, ensuring he could do little more than eat and sleep.

He didn't want to go through that again. Never again.

A soft kick against the palm of his hand tightened his throat, his eyes stinging with tears as he stared out at the trees. This wasn't right. The staff knew it, and he knew it. He should be in an *actual* home, reclining on a mountain of pillows, maybe tucked up into the side of—

Crimson bleeds from his eyes until their original color returns. Pale silver splotched with deep, vibrant green like moss growing heavy on the bark of birch trees, framed by the longest black lashes he'd ever seen.

When a tear trailed down from the corner of his eye, he batted it away without a second thought.

It should be his alpha's pup inside of him if anyone's, but he would never see Roman Kane again. The odds of him even surviving that night were slim to none, the gorgeous alpha with blood dripping from his teeth and a wild, hungry look in his gaze. A gaze that slipped back to humanity from a feral state, but only for Sidian.

His best friend. His fated mate.

Bitterness surged in his chest as he slumped in his chair, propping one socked foot up on the edge of the windowsill. The center had taken everything from him moments after he discovered he had something worth taking. Years of his life spent cowering and pathetic, months spent cold and numb, and mere moments of warmth and acceptance and tenderness ripped away so violently the edges of the wound were still raw and bloody.

He'd never get that back. Never get *Roman* back. At the center, he was doomed to be nothing but a set of holes for Pack Kincaid to use until they either turned him into their permanent fuck doll or kill him. At least death would deliver him from that, but the thought of slipping out of the world without ever ensuring the safety of his children left him cold all the way to his core.

No way out. No way to get to her, to get to the one they'd already ripped from his weak and trembling arms.

He took a deep breath and pressed down on the frustration until it sunk into his core, tangling itself with the resentment, the rage, the desire for spilled blood and torn flesh and splintered bone.

He would get out of there, and he would get his daughter back from those psychopaths no matter what it cost him.

As long as his children were safe, he didn't even care if it cost him his life.

Chapter Two

"The Bell Breeding Center ain't any different from the places we've already hit." Captain Jagger Hawthorne paced back and forth across the front of the room at a leisurely pace, uncaring of the way his body cut through the flashing images projected on the wall next to him. "If anything, it's more remote. Given the usual clientele involved, it might be to ensure they have as much privacy as any sick fuck could ask for."

Roman's eyes raked in as much detail as possible as the projector clicked through the expected slideshow. The Bell Breeding Center was a crumbling brown brick structure in a thick copse of trees, the grounds shaggy and unkempt beyond a single concrete path that wound around the building, snaking through the tall grass. Each window bore a set of iron bars that would make it impossible for the omegas within to escape even if they shattered the glass. If the windows were like the ones that came before, then several layers of glass made them difficult to break at all. Every inch of those buildings was designed to keep the prisoners within secure.

Roman's jaw twitched at the thought, and he clamped his teeth tight together as the photo of a man he'd never seen before filled the screen.

Jagger spun toward them, spine straight, hands folded behind his back. "Doctor Richard Barnes. Forty-two years old. Beta male. Began life as a promising OBGYN before being head-hunted by the former head of this breeding center to join their team. He runs the place."

"Ugly fucker," Mal whispered next to Roman, and he bit down on the corner of his mouth to stifle a slight smile.

Jagger grinned, though, his canines too long, sharp and white in his smile. "Overnight, the center employs about twenty staff members to oversee the patients. You could almost consider this mission to be overkill on our part."

Ghost spoke up from his corner of the room, his shock of hair blending in with the flat white plaster behind him. "Why's the boss got us going if it's this simple?"

"Wants to make sure we scrape the place raw. Collect every single physical file we can find." Jager jabbed a finger in Silver's direction. "You hit up every computer in the place before the systems go down, and go hard on Barnes's personal network. Rip out everything you can before we hit the bricks."

Silver raised an eyebrow in response. "Is there something about this place we need to know?"

"Boss doesn't share that kind of information with me." Jagger shrugged a shoulder; Roman felt the ripple of unease that rolled through the team, but he felt nothing. "Not our monkeys, not our circus. We go in, we do what we need to do, we get out. Extraction will join us after twenty minutes to escort the omegas to safety. Questions?"

Roman raised his hand, and Jagger cocked his head in response. "Is the doctor going to be in?"

"Why?" Jagger smirked. He knew Roman far too well for comfort despite the limited time the two of them had worked together, though Roman had forced himself to make peace with that. What else could he do? "You want that one to yourself, Kane?"

Mal barked a laugh, his head falling back; a casual glance in his direction revealed he stared straight into Roman's eyes. "Getting bored, Killer?"

"A little," Roman admitted, and the room erupted into laughter.

When the noise died down, Jagger struck the image of Barnes with a closed fist. "Do your worst. He works late nights on the weekends. You catch him, you have fun, but remember. Fifteen minutes. In and out. Once extraction finishes their work, we torch the place."

Every mission was much the same. Cut the signal to give Silver enough time to infiltrate the system, then cut the power to cloak their movements. Infiltrate, dispose of the staff, and extract the omegas within so they could be taken to safety. Spread accelerant through as much of the building as possible, then light the place up so that by the time the first responders arrived, there was little they could do but quell the flames. No survivors. No evidence. By the time Roman joined the team, the Vipers were a well-oiled machine. All they had to do was teach him the ropes.

Seventy-two days to be brought to standard, per the boss's orders, and Roman was more than happy to rise to the occasion.

The photo of Barnes flashed to a floor plan, each window and exit marked as Jagger turned to walk them through the step-by-step. "Standard front entrance, back entrance, and side entrance. Mal, you and Kane take the front. Ghost, I want you and Silver to take the back. Watch his back while he gets what he needs. Locke and Keay, you two are with me on the side entrance."

"Yes, Captain," the room chorused.

He turned to them just as the images cut, leaving the board behind him an empty white slate. No evidence. "The boss has been up my ass about this from the moment he brought it up. Do not fuck this up, or I'll have your knots for it. Dismissed."

The interior of Roman's room within the Viper's Pit was bland, practical, and impersonal. The smooth gray walls were devoid of nails or screws, given he had no memories worth keeping to surround himself with. His nightstand bore only functional items: a single reading lamp, an alarm clock with a blaring siren-adjacent alarm, and the charger for his cell phone. The device itself was for work only; the boss did not allow any of his Vipers to be anywhere where he could not contact them.

Roman plugged his phone into its charger and sat down on the edge of the mattress, knee bouncing as he fixed his gaze on the top drawer of the nightstand. Another mission meant another chance to let his hindbrain loose, if only for a short time, and he looked forward to it.

Missions were the only acceptable place to lose control, and only if he could regain his composure when his fifteen minutes were up. But for one glorious moment, forebrain and hindbrain could meld together into a cacophony of violent efficiency, maximizing the pain of the target as much as possible. Brutality was the way of the Vipers, after all. Ouroboros trained their branch for bloodshed, and taught them to be cold-blooded killers. The occasional sadistic streak was welcomed; intelligence wasn't one of the Vipers' strong suits, aside from Silver, and it didn't have to be. Their missions were short, simple, and to the point.

The Vipers had recovered the highest number of omegas, secreting them away into the safety of the Nest where they could access the resources they needed to heal. For what it was worth, it struck some pride into Roman's heart, though very little else reached him.

A quiet knock at the door startled him from his ruminations, and he shook himself back to awareness just as the door swung open. Little privacy existed in the Pit, though he'd become used to it over the long and exhausting months. None of the alphas within Ouroboros could build a pack, all of them too damaged to manage much more than teammates, so decorum was not to be expected.

Mal stood in the entrance to Roman's room, shoving one broad shoulder against the doorframe like he belonged there. "You up for a round of sparring, Kane? You're restless."

"Sure," Roman muttered. Maybe slamming his fist into something solid and alive would help steady him.

Mal's onyx eyes narrowed as he straightened up, his nostrils flaring as he no doubt tried to get a read on Roman's scent. "Something's got your blood hot. What's going on?"

"Just thinking about the mission." About listening to that pig of a doctor squeal while Roman peeled flesh from muscle and muscle from bone.

He hated betas more than the rest of the Vipers did, though none of them were fans. High and mighty pricks that run the world, delegating the lives of alphas and omegas from their lofty positions of power with no thought or concern as to the damage they did. Alphas suffered, but omegas suffered the most, and the breeding centers were proof of that. Dens of anguish where omegas were kept, their heats sold, their children ripped from their arms moments after birth to be placed in the care of their mothers' rapists.

There were no innocents who worked in such a place. Not anymore.

Mal grimaced, waving a hand in front of his nose. "Forgot how much you fucking *burn* when you're pissed off. Come on. It's been too long."

Every Pit was much the same as the Vipers': a sprawling manor with well over a dozen rooms to house the members of the team, the largest room reserved for when the boss visited and stayed overnight. They had all the amenities they needed at their disposal both inside and out. If Roman wasn't downstairs throwing his body at the equipment made available to all of them, he was out on the trails running as hard and fast as he could until his stomach turned itself inside out from the stress.

Alphas had higher endurance and stamina than omegas did, but it could never be high enough. Not to him. Not for the work they did.

One side of the gym downstairs was nothing but matted floor, giving them plenty of room to spar as need be. It was there that Mal led Roman, running his tattooed hands through his long, wine-red curls so he could tie them back with a slim black elastic. Considering he never played fair, Roman made a note of that for later. Hard to see with all that hair in the eyes, after all.

Who he'd been before the Vipers was unknown, but then, none of them knew Roman, either.

Mal glanced over his shoulder as he walked to one side of the wide floor, rolling his neck until the muscles flexed. "What are you thinking about doing to the guy?"

"I have a few options in mind." Roman stretched his shoulders and legs out, making sure he was limber enough to do what needed to be done. While he was the largest Viper on the team, Mal had always been the fastest. Keeping up with him was a pain on a good day.

Mal cocked his head, flexing his fingers until his knuckles popped. "Paint an image in my head, Picasso."

"Skinning is my favorite." The scent of bloody meat, the ribbons of muscle and cords of sinew, the flashes of white bone beneath. Roman watched as Mal's eyes lit up, the delighted and twisted smile reminding him who he was dealing with as if he could ever forget. "Wish it lasted longer."

"You're one sick fuck, Killer Kane." Mal licked his teeth, then dropped into a crouch. "That's why you're my favorite."

He broke into a sprint, and Roman's vision bled scarlet.

Sparring was about nothing more than tension and exertion and nerves, his body moving of its own accord as his hindbrain seized control of the moment. Dancing this dance was always dangerous, but it was Mal's favorite choreography, with twists, pivots, and dips filled with pain. Bruises and blood spilled; it was all the same to Mal, and all the same to Roman.

It was the only way any of the Vipers could bond.

Mal's back slammed into the mat so hard that any further force might break his ribs or crack his spine. Roman's vision snapped back with frightening clarity, one hand closed vice-like around Mal's wrist to twist it over his head and the other coiled around his throat. He planted his knee on Mal's sternum, and from the way Mal panted and heaved against it, he needed the air.

He stared up at Roman for a long moment before his head fell back against the mat, dark eyes sliding shut and the pale length of his throat exposed. "I concede, fucker."

"Smart move." Roman was off of him in seconds, not stupid enough to linger and risk a retaliatory sneak attack.

Mal just threw an arm over his eyes, sucking air into his lungs while Roman took stock of any damage he might have received. There were going to be some bruises along his right side and back, as well as his upper left thigh, but he'd had worse in the past. Either Mal was off his game, or the beast that slept in Roman's blood was much closer to surfacing than it should have been.

At least the mission should lure it back to sleep long enough for Roman to resume his iron control.

Losing control had already destroyed his life once, and he refused to let it happen again when he knew the penalty for costing the boss a Viper was a quick and speedy death.

Chapter Three

"I don't want to have this conversation with you," Sidian's favorite nurse said a few days later, sitting on the edge of the chair next to Sidian's bed. "The dark circles under your eyes are getting pretty intense. You haven't been sleeping, have you?"

Sidian bit back the urge to scoff as he stared down at his lap, contrition tugging at his hindbrain and demanding he do anything to rectify whatever mistake he had made to put that edge in the nurse's voice. Of all the staff members of the center, Tanner Matthews was the only one Sidian sort of liked, steadfast and reliable in a way that none of the others were. He never forced Sidian to do anything he didn't want to do, talked him through every new test and exam, and checked after him like he was concerned for his well-being and not just doing his job.

He was also an omega. Though Tanner wore scent blockers that smothered most of his natural scent, Sidian's nose was sharper than most. He'd always been able to smell right through them.

Sighing, he lifted a sleeve to his mouth and caught the white fabric between his teeth, worrying it as he tried to think of how to respond. If Tanner was bringing it up to him, then there was a damned good chance Barnes was making noise that Sidian did not want to hear. This might be the only chance he had to fix his sleep schedule before the endless rounds of sedatives began.

He regretted letting it happen last time. So many precious hours with his daughter, his precious Amethyst, lost because he refused to do something he knew he needed to do for her sake.

"Sid," Tanner murmured, the nickname pricking at a barely healed wound in Sidian's heart, "they're talking sedation, okay? I don't want to see that happen to you again."

His pulse quickened. Sedation did not just mean loss of time with his son; it meant an added layer of vulnerability, and while the staff at the center was disinterested in their so-called patients, some of them weren't. Some of them had wandering eyes and wandering hands, and the thought of being unable to shield or protect himself while pregnant threatened to send Sidian's hindbrain into a panic. Being trapped in a cycle of his own anxious thoughts never failed to give him a migraine.

And the extra-strength pain pills were bad for the baby, so he'd have to suffer through it alone.

He sighed and tipped his head back against the pillows, staring up at the ceiling above him. "I'm trying my best to sleep," he muttered, smoothing a hand over his stomach just to feel the baby kick. A boy, his *son*. "Do you think I could just try some hot tea before bed? Maybe that'll help."

"I drink some before coming to work," Tanner said after a moment, and Sidian flashed him a weak smile. "We can try that, I think. Couldn't hurt, right? Gimme a second."

He slipped out of the room with the soundless steps that only an omega could perfect, and Sidian breathed a sigh of relief and sank back into the pillows behind him. He stroked nervous hands over his stomach, smiling faintly when the baby shifted under his touch. How much longer did he have left with this child? How many more would Pack Kincaid expect out of him?

His omega status wreaked havoc on his body when he was pregnant, his desire to cause as much trouble and chaos as possible warring with his instincts to submit, to give in, to do everything he could to shield the baby from danger. But he knew better. Even if he behaved himself, nothing would save him when his next heat arrived. Because Pack Kincaid would come knocking. He already expected seeing them at the birth of his son, much as he loathed the thought.

His mind conjured up the memory of that leering smile, foul breathing fanning the side of his face as Dax Kincaid rested a hand low on his stomach. Right above the throbbing, bloody ruin of his torn cunt. *"Too bad they won't let me fuck you like this. I'd love to hear that pretty scream again."*

Sidian's omega whined, but he swallowed the sound down. No one who could hear it mattered; omegas didn't respond to each other's vocalizations like that, and the betas did nothing more than walk by as if they'd heard nothing at all. What did Tanner think of such things, though? Sidian was curious. He wasn't broken and bruised and hurting like the patients here. Did he have a pack who waited for him back home, an alpha who paced the halls until his car pulled into the driveway? What would someone like that think of a job like this?

Maybe it was just a paycheck. Nothing more and nothing less.

The tap of soft-soled canvas shoes drew Sidian back into a sitting position just as Tanner reappeared, a steaming mug in hand. "I added a little milk and honey to sweeten it up for you. If it helps you sleep, I'll see if I can get Barnes off your case about it. Sound fair?"

"Hell yes." Sidian offered him a small, halting smile, and Tanner returned it with a grin of his own.

Because there were notes about what he'd do with a good sharp piece of plastic or glass, Sidian wasn't allowed to just sit with a ceramic mug. Tanner sat back down in his chair, relaxed as ever while Sidian sipped the tea, sweet and comforting when nothing in this place had been. He supposed it was because it came from Tanner, who made it hard to know what to expect of him.

His first impression of Tanner was a good one, one that would be hard to live up to for anyone who might come after him. Blood-soaked and bruised, unraveling at the seams and almost broken, Sidian was thrust into Tanner's hands to be cleaned up following his first heat spent with Pack Kincaid, and it hadn't been a pretty sight. He'd broken the first mirror he'd seen as soon as his eyes landed on the handprint-shaped bruises around his throat, but all Tanner did was sweep him off of his feet and carry him somewhere where the glass slivers didn't threaten his bare skin.

As far as he could tell, Tanner was a good guy. Pretty as hell, too, broader through the shoulders than most omegas but with all the right curves, sporting short black hair that looked soft and the kind of brown eyes that made Sidian think of sweet, adoring dogs rather than people. The harsh white lights of the center washed out everyone who stood beneath him, but there was still a flush of good health to Tanner's fair skin, and his black-rimmed glasses softened an already gentle face.

Looking at him like that felt like bitter poison, though, so Sidian tried not to do it often.

"Still not messed with any of that?" Tanner tilted his head toward the neat stacks of pillows and blankets on the far side of the room, all waiting to be woven into something resembling a nest.

Sidian snorted. "You think that instinct ever hits in a place like this?"

"No." Tanner watched him sip the tea, his gaze softening to where Sidian wanted to cringe away from the kindness of it. Such a thing wasn't for someone like him. "Shouldn't be nesting in an open room like this, anyway. Nesting rooms are off the main pack bedroom for safety."

"You have one of those? Fancy nesting rooms, I mean." Was it overstepping to ask such a thing?

Tanner's eyes grew distant, almost uncertain. "Yeah. Haven't used it in the last couple of years, though. You almost done with the tea?"

The sudden shift of conversation told Sidian all he needed to know; he drained the rest of the mug and handed it over. "Yeah. Thanks, Tanner. Promise I'll get some sleep tonight if you're good on your word about getting Barnes off my back."

"I am. I will be." Tanner stood from his seat, and though it was long past time for him to go, he lingered like stepping away was the last thing he wanted to do. "Goodnight, Sid. Sweet dreams."

Sidian wished he could pick up what Tanner's scent was through the blockers, though it eluded him. There was just enough of it there for him to know what he was looking at, who he was looking at, disarming in a way that no beta's scent could ever be. But the actual notes of it were missing, with only the barest hint of a pheromone breaking through.

Sidian curled back into the pillows, reaching for the thin blanket beneath him. "Night, Tanner."

Despite the comfort of the tea, sleep eluded him. Sidian stared at the wall opposite him for a long time, counting down the seconds while he stroked soothingly over his belly. A few answering kicks made his breath catch, his lips twitching despite the utter misery that plagued him day in and day out. Nothing about him was a proper, true omega... Except that he bonded with his children instantly, anticipating every stage of their development with a glee that couldn't be ripped from him.

Even though he knew Pack Kincaid would take his son from him, he couldn't help but marvel over every little flutter of movement inside of him. For a few more precious months, the two of them were one, and he'd be able to feel the baby grow stronger and more mobile with every twist and stretch and kick.

He just wished he had his mate to share it with.

If Roman was there with Sidian... He imagined a broad chest spooned against his back, hand resting on top of his, a subtle added protection for their son. Soft kisses pressed against his hair or the back of his neck or wherever Roman's mark lingered on his throat, big body warm enough to chase all the chill away from Sidian's. It was such a pretty fantasy.

But Sidian had fucked it all up without even trying.

His eyelids started to flutter shut if only to escape the future he could never have, and then everything went pitch black.

"What the fuck?" He forced himself to sit up, head swinging from side to side as he shoved his back against the pillows, goosebumps rippling over his flesh when several shrieks sounded through the darkness. It took a moment for his vision to adjust; alphas and omegas could see somewhat well even in darkness that deep, though it offered little more than the edges of the surrounding objects. Enough to navigate by, which was something.

When the emergency lights didn't kick on, a nervous skitter of uncertainty rolled through his gut.

"What's going on?" someone called out in the hallway.

Sidian eased off the bed and crept toward the door, holding his breath so as not to be heard. If the power was cut, were the cameras offline? What happened to the security on the doors? If he pushed one of them open and made a break for it, would anything alert the rest of the staff? There weren't that many people in the building at night, just a handful of nurses and Barnes sometimes, because omegas didn't need armed guards. Pretty, docile, empty-headed bitches weren't that dangerous.

Except for Sidian.

Go. He tried to urge himself into the hallway, peering out just to see a pair of nurses whispering to one another in the hall. Neither of them was Tanner, just a pair of female betas who he'd seen in passing. Had Tanner already gone home for the night? Was he somewhere else in the building?

Not that it mattered. Sidian could run for it. He didn't know how far he'd get or what he'd do once he was outside, but he could run. He could do it.

"What is the meaning of this?" Barnes's voice echoed down the hallway, and Sidian shrunk back into his room on instinct, pressing himself against the wall next to the open doorway. "I was just sending off an email to the Board when the power cut. What's happened?"

One nurse stammered in confusion. "We were just doing our rounds. How are we supposed to know?"

"This is the one time none of you are carrying your phones on the floor." Barnes huffed in indignation. "There are flashlights at the nurse's station. Go grab some. We need to secure the patients and call for help."

Sidian stuck his head out into the hallway after the nurses rushed past, debating his chances. Barnes stood in the middle of the hallway, either waiting for the pair to return or not sure what to do with himself. He was there late some nights, and he was likely regretting making tonight one night he stayed behind. He could have been at home in bed and not having to deal with an unexplained power outage at his precious omega factory farm.

Someone from another room called out. "Doctor Barnes? What's going on?"

"There's nothing to be concerned about," Barnes said. "Just a power outage. That's all."

Something lurking at the end of the hallway caught Sidian's eye; he lowered his head and leaned further out, narrowing his eyes to squint through the shadows to get a better look at what it was. Something... Big. Something huge moved through the darkness with the lupine grace of a predator, footsteps silent as it advanced, though Sidian couldn't make out any discernible details from where he stood.

One of the nurses? He didn't know all of them, but somehow doubted it. Maybe it was someone new just come to see what was going on, except... No. The figure moved with far too much confidence, avoiding a rolling cart left in the hallway. Whoever it was could see where they were going.

Barnes turned in that direction, his voice sharp and irritable. "I understand that this is an odd occurrence, but everyone, please stay in your—"

"Richard Barnes?" The voice that answered him came from the figure—Sidian was sure of it—though the sound set his knees trembling beneath him.

The voice was smooth and dark, pitched low, a husky rasp that threatened to draw a whine from his lips. *Alpha,* his hindbrain all but purred, as a relief swept through him and left him breathless. And then he remembered where the fuck he was and stepped out of the room, trying to stay low and out of the alpha's line of sight. Whoever he was, he wasn't here for Sidian, and Sidian had no desire to give him any reason to change his target.

Why would an unknown alpha be creeping around in the middle of the night?

"What?" Barnes scoffed in response. "Of course I am. Who are you to be skulking around my halls like this?"

The alpha moved so quickly that Sidian could barely make out the movements in the dark, but the wet, crunching *rip* followed by the anguished scream told him that was for the best.

Omegas all around him yelped and shrieked and cried out in surprise. Sidian watched, mesmerized, as Barnes fell to his knees, a curious nothingness where his right arm used to be. The right arm that the alpha swung upward in a high arc before bringing the still-jetting stump down on the top of Barnes's skull.

The purr that stumbled from Sidian's lips shocked him, as did the moment the alpha's head whipped up in his direction, features obscured by what looked like a mask of some kind. Before he could so much as take a step back, a rumble answered him, so much deeper, pulled up from a broad chest whereas Sidian's own just vibrated its way up his throat.

Fuck that. Freedom was within his grasp. He had to go.

So without a second thought, he turned on heel and bolted for the stairs and the promise of freedom waiting for him to grasp it.

Chapter Four

The sweet, trilling purr of an omega struck Roman with all the cadence of a chorus of angels serenading the damned as they writhed in the flames of hell.

Every ounce of his attention shifted from the groaning, sobbing beta at his feet to focus on the little slip of a shadow in the hallway before him. The silhouette carved a delicate shape through the darkness, a petite creature whose waist looked swallowed beneath the width of Roman's hands. That gorgeous sound spilled from the omega's lips, arousing a response from Roman's alpha before he could stop himself. His own deeper rumble crawled up from his gut, the entirety of his torso buzzing with the force of it.

An automatic reaction beyond his scope and control, a response that could only mean one thing for it to be instinctive.

It wasn't possible. It just wasn't possible.

"There are no records of him we can find. Not sure what that means, to be honest, but we're going to keep looking, Roman. I promised you that much. We won't stop looking."

All the time the Vipers had been searching, and Sidian Vey had been in the middle of a fucking breeding center.

Rage closed Roman's throat just as Sidian turned to run, lithe legs carrying him away from Roman so quickly that it shocked Roman out of the anger. He didn't have time to be angry. Didn't have time for violence. Blood slicked his hands and soaked into his shirt, but he left the doctor convulsing in a pool of his own spreading viscera, boots sliding in the mess as Roman gave chase.

As soon as he crossed the tiles where Sidian had stood just a moment before, the scent of lilies washed over him in a wave so sweet it nearly knocked him on his ass.

For just a moment, his vision bled red.

"Don't touch him. Don't fucking touch him!"

The words ripped their way free of his chest before he could stop himself, his steps so rapid it felt like he was flying at the white-haired alpha with his hands wrapped around Sidian's shoulders. The rage that consumed Roman was unlike anything he'd ever felt before, burning through him with a righteous fury that drew a thundering growl from his chest. His hands cinched around the alpha's forearms so hard, so fast, that he almost missed the crack of bone, the way it jutted through torn skin and grazed his palms.

How fucking dare this alpha try to take his mate away from him?

"Kane!" Mal called after him, the rough grate of his voice snapping Roman back to reality. "Where the fuck are you going?"

But he couldn't answer. He had to get to Sidian before it was too late. Roman couldn't save his omega then, not truly, but he was more than capable of saving Sidian now.

And like hell was Roman going to let his mate slip away from him once again.

Sidian's scent was a siren song to Roman's alpha, a sweet melody that wound between the cacophony of surprised and pained cries that filled the breeding center. Frightened omegas whimpered and whined in confusion, but Roman forced himself to ignore their vocalized pleas for help as he focused his attention on the shadow slipping away from him. Sidian was fast; omegas were, but even Roman's long legs weren't giving him the advantage he needed to catch up with the omega.

Where was Sidian going? Why was he running away?

There was nothing around the center beyond trees and trees and more fucking trees leading all the way up the base of the nearest mountain. Did Sidian intend to disappear into the shadows? Maybe he did. Maybe he thought he could do this on his own, but he didn't have to do that.

Roman was there now. He could protect Sidian.

Someone tried to intercept Sidian at the stairs, a flash of pale hair ripping a growl of warning from Roman's chest that sent Ghost stumbling back and away from his mate. No time to explain; Roman flew past just as Sidian disappeared down the first flight, all but leaping down with such impressive grace that Roman's breath caught in his chest.

Sidian had been beautiful the time they first met. Roman almost could not believe there was still room for Sidian to devastate him like this.

"Sid—" Roman tried, but Sidian banged through a door at the bottom of the stairs and out of his line of sight once again.

Panic overwhelmed him at the thought of the Vipers catching his mate on the ground floor, but he reached it in time to see Sidian burst through the doors and out into the parking lot. The others must have all already been inside, where Roman should have stayed until the center staff were dead and extraction was on the way. But the only person in the world he had eyes for was Sidian Vey, and now that Roman knew where his mate was, the only thing that mattered was getting to him as fast as possible to keep him safe from the sharpest edges of the world.

Sidian was afraid. So afraid that the rotten ichor of it was wrapped up in his sweet honeyed florals, petals rotting and curling as they drifted from their stalks. Roman's poor, sweet, frightened omega mate.

Socked feet thudded against the asphalt as Sidian bolted for the trees, and Roman followed in his wake without a second thought. The richness of the forest melded so well with Sidian's scent; this was where he should be. Roman would take him far away from society, secret him away somewhere lush and beautiful and real. Watch him bloom, watch him flourish. He just had to catch up to Sidian before he somehow melted into the shadows and disappeared from sight.

Roman couldn't lose Sidian again. He didn't know what he'd become if he lost Sidian again.

Time slipped from his grasp as the forest closed in around them, swallowing them whole. It was only when the faint sounds of the infiltration faded away, when there were only the sounds of the forest and Sidian's frantic breathing, that Sidian spun around, something glimmering in his hand as he loosed a growl deeper and more vicious than any omega Roman had ever met.

The sound jerked him to a halt before he could process it.

"Stop right fucking there." Sidian brandished his weapon without a hint of fear, and Roman's pride swelled at the sight. "Come any closer to me, and I'll cut your fucking knot off. You'll still be howling from the pain when I shove it down your throat."

That threat had no right to stir Roman's cock the way it did. "Wait—"

"Don't." Sidian lifted his chin, jaw tight, and Roman took in what he could see of his mate through the shafts of moonlight spilling through the leaves above them.

Sidian Vey was beautiful. He was the loveliest omega that Roman had ever laid eyes on, and not only because Sidian was his mate. Before Roman knew that the universe carved hs soul in the shape of Sidian's name and left his heart incomplete so Sidian would come along one day and make it whole, the omega had dazzled Roman. As a stupid teenage boy with no cares or responsibility in the world, Roman had taken one look at the wild-haired boy from his father's psychiatric ward and fallen in love with him.

And he was far more beautiful now, a fully matured omega. His lily scent belied the danger that inhabited him, the glint of the scalpel clasped in his fingers an obvious warning. Wild tendrils of messy umber hair framed his delicate face, feathering the sharp lines of his cheekbones and the stubborn set of his jaw that contrasted so well with his pouty little pink mouth. The sharp hook of his nose twitched as he inhaled, trying to get Roman's scent, but that would be impossible this time.

The Vipers had to spray themselves with de-scenting cologne before each mission. The boss wanted no traces of their scents left behind.

Roman's eyes traveled from Sidian's face to the slim column of his pale throat, the lean shape of his petite form, and the tempting swell of his hips and thighs that accompanied almost every omega. All Roman wanted to do was sink down to his knees in open worship of the perfect creature before him, his gorgeous little omega mate.

Sidian's eyes glittered with anger, the vivid violet shine so unique to him that Roman had never seen another omega like him. There was only Sidian, his gemstone eyes fixed on Roman as pure hatred twisted his lovely features.

But the dark circles beneath those eyes worried Roman.

"I don't know who you are or what you're here for, but if you come any closer to me, I'll make you pay for it." Sidian took a step forward, the long grass brushing his slender ankles. "I'm done with alphas. Done with you sick fucks, and I'll take all my anger out on you if you push me."

Roman's chest tightened at the words, but he ignored the childish desire to whine at Sidian for it. Alphas did not *whine,* and given where he had just escaped from, Sidian wasn't speaking to or about him. Not really. Sidian didn't know who Roman was, and he could only imagine what Sidian must have endured depending on how long he'd been in the breeding center.

Roman would find every single alpha who ever laid a hand on his darling and cut off their fingers one by one.

Sidian winced, the scalpel lowering just a touch before he jerked it back up. "You stay here like a good little dog. I'm leaving."

"Wait." The word was a barely audible rasp, but Roman's desperation permeated his very being, making it impossible for him to bite it back.

Because Sidian could not leave him. Because Roman had already lost Sidian once, and two years without him had been more painful than he knew how to put into words. He needed Sidian at his side always, tucked in against him where he could ensure Sidian was safe and sound, where no other alpha had any hope of reaching him. And the woods were not safe. There was nothing out there but the wilderness, and it was so easy to die unprepared in the wilderness.

Sidian's muscles locked as if the sound of Roman's voice alone had an effect on him; Roman's alpha preened. "Shut the fuck up. Who gave you the privilege of speaking to me?"

An alpha's command, dominance woven into every syllable, was about as unsubtle as a sledgehammer to the face. The boss had strict rules about the Vipers never using their commands within earshot of omegas because of the trauma it could cause them after being locked within the breeding centers, some of them imprisoned for decades of their lives, and some still children. Just the same, Roman knew what an alpha's command sounded like. Requisite training for the Vipers ensured they could always shrug it off if need be, though even the boss could not infuse enough dominance in his voice to bring Roman to his knees.

Sidian silenced him with a single sentence.

He's perfect in every way it's possible to be.

Roman needed to touch Sidian. He needed to hold his mate in his arms and feel all the tension wound tight through Sidian's body relax as he realized he was safe in Roman's embrace. Such a powerful, unique, perfect omega deserved nothing but the best Roman could give him.

And he wanted to give Sidian everything.

Sidian took a step backward, but the slight tremble that rocked his frame told Roman just how exhausted his mate must have been. The adrenaline was likely weakening in his blood.

When Roman tried to draw closer to him, Sidian snarled. "Get down on the fucking ground!"

And Roman's knees struck the dirt.

The impact jarred up his spine, a grunt leaving his lips. He did not try to fight whatever the hell was going on, though, his eyes for Sidian and Sidian alone. Whatever that was, whatever Sidian just did to him, it sparked pure electricity in Roman's veins, zaps of anticipation sizzling beneath his skin. Blood filled his cock, which would have been embarrassing in any other circumstance, but not this one.

He knew Sidian was special. And now he had the proof.

And Goddess help anyone brave or stupid enough to rip his omega from his arms again.

Chapter Five

The sight of the massive alpha sinking to his knees on command stirred an unwelcome heat between Sidian's thighs. His hand trembled where it gripped the scalpel, his breathing quick and tight as he took in the broad silhouette. *Massive* might even be an understatement on his part; even on his knees, the alpha was huge. Broad-shouldered and built thick through the thighs, the narrow cut of his waist made Sidian imagine the solid wall of abdominal muscle likely hidden away beneath layers of what looked like all-black fabric. Even the alpha's gloved hands, hanging at his sides, looked large enough to swallow Sidian's entire face.

Not that he planned on letting anyone touch him ever again. He could live without seeing what the comparison was.

His feet ached from running through the woods with nothing but socks to protect him, his lungs burned with each breath, and a stitch throbbed in his side. Though he was active before being locked away, he'd been doped up and confined inside so much that he could feel how much he'd weakened, and it sickened him. But no more. He didn't know what the hell was going on, but he was free.

And no one was going to take that away from him.

He took another step back, his mind whirling through a thousand possibilities. *Keep running and don't look back.* If this alpha followed him, he might have to figure out a way to kill him. Bred omegas shouldn't trigger an alpha's rut, at the very least, but if something happened to his baby... His heart sped up at the thought, his throat threatening to close. No, nothing could happen to his son. He was going to be just fine, and when Sidian had the chance, he'd hunt down Pack Kincaid and get his daughter back, too.

He could do it himself. He had to do it himself because everyone else was fucking useless. Everyone who ever offered him anything tied a high price to it, higher than he ever wanted to pay ever.

All he wanted was to be left alone.

Another step back, however, and the alpha on the ground let out a low, crooning sound. It sank into Sidian's bones, and some of the tightness in his muscles loosened.

How the hell was the alpha doing that? More to the point, *why?*

Pack Kincaid was never interested in offering him comfort. They used every vocalization to speak to his heat-addled brain, to get him to spread his legs or arch his back or slick their cocks on command while he wished they'd snap his neck and be done with it. Just the memory alone was enough to make him whimper, his resolve wavering.

He was exhausted. If the alpha stood up, he didn't know if he'd have the energy left to kill him.

But Sidian had to. If the alpha got up, if the alpha came after him, then he had to stick his blade in that thickly corded neck and run.

He imagined it. Toyed with the idea of it. Visualized lodging the thin silver blade into the alpha's jugular, watching the flesh split open and blood jettison out. He imagined the warmth dripping over his skin and soaking into his clothes, the rich copper scent following him as he fled into the night.

Copper. Blood. Familiar, but... Not for the usual reasons. For his antics at the center.

The alpha crooned again, softer this time, and the noise drew Sidian one step closer. His omega yearned for comfort and safety in the wake of everything he'd survived, but he knew it was a trap he couldn't fall into. Not here. Not now.

"What?" he demanded, but the alpha didn't answer him. "Talk, damn it. What the fuck do you want?"

The alpha's voice was muffled behind the black mask he wore, a dark mesh over his eyes likely allowing him just enough visibility to see while keeping his identity concealed. "Sidian, please..."

Sidian's name rolled off of the alpha's tongue like a benediction, like a prayer. A soft keen rose to his lips before he could stop it, a desperation clawing at him he didn't recognize. He'd always been careful around alphas, but one of them talked sweetly to him, and he wanted to fall over and show the alpha his belly? Fat fucking chance. He should just kill the alpha to put an end to whatever bizarre power the alpha seemed to have over him.

And then something clicked, his brows furrowing as he lowered the scalpel. "How do you know my name?"

The alpha didn't answer. Instead, he stared at Sidian through the dark fabric covering his eyes, his fingers twitching like he wanted to do something. Reach out? Grab Sidian? Maybe reach for a weapon. Hard to tell when Sidian did not know who the alpha was or why he would even be here. Some kind of government agent? Somehow, he doubted it because most of the breeding centers were government-sanctioned at the very least.

Black Ops of some kind? Why would they be out there? Why rip Barnes's arm off at the shoulder like that and beat him over the head with it?

Why stop just to chase Sidian down?

When the alpha didn't answer and yet made no move to stand, Sidian took a deep breath and shifted closer a few steps, weighing his options. If he got close enough to strike a killing blow, if he rammed the scalpel in the general direction of the alpha's throat, would the alpha lift a hand to stop him? Sidian assumed so, because who would just stay kneeling in the dirt with their life on the line? But it was hard to predict the movements of someone who already wasn't like any of the alphas that Sidian had met.

That was at least more of a blessing than a curse.

A ragged breath made his spine tingle, and he bit down hard on a pathetic omega whine.

"Mask," the alpha breathed, but nothing else.

The mask? Was the alpha trying to take off the mask?

Sidian glanced toward the line of trees at his back before stepping forward, his fingers sliding over the slick black fabric so he could gather just enough of it to secure a good grip. It fit tight and almost seemed like it didn't want to come off, and he felt a slight sense of gratification that the alpha might be in any discomfort at all. After all, it wasn't the alpha who was in the middle of the woods, almost barefoot and pregnant, trying to claw back the freedom that was ripped from his hands.

Sidian ripped the mask off, and the alpha gave his head a shake, freeing a mane of glossy black curls and raising familiar eyes.

Vibrant moss, thick and green on the bark of pale, silvery birch trees. Long black lashes against smooth olive skin. *Almost* smooth, he corrected himself, noting the slit in the alpha's right eyebrow, the knick of a scar beneath his left eye, a jagged twist of white tissue along his jaw.

He didn't look the same as he did back then, but alphas matured quickly after their presentation. The lines of his face were harder now, a powerful jaw and aquiline nose, sharp cheekbones and dark brows. The quintessential alpha face, though the bright glitter of wonder and awe in his eyes softened his features to an incredible degree.

Roman Kane in the flesh.

"What the fuck?" Sidian tried to dart back away from him, but his wobbly legs refused to allow him more than a shuffling half-step. "Roman? Is that you?"

How could his mate be here of all places?

Roman nodded from where he knelt, never taking his eyes off of Sidian—off of his face, Sidian realized, not the blade in his hand as if that concerned Roman not at all. After the amount of violence he saw Roman commit the first time the bloodlust rose in him, it was no wonder he wasn't worried about Sidian and what he might do. If Roman wanted to, he could snap Sidian's spine in half.

He watched Roman wet plush lips with the tip of his tongue, and Sidian's stomach tightened at the sight. "Bullshit. I know what you smell like. Why can't I smell you now?"

"Mission protocol. De-scenting cologne before each mission." The words were clipped, smooth, but breathy as Roman looked Sidian over. Sounded just like him, not that Sidian thought about it, albeit deeper and huskier. "I didn't know you were here."

A flare of white-hot rage consumed Sidian for just a moment, his teeth gritting at Roman's words, before it flickered down to nothing but embers. Embers that were being smothered by relief and his omega keening with excitement in his hindbrain, wanting to preen and dance and coo over his mate reappearing after all this time. All those months of desperate, useless hope just for Roman to show up when Sidian thought he'd never see him again. Impossible.

And yet there Roman was, changed enough that Sidian knew he couldn't be hallucinating him. Staring up at him like Roman had seen nothing more important in his entire life.

Sidian's knees trembled beneath him, his body slumping forward without his permission. The exhaustion crept up on him so slowly he didn't notice it until then, but it coiled through his muscles, forcing his body to bow. His lack of physical activity and wretched state in that fucking facility had left him far too weakened by something like running through the woods, and he couldn't have that.

He had to be quick on his feet. He had to have the stamina necessary to escape any time another alpha tried to cage him.

Before he could hit the ground, Roman shifted closer with terrifying speed, his arms cinching around Sidian's waist. Sidian didn't have time to swing his arm out of the way, and a choked noise caught in his throat when the scalpel sliced through the meat of Roman's cheek just enough to break the skin. The sight of dark blood bubbling out of the shallow wound stirred a part of him that wanted nothing more than retribution for all the pain he'd suffered, a visceral pleasure at seeing someone else hurt for once.

But Roman paid it no mind as he stabilized Sidian, letting him throw an arm around Roman's broad shoulders to brace himself. "Easy, Sid. That was an impressive distance to cover."

"Fuck off," Sidian muttered, but there was no heat in the words. Not like there should have been.

Roman chuckled but made no move to touch Sidian further, his arms warm where they rested against Sidian's skin, his gigantic hands fanning across Sidian's back but otherwise remaining well above the waist. The heat that radiated off of him cut through the chill that had sunk deep into Sidian's bones, soothing him in ways it shouldn't have been able to. But of course, Roman was an alpha, and alphas and omegas were made for each other.

Sidian slumped forward against him, letting his face rest against the mop of Roman's soft curls. He was so tall that even on his knees, Sidian didn't have to bend down too far to reach him. "Feels like I'm not gonna be able to make it back."

"It's all right," Roman soothed. "Just rest. When you're ready, we'll go back together."

Sidian's throat threatened to close as the thought of being left in the ruins of the center, separated from Roman yet again, even though he was furious at Roman for not being with him until now. "What happens next?"

"That depends on you. Think about it while you rest." Roman bumped his forehead against Sidian's chest right above his stomach, and Sidian tensed.

Had he noticed? He had said nothing about it, but why else would Sidian be at a place like the breeding center if not to be sold and bred?

What else were omegas even considered good for?

That Sidian couldn't pick up Roman's scent at all prickled his nerves, his omega disquieted even if he knew this was his alpha. Pretty unreasonable to expect the guy to just walk around the way Sidian wanted him to, but the scent said so much between mates that now, he craved it.

Roman leaned back to look up at him, and Sidian allowed him to do that, studying the strong lines of his face. "You look just as stunning as I remember."

"Fucker. Last time you saw me, I was covered in blood you got all over the living room. And all over you." Sidian shifted so he could trace a hand down the side of Roman's face, remembering the smear of crimson that dripped down his jaw.

Roman rumbled deep in his chest, pressing into the touch like a cat as his eyelashes fluttered. "Goddess, I've missed you."

Something in those words threatened to undo Sidian when he was already too weak to do much more than stand there. Roman was here. When Sidian was so sure he was dead in the ground for what happened—what Roman did for him, because of him, to protect him—he showed up. He was there, alive and well.

The only time he'd ever kissed someone by choice was Roman, his mouth wet with blood and tongue slick with copper. Sidian was bad at it then and maybe worse now, but he still mashed their lips together with a ferocity that shocked even him. His hands framed Roman's face, nails digging in so the alpha couldn't escape. A growl rumbled up his throat when Roman tried to shift, but it was only so their lips met seamlessly, warm and wet and so perfect it made his cunt throb.

Roman's arms tightened around him, and the ground disappeared from beneath his feet as Roman stood, holding Sidian above him with an ease that made Sidian whine against Roman's lush mouth. He should have been scared out of his fucking mind that Roman could do that, but he just wrapped himself around his mate as much as he could, clinging to Roman, shuddering when Roman's tongue slipped into his mouth and curled against his own. It was slick and left him wanting more, and while the only thing that would make it better was Roman's scent closing in around him, Sidian would take what he was given.

The kiss grew almost frantic on Roman's end. Harsher, wetter, more demanding, his mouth devoured Sidian's as his grip on Sidian tightened. Not to the point of pain, but if Sidian didn't know any better, he might think that Roman was just as afraid to lose him as he was scared to lose Roman.

He only ripped his mouth away from Roman's so he could breathe, and Roman barely let him do that, brushing chaste little pecking kisses against Sidian's lips as he set him down on his feet. The height difference between them meant that even on Sidian's toes, Roman had to lean down to reach his lips, but Roman didn't seem to mind. With one hand braced in the small of Sidian's back, the other threaded through his hair to draw him closer.

He didn't know an alpha could be so gentle.

"I'm sorry I wasn't here sooner." Roman kissed Sidian's forehead, his nose, his cheeks, his eyelids, before returning to his mouth with a low, soft groan. "I looked. We couldn't find you. But I looked." Another harsh kiss left Sidian panting. "And I will never let you go ever again."

Sidian grasped Roman's arms as tight as he could. He wasn't going anywhere.

Chapter Six

"Here." Roman stripped off his long-sleeved black shirt and handed it to Sidian, who yanked it over his head without a word. "We should head back."

He wasn't sure how long they had been gone, but the rest of the Vipers should be gone by now. Extraction would be well on their way to taking the omegas to safety, and Jagger would be losing his mind at a disappearance; Ghost would have to explain what happened, which did not bode well for Roman. He would have to contact his captain, but it was the last thing on his mind.

His cell phone remained silent. An excellent sign.

Sidian slipped his hands beneath the fall of his raven hair to free it from the neck of the shirt. It was long enough to need that now, brushing the very tips of his shoulders as he ruffled his fingers through it. With Roman's shirt looking more like a dress on Sidian's lean frame than anything else, the omega looked so achingly beautiful that Roman had to blink to keep from tearing up.

It had been so long. So much longer than he wanted to think about. So much longer than he ever wanted it to be.

"What the fuck was all of that, anyway?" Sidian asked, fidgeting with the sleeves of Roman's shirt. "I'm assuming you're responsible for that freaky power cut shit."

Roman shook his head, leaning down to pick up his fallen mask to stuff into the back pocket of his jeans. He did not know when or if he would need it again, but leaving any evidence lying around was likely to get him beaten when he made his way back to the Pit. "No. Not my area. They task one of my teammates with it. Standard protocol."

Sidian's brows furrowed. "Standard protocol? The Vipers? Are you bullshitting me?"

Roman blinked at him, not sure how to answer that question. Why would he do that in the first place? He'd always been frank in his honesty; it was one of the many traits that Sidian had seemed to like about him when they first met. "No, of course not. I joined after... The incident."

"Since when were you all about that mercenary squad lifestyle?" Sidian sorted as if the thought amused him, taking a shaky step forward only for his knee to buckle.

Roman caught him by the shoulders to hold him upright, unwilling to let his omega suffer the indignity of falling after the impressive distance he'd run. "I'll carry you back. How would you prefer it?"

"You know what? Yeah. That's what you're gonna do since it's your fault I'm all the way out here." Sidian let himself lean against Roman's chest, and Roman tried very hard not to let it show just how much he preferred that position. "Piggyback. Crouch down for me."

Though Roman would have preferred a bridal carry himself, he nodded and turned, crouching down low enough for Sidian's arms to snake around his neck. Sidian's lean chest pressed up against his back when he stood, and his hands slipped around to find the bends of Sidian's knees, cinching Sidian's legs around his torso as best they could manage together. Though it wasn't easy with someone as broad as Roman was, Sidian managed just fine, dropping his chin down on Roman's shoulder with a relieved little sigh. His lily scent bloomed soft and sweet in the air, laced with obvious omega pleasure that had Roman's alpha rumbling contentedly.

Sidian didn't weigh enough for Roman's preference, but that wasn't something he needed to dwell on when they couldn't do anything about it yet. "Are you comfortable?"

"Comfortable enough." Sidian tilted his head just enough for Roman to feel the tip of a cold nose graze his ear, and his cock jumped in answer. "What made you decide to join the Vipers in the first place? Doesn't seem like your rodeo."

Roman pursed his lips. "The boss offered me a spot. Money can make three homicides go away."

"Should've just been the two. You didn't mean to kill your old man."

No, Roman hadn't meant to do that. The words resurrected his barely buried guilt, the sharp spines of it digging into his guts as he started back toward where he knew the charred remains of the center were likely waiting for them. Of course, the world at large did not care that his father's death was nothing more than an accident. All he wanted to do was slow Roman's rampage and help him get himself back under control, but Roman's agitated hindbrain refused to see his father as anything more than yet another enemy trying to come between him and his mate.

He regretted it. Anyone would, and Goddess knew he did despite the boss's insistence that regrets only existed to weigh them down. It was the only one Roman could never let go of, the reminder that no matter what happened, he must maintain control of himself as much as possible. That there were others around him, and that he needed to remember what he was capable of rather than risk losing everything because the heat of the moment sank its raking claws into his bones.

Sidian drew his cheek along Roman's shoulder, and his alpha rumbled at the sensation of being scent-marked by his omega. "How long have you been with 'em, then? Since they put me away? Must have been because I doubt the state was gonna let you rot in prison over the needle."

Roman's jaw tightened at the thought. "Yes. I've been with them for that long. And no one will ever lock you up again."

"I know that." Sidian dug his knees into Roman's sides just enough for Roman to feel the dull pressure. "Might not know as much about you as I used to, but if you burn breeding centers down, then I can trust you to make that promise for real. And if you let it happen again, I'll fucking gut you."

As expected, the Bell Breeding Center was aflame when they emerged from the treeline, the fire twisting its way up toward the glittering stars overhead. The sight always instilled a peace within Roman's soul, the fractured pieces of it soothed by the knowledge that the hands of the Vipers had split apart at least one more den of evil. While they might not have been righteous people—they did what they had to do, whatever that entailed—they at least had respect for omegas. Like proper alphas are meant to.

Sidian sighed in Roman's ear. "Now that's a sight for sore eyes. Doesn't look like anyone's around. Your guys take off that fast?"

"Someone may have reported the fire," Roman admitted, though he didn't know how far the smoke had traveled or if anyone lived nearby. He eyed the parking lot; none of the vehicles that had been parked when the Vipers arrived had been disturbed. That was good. "We should go, I think."

None of the staff had escaped, not that they ever did. But at the very least, it looked as though he and Sidian could borrow a pair of wheels.

Sidian slept curled up in the passenger seat of the Nissan Ultima that Roman chose, his cheek resting against the window and his arms coiled around himself despite the heat pumping through the vents. It was too much for Roman, who had to crack a window as soon as his mate dozed off, in desperate need of escape from the overwhelming warmth. Alphas ran so much hotter than omegas did, but he would put up with as much of it as he could for Sidian's safety and comfort.

Unable to help himself, Roman kept stealing looks at Sidian, tracing the curve of his cheek, the bow of his bottom lip, the fall of his hair. All he wanted to do was touch, to caress every inch of Sidian's body until Roman had the lines and curves and contours of him memorized. So that he would know Sidian by touch alone even if his eyes one day failed him.

It seemed unreal to have Sidian so close once again.

Not that he deserved it. He gritted his teeth and dragged his eyes back to the road, glancing at the rearview mirror to ensure no other cars had come up behind them. Especially no pigs. If the police pulled up on them, then Roman would be forced to kill them. He was fine with doing so if need be, but that made matters so much messier than they needed to be, and he would know. He'd had to do it.

He drummed his fingers on the steering wheel as he pored over the last two years in his mind. The Vipers had checked every single database across the country that Silver could access, though Roman would have to comb through the records of those searches to ensure they checked Bell before he would have any peace of mind. Some of the documentation they had come across had been lacking, to say the least. Missing and nonexistent records were common in breeding centers if there was something worth hiding, though Roman wasn't sure if that was the case.

What was there about Sidian that needed to be hidden?

The rough shape of a motel materialized in the darkness an hour after they crossed the state line into Oregon, which should keep them secure until Roman had the time to figure out a proper plan. The boss was going to have his ass for disappearing in the middle of a mission, but hopefully Ghost could give the others enough context that they could draw their own conclusions. After all, the boss especially knew how much Sidian meant to Roman, and he had to understand how important it was that Roman kept his omega safe.

A breeding center. Goddess's sake, a fucking *breeding* center.

Roman parked the car in the motel parking lot, making sure the license plate was not easily visible from the road. He gave the lot a cursory glance as he climbed out of the car, then glanced down at himself. Though the scent of blood on his skin was still noticeable, there was little he could do about it. At least the patches of blood on his undershirt and pants looked to have dried enough to be unnoticeable. Nothing stood out to him, though he hadn't been around civilians enough to know if he gave off an unsettling air like he did to the Vipers.

Guess he'd just have to find out.

A middle-aged beta sat behind a stretch of cracked counter on the far side of the motel lobby, his attention focused on the phone in his hand until the bells over the door jingled. The beta glanced up before setting the phone down and standing, smoothing out his shirt. Roman appreciated the lack of a polite smile; he was too tired to muster up a facade of his own and didn't want to bother.

"How can I help you tonight?" the beta asked, glancing behind himself at a stained, weathered clock hanging on the wall. "My, my. Cutting it pretty late tonight, are we?"

Roman noted the beta's nametag, committing the name *Larry* to memory in case it came up again in the future, though he doubted it would. Force of habit. "I drove later than I expected to."

Larry scoffed and waved it off with a hand, the silver band of a wedding ring glinting. So he might have someone who would miss him if he were gone. Good to know. "Nah, don't worry about it. Ain't many places out here in the middle of nowhere. Makes it real easy to lose track of time, doesn't it?"

"It does." Roman drew his wallet out of his back pocket, fanning it open. The Vipers only carried cash on them in case of an emergency, but he doubted it would be much of a problem in an establishment like this one. "Do you take cash? We need a room for one night."

Larry typed something into the computer on the counter, the monitor worn and cracked at the corners, before giving a brief nod. "Sure do. Ain't really bother with cards out around here if I can help it, though my daughter says I need to acclimate. Anyway, gonna be fifty for the night. What name you want it under?"

"Ethan Rhodes." The name rolled off of Roman's tongue with ease as he extracted a crisp fifty from his wallet, then smoothed a twenty on top of it. That should keep Larry quiet. "For the trouble."

"Enjoy your stay, Mr. Rhodes." Larry snatched the bills before Roman could change his mind, turning to pluck a key off of the corkboard of fobs mounted on the wall. "Room One at the far end should do ya for the night. No other residents on that side of the building, so it'll be nice and quiet for you. King-sized bed, too, nice and comfy. Mattress is just a year old."

"Thank you." Hopefully, the quiet would allow Sidian to rest for as long as he needed to before they moved on again.

You need to sleep, too, Roman reminded himself, stepping back out into the cool night air of the Oregon woods. He did not know what town they were in, but for the time, that didn't matter. *You'll be useless to him if you can't keep your eyes open.*

Sidian didn't so much as twitch as Roman opened the passenger door of the Ultima and unbuckled his mate's seatbelt, scooping the sleeping omega into his arms. Sidian's head came to rest against his shoulder, lips parted with each gentle breath. Maybe Sidian would get enough rest to do something about those dark circles. If not, Roman would ensure they had long rest periods until he had recovered in at least one small way.

Room One was at the far end of the building, as Larry promised. Roman shifted Sidian's weight as carefully as he could while he unlocked the door, ensuring the movement did not jar him too much. Inside, the room was clean and warm enough to suit their needs, and Roman's nose detected nothing out of the ordinary that would put him off staying overnight. The scents of black mold or cockroaches, for instance, were easy for an alpha to detect. Not so for a beta, he supposed.

With one flick of the wrist, Roman drew back the comforter so he could tuck Sidian beneath it, smoothing his fingers through his mate's dark hair. Sidian sighed in his sleep, nuzzling into the pillow, which was good enough for Roman. It wasn't a nest, but it was something. And once Sidian had gotten some much-needed rest, they could sit down and discuss where to go next. What the plan was.

He could take Sidian back to the Vipers' Pit, but he wouldn't make that decision for them. Instead, he unlaced his boots, double-checked that the door was locked, and slunk into bed behind his omega.

It was time for a good night's sleep.

Chapter Seven

The scent of sunlight warming iron tickled Sidian's nose, the metallic richness of it drawing a purr from his lips. Beneath it was something sweet and smoky, flames licking at oiled wood. A funeral pyre.

His cunt twitched, slick gathering between his thighs as he shifted on what felt like the softest bed he'd ever slept on. Something solid brushed up against his back, and he pressed into it without thinking, a wall of solid muscle that vibrated against his back as he arched into it. One large hand gave his hip a brief squeeze, but he whined because that wasn't where he wanted to be touched. Not even close.

Lips feathered a kiss across the top of his head. "Looks like the shower did the trick, then."

"Hmm?" The voice was rich, dreamy, and familiar.

Where had he heard that voice before?

"Slept a few hours. Took a shower. Slept a few hours more." A mouth trailed kisses through Sidian's hair before pressing one just behind his ear, stubble tickling his skin. He could imagine what it would feel like on his thighs. "You didn't like the de-scenting cologne. Better now, Sid?"

Only one person in the world could call him that.

Memories from the night before flooded his mind as his eyes snapped open, his head twisting back until he could see just enough of Roman's face to confirm he was real. There was a light shadow of facial hair along his jaw, which only made him look sexier than he did last night. His green-gray eyes gazed down at Sidian with a look of such utter warmth that Sidian's omega whined at the sight. Two years without his mate. Two years of pure and utter suffering, but Roman was there now. It didn't seem possible, but he was solid and warm and *real.*

Sidian pressed back into the solid heat of Roman's chest, his eyelids fluttering as he enjoyed his mate's touch. "It's you. Holy shit. Thought I might have dreamed you."

"A pleasant dream, I hope?" Roman grinned down at him, his eyes crinkling as he dipped his head to press a kiss to Sidian's forehead. "You have a gorgeous purr when you sleep."

"I purr in my sleep?" Sidian doubted he'd purred once in the last two years. If anything, he'd only purred the night he kissed Roman and licked the blood off of his tongue.

"When I was near. You were quiet on your own." Roman's hand crept along Sidian's hip and feathered over his chest, fingers brushing over Sidian's throat until cupping his chin, holding him still for another light forehead kiss. "You smell so sweet. I knew it was you in an instant. Nothing else mattered."

"How much trouble are you gonna end up in for chasing me?" It was a stupid question; an elite mercenary group was not likely to forgive and forget, but it didn't bother Sidian.

Chuckling, Roman nuzzled into Sidian's hair, breathing him in, and for a moment, he tensed... Then relaxed. If Roman hadn't noticed the pregnancy yet, then maybe Sidian would get lucky. Maybe Roman wouldn't notice at all. "The boss will be annoyed with me. He can deal with it. You're more important to me than any mission."

Sidian wrapped a hand around Roman's wrist, dragging his scorching touch down his body. While that was sweet, and he wanted to hear every honeyed word Roman planned to shower him with, his pussy was intent on making its demands clear.

His clit pulsed with every beat of his heart; it had been too long since he'd *enjoyed* anything intimate, but with Roman, he planned to indulge. If he didn't, he was going to be soaking wet and irritated until he indulged in his own desires.

And he desired so much.

The moment Roman's fingers skimmed the waistband of Sidian's pants beneath his directing touch, Sidian's body lit up from the inside out. His cunt tightened around air and a needy whine spilled from his lips, his hips bucking to draw Roman's hand where Sidian wanted it.

"I think that's the mate bond talking," Roman murmured, though he slid his fingers the rest of the way down, tracing them over Sidian's mound through the thin white cotton.

"Probably," Sidian rasped out, closing his eyes as he arched into that knowing touch. The slow glide of fingers over barely covered skin made every nerve spark, his teeth gritting against the need that pulsed through him. Goddess, his heats with Roman were going to be *unbearable*. "Heard it's not unusual for scent matches to fall over fucking each other before they know each other's names, but I'll settle for you getting me off for now."

"We already know each other's names." Roman nipped his ear, and Sidian bit back a curse when those thick, callused fingers found the very top of his slit. "You should take these off."

"Fuck yeah. Good idea." Sidian wriggled away from his alpha just long enough to shove the pants down and off, as well as the sorry excuse for underwear the center had given him. It didn't even absorb slick, the cheap piece of shit. "You know how to get an omega off, I'd hope."

Roman huffed and drew Sidian back against his chest, one arm slipping beneath Sidian to cradle him closer while Roman's free hand guided Sidian's thigh up and over his own leg. "I've done some research."

"In person research?"

"No, never." Roman wrinkled his nose, and Sidian bit back a small snicker of satisfaction. "Videos and books exist. Those have been suitable."

Sidian wanted to laugh at the image of Roman poring over books or pornography to understand how to please an omega, but before he could, warm fingers stroked along his inner thigh before touching his cunt.

There was something hot about being held like that, well aware that Roman was so much stronger, able to manhandle Sidian any way he liked. But he was gentle with his touches, the hand wrapped around Sidian's thigh heavy with possession while the fingers that stroked along his soaking wet slit were gentle and careful. They traced their way down his slit before dipping between his folds, spreading them as Roman's fingers stroked back up.

"Oh, your research was excellent." Sidian let his eyes fall shut, giving himself over to the little sparks of pleasure that burst in his blood.

"I'd hope so." Roman kissed behind Sidian's ear again, touch honing in on his clit, tracing smooth and leisurely circles around the puffy swell of it. "I didn't want to risk disappointing you."

Sidian's head lolled back against Roman's chest as he moaned, his hips rolling into each teasing touch as he all but begged for Roman to touch his clit. Instead, his alpha took his time, fingers dipping down to stroke over Sidian's fluttering entrance, gathering the slick there to drag it back up to his clit. Every stroke was slicker, sliding over swollen flesh until Sidian's toes curled and another needy whine broke from his throat. He wasn't always so desperate to get off unless he was in heat, but Roman's smoky scent was like an aphrodisiac.

Teeth scraped along the side of his throat. "You smell like heaven."

"You smell like fire and death. Sexy, though." Sidian swore, feeling himself clench as Roman touched his clit. "Not gonna be enough. I want your fingers in me *now*."

The purr of the command slipped over his lips, and Roman's other hand shifted down, fingers sliding through slick before two of them wedged inside of Sidian without hesitation. The sudden stretch sent him writhing, panting harshly and hot as Roman played his body like a fucking violin. Wrapped up in the alpha's arms, riding the thickness of his fingers while he stroked Sidian's clit in tight circles, Sidian was in fucking heaven. Or at least as close to it as he could be.

"Are you always this wet?" Roman asked, curling his fingers forward until he massaged Sidian's G-spot with ease, the pressure drawing a ragged cry from Sidian's lips. "Or am I doing a good job?"

"S'all for you. Just you." Only under command had Sidian ever slicked up like this for anyone else, and he'd been in heat then. It didn't count.

None of it counted as far as he was concerned. Just Roman's big hands between his thighs, worshipping his pussy, overflowing waves of heat washing over Sidian like tender caresses, pushing him closer to the edge while he dug his heels in, desperate to make the high last as long as possible.

Roman pressed their cheeks together, rubbing just enough that a burst of his scent fanned over them both. Scent-marking between mates was fucking sacred, a claim of ownership long before a bite was ever placed. Of course, Sidian knew that; he'd scented Roman as he'd been carried out of the woods, determined that if Roman didn't smell like himself, he'd at least smell like Sidian.

But, fuck, he was *delicious.* Aromatic oil slicking fragrant charred wood, flames licking against Sidian's skin, the metallic bite of it almost overwhelming. He didn't even realize he was moving faster, his hips bucking in quick, frantic movements as his hindbrain took over and sought release.

Roman sighed against his skin. "There you go, darling."

The pet name shoved Sidian over the edge, his lips parting on a cry as heat burst over him, every muscle clenching as he rode the waves of pleasure. Roman worked him through it, his hands never slowing until Sidian clawed at his forearms to make him stop, oversensitive and trembling. The wet sucking noise of his cunt as Roman eased his fingers free should have been embarrassing, but it felt right.

That orgasm was the best he'd ever had. Bless his mate and his touch.

"There you go." Roman sucked a kiss into the side of his neck, and Sidian hummed, letting himself slump down onto the mattress. "Just lay here and relax, and I'll get you cleaned up."

Like Sidian was going to argue with that.

He peered over a shoulder as Roman stood, watching him suck the wetness off of his fingers, his scent spiking hot and hungry in the air. But almost immediately, that was far less interesting than the planes of olive muscle on display, his back flexing as he rolled his shoulders, and when he turned just so, Sidian caught a flash of firm pecs and a smooth, flat stomach.

There were a few scattered scars, and he longed to trace the knotted flesh with his tongue, sink his teeth in to rip them open again.

Roman disappeared around a corner, then reappeared a moment later, shaking out a wet washcloth that was warm and damp as it glided over Sidian's thighs and over his still-tingling pussy. "Was that good for you?"

"Kind of stupid question is that?" Sidian bit his lip as the terrycloth drew lightly over his still-swollen clit, but he was well and truly done for the time being. "Let me make one thing clear ahead of next time, though, in case we go any farther. You do anything I don't want you to do, anything I don't like, and I'll rip your throat out. I'll make what you did to the doc look like amateur hour. Goes for you and anyone else you might be packed up with."

Instantly, Roman's eyes darkened. "No pack. I'm not sharing. No other alphas deserve to serve you."

"And you think you do?" It was hard not to tease him.

"No." Roman leaned down and pressed a kiss to the slip of bare stomach just above Sidian's cunt, and for one terrifying moment, he thought Roman knew, but nothing showed in his eyes or flared in his scent. "But I aim to be worthy."

That sounded good to Sidian.

Roman tossed the washcloth aside and stretched out on the bed next to Sidian, who leaned down to tug his underwear and pants back up. They weren't ideal, but considering he had no other clothes, he wasn't sure about changing.

For now, though, Sidian was content to roll over and tuck his face into Roman's bare chest, fingers brushing through the wispy line of chest hair between his pecs. Every inch of him was bronzed perfection, and Sidian *knew* he'd have a good time taking Roman all the way apart and seeing just how far that servitude went. If he were half as devoted as he portrayed himself to be, then Sidian was going to enjoy what a potential bond between them might look like.

That was for later, though. Only when he had Amethyst back.

He traced his fingers over a line of scar tissue along Roman's collarbone, leaning up to taste the texture of it with his tongue. "You got so sexy."

"I'm glad you think so." Roman sighed, his eyelids fluttering shut. It seemed almost miraculous he'd asked for nothing at all, not even Sidian's hand on his cock, though Sidian didn't think he'd agree just yet.

Maybe one day soon, but not right then.

"What do we do now?" he asked, looking up into Roman's relaxed face. "Or did you think about what would come next after running off?"

Roman's brows furrowed. "I thought I would let you choose. The Vipers will not be thrilled I ran, but I won't be punished. But if you don't want to go back, we don't have to."

"I don't." Not yet. There was only one thing that Sidian wanted, and he wasn't sure that Roman would let him have it. "I know what I wanna do, though. Gonna depend on how up for it you are, though. "It will not be pretty, but it's in your wheelhouse."

"What is it?" Roman opened his eyes, his expression curious. "If I can give it to you, I will."

How did Sidian explain this without divulging more than he was ready to tell? Roman wasn't stupid; he lived simply, sure, but he had never been unintelligent. He could likely draw the most logical conclusion about what happened in breeding centers, which meant that Sidian had to tread carefully. Roman didn't know about Amethyst, not when he didn't know that Sidian was even in a breeding center.

And he couldn't know. Sidian wanted to tell him, but he could not bear the possibility that Roman would say *no* if he knew there was a child involved. When they'd been younger, neither of them had wanted children, and even a potential bond might not have changed Roman's opinion on that. Sidian would just have to hope that meeting Amey in the flesh would change his mind.

She was perfect. Roman would see that for himself.

"There was a pack who came to see me during my heats," Sidian said, feeling Roman tense up under his hand. *Good boy.* "I want them dead. For everything they did to me, I want them dead. I want to see them on their knees, begging me for forgiveness, and then I want you to rip their guts out for me."

Roman's eyes snapped open, his face creased with a rage Sidian had never seen before. "What did they do to you, Sid?"

Sidian thought of Amethyst. He thought of her tiny face staring up at him for the brief seconds he held her. She didn't cry when she was born, but she looked around the world that surrounded her like she wanted to take as much of it in as possible. Given how quickly she was ripped from his arms after the doctor placed her there, maybe she knew it would be the only time she'd get to see him. It had been well over a year since that day, but every single detail was all but emblazoned on his memory.

Her wide, dark blue eyes. The agony of feeling like his entire body was being torn apart. Pack Kincaid leered and laughed and did everything possible to shred the tiniest hints of safety so that Sidian was never under the impression that the doctors and nurses telling them to stay back could stop them. It was by their own power, and their own power alone.

That one last, dizzying remark right before they vanished with Amey. His firstborn child.

He stared at Roman's chest, fingers smoothing over the scar tissue on Roman's collarbone. "What didn't they do to me?"

"Sidian?" Roman nudged their noses together, and Sidian squeezed his eyes shut. "I'll kill them. Just for you, however you want me to."

"That's what I like to hear." He rewarded Roman with a kiss, smiling at the deep alpha rumble that vibrated against his lips. "Do you care if I hop in the shower?"

Roman shook his head, leaning back just enough so Sidian could sit up, though he still felt shaky from the force of that orgasm. "Take your time. When you're ready to go, we'll go."

Sidian stole one last kiss before heading to the shower, intent on scrubbing off the memory of Dax Kincaid's fingers on his bloody skin.

Chapter Eight

The motel was a few miles from the highway, which carried Roman and Sidian down to a small city called Summit Falls. The fact it was just off the highway meant no one paid Roman any attention as he made the handful of stops necessary to gather what he thought they might need for the trip ahead, and no one looked twice at where Sidian slumped against the passenger side door. The pleased little smile that curled the edge of his lips filled Roman with a stupid sort of pride, his alpha swelling up in his chest at the knowledge he'd pleased his mate.

As long as Sidian was happy, Roman was content.

Though Roman was not fond of cities, they meant larger stores brimming with thousands of customers per day and dozens of disenchanted employees who paid him no mind. A couple of people seemed concerned when they looked at him for too long, but no one spoke to him beyond the bare minimum, which was his preference even on a good day. Roman had never been much of a talker growing up despite his father's desperate attempts to socialize him.

By the time they pulled into a truck stop to gas up the Ultima, the day was looking brighter despite the dreary clouds that hung low overhead, painting everything with the same muted, gunmetal hue.

Sidian disappeared into the truck stop's bathroom with a drawstring bag of clothing slung over one shoulder while Roman filled up the tank, sitting in the driver's seat with the door wide open. He stared at nothing in particular, mapping out his purchases in his head as he tried to figure out where they would go next. He'd spent a good portion of his time selecting as much clothing as he could afford, having chosen a store that had plenty of clothing at fair prices. Then he'd picked up a pair of drawstring bags from the sports department because carrying plastic bags of clothes into a gas station of any kind would look too suspicious.

This was better, but at least it was something.

When Sidian returned to the car, it was in a fresh pair of baggy jeans, a black t-shirt, a heavier plaid jacket with a gray hood tugged up over his soft dark hair, and a pair of sneakers that had looked his size. He looked like *himself* again, which also pleased Roman's alpha enough that he felt a rumble deep in his chest, clearing his throat to shake it off.

It was just clothing. He needed to calm the fuck down.

"Don't think anyone paid attention to little ol' me. Too busy digging through clearance snacks and shit," Sidian said, settling back into the passenger seat. He cocked his head in Roman's direction, eyebrows raised. "So. We got clothes. We got gas. What comes next?"

That was a good question. What they needed was information. "I need to think about that. And I would like to find a nicer place to stay."

"Sounds good to me." Sidian adjusted his seat so he could lean back, tugging his hat down to shadow his eyes as he stifled a yawn against his palm. "Might take a nap on the drive. Once we find a place, though, how do we go about hunting down Pack Kincaid?"

"If we're lucky, I might be able to look them up." A task that would be easier with Silver, but Roman wasn't ready to radio back in to his captain just yet, and Jagger hadn't called him.

"Look 'em up?" Sidian clarified, then snorted. "Fair enough. If they could afford that place, they're probably a bunch of rich assholes."

Roman knew they would be. It would make killing them a messier affair because they had people to miss them when they were gone, but he would do what he needed to do for his omega.

He slid out of the car to slide the nozzle back into the pump and screw the cap back on the tank, then rejoined Sidian in the car and pulled the door shut behind him. This was as close to civilization as Roman had been in the last two years, and though he was pleased, he could still affect civility when necessary, he was still unnerved. The quiet of the Pit, broken only by the occasional shouts and arguments and scuffles, was still far and away more peaceful than this was.

Sidian adjusted himself in his seat before settling, and for just a moment, it was easy to pretend this was just a normal day for a normal couple living a normal life without the Vipers or the center of the bloodbath that prevented Roman and Sidian being ripped away from each other. In a better world, they would just be stopping for gas on the way home, or maybe on the way to a vacation spot where they could sequester themselves away from the world for a week or two.

Fucked that one up, didn't you, Roman?

Sidian punched him in the shoulder, shaking Roman out of his daze. "Go get dressed. I want a cheeseburger. Fuck that, I want *three* cheeseburgers. And you're paying for them."

"Of course, Sid." Roman picked his bag out of the backseat and slid out of the car once again, letting himself stretch out his muscles to prepare for what promised to be another long drive.

He would find somewhere quiet. More than anything, he needed to think.

Three hours outside of the city was the town of Angel Ridge, Oregon.

Tucked into the forest with narrow, cracked streets and worn buildings, it was the perfect place to stop for a bite to eat. The Ultima was only slightly newer than most of the cars in the diner's small parking lot, and luckily, it wasn't painted an ostentatious color that would make it impossible for them to blend in. Hopefully, though, no police drove by and felt the itch to run the plates of an unfamiliar car. Roman didn't know why they would, but it was a concern. Even though the town gave him an air of people who kept to themselves, he knew better than to drop his guard for even a moment.

Especially with Sidian involved.

The interior of the diner was all wide glass windows and paneled wood, smelling of lemon cleaner and greasy food. Roman cast a glance around just the same, making a note of each person who sat at a booth as well as the elderly man seated at the counter.

"Just sit anywhere," someone called out to them. "I'll be with you in just a moment!"

Sidian made a beeline for a booth in the back tucked next to a window, and Roman followed him without a word. The seats were smooth with no cracks, which was a pleasant surprise given the relative age of the building.

Within maybe two minutes of sitting down, a pretty blonde waitress with a fairytale princess amount of curls drawn back into a high ponytail hurried up to the table. She plucked a notepad from her apron and a pen from behind her ear; the nametag pinned to her waist read *Fable* in cursive script; it suited her. She smelled of watermelon sugar, which told Roman that there was an alpha skulking around the kitchen. No one would let an omega work the front of the house without some kind of back-up.

And that was useful information to know.

"Sorry to keep you waiting," Fable said, smoothing down her apron before she straightened up. "What can I get for the two of you?"

Sidian, who had retrieved a menu tucked behind the small rack housing the salt and pepper shakers, glanced up at her. "You guys serving lunch, or is it still too early in the day for that?"

"Don't even worry about the time, sweetheart. Anything on the menu is available whenever you want it." She flashed him a pretty smile, her nose scrunching up just a bit before her sapphire blue eyes softened. "Anything you want, it's yours any way you want it."

Sidian seemed to pause before he sat up and slid the menu to Roman, who peered down at it. "Three cheeseburgers with everything on them. Fries, uh, but maybe hold the salt on those. Wouldn't wanna have high blood pressure, right?"

Fable giggled and nodded as she scribbled away on her notepad. "Of course not. And what would you like to drink?"

"Tea, I guess. Sweet tea." Sidian leaned back in his seat, looking very pleased with himself.

When Fable turned her attention to Roman, he kept his expression as neutral as possible. Though he knew Sidian had no reason to doubt him at all, there was no reason for him to offer any fuel for a potential fire. He could control himself. "Just a breakfast platter and some black coffee. We've been on the road for a while this morning."

"I'll have that right out to you two." Fable headed for the counter, giving them a moment alone.

"So, what do we do now?" Sidian asked as soon as he deemed her out of earshot, though Roman wasn't so sure if she was. "How do you look up Pack Kincaid? I've seen your phone, Roman. You can't have actual fucking data on it."

The phone had no data. Every phone owned by a Viper existed only to make and accept calls to one another, the captain, and the boss as needed. "I need to call my captain. One of our members is good at collecting information. He may help us."

"You sure about that?" The fervent glow in Sidian's violet eyes would have unnerved someone else, but it never disturbed Roman.

He wondered if that was what Sidian thought about in the center. What he would do when he escaped, plotting ways to slip out of those barred windows, secured doors, security cameras. How to survive in the countryside just long enough to find someone who might indulge in his lust for revenge. Two years was more than enough time to lose hope under the crushing system designed to break omegas down at the core of their beings.

Sidian could never break, though. Roman was certain of that.

"That depends," Roman said, keeping his voice low and soft. "But I will make the call. Silver should be willing to help us."

Sidian grinned, all bright white teeth. "Fuck yeah."

With that settled, Roman turned his attention to the window next to them, studying the still-green trees and the miles of forest that stretched as far as the eye could see. When he'd been younger and his mother was still alive, they'd gone on a few family camping trips that allowed his parents to have some alone time while he explored as far away from the tent as possible, using his nose to lead him back. If he stepped out of the perimeter where he could pick up their scents, he would backtrack until he was somewhere he deemed safe once again. Dad never worried about him because he knew Roman would always find his way back to them as long as his nose still worked.

He tried to imagine that for Sidian, for himself. A cute little tent, a bonfire, Sidian tucked away in Roman's lap while a child dug through the underbrush for snakes and beetles and Goddess knew what else. It was hard to imagine normalcy given how far from that path Roman had strayed over the years.

Snapping someone's neck for the first time had given him a different perspective on life.

Fable returned to their booth with two steaming plates, a mug of coffee for Roman, and a tall glass of iced sweet tea for Sidian. "You two let me know if there's anything else you need, and I'll bring it to you. Eat up. And there's plenty more where that came from."

Sidian stared after her for a moment before tucking into his first burger, muffling a moan after the first bite that nearly made Roman drop his fork. The sound traveled straight to his cock, which was only slightly mortifying given they were in public, but he did his best to ignore it as he dug into the half-cooked yolks of his fried eggs. Given that he'd only gotten Sidian off this morning and asked for nothing himself, it wasn't surprising to learn his body was still far more responsive than usual. When Sidian was interested in reciprocating, Roman would be thrilled. But he'd wait until then.

Sidian met his eyes over the table, licking a smear of ketchup from the corner of his mouth; for a moment, Roman imagined it was blood, and his dick throbbed. "You good over there, Roe?"

"I'm fine." His self-control was better than that. He could sit in public, enjoy a meal with his mate, and not sink into the most pathetic displays of animal instinct possible.

"Oh, are you?" Sidian licked his lips for real, then turned back to his burger.

It was a relief to see him acting this way. Roman couldn't imagine what Sidian had suffered at the hands of whoever Pack Kincaid was, and as soon as they found them, Roman would visit as much brutality on them as possible. But at least they had not fractured Sidian's soul.

That would be unforgivable. Roman would let go of himself, and he wasn't one hundred percent certain he would come back in one piece when all was said and done.

Sidian ate with gusto while Roman took his time with breakfast, continuing to eye the rest of the diner and spare occasional glances toward the door. No one paid them any mind, but he was paranoid from force of habit and would not drop his guard in a strange place. Only when they were alone would the sensation of someone watching them fade from his shoulders.

"How do you feel about staying here overnight?" he asked. "In Angel Ridge, I mean."

Sidian seemed to think about it for a moment. "It's fine with me. Find a nice place like last time."

Roman would ask the omega waitress on the way out. He could use a nap before they hit the road again.

Chapter Nine

"Excuse me," Roman said when the waitress returned to give them the check, "what accommodations does your town have for visitors, if any?"

The omega—Fable, Sidian reminded himself—brightened at the question as she handed the receipt to him. "Are you looking to stay for the day? We have an inn just up the road before you get to the campgrounds. Some people have reservations, but it always has some rooms available. You can still call ahead if you want to make sure. I can even give you the number if you'd like."

Roman smiled just as he set a healthy wad of cash down on the table. "That would be lovely."

"Of course." Fable flipped the receipt over, scrawling a number across the smooth white backing. "You should ask if they have any nesting rooms available. It's *just* a nest, no bed, but it'd be more comfortable for you and your mate!"

Was it that obvious, then? "Thanks for the tip. We'll ask about that," Sidian said.

"I sleep in my nest all the time, no matter what. It's warm and cozy, so why would I ever change it?" Fable glanced between the two of them, and for the first time, Sidian noticed how it seemed like she had to contain herself. "How long have the two of you been together? Male omegas are so rare around here."

Ah, that explained it. "Uh, we've known we were mates for the past two years, but we were kinda fucking around with each other even before we knew."

It struck Sidian then that he'd never been able to talk like that with another omega. A normal conversation, talking about normal relationship stuff. Other omegas avoided him in school because he was a freak and an outcast, and he'd been too angry in psychiatric care to make friends.

No one made friends at the center. They were just poked and prodded by the nurses. How was he sleeping? How did he feel, how were his energy levels? Any mysterious aches or pains? Could he please stop wriggling around in the stirrups so they could do an ultrasound?

"Hold his legs open for me, boys. If he wants to put up a fight, we'll show him how powerless a bitch in heat is."

Sidian's stomach roiled, and he shoved the memory away.

Fable's smile dimmed, her gaze sliding to Roman for a half-second before she leaned down and hooked her arm with Sidian's. "Hey, why don't you come up to the counter with me real quick? I think we just pulled a batch of cookies out of the oven. We give them to little kids as a treat to take home, but I've never met an omega who could turn down fresh, warm, chocolate chip."

Roman gave Sidian a brief nod as he slipped out of the booth, receipt in hand as he fished his phone out of his pocket. Looked like they were staying in town after all.

Unease prickled at Sidian's skin as he allowed Fable to draw him out of the booth and lead him up to the counter. It was reasonable to believe that Roman would have known if she was some kind of threat, and even without mercenary training, Sidian wasn't stupid enough to think she was dangerous. Whatever she wanted, it had to be borderline harmless.

As soon as they reached the counter, Fable dropped her voice so low that Sidian almost did not pick up the sound of it. "Are you okay? Because we have two alpha chefs in the kitchen who can hand your alpha his ass if you need them to do that for you."

"What?" Sidian almost barked a laugh at the thought.

"You just seemed upset for a second, is all." She gave his arm a gentle squeeze while she flagged down one of the chefs. "Sometimes, alphas... They act better than they are until they get their claws into you, or their teeth, or a baby, and then you feel you have nowhere you can go. But if your alpha hurt you or scared you or anything like that, we can help. I promise."

She wasn't dangerous. She was as far from dangerous as possible, and that only made her more charming. "It wasn't him I was thinking about. He's the only good thing that's ever happened to me."

Her face softened. "I'm sorry to hear that, but I'm glad you have him."

Sidian didn't know what to say about that. Roman was the only constant in his life for a long time; he'd been fourteen years old, surly and unmanageable at the psychiatric ward until Roman came along and gave him something worth behaving for. He'd been a rare spot of light in a lifetime of darkness, and when Sidian had lost him... But he had him now. He had Roman back, and nothing was going to separate them. Nothing *could* separate them.

Except for Amey, right?

No. Bullshit. Roman would *love* her. He just needed to meet her first, that was all. And he needed to continue not noticing the pregnancy, which Sidian would get away with for another few weeks until he started to show. But that was something to worry about later.

He forced himself to take a deep breath, offering Fable a smile that he knew didn't reach his eyes. "I was in a pretty terrible place before I met him, but he's safe. I guess I'm just not all the way out of it yet. Takes a fuck of a long time to get out."

She glanced back at Roman with his stupid little flip phone pressed to his ear, then to Sidian, before pulling her notepad out of her pocket. "I know how that feels," she said, scribbling something down before tearing off a sheet of paper. "I don't know how long you two are in town for, but if you need anything, you just call me, okay? It's a small town, but I promise everyone's friendly."

Considering Sidian didn't know how long they were staying anywhere, he accepted the number without an argument. "Thanks."

She sent him back to his mate with the cookies she promised, and Roman offered nothing more than an absurdly handsome, bemused smile.

The Angel Ridge Inn was the nicest building Sidian had seen so far, at least compared to the rest of the town. Two stories and large, situated so that the back-facing windows had a pretty view of the forest beyond. The lot was half full, and Roman only needed to sweep by the front desk long enough to grab their key before he led Sidian toward the set of wide wooden steps that led upstairs. The staircase was at least twice as broad as a normal one, with a balcony that wrapped all the way around the second floor. It shadowed the entrance, the front desk, and the sitting area situated before a cozy fireplace.

"We're in the back of the building," Roman informed Sidian, leading him down a hallway. "Got one of the nicest rooms they have. What did the girl want with you beyond the cookies?"

Sidian snorted. Of course, Roman noticed something unusual going on. "She thinks you beat me."

"Thinks," he echoed. "Did you tell her it was the other way around?"

Sidian gave him a half-hearted shrug before snickering at his indignant little pout. "Nah. Told her you saved me. She seemed to think a little better of you after that."

"It was kind of her to check on you." Roman unlocked a door and pushed it open before ushering Sidian inside, dropping the two suitcases that contained the clothes he'd purchased them before twisting all the locks with a quick, paranoid touch.

The room was beautiful. Dark wood-paneled walls contrasted with the white, gauzy curtains overlaying a pair of windows, giving the room a cozy vibe that Sidian appreciated. A large nest was pushed against the far wall, with a loveseat and an armchair positioned in front of a brown brick fireplace. A door off to the side made him think bathroom, which was probably on the nicer side, too.

"Good choice," he said, kicking off his shoes.

"I'm going downstairs to nose around. See if I can get a feel for the place." Roman slipped an arm around Sidian's waist to reel him back against that broad chest, dragging one scruffy cheek along the side of Sidian's head so that the delicious molten metal scent marked him. "Get comfortable. Nest to your heart's content. I'll be back as soon as I can."

Sidian had never built a nest in his life, so he wasn't sure how Roman thought that was going to work. "Get back soon so I can take an actual shower. This place probably has pretty nice soap, but I'm not gonna risk slipping and cracking my head open without you somewhere nearby."

Roman made a low, displeased noise at the idea. "You have soap in your suitcase." He kissed the top of Sidian's head, then pointed to one of the front pockets of the suitcase while Sidian purred from the tiny brush of warm affection from his alpha. "An employee showed me where the omega-grade bath products were. Maybe somewhere else in town will have more supplies. It couldn't hurt."

Supplies. Like it was the end of the fucking world or something. "Sounds good to me. Have fun."

Roman rumbled against his back, a petulant noise, so Sidian tilted his head up so Roman could press a brief, rough kiss to his lips. His thighs pressed together at the touch of Roman's mouth, the promise of so much more, but he made himself step away from Roman before he ended up jumping him right here and now. It amazed him he could think about fucking Roman at all with Pack Kincaid lurking at the back of his mind, but they couldn't touch what Roman was to him.

Thank the Goddess for that.

Roman hesitated as if there was more he wanted to say, but he drew back and slipped out the door, soundless enough to make the hairs on the nape of Sidian's neck prickle. He reached back to smooth them down, shuddering at the drag of sensation over the sensitive mating gland there. His hair was long enough to cover it, which he was grateful for, but being around Roman made him so much more aware of everything around him. Of what *they* were to each other.

He locked the door and rubbed his hands over his face, trying to gather his bearings as his stomach tightened. How could Roman disarm him with such ease? How was it possible that he slipped into Sidian's head, where so much nasty shit lived, and just banished so much of it away?

Sidian would never let Roman go. Not just because they were mates.

A padded trunk sat at the foot of the nest, and Sidian sat on it, wrapping his arms around his stomach as he allowed his guard to drop for just a moment. He smoothed his fingers over his belly, willing the tiny spark of life there to understand they were safe now. It felt sort of odd to go from having an ultrasound almost every day—the staff did not trust him with a life that wasn't his own—to knowing nothing about what was going on with his baby. Nerve-wracking, but he was trying not to let it bother him too much. What was he supposed to do about it?

You could always just tell him the truth.

He gritted his teeth at that, but shook his head at himself, leaning against the foot of the nest instead. No, it wasn't time for that yet. When they had Amethyst back, then Roman would understand how special she was, and he would want her. He'd want the baby growing inside of Sidian, too. He'd accept them both as his own, and that would be that. That would be their happy ending.

A blood-soaked one to be sure, but it would be fucking worth it.

Chapter Ten

A single black bag sat on the driver's seat of the Ultima, the smooth leather gleaming in the dull gray light from the sky overhead.

Roman's heart jammed itself into his throat as he scanned the parking lot around him, his eyes narrowing as he tried to gauge how safe it was to be standing around out there. Certainly, nothing about Angel Ridge gave him the impression that anything about the town was more noteworthy than the many dozens just like it all throughout the mountains. Just the same, it would have been dangerous to pretend as though he and Sidian weren't traveling with targets poised on their backs.

The staff of the Bell Breeding Center had families and friends, not to mention government connections. What alphas might have been serviced in that wretched place, and what might they do to recover the omegas who might be bearing their children?

How would they even know where to find us?

He opened the car door, something catching his eye as he reached for the bag. A small slip of white paper was folded up and taped to one of the bag handles, likely to prevent it from falling off without him noticing it. I peeled the tape off as carefully as he could, unfolding the note to discover seven simple words greeting him in a cold, impersonal script.

We are the same. Control yourself. - Devereaux.

How did the boss know where they were?

Roman stared at the message for a moment before pocketing it and slinging the bag over his shoulder, not sure what he would find inside but no longer concerned it might be something like a bomb. He doubted the boss trailed them in his own car; he wouldn't have gone to the trouble just to drop off a bag and a note, busy man that he was when he wasn't staying with the Vipers. Though he'd never said much about what his business life included, the Devereaux fortune was vast enough to tip Roman off it could not all be legal.

But the boss funded one of the seven branches of Ouroboros. It made sense he had enough money for a messenger. Roman just didn't know how he knew where to send that messenger.

He made a mental note to call the captain as he headed back into the inn, hoping he gave nothing away as he mounted the stairs. The elderly woman behind the front counter didn't so much as glance at him as she focused on what looked like a knitting project spread out across the faux granite. There were a handful of betas sitting on plush couches next to the enormous fireplace across the room, but none of them looked at him. Everything in Angel Ridge was peaceful.

A tourist spot was a good sign. Most small towns had motels and prepared to see visitors at their establishments every so often, but for plenty of places, that was a courtesy. It didn't mean they wanted visitors; it meant they prepared for them because they knew such things could be inevitable, especially in a town just off the highway or on the way to a larger city or tourist site. He and Sidian would hopefully stay long enough for him to get the information he needed to ferry them right to the front door of Pack Kincaid.

Roman would bring them to their knees as soon as he met them.

It was the least he could do for his mate's sake.

He knocked on the door to their room, and Sidian answered a moment later, his hair slightly ruffled as he stepped back to let Roman inside. He'd lost the jacket and, Roman realized with a raised brow, the jeans. In just a pair of boxer briefs that clung to his plush thighs and a baggy t-shirt, Sidian looked adorably rumpled, and Roman wanted to pick him up and toss him in the nest so he could—

Stop that. You have more important things to discuss.

"Coast is clear," he managed, ignoring how husky his own voice sounded. "What have you been up to in my absence?"

Sidian locked the door for him, then tilted his head toward the nest. "Just, uh... Getting that shit all sorted so we have somewhere to sleep tonight. Did a pretty good job for an amateur."

Most nesting beds were similar to the one in the inn; overly large and lush, made to be comfortable for as many members of a pack as were willing to cram in beside each other. Despite that, the padded walls of the nest were piled so thickly with pillows that Roman doubted more than just him and Sidian could fit inside. The pillows were secured in place with a tangle of sheets, and a pile of blankets draped across the center of the bed made him long for something soft and warm.

He wanted entrance into Sidian's nest. He just hoped his mate granted it.

A slight pressure on his shoulder dragged him back to the present, where Sidian was busy giving the zipper on the leather bag another yank. "What's in here? Where did you get this?"

"Lorcan Devereaux had a delivery dropped off." Roman allowed the bag to slide off of his shoulder so Sidian could carry it to the trunk at the foot of the bed, already giving the rather large zippers more vicious pulls, the rasping of metal on metal echoing off of the walls. "I don't know how he knows where we are, but he is an ally. He's the reason I became a Viper."

Finally, the bag gaped open. "You have an awful lot of trust in a guy you haven't known that long."

"He is a better person than most. I believe at least that much." Roman kicked his boots off at the door and shrugged out of his own jacket, tossing it across the small console table pushed up against the nearest wall. Enough time had been wasted. He would call Jagger, and then—

Sidian's scent intensified very suddenly, honey-sweet lilies almost syrupy with desire. "Holy fucking shit. I think I love this guy."

Roman glanced toward his mate just in time to see him holding up a leather and steel contraption that Roman had only seen once in his life: when it was used as a threat against him during his early days at the Pit. Getting used to living with six other alphas was a lot to ask of someone who'd just killed three people without thinking twice about it, and having Sidian taken from him did not make him feel any better. So the boss, infinitely impatient, gave him one single option.

Get himself under control, or wear the muzzle until everyone was content he could be trusted.

Sidian turned to him, eyes wide. "What's this for?"

Control yourself. How funny. "I was told I would have to wear one if I lost control. I never gave the boss any more trouble after that day."

A small pink tongue darted out to wet soft lips as Sidian considered the muzzle, then Roman, then the muzzle again. Roman felt a slight buzz of anticipation as those violet eyes absolutely lit up. "I was gonna take a shower, but I think I'd rather have you get me dirty instead."

Roman crossed the room to Sidian's side to empty out the rest of the bag. A frankly cartoonish wad of unnecessary cash, a couple of cans of de-scenting cologne that Sidian would hate, a couple of fake IDs—message loud and clear—a pair of hand-guns, one sized for Roman's hands and one on the smaller side, likely for Sidian, with a respectable amount of bullets for each, a thick leather collar, a First Aid kit, and a black fabric roll bearing a set of four small knives.

What exactly was the boss expecting them to do with all of this?

Sidian snatched the collar out of Roman's hands as soon as he saw it, bending the supple leather between his fingers. "Your boss has a good eye for this," he said, eyeing Roman's neck.

The collar and the muzzle painted a very specific image of what the boss meant when he said *control yourself,* though Roman wondered if he knew who was in control after all. "What are you thinking about?"

"I think you already know. You're not a dumb dog by any means." Sidian unbuckled the collar, running his fingers along the smooth interior. "Get down on your knees. I want to see how it looks before I decide if I'd like to replace it with some-thing else."

Sidian wasn't asking. The weight of his words dragged Ro-man down to the floor, the pressure of pleasing his omega just as intense as it was in the forest. It had taken everything in him to get out the single word needed for Sidian to remove the mask; something had always been odd between them, but Roman didn't think about it too much, nor did he care. The delight that danced through Sidian's eyes as he combed a hand through Roman's hair, nails dragging over his scalp, was more than enough for Roman. If Sidian wanted him on his knees, then he would stay where he was like a good dog.

"You look good like that," Sidian said, voice low as he looped the collar around Roman's neck. "Let's see what we're working with here."

The leather was cool against Roman's skin as it settled around his throat, Sidian adjusting where it laid before buckling it closed. Warm fingers brushed the skin just below where the collar rested before he took a step back to examine it, giving Roman an eyeful of his bare thighs. The urge to lean in just to feel them against his face was a powerful one, but he resisted it.

"Okay, yeah, I like it." Sidian hooked a finger beneath the collar and tugged forward, and Roman's back bent toward him automatically. "I was never much of a dog person until I met you, you know, but you've always been such a good boy."

Dog. The word was humiliating. It should have been enough to put Roman off, but it hadn't changed his mind back then, and it didn't do so now. It was degrading, but his cock twitched and swelled under Sidian's words just the same, something in his mind clicking into place. There was a rightness to kneeling at Sidian's feet. Perhaps it was that Roman could pay him proper worship from there.

Goddess, help him. He would be crushed if he ever lost his omega again.

Sidian left him kneeling to turn back to the contents of the bag, picking up the roll of knives. "What exactly did you tell this uber-special boss about me?"

What is your little darling like, Kane?

"Everything I knew at the time." Which was precious little. They'd only seen each other a handful of times following their fateful first meeting, a product of Roman not wanting to take the bus home. It was an accident of the best kind. "You liked to start fights. You'd use anything sharp you could get your hands on. If you could, you liked to make people bleed for you."

Sidian chuckled, sliding one of the knives from the elastic band securing it in place as he turned it over between his fingers. "The breeding center had the same issue with me. I wasn't allowed to be left alone with any utensils or cups or anything I might be able to break."

"You grabbed a scalpel on your way out the front door." Smart thinking on Sidian's part; Roman wasn't even paying enough attention to what Sidian was doing beyond running to know where he snagged it from. A lone cart, perhaps.

Sidian hummed softly, fingers brushing over the scab on Roman's cheek. "You cut yourself making sure I didn't fall."

"It didn't hurt. Doesn't bother me." He'd cared far more about catching Sidian than hurting himself.

Sidian's hand slid down to cup his jaw, tilting it upward so that the cool, thin blade of the knife met Roman's cheekbone. "What would you do if I used this on you?"

"Let you." It wasn't even a question. Saying no didn't occur to him. If Sidian wanted to slice him open, then he could.

The thought of being at Sidian's mercy shouldn't be as exciting as it felt. Anticipation swelled in Roman's gut at the thought, and an unwelcome memory returned. How many times, as a stupid teenage boy who was more hormone than he was human, did he wonder what it must have felt like to be under Sidian? To be at the receiving end of whatever weapon Sidian had gotten his hands on this time?

Viper training required them to refine their natural alpha pain tolerance into something borderline superhuman. Between that and his own fucked-up head, masochism really should have been on Roman's radar before now.

Sidian trailed the very tip of the blade down Roman's skin, though he didn't add enough pressure to cut him. "You always did look good covered in blood. Brace yourself, Roe. You're gonna need it."

Chapter Eleven

Something about the sight of Roman on his knees made Sidian want to cut him open, see Roman bloody and torn in front of him.

Logic would dictate it was because Roman was an alpha, and every single alpha Sidian ever encountered in his life had wanted to hurt him, or had hurt him. The businessman who convinced his worthless father to sell him like a whore, Pack Kincaid... So few compared to the world at large, but Sidian had been wary of alphas even before he presented. Wary, and always aware of hungry eyes gazing at his immature body in just a t-shirt and jeans. As if that was enough to lure them into the thoughts of what they might do to him.

He wanted to hurt Roman because he was an alpha, and because he couldn't hurt anyone else who'd wronged him. But that wasn't all of it. He wanted to hurt Roman because he enjoyed hurting people, and that very realization kept him from progressing anywhere in his mental health journey. Roman's father saw it as a flaw, a symptom of something greater. It wasn't allowed to be a part of Sidian because a good little breeding bitch didn't want to sink its teeth in just to feel the flesh tear and the muscle twitch.

He wanted to hurt Roman because the thought of blood rolling from wounds inflicted by his own hand made his clit throb and his pussy ache to be filled.

Roman's scent always answered the bloom of Sidian's own, flames licking his skin as he watched Roman skim his shirt up and over his head. Ropes upon ropes of muscle, a feast for the eyes, shifting and flexing beneath that sun-kissed olive skin. There were more scars here and there, and a bitter growl rose in Sidian's throat because none of them were his.

Roman was his. He should belong *only* to Sidian.

"Wherever you want," Roman rasped up at him, and slick trickled into Sidian's underwear. "Whatever you want, omega."

Fuck. That single word made Sidian want to shove Roman against the floor so he could ride that pretty face of his. Sidian had been told it felt good, but none of the alphas who'd ever fucked him did more than rip him open and leave him bloody and raw. A whine tore from his throat at the memory, more terrifying than it had any right to be, because he didn't want that. Not again. He'd been hurt so many fucking times he couldn't even think straight if a gorgeous man offering himself up for the slaughter was enough to scare Sidian still.

Roman tipped his head back, baring the long line of his throat. A sign of utter submission. "What's wrong?"

"You listen to me." Sidian tapped the blade against Roman's nose, biting back a chuckle when Roman's eyes crossed to look at it. "Or you don't get to fucking *touch* me."

Those beautiful forest eyes flicked back up to his face. "You were thinking about them."

"Whole fucking pack, yeah." Sidian didn't want to think about Pack Kincaid, but he couldn't run away from them. Roman needed to know, and how much longer Sidian could hide the worst of it from him was up for debate. "The shit they did to me... You ever fucking *think* in that direction, and I won't even give you the courtesy of a quick death. I'll make sure you beg me to fucking die."

Roman's brows furrowed. "Of course. I'd let you."

It clicked a moment later, and Sidian bit back a moan, slick gushing out of him like a damned fountain as he pressed his thighs shut. Roman's submission was almost more than he could bear, omega hindbrain ill-suited for what it meant to be in control. He didn't know alphas could be so submissive, could give in so freely and so openly, and it turned Sidian on so fast he felt dizzy. And horny, his cunt weeping to be touched.

He ran his tongue across his teeth. "I'm going to cut you. I'm going to hurt you."

"I hope so." Roman shifted on his knees, his scent thick and heavy in the air.

"Not just this once. I'm going to do it as many times as I want." Sidian flicked the blade, and Roman flinched, though he didn't respond fast enough. A thin cut opened on his cheekbone opposite the one Sidian had accidentally left on him in the forest, an almost-matching set. "And only when I'm satisfied do you get the privilege of getting me off."

"I want to." Roman swallowed, and Sidian watched the collar undulate with the shifting movement. "I enjoyed making you come at the motel. It was satisfying."

Sidian chuckled and let himself wander back; that had been a good way to wake up for certain. "If you're really good, I might let you get your tongue on my pussy. How does that sound?"

"Please." Roman shifted on his knees, his hands twisting into fists atop his thighs. "Please, I want that. If you'll let me."

"I'll consider it." Sidian cupped his jaw and tilted his head up so he could trace the tip of the blade just under the pout of Roman's bottom lip. He would let his alpha have it, but only if he could put on an excellent performance and prove just what an obedient dog he was.

There was a lot of room to work with, a lot Sidian wanted to do. He took his time circling Roman's body before he stopped behind him, wrapping a hand around one broad shoulder and giving it a squeeze just so he could feel the muscle twitch under his touch. When he pressed the knife through the flesh, Roman shuddered, but he didn't move beyond that small, unconscious response.

Sidian drew a thin, neat line across his back, watching as the skin parted around the blade.

There was something so heady about the blood that oozed through the slender cut, a few droplets swelling fat and glossy before they rolled down Roman's broad back.

Excitement skittered up Sidian's spine at the sight. He stepped back and leaned down so he could be closer to the open wound, dragging his tongue over the length of it to taste the hot, coppery fluid. His clit ached in his underwear, and he dared to reach down to touch it, feeling the puffy swell of it through the fabric as he reached the end of the wound and sucked hard, pressing down on sensitive nerves.

Roman shuddered, his head lolling forward, baring the nape of his neck. "Feels so good."

"You like it that much?" Sidian tightened his hand on the blade, licking his lips as he considered what he might do. "I want to carve something into your chest."

"Yes." Roman looked back at him, pupils blown black. "Lick it clean, too. It hurt so good, omega."

Omega. It would never stop making Sidian's cunt pulse. "Fuck yeah."

Roman stretched out on his back without being told while Sidian dropped across his waist, leaning over to press the tip of the blade into the meat of one pec. Right over Roman's heart, he took his time carving his name in a loopy scrawl, giddy at the sight of the letters splitting open Roman's flesh. *Obsidian.* Black all the way to the soul; the perfect and only name for him. It looked even better etched into Roman's flesh one long, swooping letter at a time.

He pressed harder on each curve, shuddering when Roman moaned in pain beneath him.

"Good?" he asked, bringing the knife up to his lips to lick a smear of blood from the blade. The dazed expression in Roman's eyes was gorgeous to him.

Roman laughed, his head rolling to the side even as he winced. "Better than anything I could have imagined. You're so good to me."

"And you're such a good dog." Sidian tapped the handle of the blade against Roman's nose and then leaned down to get back to work, aware of his breath shortening, his heart thudding with every stroke of the knife through Roman's flesh.

As he completed each letter, he dragged his tongue over Roman's chest, licking hard enough to feel the edges of the flesh giving way, parting a little under his tongue. The taste was fantastic, but it wasn't for taste alone. Alphas and omegas had enzymes in their saliva to help close wounds and heal them, meant to solidify the mating bond, though it worked for this purpose just as well. Roman handled every letter with ragged noises and low moans, his scent peppery in Sidian's nose. Distantly, he knew that he was smearing slick all over Roman's firm stomach, his underwear now soaked all the way through.

Damn the connection between them, damn the hormones, damn Roman Kane.

"You're wet," Roman told Sidian just as he finished licking the N clean, sitting up to study his handiwork. "Fuck, you smell so sweet. Sit on my face and drown me."

That wasn't a bad idea at all. "Did you enjoy yourself, alpha? You make such a responsive canvas."

"See for yourself." Roman shifted under him, not enough to dislodge him, but enough to get Sidian to glance back over his shoulder at the front of Roman's hips.

The sight of the bulge there made his mouth go dry.

On another alpha, it would have felt like a threat. Sure had been fucking used as one more than once, Sidian's face dragged against denim seconds before he'd been pinned down and—No. Not going there. Not thinking about that. None of those alphas were anything like his. None of them would have trusted him with this, would have wanted this just as much as he wanted to do it.

He traced his fingers just over the ridge of his fly, and Roman shuddered under him. "Goddess, Sid, you're fucking perfect."

"Yeah?" Sidian twisted back around, leaning close to Roman so he could go back to work. "Glad you think so. Now let me finish, and I'll sit on your face."

It took more time to etch the shape he had in mind into Roman's skin, content to mark his territory the only way he could without a bond mark. Roman's scent stayed thick in the air, his breathing rough, little inhales and exhales catching. Every grunt or muffled groan made Sidian pause, his eyes squeezing shut for just a moment as his cunt clenched. Back at the center, arousal was a bad sign, a sign of things to come, but it was exciting with Roman. Exciting because Roman wasn't *doing* anything about it beyond lying right where Sidian wanted him, letting Sidian work on him, letting Sidian *hurt* him without putting up a fight.

He licked each delicate petal of the lily clean before setting the knife aside, his hips rolling down against Roman's stomach in an instinctive search for friction. "All done, alpha."

"Goddess." Roman offered him a woozy smile. He hadn't lost enough blood to be dizzy, so maybe he was just that turned on. "Use me, Sid. Go ahead. I'm all yours."

Use me. Fuck, he was such a good boy. "Have you eaten out an omega before?"

"Nah." Roman laughed, his eyelids fluttering shut. "Like I said, I did research. I made sure I did as much research as I could about that specific action. I wanted to make you feel good."

Roman stayed where he was as Sidian shifted off of him just enough to peel the briefs down his legs, the fabric molded to the shape of his cunt from just how much slick had soaked through them. Idly, he tossed them aside before kneeling down across Roman's face, hyper-aware of the fact that Roman had never *seen* him before. In the handful of times they'd met in the past, he'd been clothed. Sure, Roman *knew,* but there was a big difference between knowing Sidian was trans and seeing his body for the first time.

All male omegas had cunts. Sidian wasn't worried about that part. But the obvious lack of a cock was going to catch Roman's attention right away, and he didn't know how Roman felt about that. Maybe he'd be disgusted. Maybe—

Roman's hands were so warm when they settled on Sidian's bare hips, dragging him down so Roman could lick up Sidian's cunt with a moan that reverberated through his entire body.

Fuck. *Fuck.* Sidian slammed his hands down on the floor to stabilize himself, managing a squeak before Roman buried his face between his legs. Thick arms wrapped themselves around Sidian's thighs to keep him where he was, Roman's lips leaving open-mouthed kisses all along his cunt. It was dizzying. It was so fucking good it made Sidian's legs shake, his nails digging into the hardwood floor as his spine arched.

Oh, it was good. It was so good, and Sidian didn't know it could be so good.

"Tastes so sweet." Roman lapped between Sidian's legs like he was starved for it, like he'd die without it, rasping over his hole. Teasing bastard, inches away from giving Sidian what he needed and not letting him have it, stubble scraping over his inner thighs. "Fuck my face, omega, take what you need from me."

It took Sidian a minute to find the strength to move, his hips rolling as he ground himself against Roman's face. He was all sharp angles, and the friction was perfect when Sidian dragged his clit against the bridge of Roman's nose, his eyes fluttering shut. Heat burned between his thighs, the intensity almost frightening as Roman leaned back so he could get his tongue on Sidian's clit for the first time.

And, Goddess, did he give it his all. He swirled his tongue around it before sucking it into his mouth. His lips were so soft and perfect, the suction drawing a feral moan from Sidian's lips. When he dug a hand into Roman's curls and yanked, Roman responded by sucking harder, growling against Sidian's pussy.

The vibrations sizzled through his skin, and he fell on top of Roman, his hips bucking against Roman's face. "Fuck!"

"Every noise you make is such a delight." Roman swiped his tongue back and forth before sucking Sidian's clit again, uncaring as slick dripped down his chin.

"Shut the fuck up and get me off." Sidian yanked his hair again, and the resulting groan had him keening in response.

He needed to come. He needed it . The only orgasms he'd had were by his own hands and ones forced out of him, yanked from a body so bruised and beaten it was a miracle he had any working nerve endings left at all. But Roman was so good, so desperate, devouring Sidian like a last meal, eating at him like Roman would die without a taste of his cunt. His hands held Sidian tight but not too tight, letting him wriggle as much as he pleased. And when Sidian looked down, he found Roman's eyes with his and realized his alpha was watching his face, drinking in the way it contorted and scrunched and went slack with overwhelming pleasure.

And Roman held Sidian's gaze as he pursed his lips against Sidian's clit, sucking so hard Sidian's vision whited out for a moment.

The disgustingly wet noise that echoed off the walls of the room made his cunt squeeze tight, his eyes slamming shut. Roman sucked him off wet and messy, his tongue and lips working him over until the fever pitch of pleasure crashed over Sidian like a tidal wave. It felt so good it almost hurt, every muscle in his body jerking and twitching as he rode Roman's face. Too much. It was too fucking much.

He's not stopping. Fuck me, he's not stopping.

Roman kept his mouth on Sidian where he wanted it the most, working him through the crest of another orgasm before Sidian could even catch his breath. His entire body slumped, but Roman caught him, holding him where he was, keeping his pussy pressed flush against Roman's face. Only when it was way too much did Roman back off, tongue lapping at the folds of Sidian's cunt while the corners of his mouth twitched up in a stupid little grin.

He really was a dog, but he was a good one. He was Sidian's good boy.

And he wasn't done with Roman. Not even close.

Chapter Twelve

Sidian ripped himself off of Roman, his twitching cunt still begging Roman to lick up the mess dripping out of his omega. The sight of Sidian on top of him was too much for Roman, plush thighs parted wide to reveal the pink flush of Sidian's pussy, his cheeks red from exertion, his eyes hazy with pleasure and shining with want. There was still blood on his teeth and at the corners of his mouth, smeared along one cheek where he must have dragged it over Roman's torn flesh. Sticky blood on his fingers, too, where he worked Roman's flesh open with such artistic intention that he could do nothing but kneel there, feeling every slice of the knife go straight to his dick.

The arousal was almost painful. He'd suffered through every single rut with nothing to dull the ache because he refused to take suppressants of any kind. Likewise, he refused the comfort of attending an omega who might have eased the burn. Sidian was the only mate he'd ever had and the only omega he wanted, and he didn't want to touch anyone else, fuck anyone else. Just Sidian, only Sidian.

And Roman was going to *kill* every single alpha who dared lay hands on his omega. He was going to rip them to pieces. He would rend flesh from muscle and muscle from bone until their desperate cries of anguish satiated him.

And he wouldn't let them die. He wouldn't ever let them die.

"Fuck me," Sidian said, his chest still heaving with every breath, dripping slick onto Roman's bare chest. It stung in the still-open wounds, but Roman didn't care. "In the nest. Fuck me in the nest. I want it."

Roman's mind raced at the thought, his eyes trained on Sidian's face because if he looked between Sidian's legs, he'd do it. "You're granting me the privilege of fucking you?"

"It *hurts*," Sidian said, and Roman watched, mesmerized, as Sidian reached down to pet the swollen folds of his own cunt. "Dunno if it's that you're my mate or something else. I got horny as soon as I realized it was you in the woods. No better now."

Slender fingers stroked over the pretty bud of his clit and then slid down, curling so Sidian could ease his fingers inside himself. There was something hypnotizing about watching his slender, bloodied fingers work his pussy open, the slick sucking noises making Roman's alpha howl with want. His omega was asking Roman to fuck him. Did it get much simpler than that?

Goddess help him, he wanted to. He wanted to sink his knot into Sidian's beautiful pussy and hear his breath get high and thin with how good it felt, how perfect they fit together. He knew they would. They had to.

"Fuck," Sidian whined, his head tipping back as he fucked himself on his own fingers. "Roe, I need it."

"You'll get it then. However you want it." However many times he wanted it. Fuck sleep. Roman didn't need to sleep.

Sidian reached for something with his free hand, and Roman watched as his omega offered him a lazy smile, the muzzle dangling from the tips of his fingers. "You good with wearing this for me? I don't need your teeth. Just your cock."

"You can have whatever you want, omega." Roman reached for the muzzle, but Sidian jerked it back just in time to shove his slick-coated fingers into Roman's mouth.

"I want to put it on you," he said, and he almost choked Roman when he pressed down on the back of his tongue. "And then you'll fuck me in the nest I made nice and pretty for you. Be a good dog, Roman, if you want another treat."

As soon as Sidian's fingers left, Roman lifted his head off of the floor so Sidian could secure the muzzle in place. It occurred to him he should have wiped his face off first, but it was too late for that. The muzzle buckled into place at the back of his head, firm leather laid over his nose and cradling the line of his jaw. Steel bars connected the two pieces and caged his mouth, preventing him from biting no matter how much he wanted to. And he wanted to. He wanted his teeth in Sidian, but he wanted Sidian more than he wanted the mating bond.

Did that even make sense? He didn't care. He just felt that way.

As soon as Sidian slid off of him, Roman sat up just in time to watch his omega peel the shirt up and over his head. He was lean and fair-skinned, though the odd scar stuck out to Roman here and there. There was a moment, a flare of uncertainty, a souring of Sidian's sweet scent.

"Fucking gorgeous," Roman whispered, and Sidian preened at the praise. "Pretty omega, I want you so fucking bad."

Sidian laughed and stepped back well out of his reach. "Undress. Show me what you've got. If it's not up to my standards, maybe I won't want anything to do with it."

Roman's hands shook as he unbuckled his belt and shoved his jeans down, his cock smacking against his stomach when it was freed. Sidian's eyes honed in on it, the omega licking his lips before he made a dash for the bed. A delighted little laugh spilled from his lips as he leaped into the middle of it, the mattress bouncing beneath him before he turned those wild violet eyes on Roman.

There was something gratifying in how surprised Sidian was at the speed Roman could move when he needed to.

The mattress cushioned them both, so Roman didn't crush Sidian when he pinned his mate down against the mattress, wishing he could kiss him but settling for running his hands over Sidian's perfect body. He was still too thin for Roman's taste, but they would get him there. Sidian shivered when Roman's fingers traced over his sides—likely ticklish—and tensed when Roman cupped both of his breasts, rolling the nipples between his fingers. They were small, unnoticeable beneath the baggy shirts Sidian favored, but sensitive based on the way his eyelashes fluttered and his breathing tripped.

Sidian pushed Roman's hands off of him and moved up into the pillows, spreading his thighs open wide so that Roman's eyes were drawn to his cunt. "You're not getting me on my knees. Not yet. Come fuck me before I change my mind."

That was all Roman needed to hear.

Sidian's hand wound through the collar when Roman moved to kneel between Sidian's thighs, pulling his omega up into his lap to make up for the difference in size. Most of his height was in his legs, so they were much closer this way, and a groan rumbled in his chest when Sidian yanked the collar just as Roman's cock slid between slick, puffy little folds.

"You're such a fucking tease." Sidian squirmed in Roman's hand until the head of Roman's cock caught against the twitching entrance of his mate's cunt, a pleased noise pulling from Sidian's throat. "Fuck me *now*."

Who was Roman to argue with that?

A roll of his hips pushed the head of his cock into the slick heat of Sidian's cunt, and Sidian's head fell back on a choked gasp, gemstone eyes squeezing shut. A soothing rumble vibrated up Roman's chest, a gentle rhythm that relaxed Sidian, easing the tension in his muscles until the death grip on

Roman's cock eased into something almost welcoming. Every careful thrust into Sidian had the omega whining, the hand on Roman's collar tightening its grip until the leather pulled taut across his windpipe.

Choke me. You can. I won't stop you.

The burn of it was glorious, a perfect contrast to the hot velvet, the fluttering grip of muscle as Sidian just seemed to draw Roman deeper and deeper into his pussy. He was so tight, so hot, so wet that it made Roman's head thrum with static, his alpha rumbling in utter satisfaction at how prepared Sidian was for this. Sidian whimpered, and it was adorable, his thighs trembling in Roman's hands as Roman rocked back just enough to ease in a little deeper. That slight tug of friction had both of them moaning, Sidian's back arching. If Roman's mouth was free, he'd have it on those pretty little tits, but next time. It could wait.

"Feels so fucking big," Sidian slurred, reaching down to lazily stroke his clit. "So big and *thick.*"

A laugh lit his face when Roman batted his hand away, replacing Sidian's fingers with his own, feeling the twitch of throbbing flesh beneath his touch as he stroked. "Let me do that. I've got you, darling."

There was something magical about watching his cock disappear inside of Sidian for the first time, listening to the pretty little moans and whimpers the pressure drew from kiss-swollen, bloody lips. Knowing the only other alphas who had ever touched Sidian did so to hurt him made it paramount that this was good for him, that he felt nothing but pleasure. Roman couldn't imagine hurting Sidian. He was so beautiful like this, strung out on sensation and milking Roman's cock with every little thrust.

Roman's hand slid up to his belly, imagining it swollen with life as he leaned over to nuzzle Sidian's soft black hair. "I've got you now. I've got you."

Sidian clenched up tight, rolling his hips. "Prove it. Fuck me and show me you've got me."

Oh, with *pleasure.*

Sidian choked the moment Roman's knot pressed against his folds, and he let Sidian feel the weight of it, the tease against his clit before pressing him down into the sheets. Trembling hands gripped his back almost frantically when he drew out of his omega, his hips snapping forward. The friction and pressure were immediate. Sidian swore, and his thighs clenched shut around Roman's hips, his heels digging into Roman's back.

Mark me up all you want, Roman thought, hissing when Sidian's nails dug in and dragged over his flesh, the closed wound on his back tearing open until he could feel a few droplets of blood rolling down his skin. *Scratch me, bruise me, bleed me. It feels so good to be yours.*

Stamina and endurance were expected of alphas and drilled into the Vipers; fucking Sidian required both. Hot sparks danced along Roman's spine with every thrust, a pressure building low in his gut every time his knot brushed up against Sidian's pussy. Sidian mewled in pleasure and arched beneath him, nails scouring Roman's flesh until the familiar sting told him his omega had drawn blood. That was what Roman wanted. Let Sidian claim him in all the ways he wanted to.

"So fucking good." Sidian strained underneath Roman, lips parted in the cutest pout. "Gonna c-come. Don't stop."

"I won't." No matter how badly Roman wanted to chase his own orgasm, he wouldn't.

Sidian quaked under him, head flinging itself back and forth, the long feathery strands of black hair clinging to Sidian's cheeks and throat with sweat. When he came, it was pure agony, his cunt squeezing tight around Roman's shaft and every thrust demanding Roman to fuck him harder to fight the grip. Slick gushed around them, soaking Roman's thighs and knot, but he didn't slow his thrusts. No stopping. Not allowing himself to be tempted to knot that perfect pussy when Sidian needed to come again. Roman's poor, sweet, deprived little mate.

So much pain. So much pointless suffering. Roman had to make up for it. He had to give Sidian every single blissful second of pleasure he should have had all the time they'd been apart.

Sidian moaned as he bucked his hips, meeting every thrust, heels pressed into Roman's back so hard he knew they would leave bruises, but it gave Roman perfect leverage. "Need it so fucking bad, alpha. Need you. Don't you ever fucking leave me again."

That raw demand ripped through Roman, Sidian's words slotting into place in his very soul as he leaned down to press his face against Sidian's. He needed to kiss his omega, but he could suffer without, gritting his teeth behind the steel bars of the muzzle. Whatever Sidian needed. Roman would be whatever Sidian needed.

"I'm never leaving you again." He cupped Sidian's cheek, staring down into his hazy eyes. "Never. I'll kill whoever tries to come between us."

Sidian laughed, tilting his head to dig his teeth into the heel of Roman's palm. "Save some for me. I wanna help."

"Gladly." The thought of him streaked with blood had Roman gripping his mate even tighter, drilling into his cunt with renewed fervor while Sidian shook and mewled beneath him.

The second orgasm had him all but sobbing, and he kicked Roman so hard in the back it hurt. "Knot me, knot me, I want your knot alpha, plea—"

One harsh thrust choked the word off in a cry, Sidian's cunt eagerly swallowing Roman's knot. The sharp pressure of his pussy clenching tighter unleashed the clench in Roman's guts, his vision going black for just a moment as the pleasure of it hit him all at once. He spilled inside of Sidian where he was supposed to, and Sidian moaned again, his hips twitching, dragging Roman's knot against his raw, flayed nerves.

It took Roman time to come down from the high. Took him time to catch his breath, and then pure wonder choked him until he felt a sting at the backs of his eyes. He'd feared once that he'd never see Sidian Vey again, that he was ripped from Roman's arms moments after he removed every obstacle between them, but Sidian was there. Wrapped around Roman's knot like a hot little vice, trembling and sweaty, sweet and perfect and a dream come true.

Roman's. All Roman's. His sweet little omega mate.

"Fuck." Sidian's arms fell into the nest, and Roman saw fresh blood smudged on his fingertips. "Mm. Come here and hold me. I'm tired."

Laughing, Roman covered Sidian with his body as best he could in the current position, letting his omega rest against the sheets before slipping an arm under his slender back to hold him closer. His soft tits pressed up against Roman's chest, and he made a mental note to make good on how badly he wanted to get his mouth on Sidian's nipples the first opportunity he got.

Sidian nuzzled the front of his throat, sighing against his skin. "I'll take the muzzle off in a minute. Looks pretty sexy on you, though."

"I'm sure the boss will be happy to hear that." He'd sent it for self-control, or so he said, but Roman did not know if he believed that.

Now that he thought about it, he wondered if he might have let something slip when he was a teenager. Or had the boss listened to what details Roman offered and discerned what the power dynamic would be? A muzzle would prevent a bite. It wouldn't stop Roman from killing anyone.

He could do that with his bare hands, after all.

Sidian nipped his skin, the light pressure of his teeth making Roman dream of something more. "I want you to fuck me as often as possible. And eat me out more."

"I'd do that every day if you wanted." Roman could envision that: being woken up by the scent of slick, his face already caged in the welcoming heat of Sidian's pussy so that the first lazy lick would find his throbbing little clit and have his mate sighing above him.

Sidian slapped him on the chest. "Don't threaten me with a good time."

They would definitely revisit that offer in the future, then.

Chapter Thirteen

"*How nice of you to remember the skill of making a phone call, Kane,*" Jagger said as soon as the call connected, his smooth voice undercut by a slight growl of irritation. "*The boss said he contacted you and that you were fine. Good to know since you wouldn't call in.*"

To his credit, Roman only looked a *little* like a kicked puppy where he sat at the foot of the nest. "I was busy. I needed to get Sidian somewhere safe. It was hindbrain stuff."

Jagger scoffed in response. "*Whatever. What the hell went on back there? Ghost told me you chased an omega out in the woods, and you didn't make it back in time for extraction to pick you up. Is Sidian supposed to be the omega you ran off with? Who even is that?*"

"Hi," Sidian called out from the bathroom doorway, monitoring the tub as it filled up with water and bubbles while also nosing into the conversation that did not involve him. "Nice to meet you. I'm the runaway omega."

There was a pause before Jagger spoke again. "*You're letting him listen in on the call?*"

"He's my mate." There was no hesitation in Roman's voice as he combed a hand through his hair, his expression at peace as he rolled his shoulders. Must be getting sore, or maybe itchy from all the blood. "He's allowed to listen to whatever he wants."

Sidian chuckled as he adjusted his own standing position. His entire pussy felt like so much as a touch would bring him to his knees, but the sex had been well worth it. Who even knew sex could feel that good? No wonder other omegas enjoyed their heats.

"Is this the one we were looking for?" Jagger asked, sounding exasperated. *"How the fuck is that possible? Even the boss looked. He didn't find jack shit about that omega."*

Roman's mouth turned down at the corners. "We're working on figuring that out. A pack by the name of Kincaid was assaulting him at the breeding center. Any info on them?"

That time, the pause was at least twice as long. *"What are you trying to do, Kane?"*

"I'm doing what my mate needs me to do," Roman said. "You know something?"

"Pack Kincaid is one of the nastier packs in the sex trafficking rings. Ouroboros considered Dax Kincaid at one point, I think, but the guy has a short temper and doesn't play nice with others. Heard Nightingale talk about him once." Jagger sighed, though the irritation had not faded from his voice even a little. Sort of impressive. *"Kincaid and his goons are hired muscle for the auctioneers. Not our area. You'd have to ask the Mambas for any factual information about them."*

Roman winced as he reclined in the nest, the heel of one bare foot thudding against the top of the padded trunk. "What are the chances of wiping out the whole pack? They hurt my omega. I intend to put every single one of them in the ground."

Jagger huffed, world-weary and exhausted. *"I dunno, kid. Last I checked, they're somewhere out in Jersey. That's how the Mambas keep a close eye on 'em. They're on their turf."*

"Fuck," Sidian snapped, the back of his head hitting the wall behind him. "That's one hell of a drive."

"It's fine. We can make that. If the Mambas might give us some information…" Roman trailed off, teeth dragging over his bottom lip. "What are the odds of me getting involved with them without there being blowback from the Mambas?"

"It's possible, I guess," Jagger said. *"I think we were on good terms with them last I checked, but for fuck's sake, don't bring up Ghost's name to save yourself some trouble. What are you gonna do, drive out that way, ask for permission, and then kill these rich assholes?"*

Roman pressed his lips together, his nose wrinkling. "I don't see any reason the plan should be more complex. That gets to the heart of it quickly."

"All right. Okay." Jagger fell silent, though Sidian thought he could detect the man's moodiness through the phone. He might accept this, but he wasn't happy about it.

He debated speaking for a moment, not sure if that would make the situation better or worse for Roman. But how much worse could it get? "Hey, thanks for taking care of my alpha while I was locked up. You didn't do too bad of a job getting him in shape."

"Too bad of a job," Roman echoed, smacking a hand over his mouth when Jagger made the most disgusted noise on the other side of the line. Offended, it sounded like.

Baiting an alpha into getting annoyed or angry was just like teasing a dog.

"What do you mean I didn't do too bad of a job?" Jagger demanded, and Sidian cackled as he leaned against the wall. He had to make it a little more fun for himself, right?

Roman rolled his eyes before getting the conversation back on track, and Sidian slunk into the bathroom for a moment to enjoy the steam rolling off the top of the tub. Looked like it was almost full, and that was good; he was a sweaty, sticky, well-used mess. And for the first time in the last two years, he didn't feel disgusted for it. He felt like he was where he needed to be.

He returned to the bathroom door. "Alpha, the tub's almost full. Are you coming?"

"The what?" Jagger sounded scandalized, which was rich if he was the big, bad, scary captain of the Vipers. *"Right, I'm gonna go before I hear something I don't wanna hear. Kane, keep me up to date for a change. Don't fall off the radar again."*

He cut the call before Sidian could think of something else to upset him, which was no fun. He pouted as Roman sat the phone down and stretched his arms over his head, cracking his back as he rose to his feet. There was something sexy about how big he was, how graceful, how he'd used every inch of that carved body to fuck Sidian into sweet oblivion. They had to do it again.

"I think you scared him," Roman said matter-of-factly, and Sidian dissolved into giggles.

He squeaked when Roman pressed him up against the wall to steal a kiss, his lips and tongue warm and wet, and Sidian clawed at his shoulders to get closer to him. He was tempted to have Roman fuck him against the wall, rag-doll him when it would be oh-so-easy to pin him in place with those huge hands.

But the tub would flood the room, and that would cause trouble. "Bath time?"

"Bath time," Roman agreed, though he looked regretful as he took a step back.

It was adorable how petulant he could be, how pouty. He could take what he wanted, and because it was him, Sidian might even give it to him without a fight. But Roman took nothing.

He'd ask, he'd offer, but he'd never *take*. It wasn't in his nature. That was reassuring in a way few things were—the knowledge that Sidian had a mate who would always respect his wishes and honor his boundaries because he didn't know any other way to be. What a fucking alpha.

And he would be a good father. He would be. He just needed to see Amethyst, and it would work out.

For a moment when Roman was inside of him, Sidian thought he knew. Had felt that big hand fan over his stomach and was so certain that it was silent proof that Roman somehow *knew*. The barely there curve of his stomach was not that noticeable, and Roman would have said something by now, right?

He had to believe that Roman didn't know for his own sanity. That he wouldn't let Sidian walk around as if it weren't true otherwise. No, Roman was a worrier. He'd be trying to shove vitamins down Sidian's throat, worried about his health and the health of the baby. The health of their son.

Roman's expression was still pouty as he followed Sidian into the bathroom, which was all brown and green tiles, with a cute little fake plant hanging from a tall window where no one could peek inside. Steam rolled lazily off of the surface of the water as Roman sank in, getting comfortable before Sidian joined him. Roman's broad chest was almost warmer than the water, and Sidian snuggled into him with a shameless purr, letting his omega have full control for once.

This was almost perfect. This was worth all the bullshit he'd gone through just to get Roman back.

"How are you feeling?" Roman carded damp fingers through Sidian's hair, brushing it back so he could press soft kisses to Sidian's forehead and cheeks.

And here he thought omegas were supposed to be the affectionate ones. "Good. Fucked out of my mind, but good. Not gonna lie, I didn't know it was that good."

"Sex?" Roman made a low, sad noise in his throat, but Sidian leaned up to nip at him to make him stop. "That's just so fucking sad, Sid. You should know. No one should have hurt you like that. I wish I'd been there."

Sidian wished Roman had been there, too. "I don't want to think about that at all right now. You're here now, and that's good. I would have... I don't know what I would have done."

Lose another pup without you was seconds away from slipping from between his teeth.

"You never have to worry about it." Roman tightened his grip on Sidian, his hand smoothing over Sidian's hip as he nuzzled into his hair again. "I'll be here. I don't know what we're going to do after all of this is over, but I'll be right here while we figure it out."

Tears stung Sidian's eyes, but he blinked them back as he cuddled into Roman's chest, content for the first time in a long time. "Now we get to figure out our little fucked-up future together."

"I'd like that." Roman paused as if considering his words. "I don't know what I'd do if I wasn't a Viper, but if you're against it, I can figure out something else, I suppose."

"You would do that for me?" It was so surprising to just hear him say it.

Roman nodded, pressing another kiss to Sidian's forehead. He really was so affectionate for an alpha, so unlike the rest of his designation. "I would do anything for you. I understand you don't believe me yet, though. We'll get to that understanding together."

Sidian refused to cry in the middle of such a nice, cozy bath. "I trust you to get me there."

"Thank you." Roman drew Sidian's hand up, pressing soft kisses to his knuckles before giving him a gentle squeeze.

In the back of Sidian's head, in his hindbrain, he was aware of just how fucked they were. Roman might have been a trained badass, which Sidian didn't doubt, but Pack Kincaid would not be easy to kill. They weren't pushovers, and as much as Sidian wanted to rip their eyes out of their skulls and dig his knives into their knots and choke them with each other's entrails for taking Amethyst away from him... On a very primal level, he was terrified.

Their alpha commands had slipped right into his mind before he could stop them, and he did not want to admit to himself how easy it had been for them to take him apart.

Roman rumbled for him, wrapping Sidian up in his arms, but he didn't question what had Sidian upset this time. Sighing, Sidian closed his eyes and just tried to focus on his alpha. Roman's rich metallic scent all melting and hot, his comforting touch, his own omega's purrs harmonizing with Roman's rumbling—because no matter what, Sidian was happy. Being with Roman was like having the shredded pieces of his soul stitched back together, Roman's tenderness and affection filling the cracks until he felt whole again.

That was what an alpha was supposed to be like. Even when it was bad, even when the world was going to crash down on them at any moment, Roman had him. Roman *had* him.

"Thanks," he muttered, rubbing his hand over Roman's chest. "Being in control... That was good for me. Felt good and safe. Like I knew you'd listen the whole time."

Roman kissed his temple this time. "I liked it. Dunno. Taking orders wasn't easy when I joined the Vipers, but with you, it feels... Natural. Like it's just what I'm supposed to do. And you're sexy when you're bloody, too."

Sidian snorted at that, and Roman just chuckled, rubbing a hand up and down Sidian's back and letting him melt the rest of the way into Roman's embrace. Whatever came next, no matter how bad it was, at least they had each other. Nothing was going to change that.

Not even the babies. Sidian was sure of that.

Chapter Fourteen

"We can grab something to eat at the diner on the way out." Roman shifted his limited supply of clothing around in the suitcase, doing some quick mental math. If there were a place in town where they might find some more clothes, it would be a good idea to hit it up before they left. The fewer stops they made, the less likely they were to run into any trouble on the way to New Jersey.

They could meet up with the Mambas to ask them for a better variety of weapons because guns would not do the pain Roman wanted to inflict any justice. They would have to go straight through Oregon, making sure not to creep back into Washington to keep the Ultima from crossing that state line. The cops might be on the lookout for the plates now. Taking the Ultima at all was a risk, especially if the investigation widened, but Roman would push it until they had to pick up a new vehicle.

Having to ditch the Ultima and pick up another car would be simple. He would keep his eyes peeled for any suspicious police activity while he eyed a car they might snatch. That would also let them avoid being pulled over with multiple fake IDs in the car; he should choose one and hide the others. At least he didn't have to worry about a credit card giving him away.

Thank the Goddess, most places still accepted cash. Credit cards left a paper trail.

Sidian sat on the padded trunk, fidgeting with the sleeves of his jacket. He had on a long-sleeved, dark purple shirt that matched his eyes, paired with black jeans. Pretty little thing; for a moment, the methodical planning slipped away in lieu of appreciation, and Roman imagined dragging his mate back into the nest and making him fall apart under his mouth all over again.

Sidian's eyes snapped up to his. "Insatiable fucker, aren't you?"

"You do that to me." Roman cupped Sidian's cheek, and his alpha thrilled when Sidian nuzzled into his touch with no hesitation, his eyelashes fluttering. "I can keep my knot under control, though. I promise."

Sidian snorted up at him. "That, I don't doubt. Hell of a lot sexier than a guy who's on the edge of losing control."

"I care little for the alphas who are like that." If he could, Roman would kill them.

Sharp teeth nipped at the palm of his hand. "That's why we're mates, isn't it? Because you're the only alpha in the world who suits me like I need you to."

"All I want to do is please you." He pulled his hand away before he made a mistake, but the glowing grin he earned, sharp white canines exposed, was well worth it.

He zipped his suitcase shut and picked it up, and Sidian shouldered the leather bag. The drawstring bags were out in the car, still filled with Sidian's clothing from the center and Roman's clothing from the mission. Until he could find somewhere safe to dump them, they were staying right where they were. Only took one curious person and one call to the police to blow everything wide open, and Roman had no desire to be considered a fugitive from the law.

The Vipers operated illegally. They didn't have a choice. Ouroboros's money protected them mostly, giving them ample resources and paying off police and judges as need be. The original founder of the organization had set up a sting and handed the law so much evidence about an omega trafficking ring they chose to look the other way, building the foundational precedent for the status Ouroboros had now.

But it would only take one moron to fuck it all up, and Roman did not intend to be that moron.

"We're going to hit Main Street after breakfast," he said, and Sidian bobbed his head in understanding. "You see anything you think you need, let me know, but try not to grab too much so we can still travel light. If it's not something we can fit into one bag, I'd prefer to leave it for now and spoil you with it later."

The corner of Sidian's mouth twitches. "You seem like you make spoiling money."

"First thing on the list is a big, cozy nest for you to laze around in all day." Somewhere permanent, somewhere real, somewhere Sidian could load it up with all the pillows and blankets he could ever want.

Sidian leaned up on his toes, pecking Roman on the lips. "Long as I have you, I'll have just about everything I could need."

They checked out at the desk and loaded the car back up, though the nerves in Roman's stomach wouldn't be soothed until they were on the road. While taking back roads came with certain risks—easy to be chased, easy to be cornered, and even if the Ultima was an off-road vehicle, the trees couldn't be driven through—the reward outweighed the risks. It would be so much harder for them to draw attention to themselves if they were out where no one was looking, and small-town police were rarely called in to work larger cases.

That was how it had to go until they were back with the Vipers. Once they made it to the Pit, Roman could finally breathe easy.

Fable waved to them from the counter while Sidian shot toward the table from yesterday, settling down in the booth with a relieved sigh. Though he'd only been with Roman for a couple of nights now, he looked so much better. His color was back, his eyes were glowing, and the dark circles were slowly fading away.

I can take care of him. I knew I could do it.

"Nice to see you two again this morning," Fable said as she sidled up next to the table, notepad in hand. "Tell me what I can get for you this fine morning."

"What my dog had yesterday," Sidian said, nudging Roman's foot under the table. "Double all the meat, though. I'm starving to death."

Fable let out a nervous little giggle, only relaxing when she saw Roman didn't even respond to the supposed jab, and scribbled down the order. "What to drink? We have decaf if you want it, but it's pretty nasty, like you'd expect it to be."

"Orange juice today sounds just perfect." Sidian fluttered his lashes at Roman, and his chest tightened. He felt like a stupid fucking teenage boy all over again. "And what do you want for breakfast, Roe?"

"Pancakes sound nice today." Something filling and heavy; he would need the energy while they were on the road. "And a side of sausage links, if you don't mind, with black coffee."

"Coming right up." Fable turned and half-skipped back to the counter, and Roman wondered for a moment if she had a mate of her own somewhere.

She was sweet. He hoped someone treated her right.

"The one thing that I keep thinking about is something you mentioned last night," Sidian said, and Roman blinked at him, stirred from his thoughts. "You said you'd leave the Vipers if I wanted you to. I'm not saying I do, but are you sure you'd be fine with doing that if I asked?"

What kind of question even was that? "I care more about your happiness than I do their mission. It was good to help, but..." But Sidian was more important. It was selfish, in a way, but Roman did not care. He would always put Sidian first. "But I would choose you, over and over."

Sidian glanced around the diner before leaning across the table. "What, like... *Is* all the stuff you get up to? People talk, obviously, but everyone talks. I don't think anybody knows shit."

Sidian was right; talk meant nothing. Most alphas and omegas heard rumors about Ouroboros growing up because they remained a persistent thorn in the side of the beta-led government. Most of the large-scale attacks on government facilities or buildings were attributed to them, though becoming a Viper meant discovering that half of those were blamed on Ouroboros for the sake of bad press. Some of that blame was to allow the police to avoid the fact that they couldn't find the culprits they were searching for.

And to this day, the police still refuse to admit when Ouroboros assisted in an investigation. Not that they ever asked for help, but every so often, goals aligned.

"Ouroboros is an organization run by a group of very elite alphas, omegas, and one epsilon. And that's the boss." Roman watched Sidian's eyes widen. "Jagger is my captain, and he answers to the boss. In order to even be around alphas, Devereaux has to wear a gas mask."

Sidian whistled and leaned back in his seat, his eyes wide with intrigue. "Guess it's a good thing I'm an omega in case I ever meet him."

The edges of Roman's vision flickered crimson for just a moment. *Calm down right now.* "The boss himself is harmless, at least to omegas. He runs the Vipers. Each leader hand-selects their teams and trains them. There are five more Vipers besides myself and the captain, and I assure you they'd all be thrilled to meet you."

"Do they know about me?" There was a halting quality to Sidian's voice, an uncertainty that made Roman's stomach twist. "I mean, not that you had to tell them about me, but—"

Roman cut him off. "We aren't a close group. We're not a pack. But the boss knows your name, like I said."

"Right. Cool." Sidian dropped a hand to his stomach, then shoved both of them behind his thighs, nervous, it seemed. "So, the whole breeding center thing. That's your MO?"

"The boss's, but yes. The Vipers occupy ourselves with that program while the other branches handle something else. The Mambas, for instance, prefer to focus their time and effort on taking down trafficking rings. The Cobras concern themselves with political work."

"That's so much shit to get into at nineteen. Well." Sidian smiled, though it didn't reach his eyes. "I mean, not that what I got into was any better, I guess."

Roman reached across the table, and Sidian gave him his hand, letting their fingers twine together. "You were worth it. I was trained to be the alpha I needed to be for you, and I'm grateful for it. I'll always be grateful for it."

Fable bustled over a moment later with their plates and drinks, and Sidian dug into his food with vigor once again. Roman made a mental note to plan more stops for hot food, though he had every intention of hitting a gas station on the way out to load up on as many snacks as possible. Anything healthy he could lay his hands on, as well as anything that would keep well. Sidian needed to continue eating as much as he wanted to reach a healthy weight, after all. Roman had to take care of him.

Sidian knocked their ankles together beneath the table just as Roman finished up his second pancake. "I appreciate it. I suck at showing it, I know, but I do fucking... Appreciate every-thing. You. You're a damned miracle to me, Roe."

Roman's chest tightened. "That means a lot to me."

Sidian nodded, stabbing his fork into his eggs. "I'll try to do a better job at showing it because you do so much for me already. It's the least I can do for you in return."

It was second nature to insist it wasn't necessary. "I'd like that, but don't feel pressured."

"I won't." A small, sweet smile made his heart beat even faster. "Not by you."

Roman shoved a bite of pancake into his mouth to keep from tearing up in front of the handful of people in the diner, as well as his mate. When he'd first met Sidian, when the first bur-geoning attraction to him began, Roman didn't know how to express it. But seeing Sidian that night during the infiltration, scared and scrawny and ready to kill to protect himself, made it so easy to be sweet to him, to give him the easy affection every omega in the world deserved.

And Roman would keep doing it. He would never stop.

He left Fable a healthy tip for her services, his mind return-ing to planning as soon as they exited the diner.

A handful of stops and then back on the road until the fatigue hit him and they had to stop for the night. As late as possible, as far as possible. They could do this.

With Sidian at his side, there would be no stopping him.

Chapter Fifteen

Sidian didn't know when he dozed off on the drive, but he woke to the sight of the sun sinking below the clouds, throwing long shadows across the road. Part of him wanted to apologize for falling asleep and leaving Roman on his own during the drive, but when he glanced over at his alpha, Roman looked peaceful. His eyes remained focused on the road, though he looked at Sidian after a moment, his eyebrows rising as he offered a small smile.

"Feel better?" he asked, chuckling when Sidian just grunted at him. "You needed that, I think. You were out maybe ten minutes after we left Angel Ridge."

That fucking long? For fuck's sake. "Maybe I have narcolepsy."

"I think your body is calming down enough to heal," Roman offered, which was not something that Sidian expected to just have thrown at him like that. Though, he supposed, Roman was right; he'd been in a hypervigilant state for so long that sleep came when he needed it, and the pregnancy did not make that easier on him. "You went through a lot of traumatic shit. I think you can grant yourself some grace."

Sidian wanted to laugh at the thought of that, but Roman had a point that he hadn't thought about too much. The concept of healing was foreign to him; he hadn't been getting any better at the psych ward back home, deteriorating further every single day he spent within those sterile white walls. And he would have been content to rot there for the rest of his life if not for his fucking father.

Sighing, he picked at the seam of his sleeve, trying to loosen a thread to tug at. "Do you think it's possible for someone like me to get better?"

"Hmm." Roman cocked his head like a puppy. It was so fucking cute. "I don't know why it wouldn't be possible, admittedly. Maybe there's something I'm missing here?"

Maybe he was just too sweet for his own good. "I'm just saying, y'know, I was pretty fucked up when we first met. It wasn't like I was some innocent little breeder back then. I stabbed three nurses before you met me the first time."

"Three?" He whistled. "I knew it was at least one, but Dad didn't want to give me any of the details."

"Your dad was a pretty all right guy, all things considered. Just thought he could fix me, and that was off the table." Not that he didn't try. Dr. Kane would do just about anything to help Sidian, and to this day, he wasn't sure what he did to deserve that level of sympathy, or if he ever deserved it at all.

There were other patients in the ward. Smart, hopeful patients who might have a future laid out before them if they just buckled down and got to the root of their problems or something like that. Sidian had seen kids come and go in the two years he stayed there, some of them just post-suicide visits and some of them long-term patients. Hell, some patients who were there when he arrived had the chance to leave before he did.

"Why was it off the table?" Roman asked.

The last thing Sidian wanted to talk about was those days. His life had been shit for years; there had been so little good in it, but revisiting the past just hurt. "Didn't want to go home to my dad, y'know?"

When they reached a stop sign, Roman turned to look at him, his gaze quiet and intense. He'd been like that the first time Sidian saw him, too. Even before presentation, he knew he was looking at an alpha; there was just something about them that gave it away even before their scents developed and their pheromones kicked in. But whereas it was kind of threatening in other alphas, it was just... A part of Roman.

Hard to think of him the way Sidian thought of people like Pack Kincaid when Roman had been so willing to hand over the reins of control.

"Am I allowed to say I'm glad I killed him?" Roman asked, and Sidian scoffed and leaned over, shoving his face away. "What? I mean, it's not like I was *planning* to do it. It just sort of happened, but I don't regret it. Someone who'd sell their kid off like that doesn't even deserve children."

On that point, they agreed. "If it meant your dad survived all that shit, would you take it back?"

"That's a good question. I don't know." Roman shrugged and turned back to the road, foot pressing down on the gas pedal. "Because I don't know if we would have found each other again. That alpha could have taken you and vanished halfway around the globe."

Sidian thought they would have found each other again, but he was content to keep that to himself as he tilted his head back into the headrest, his eyes fluttering shut again. Maybe it was stupid to think of it like that, like it was just some twist of fate after all, but he would like to at least believe he and Roman would have found each other again. That their paths would have crossed elsewhere if not at the center, that Roman would have picked Sidian out of a crowd. He didn't know if Roman could pull that off because damn, was he so much taller, but if their eyes met, then Sidian was certain it would happen.

It was some kind of progress to admit he'd pick Roman out of a crowd, too. Just too bad the doc wasn't there to see him make it.

When Roman fished his phone out of his pocket midway through a turn, it was to toss the vibrating device into Sidian's lap. "Answer that for me, will you? I don't want to take my eyes off the road. Crazy turns out here."

"Sure." Sidian didn't know who *Mal* was supposed to be, but he answered the call. "Roman's driving. What the fuck do you want?"

There was a pause on the other end of the line before a disbelieving little laugh tripped over someone's lips. *"Are you the omega spiriting him off to the middle of nowhere, then?"*

"Who is it?" Roman asked, his eyes on the road.

"Someone named Mal," Sidian replied, and Mal—whoever he was—made a hurt noise on the other end of the phone.

"I can't believe he hasn't already told you all about the group," he said, pouting how Sidian had heard so many alphas pout before. It would almost be cute if it weren't so fucking annoying. *"I'm one of the Vipers. Thought I'd check in on the kid after the captain said he wouldn't be back for a while."*

Roman raised his voice. "You wouldn't call for that reason, Mal. What's going on?"

"Fine, fine. Fuck me for trying to care about you." Mal cleared his throat, his tone shifting to all business. *"Pack Kincaid is out of state for the time being, but they should be back soon. Doing a job over in Manhattan. The Mambas had plans to infiltrate, but it*

looks like someone got wind of that and changed locations at the last second."

Sidian's mood soured at the words even though they weren't anywhere near Jersey yet. It wasn't like it mattered if Pack Kincaid were out of state when he and Roman weren't even in state yet, but it still unsettled him. How long was it going to be before they figured out what had happened at the center? Were they going to care that Sidian had vanished with their second child? Were they going to come looking for him and the baby?

He wanted to believe he wasn't significant enough for them to track down, but he knew better than to assume. That might just put him in more danger.

Roman squeezed his eyes shut for a brief second. "An auction, I'm assuming. Any idea who's involved?"

"It's not our area to know shit like that, and the Mambas don't like sharing intel unless they have to, so be prepared to give them something to get what you want." Mal heaved a put-upon sigh, and Sidian wondered how Ouroboros functioned if they were all supposed to be working together but did not like to share with each other. *"Someone important, but rich enough to jump ship on location. Given how many omegas they have to transport, it's not a small amount of money to burn through."*

Sidian's mouth dried at the thought. "How do you know how many omegas they're selling if these people don't talk to you about shit like that?"

Mal didn't answer him right away, and Sidian realized he wasn't supposed to be listening to any of this. He wasn't some fragile fucking doll who couldn't handle the reality of the situation he was in, but he also wasn't a trained assassin or whatever it was the Vipers were considered. Even though he was pretty sure he could blow someone's brains out if given half the chance, he'd not been able to do anything to stop Pack Kincaid either of the two times he'd seen them.

Roman's hand lit on his knee for one moment. "The Mambas don't have to share those numbers with us. Those are spread through Ouroboros as a law so that we all understand the stakes of our failures."

Mal cleared his throat. *"It's somewhere between twenty and fifty depending on how big the auction is, and this one was supposed to be big. Mambas might have gotten too close and spooked 'em, though."*

"They've got a few who are careless," Roman agreed, "but that's fine. Thank you for letting us know. We're making our way to New Jersey, but we need to take our time." His hand returned to Sidian's knee, fingers splaying over his thigh, and Sidian just let him. Maybe there were things Roman needed to seek comfort from, things Sidian would never know or understand.

Mal snorted. *"Shit always gets back to the lowlife bottom feeders of the world. Take care of yourself, Kane, and let us know if you need anything else."*

The call ended, and Sidian looked up at Roman, not sure what to say. Twenty to fifty omegas at a time? Given how rare omegas were, the amount they'd have to capture to pull those kinds of numbers on even a semi-regular basis was nauseating. How many of them were mature? How many of them were just kids like Sidian was when his father slipped into his room for the first time, sold off for potential?

Roman rolled his tongue along the inside of his cheek. "I'm sorry. That's the reality of our work. Breeding centers can't be packed up and moved without a moment's notice, but anything temporary can be."

"Are they going to find a new auction location?" Sidian didn't know why he was asking. He didn't know why he cared.

Anyone would care. It's basic fucking empathy.

"I can't give you a definitive yes or no. I don't know what they get up to. But if you want, you can ask the Mambas when we have to talk to them ourselves." Roman lapsed into uneasy silence. That must be the best he could offer.

Sighing, Sidian reached over and punched his shoulder. "Sometimes I get so wrapped up in how fucked up my life is that I forget that results from the rest of the entire world also being this way. Sucks."

"But it is over," Roman said, and Sidian heard the steering wheel creak under his grip. "No more fucked up shit happens to you. Not on my watch. Once we deal with those assholes who hurt you, you can do whatever you want. I'll make sure of it."

He was sweet. Misguided though he was to think he could take on the entire world for Sidian, it was sweet of him to try.

Still, Sidian filed the whole auction thing away for later and settled back in his seat. No use in letting himself get dragged down into the things he was incapable of doing anything about, just another injustice waged against his designation with only a handful of people who cared enough to stop it.

At least he had the best of those people at his side.

Chapter Sixteen

I f Roman drove straight to New Jersey, taking the straight-est possible route laid out before them, he was certain he could reach the East Coast in a couple of days at most. There were a few dead zones he had to worry about, places where even his limited cell phone signal would drop, but otherwise it was possible. Skulking through small towns tucked away from the rest of the society and choosing motels half-hidden from every main road was just a precaution to ensure they stayed safe.

Working for Ouroboros had taught him there was no such thing as being too worried, too prepared, and he had taken that to heart where some others—like Mal—had scoffed at it.

"I don't get it," Sidian told him on their last night in Ne-braska, stretched out on his back with his legs resting against the headboard. "Is there someone you're afraid of running into or something?"

It was a good question to ask. "I'm concerned more about the police than anyone else. Our identities within Ouroboros are kept secret, so no one should know my name or face."

Sidian cocked his head as if considering this. "So that's why the fake IDs? Because nobody knows who you are any-way, it's not like it matters what the card says. They'd have to scan it to clock that you were lying to them. Do you even have an ID of any kind on official record?"

"I don't. The others might, but I hadn't taken my driver's test before everything happened." Roman leaned his own back against the headboard, unsurprised when Sidian rested a foot on his shoulder.

"So did they have to teach you how to drive?" Sidian asked.

Roman curled a hand around Sidian's ankle just to touch him, just to feel the warmth of his omega's skin beneath his fingers. "They did. Jagger had to, in particular. I don't think any of them were thrilled with me not knowing how." Though it had been amusing to watch the captain bite back curses while Roman sat behind the wheel, concentrating on not getting either of them killed.

"Sounds like a good time. I still don't know how to drive," Sidian admitted.

"I can teach you," Roman offered, and Sidian hummed but didn't respond. He didn't need to know how to drive if he didn't want to know; they could always find a quiet place with plenty of sidewalks, a pleasant neighborhood where he could stay while Roman handled any actual driving. He wasn't a car person by nature, but cars were fine. He was okay with driving.

He wondered if the other Vipers had ever stopped to have these thoughts. If they'd ever pondered what they might do with the rest of their lives, should they ever find mates of their own. Did they sit around and think about where they might take that omega to live, or where they might find them? Did they all imagine the breeding centers? It wasn't like they went elsewhere very often.

Roman should have asked one of them about it, but he'd been committed to talking as little as possible around the Vipers. He had no genuine desire to change that aspect of himself now.

Sidian clicked his tongue, hooking a finger through one of Roman's belt loops and giving it a firm tug. "Did you ever think about moving up the chain of command?"

"No. I have no desire to be captain. The others wouldn't listen to me."

From a distance, Roman could see how Jagger struggled to maintain control of the Vipers even on good days, even after successful missions. Though he was confident he had never given his superior much reason to struggle with him, the others had.

"Who are the others?" Sidian nudged him with his foot again, and Roman wondered if the sudden questions were from boredom. Perhaps the trip was taking too long for his mate's taste. "Who called you on the phone the other day? Like, what's everyone's deal?"

"That was Mal. Short for Malice." Roman winced the moment Sidian snorted, smashing a hand over his own mouth to keep himself from laughing. "I know. He's my primary sparring partner. Most of the others struggle to keep up with me."

The smile faded from Sidian's face. "That's because of me, right? Because of what happened that day. Because of going feral."

Going feral seemed like such a delicate way to phrase it. Through be told, Roman had been more or less able to keep himself stable, but that was because he let himself loose on every single mission. It was where Killer Kane came from; the first time he lost it on a member of the breeding center staff, it had become a tradition to let him pick one target to unleash his frustration and bloodlust on. Just something to feed the violence that had taken up residence within his chest.

He didn't know what it was in the literal sense. He didn't know if it was always bound to be a part of him or if it was the result of a young alpha losing himself because he'd had his mate taken away from him.

Maybe now that he had Sidian back, he would get better.

"It could never be your fault," he reassured Sidian, leaning over to cup the omega's cheek, smiling when Sidian scrubbed his face against Roman's thigh. Very possessive scent-marking, he noted. "I've got it under control."

Sidian nodded, though he didn't seem to believe that. Roman couldn't blame him for it; it would be something he came to see for himself in time. "What about the others? Four others and the captain guy, right?"

"Correct. Jagger is the captain. He's older than the rest of us, about thirty-two, I think. Strict and old-fashioned, but a talented trainer. Did a good job with us." Or as good of a job that could be expected of someone without as much experience as Roman expected him to have. He didn't doubt the captain; the boss saw something in him, something that Roman wasn't capable of seeing.

And he doubted he ever would. The boss's perspective had been created through circumstances and experiences that Roman knew he himself would never have. And he was thankful for it.

Sidian tilted his head so he could dig his teeth into the denim covering Roman's thigh. "What about the other Vipers?"

"Silver is the one who handles information and file recovery. He tries to name and place all the omegas we save." Or at least find a safe place to put them until the Vipers could figure out where to ferry them off to next. "Physical paper files and digital files."

"Do you get the digital shit before you cut the power? Or does he just steal hard drives?" Sidian asked.

"Hard drives, I think. Not my area, though." Roman had never asked about that. It was something he never needed to know; Silver was already a professional long before Roman showed up. "Ghost used to be aligned with a criminal pack, but the boss stepped in when he was arrested. I think he was going to take the fall for something heinous. He won't share the exact details, and neither did the boss."

"And the last two?" Sidian pressed.

"Locke and Keay." Roman rolled his eyes when Sidian snorted; he'd had plenty of time to get used to their ridiculous names. "Not their real names, I don't think. I don't know where they came from, and they keep to themselves. Less social than I am. They're our main infiltrators. Physical locks, digital locks if Silver can't access them. I'm not sure what goes into that."

Sidian fell quiet for a moment, staring at nothing in particular before he knocked Roman in the shoulder with his foot again. "What was your specialty in the group? Anything important?"

"I killed people." Would he have been surprised if it were anything else? "That was what I was chosen for. I'm stronger, faster, have higher endurance and stamina, and a much higher pain tolerance."

"Sounds about right." Sidian swung his legs over so he could sit up, stretching his arms and stifling a yawn against his palm. He still dozed off in the car, but his dark circles were almost gone. "They wouldn't believe me if I told them you used to be a bookworm."

Roman still spent a fair amount of time reading, but that was time he spent with his bedroom door shut, and the others only came to bother him if they needed something in particular. "That's fine. That's not who I am anymore. At least, not to them."

Who did he used to be? Quiet, soft-spoken, polite to a fault. He shoved his nose in books because fictional people were easier than real people, and stories let him escape the mundane quality of his lackluster life. Sidian was the first genuine spark of color amidst the black and white, someone who was real and alive and who captivated every moment of Roman's attention. He was always important, mate or not.

He was more important now. Roman's life had slipped back into black and white, spotted with crimson from time to time, but he could recognize how easy it had been to fall into old habits. Working out kept him healthier than staying in his bedroom all the time, but it was similar.

His mind was far more active now; he needed to keep them ahead of whatever might be coming for them, to plan out their course, to prepare for what it might take to kill a pack of alphas. It wasn't just sitting around and waiting for orders; Roman wondered if he'd ever have broken out of that rut if Sidian hadn't come back into his life.

He would have just continued to exist, waiting for something to change.

Sidian leaned his shoulder against Roman's, snuggling up to him, his lily scent subdued. "Did you know I wanted to be a mom? I don't think I ever told you about that."

"What?" Roman blinked at him, caught off-guard. "We never discussed children."

He thought he might have imagined Sidian wincing. "I mean, it's not something you just talk about with people when you're locked up in a psych ward, but... I thought about it. My mom was a piece of shit who let my dad do whatever he wanted to me, but I always told myself I'd be different. Pick a good alpha. Take care of my kid."

"Just one child?" Roman tried to imagine that, but he found it was far simpler to visualize than it should have been. An omega, perhaps, with Sidian's black hair and violet eyes.

"Well. I guess as many as we wanted. It'd depend on a lot of things. Money. Fertility. How hard it was to raise the first one."

Sidian wrapped his arms around himself, and Roman frowned at his words. He must have been thinking about it an awful lot at the breeding center. "Guess I'm lucky my heats never worked out for Kincaid. I don't know what he'd have done if they had."

Bile rose in Roman's throat at the thought of his omega forced to carry and birth a child he would not get to raise. That would never happen. If Sidian wanted a child, they would discuss it when they were in a better place. "Do you know why they didn't?"

"Ttress. Omegas don't conceive when they're super stressed." Sidian shrugged, and the slight change in his voice told Roman the conversation was over.

They sat in silence for a while before Sidian slipped off the mattress, mumbling something about taking a shower, and Roman watched him go without a word. He could feel the frustration still simmering under the surface, but there was nothing he could do about it. Even if they ended up in New Jersey tomorrow, there was no guarantee that Pack Kincaid would be back in town. And while Roman wanted justice to be served, he wanted to be prepared. No rushing in just to get killed.

The anger swelled and shifted inside of him for a moment, choking him from the inside of his throat. Blood and viscera, gore and death, bodies strung up and ripped open, oozing and gushing and dripping. Bone jutted through pallid flesh, organs glistening on the floor.

It took several deep breaths and standing to pace around the small, cramped room for the anger to abate. At least with no target to fixate on, it lolled back to sleep, returning Roman's clarity.

He wondered if he would make it once they reached Pack Kincaid, or if losing his self-control over his mate's rapists would push him beyond the point of no return.

Chapter Seventeen

When the fuck is Pack Kincaid supposed to go home?

The question dug its claws into Sidian as he stared at the scenery passing by outside the window, his jaw locked and pure tension coiling through every part of his body. Not having answers was pissing him off. He knew it wasn't Roman's fault; he knew it wasn't the fault of the people Roman kept in his life, but the anger was there just the same. The irritation at the fact that those assholes couldn't be in the one place Sidian needed them to be, the one place they *should* be. He wanted Amey back, and he wanted the pack dead.

They would never suffer enough for what they did to him, so he would just have to settle for the grave.

The monotony of driving was getting to him, too. While he liked just having time with Roman alone, the long hours were wearing on him. He could only sleep for so long before an inevitable pothole or dip in the road shook him awake, and besides, he didn't want to just sit around and sleep. He wanted to do something. He needed to.

Something more productive than just sitting there and waiting.

"Can we stop somewhere?" he asked, and Roman cocked a brow at him. "Just... This is going to sound fucking stupid, but the car's gonna give me cabin fever. If we can't go straight to

Jersey, is there anywhere we can just hang out for a little while? Just today?"

Somewhere outside, fresh air and green leaves and nothing but the wilderness surrounding them.

Roman checked the rearview before pulling over, digging the map he'd pilfered from the last gas station out of the glove box. "What did you have in mind?"

"I just need to walk around somewhere we don't have to worry about being seen. That's all. And you need to stretch those long legs." At least, Sidian knew he did, and he wasn't that tall.

Roman was quiet for a moment, alternating between glancing in the mirror and studying the map, finger dragging along squiggling lines in various colors. As long as Sidian got what he wanted, he was content to wait as long as Roman needed him to, his head resting against the cool glass of the window next to him. The Ultima stayed warm, but he'd still rather be curled up in a cozy nest somewhere than out there on the road. Maybe after all of this was done, he could do just that.

Roman had said something about a fancy nest for him one day, hadn't he?

"There's a state park not that far from where we're driving. We're heading in its general direction." Roman folded up the map and slipped it into the glove compartment, satisfied. "Some trails look easy enough. We can walk around for a while before finding another motel. I doubt many people are going to be hiking in the middle of the work week, anyway."

"Lifesaver," Sidian murmured, letting his eyes fall shut. "Wake me up when we get there. I'll give you a treat tonight since you're being such a good dog."

The sharp little inhale of breath made him chuckle. Roman was a good boy.

They pulled off into a small parking lot with just a couple of other cars. Sidian took the time to stretch before zipping up his jacket, letting Roman pull him in close without a word as he steered them toward the trees. Roman was warmer than Sidian was; being close to him was nice. And even better were the fresh air, the wide open space, and just the two of them to enjoy it.

Despite the other cars, they didn't see anyone else on the trail Roman chose for them. It wasn't much of a trail, more like a little dirt path that led to a walk along a river, but it was beautiful. The water had a clean, fresh, metallic scent, and the trees were lush and green, leaves rustling in a breeze that was only slightly chilly.

It was what Sidian needed. "Thank you, alpha."

"It's not a problem. I like it out here more than I do in town or in the city, anyway." Roman rubbed his hand up and down Sidian's back, though it resumed its place at Sidian's hip as if Roman thought he was going anywhere. *As if.* "I'm sorry for that, by the way. I should have been clearer about what this was going to be. About how much patience it would demand."

It would have been nice to know just for the sake of preparation, but Sidian could never be angry with Roman. Not in a way that mattered. "It's fine. I mean, I'd rather drag ass on the way to Jersey than get picked up by the cops. I don't even know what they'd end up doing with me."

"I don't know, either," Roman admitted, his hand tightening just enough that Sidian could feel it. Oh, he was *worried,* and that was fucking adorable. "We take all the omegas from the centers somewhere safe. I do not know what would happen to them if we didn't do that."

It wasn't a surprise that the trained mercenary chose caution, then. Sidian didn't know what that life demanded of Roman, but he knew he could at least trust him to understand the danger they were in. "How many alphas do you think would be pissed off in their unborn children vanished?"

Roman wrinkled his nose. "The children do not *belong* to them. They belong to their mothers. And I don't know. I guess it would depend on whether the packs in question wanted children. Breeding centers are used as brothels just as much as they are anything else.

"And some of 'em just wanna be cruel for the sake of it," Sidian muttered, and Roman's grip tightened further. "Relax. I'm not going anywhere. It's not like they're hiding in the trees."

Roman's head jerked as a breeze rustled some leaves nearby. "Don't put that into the universe."

A wooden bench appeared on the path ahead, and Sidian wriggled away from Roman's side to sit down on it, letting himself lean back against the wide, comfortable slats. The river stretched out before them, the rushing waters adding a nice ambiance without being too loud or distracting. If they were just traveling, Sidian might have liked to stop there just to take a breather.

Roman draped his jacket over Sidian's shoulders before sitting down, and Sidian burrowed into the smoky, metallic scent that clung to the fibers. "We *are* going to kill that pack. No matter how long we take to find them. I want to repay them the favor for what they've done to you."

"I know, big guy." And what would he do when he learned the truth? Sidian didn't want to think about it. Instead, he shifted closer to lay his head against Roman's arm, purring when

Roman lifted his arm and tugged Sidian's head against his chest instead.

The low, steady thrum of his heartbeat, elevated as it was, was comforting.

For just a moment, Sidian gave in to his omega's instinctive need for comfort and touch, letting Roman hold him close and just basking in his presence. He could not have mated a better alpha, but he knew that the moment he realized he was scenting Roman through the blood and flesh. No alpha could ever compare, but it still felt like the universe threw the worst possible alphas at Sidian to mock him.

As if he ever needed a reason to appreciate Roman more than he already did.

"The Pit's not as forested as this, but it's in the countryside," Roman said, stirring Sidian from his relaxed state. "The boss wanted us to make sure we got fresh air when we needed it. Some vitamin D bullshit, but we can walk around there like this. If you want to go back, that is.

Sidian thought about it for a moment. "Is the Pit what you call your guys' house or something?"

"It's the name of the entire collection of buildings. The main buildings, the dorms, the storage, and so on." Roman gestured with his hand, the other cupping Sidian's elbow and tugging him closer. Maybe teasing him about the trees was the wrong move after all. "The names are silly. I'm not sure who came up with them, but that's what we call it."

Themed naming for a collection of mercenary groups was indeed stupid as fuck, but Sidian found it charming in an immature way. "The guys wouldn't bother us if we went, would they?"

"No," Roman said, his brow creasing. "If they tried, I'd chase them away. You don't deserve to be harassed when you're just trying to take a walk. They can be a bit much."

Goddess, he was so stupidly protective, and it was cute. Not threatening or off-putting at all. It was so sweet. "Are you gonna snap and growl at them every time they get too close to me?"

Roman pouted, and Sidian grinned as he leaned up to kiss the corner of his alpha's mouth. Baiting Roman was too easy; he was like a dog. But it was fun just the same, watching him get a little wound up, a little annoyed. He'd been so put together as a teenager right before everything went to shit, so it was good to see him relax. To see the seams of his person relax for just a moment.

And then he threw Sidian a curveball. "I've been thinking about children on the drive."

"Oh?" Sidian eyed him. Were there any signs that might have slipped during the drive? Did Roman notice something he otherwise hadn't before?

Roman took a deep breath, schooling his expression before looking down at Sidian, his eyes twice as vibrant as the surrounding forest. "If you want to be a mother, you should have that opportunity. I would be honored to be the alpha in your life when that happens."

What was Sidian supposed to say to that? He opened his mouth, but no sound came out, his stomach clenching as the weight of that proclamation settled on his shoulders. A pang of guilt tightened his gut, and when the baby fluttered inside of him, he wondered if Roman could ever forgive him. If he could ever forgive *himself* for what he was doing.

Maybe he should just tell him. Maybe he needed to get it out. "Roman, I don't—"

But Roman cut him off with a soft kiss, and Sidian swallowed a whine. No, he *couldn't* tell Roman yet. As much as he wanted to, as good as it would feel to get it all off of his chest, he'd been hiding it for a reason. He had to put his son first because what kind of mother would endanger their child? And as cavalier as Roman was being, Sidian couldn't bank on his reaction.

Not until he saw Amethyst. Not until he understood what this would mean for both of them.

"I want to do this for you," Roman said, and Sidian bit down on his bottom lip. It would be okay. He'd get to see Roman hold Amey for the first time after every single Kincaid was dead, and Roman would come through for him one last time. He had to. He *had* to. "If you'll let me, that is. We can do whatever you want to do as soon as those bastards are dead."

Sidian scoffed and kissed him again. "Idiot. I don't want anyone else but you."

They sat for a while longer on the bench before the temperature dropped enough for Sidian to miss the warmth of the car. Roman kept his jacket wrapped around Sidian on the slow walk back, his eyes drifting from tree to tree, resting on the river for a moment. It didn't occur to Sidian just how tense Roman had been until he saw him relaxed, his steps easy and meandering rather than purposeful. Maybe he also needed to get that conversation off his chest, too.

When all of this was over, maybe the nice house and the white picket fence was a possibility.

Sidian tugged Roman's belt to get the alpha's attention, shivering when those inquisitive eyes met his. "I think you deserve a treat when we decide to stop for the night.

Roman's scent grew so hot in the air that it chased away all of Sidian's chills for just a moment. "Well, I'm glad you enjoyed your little rendezvous in the forest, then."

Sidian knew what he wanted to do to Roman, and what he wanted to try. Something different from last time, something more involved on his part, something he would do at his own speed. Pack Kincaid would never allow it, but Roman would let

Sidian gag him and tie him up in order to feel that necessary control. And Sidian thought he might do just that.

Roman would look so sexy with his hands behind his back.

Chapter Eighteen

As soon as the motel room door clicked shut behind them, Sidian tossed his suitcase on the floor and stalked toward Roman, something dark in his gemstone eyes. Dark and hungry.

"I want your belt," he said matter-of-factly, holding his hand out for it as if that was all he had to do to get what he wanted. In reality, he had to do even less. "And I want the collar. If you have another belt somewhere in your bag, then I want that, too."

A tiny thrill in Roman's hindbrain reminded him that Sidian had knives he could use against Roman should he want to do that, but the danger was the point. Roman unbuckled his belt and tugged it out of the loops, handing it to Sidian before tossing him the leather bag so he could retrieve the collar. Sidian was lucky; Roman had a couple of other belts because they were on sale when he picked up their clothes, and he had to buy more than one belt to trigger the sale price.

Stupid fucking retail stores.

"On the edge of the bed." Sidian draped the belts over his shoulder, unbuckling the collar as he approached Roman. "You were a good dog. You still want your treat, right?"

Fuck yes, he did. "Yes, please."

"Very polite." Sidian fastened the collar around Roman's neck, curling his fingers beneath it to test the tightness before pressing a rough kiss to Roman's lips. "Hands behind your back.

You're not going to be needing them, so you might as well not have access to them."

Roman had two seconds to process that he was being tied up, but his hands were already in the small of his back by the time Sidian slid behind him. One belt wound around his wrists nice and tight enough that the leather bit, though he'd be able to rip it off in an emergency. He didn't realize what Sidian was doing with the other belt until he yanked at the collar, then did *something* that pulled on the supple leather.

"I tied your wrists to your neck," Sidian said as he crawled off of the mattress, the tempting swell of his ass catching Roman's eye. He came to stand in front of Roman, combing his fingers through his hair. "I figured I'd suck you off, but I don't enjoy having my hair pulled, so you're not allowed to touch me."

"I wouldn't pull your hair," Roman said, feeling he needed to make this point. "But I like this."

Sidian chuckled, nimble fingers unfastening Roman's jeans. Roman lifted his hips just long enough for his omega to get the denim and the thin pair of boxers beneath all the way down, leaving them in a tangle around Roman's ankles. The way Sidian's eyes lit up when he freed Roman's cock made it stiffen the rest of the way in seconds, and Sidian let out a little trilling noise as he sank to his knees. It was so unlike him it made Roman's head spin, his blood threatening to catch fire. If not for the leather keeping Roman where Sidian wanted him, he'd almost think Sidian was trying to mess with his head.

"Didn't like this the first handful of times I did it, so be warned," Sidian said, wrapping a hand around Roman's shaft. He stroked it once, fingers tracing the veins all the way to the swollen tip. "I might just leave you here if I decide this isn't worth my time."

Sidian let that hang in the air—half-promise, half-threat—and shifted forward on his knees so he could run the flat of his tongue over the flared tip of Roman's cock. The sensation was unlike anything Roman had ever felt before, the smooth glide of that soft pink tongue making him shudder at his hands twisted in his bindings. His hips twitched, and Sidian grinned up at him like he knew, planting his arms across Roman's thighs like he was strong enough to keep him right where Sidian wanted him.

"Stay," he said, and something in that silky little word fired synapses throughout Roman's brain.

He couldn't move even if he wanted to.

Sidian watched Roman's face as he rolled his tongue over the tip again, letting out a pleased little noise when Roman's eyes slammed shut. A shaky exhale left his lips, his fingers twisting in the leather for something to ground himself with. Muscles tensed in his thighs as if his hips were going to buck, but he couldn't move at all. With one word, Sidian kept Roman pinned to the mattress, his obedience in the palm of Sidian's hand.

Just like a dog.

"You taste a lot better than I expected," Sidian mused, stroking Roman's shaft as he pressed a wet, sucking kiss just under the head. "Good news for you, Roe. Guess that means you'll get to come after all."

"Th-thank you," Roman stuttered out, and Sidian grinned at him.

Sidian's tongue continued its leisurely path along Roman's cock, and when he looked down at the omega, it was to the sight of Sidian lathering spit on his tongue so he could leave one long, wet lick, his fingers sliding through the mess he made. The soft, slick sounds were loud in the quiet motel room, and Roman had to bite back a moan.

"Don't be quiet now," Sidian said, sweet little mind reader he was. "How am I supposed to know if I'm doing a good job or not? You gotta tell me, alpha."

"You're doing... A good job." A shudder rocked Roman's spine as Sidian licked his cock again from the top of his knot to the tip, using the flat of his tongue that time. "Goddess, that's—"

"I'm the only god you should call out to." Sidian stroked down, wrapping his fingers around the swell of Roman's knot, squeezing just enough to choke a whine from Roman's lips. "Remember, stay still. Good boys get treats, but bad boys get punished."

He parted rosy lips to take the head of Roman's cock inside, his eyelids growing heavy as he eased his way down. The inside of his mouth was warm and wet as he sealed his lips around Roman's shaft, letting them glide through spit and pre-come. Roman watched Sidian's nostrils flare as he took a breath just as his tongue flicked up against Roman's cock. And Roman whined, not very alpha-like, but he did not give a fuck.

Sidian's lily scent bloomed thick and sweet in the room as he laved Roman's cock with his tongue, taking it in just an inch at a time, slow and steady. Roman's entire body tensed and trembled, but he couldn't move. Not *wouldn't*, he realized, but *couldn't*.

Sweet little omega witch. How had he pulled that off?

It was slow going, but Sidian got most of Roman's cock down without issue until he choked near the base, backing off to breathe through his nose. Violet eyes met Roman's as Sidian allowed his lips to glide around the shaft, bobbing his head in one smooth motion. And then he eased down again, swallowing this time, until the tip of his nose brushed up against Roman's knot.

Fuck. Holy fuck. Roman didn't know he could do that.

Mischief glinted in Sidian's eyes as he stayed there for a moment, showing off, his tongue rubbing up against Roman's cock before he eased back again. Soft fingers massaged Roman's knot, the little sparks of pleasure making him twitch. He moaned at the sensation, his head falling back because he couldn't move, couldn't do anything but sit there and *feel* it.

When his hands strained too hard at the belt on his wrists, it yanked at the collar, pulling the leather taut across the front of his throat. The sharp discomfort knocked him out of disobedience while Sidian lazily slurped around his cock, easing off and back down, slowly working his way up into a wet, teasing rhythm.

Roman wished he could touch his omega. He wanted to pet Sidian's face, cup his chin, feel his throat flexing as he sucked and swallowed. The pretty flush in his cheeks and his warm, sleepy eyes told Roman that Sidian was enjoying it, that it wasn't just for Roman's benefit, and that was far more thrilling than the pleasure on its own.

Sidian eased off of Roman's cock and rubbed his cheek against it, and Roman half-choked on a laugh at the sight. "What? Gotta make sure no one touches what belongs to me, right?"

"No one h-has," Roman reminded him, but Sidian just huffed up at him, leaning down to run the tip of his tongue over the swell of Roman's knot.

He was such a tease, and Roman loved every second.

Sidian swallowed him back down with far more ease the second time, bobbing his head in quicker, shorter strokes as he kneaded the sensitive flesh of Roman's knot. The pleasure was more intense, building faster, the pressure and the slick stroke of his tongue pushing Roman, driving him crazy, but he couldn't move. All he could do was watch Sidian, his chest heaving, sweat beading on his forehead and the nape of his neck, groaning as Sidian took him all the way down and swallowed *hard*.

Violet eyes met Roman's as Sidian squeezed his knot, and something in that gaze ruined him.

It was intense, not being able to move when he came. The sudden, sharp intensity left him gasping and quaking while he spilled down Sidian's throat, and Sidian swallowed until there was nothing left, falling back on his knees as Roman's cock slid off of his tongue. Breathless, Roman watched as Sidian dragged his thumb through the white dripping out of the corner of his mouth, then sucked it clean.

"Not bad," he said, using the edge of the mattress to pull himself to his feet. "Aren't you lucky? Maybe I'll do it again just because I liked it so much."

"Extremely fucking lucky," Roman slurred, and Sidian laughed and kissed him, his tongue curling inside Roman's mouth.

He could taste the salty, bitter flavor of come on Sidian's tongue, but Roman kissed him through it, anyway. What he wanted was to touch him, to pull his mate close, pet him and praise him and cover him in kisses, but Sidian didn't allow that. Instead, he pushed Roman back on the mattress, straddling his waist, head tilting to the side.

"You stay here," he said, giving Roman's cheek a pat. "I'm going to go get showered off, and then I'll let you up to do whatever it is you wanna do. Okay?"

Sidian was going to leave him trussed up. That was fine. "Okay."

"Good dog." Sidian kissed Roman again, sharper this time, his teeth scraping over Roman's lower lip until it stung, and then he lapped the blood away with a satisfied little purr and left Roman gasping on the mattress to go shower.

Roman stared up at the ceiling, trying to process while his breathing slowed down. Where the fuck had that come from, and why, and how in the hell did Sidian tell him to stay still, and Roman just did? No wriggling, no struggling, no having to fight himself to avoid trying to fuck Sidian's pretty face. Every time Roman jerked himself off, especially in rut, he had damn near lost control.

What was it that Sidian did to him? He didn't understand it.

Sidian returned at some point, wearing another one of Roman's shirts, his hair damp and wild. Instead of letting Roman go, he crawled up onto the mattress and lifted Roman's head from the comforter, laying it across his bare thighs as he combed his fingers through Roman's hair.

"Did you like that?" he asked, his voice low and soft. "The being tied up part, I mean."

Roman did. Whatever it said about him, he didn't care. "It's nice. You should tie me up more often."

"I'll keep that in mind." Sidian slid his fingers beneath the collar again, teasing the tips of them over Roman's Adam's apple. "But for now, I think I'm going to keep you just like this. Be my good dog for just a little longer."

As if Roman would ever complain about a request like that. "Happily, darling."

Chapter Nineteen

Roman's phone lit up in the middle of the night, the insistent buzzing waking Sidian from his light doze and tearing a snarl from his chest. He buried his face in Roman's chest and whined at him, unwilling to relinquish his hold as Roman tried to roll over to grab the phone. Fuck him and fuck phones; it was the middle of the night, and Sidian wanted to *sleep* when everything was warm and cozy.

To his credit at least, Roman wrapped himself back around Sidian, cradling him in warmth as he answered the phone. "Kane."

"*The boss told me you're interested in something within our territory.*" The smooth, masculine voice that issued from the speaker was unfamiliar to Sidian, though he bared his teeth at it just the same as he snuggled back into his alpha's chest. "*I was given the clear to contact you. Where are you stationed?*"

Roman snorted. "Eastern Nebraska, right on the very edge of it. Nowhere special. What do you need?"

"*Information.*" There was a beat of silence during which Roman made a low noise of confusion. "*Our captive won't talk. It's been a very frustrating couple of days. We need the information he has. In return, we'll grant you the personal home address of Dax Kincaid, which is what you're looking for.*"

"What?" Sidian's head snapped up, his eyes wide with hope.

Roman's brow furrowed. "Why are you making it an exchange? What do you stand to lose if we kill them?"

"We've been monitoring their movements and using them in order to locate potential auction sites," the man on the other end of the phone said. *"Allowing you to kill them would make our jobs harder than they already are, but this is out of my hands."*

"You don't sound happy about that, Hadeon."

Sidian tapped Roman on the chest, and the alpha glanced down at him. "Who are you talking to?"

"Is someone else there?" the man—Hadeon, Sidian guessed—demanded.

Roman loosed a little growl, tucking Sidian more firmly against his side as if the other man could reach through the phone and do something about him listening in. "That's my mate. The entire point of taking down Pack Kincaid is doing it for his benefit. Make sure you hold your tongue. And to answer you, darling, he's a Mamba. One of the very best."

Hadeon grumbled something just out of earshot. *"No one told me someone else accompanied you. Is he a recent acquisition of the Vipers?"*

"No," Roman growled, and Sidian bit back a delighted giggle at how needlessly territorial he could be sometimes. But it was sexy watching Roman act like that.

"Regardless, bring him along. He might prove useful for our needs." The call cut, the phone screen going dark.

Roman let the phone fall to the nightstand before rolling back over to wrap Sidian in his arms, nuzzling down into the top of Sidian's head. It was just another little shred of evidence that the two of them were leading different lives because how could Roman just go back to sleep after that conversation? Did he hear a single word that Hadeon guy just said? Did he just agree to torture someone for possible information?

"Hey." Sidian patted him on the back, and Roman grumbled against his scalp. "Roe, what was all that about?"

Roman dipped his head down to kiss Sidian's forehead. "Talk to me about it in the morning. I'm tired."

Sidian could push Roman, and Roman would speak, but he let him rest and snuggled back into his chest instead. Maybe he should show a little mercy considering how good Roman was for him. And besides, it was late. They needed to sleep.

But did Roman just volunteer Sidian to help *torture* someone?

"Hadeon is one of the elite Mambas. He's on a similar level to Mal on our side of the fence," Roman explained to Sidian the next morning, letting him comb his fingers through Roman's hair to tame his wild, damp, freshly washed curls. "He's not a friendly person. I believe he's from Oregon, but I know nothing more than that. Like Ghost, he appeared one day, and they took him in as one of their own."

Sidian frowned down at where his alpha's head lay in his lap. "Seems like they're just willing to take anyone into the super-secret mercenary group."

"It's not like that," Roman said, even though that was what it sounded like. "Wayward alphas have very few places to go. Ouroboros can put them to use provided they can prove they can handle it. And if they're not, they're cut loose. The leaders are excellent judges of who can make it and who can't. We don't take in anyone we cannot be sure will thrive."

"He sounded like a prick on the phone," Sidian muttered, and Roman muffled a soft laugh.

"That would be because he is." He reached up to give Sidian's thigh a little squeeze. "When he meets you in person, he'll be on his best behavior. But he is an asshole every chance he gets."

Figured. Roman's buddy sounded polite on the phone, but Sidian guessed expecting the people who lined up to commit murders as part of their job to be nice was a bit of a stretch. Or maybe it was just stupid to give a fuck about it; the Mambas took down omega auctions, so maybe that gave this guy a free pass to be as much of an asshole as he wanted. Granted, Sidian didn't know if Hadeon was involved in the work, but still.

"Why are we torturing someone? Are they not capable of doing it?" Given they were *mercenaries,* it seemed like they would have been able to take care of it themselves.

"I'm not sure. They are, in fact, capable of doing it." Roman shrugged, then turned his head and pressed his face into Sidian's stomach. "I'll do what it takes to get that address."

Sidian tensed, not sure he liked Roman anywhere near his stomach, but he had said nothing yet. He couldn't have noticed. "And then we can go kill Pack Kincaid once and for all."

"That would be the plan." Roman tilted his head back, and Sidian brushed the curls off of his forehead, tracing the scar through his eyebrow with the tip of one finger. "They just lost an auction location, so maybe the captive is supposed to know something about that. It's possible."

Sidian sucked his bottom lip into his mouth, considering. "Like the location details?"

"No, it's been a couple of days, so the auction might have already happened." Roman didn't note the obvious; Pack Kincaid might be on the way home if the auction had already happened, but Sidian chose not to bring it up. Not yet. "It might be more about an information leak. How would the traffickers have known the Mambas were closing in on them if not for a leak?"

"I guess that makes sense. A rat in the snake pit. How nice." And how fucking worrisome to think about.

Sidian could tell it was a stressful job for everyone involved, much less with someone feeding information to the worst lowlifes in the world likely for a quick buck. He didn't understand how anyone would go through the trouble of joining Ouroboros—and it had to be trouble—just to cash in their morals at the last second for someone who didn't even deserve to draw breath.

No wonder the Mambas were ready to outsource help. Maybe they didn't trust who they had available to do the torturing. "What makes Hadeon think we can get the information? He's used to torturing people. I've never done it before."

Roman puckered his lips. "I think you can get it out of the guy if you want to. Knives go a long way toward loosening someone's tongue, sometimes, but still. You can do a lot of damage with blades alone."

"Why can't Hadeon do that damage instead?" What was it about the guy that made him not willing to trust even himself to get the job done?

"He's impatient," Roman murmured. "He might have called us in to take the guy off of his hands before he kills him, which wouldn't be the first time. If their information is slipping through holes, then he's likely desperate to get a foothold in what's going on, and this might be the only way for him to do that. I don't think he wants to risk fucking it up over his anger issues."

That sounded pretty reasonable, even if Sidian still had severe doubts about what they were expected to do. "So we just carve the guy up and hope he talks?"

"Carve him up, splash him with some alcohol while he's bleeding. Maybe I can break some of his fingers." Roman cracked his knuckles, and Sidian's clit twitched in response. "If you're up for it. I won't make you do it, but... We could do it together. We could enjoy it together."

Together. The thought of bleeding some asshole alongside Roman was far too attractive of a concept to just write off. "You wanna do that with me?"

"I'd like to see what you could do to someone if you knew you didn't have to hold back." Roman grinned at him, and Sidian studied the sharp points of his alpha canines.

He considered the idea, wondering what it would feel like to hurt someone alongside his mate rather than doing it on his own. Though he wounded his fair share of people over the years, he'd never gotten to dig into them the way he wanted to. No one at the center would let him near anything resembling a weapon, but he'd done some pretty significant damage at the psych ward.

If only he'd stood up for *himself* that night...

Let it go, he urged himself. *Roman's waiting for you to give him an answer, idiot.*

When he brushed his fingers over Roman's lips, Roman parted them just enough for Sidian to slip them inside. A warm tongue laved his fingers before Roman sucked, reminding Sidian of last night, of Roman's cock heavy and hot on his tongue. When Pack Kincaid came for his heats, they'd dragged him down to his knees even with his cunt inflamed from how desperate he was, but that was nothing like what he'd done for Roman. There was no force, no violence, nothing but him restrained and beautiful and letting Sidian suck him off.

Sighing, he leaned down to kiss Roman's forehead. "Yeah, Roe. I'll torture a guy to death with you. Sounds like a fun date night idea."

"I know." Roman sucked his fingers harder, and Sidian's cunt throbbed. "You're going to look so sexy covered in someone else's blood. I don't know if I'll be able to control myself."

Now there was an image. Sidian considered what Roman might look like caked in someone else's blood, gorgeous and wild like when they were kids. It might be risky to take him into the middle of that, given what happened last time, but as long as they got the information, did it matter what happened after? Maybe they could see how many pieces they could chop the guy into before he hit the incinerator.

The only drawback was Hadeon. Sidian was not looking forward to meeting another alpha.

Roman drew his hand down and pressed a kiss to the inside of Sidian's wrist. "If you don't want to do it, I can handle it on my own. Won't differ greatly from what I already do to people who piss me off."

"I do wanna do it with you." Fuck it. Roman came back to him last time. Sidian could get him to come back if he lost Roman again.

Roman nodded and straightened up, rolling his back. "We should get a move on, then. We're still a couple of days out from the Mambas' Pit. Hadeon should be waiting for us since it seems like he's expected to arrange this. And trust me when I say that no matter what, he's harmless to you. An asshole, but he would never harm an omega. Especially not my mate."

"Time to pack it up?" Sidian asked, hopping to his feet.

"Time to pack it up." Roman caught him around the waist and kissed him, warm and slow. "And when the guy's dead and we have what we want, I hope you'll grant me the privilege of fucking you."

Oh, Sidian was *down* for that.

Chapter Twenty

Hadeon Warner was one of the few Mambas that Roman had been willing to work with over the years.

The Mambas specialized in surveillance and espionage, collecting as much information on their targets as possible before moving in to strike in one fell swoop. Focusing their attention and efforts on omega trafficking meant they needed to keep their heads down as much as possible and rarely had the time to enact the brutality that Roman preferred. He respected their mission as much as any other, but it wasn't the sort of life he would have been able to lead. His abilities were drenched in bloodshed and violence, not patience and planning. He preferred to keep it that way.

But Hadeon was unlike the other Mambas, and every so often, he and Roman could collaborate when their goals aligned. Like now.

Hadeon waited for them outside the main gate of the Mambas' Pit, his back resting against the wrought iron as Roman parked between two trees. Sidian eased out of the car more slowly than before, his eyes pinned on Hadeon's silhouette in the darkness, his lips twisted away from his teeth in a snarl that belied just how he felt about the situation. Not that Roman blamed him; alphas had harmed his mate more than any other designation, and mistrusting a stranger was a natural response.

Hadeon pushed himself off of the gate as they approached, Sidian walking a half-step behind Roman like he wanted to stay as far away from the Mamba as possible. "Who the fuck is that?"

"My mate. We spoke about him on the phone." There was no need to hide Sidian's identity, not here where they were among allies. "He's going to assist me in the interrogation."

"Him?" Hadeon tilted his head, his pale blue eyes trailing down Sidian's body and back up, and Roman bit back a growl of his own at the sight. There was curiosity, and there was disrespect; Hadeon always walked a fine line between the two. "That's fine, I guess. As long as you get the information I need, you'll get what you want. Follow me inside. The boss knows you're here, but it's just the team for the night. Kept us waiting a long fucking time, didn't you?"

Roman rolled his eyes. "Just a few days. It didn't sound like you were in a hurry."

"I guess so." Hadeon scoffed anyway, shoving his hands into the pockets of his jeans. "Well, welcome to our illustrious shithole. Same as it's always been."

The Mambas' Pit was much the same as the Vipers' Pit; squat brick structures, extreme amounts of armed security, and the distinct air of danger that lingered in such places. To Roman, it was nothing, but he knew well that this was not the norm for Sidian and so allowed his mate to cling to his sleeve for security. Those wide, beautiful eyes flicked from building to building, guard to guard, likely trying to make sense of everything he saw. Roman's explanations paled compared to the reality; the way they had to live in order to achieve efficiency was not for the weak.

Hadeon led them to the main building, the largest in the Pit and likely where most of their mission work was conducted. The Vipers had something similar, though Roman was never there outside of direction and debriefing. Unlike Silver, he never needed to bring his work home with him.

"The guy's a beta," Hadeon explained, holding the door open for them and all but ensuring Sidian plastered himself against Roman's back with a low, threatening noise. "Easy, omega, I'm not interested in you." To Roman, he continued. "We picked the guy up right after he accepted a hand-to-hand cash payment from one of our primary targets, and he won't tell us what it's for. Boss says we're too close to the mission. Your boss called us at just the right time."

The boss is involved? Roman filed that away for later, though he wasn't sure what knowing it meant, or why Devereaux would even get involved. "Anything special about this beta?"

"His pain tolerance is shit, but that's about what you'd expect. He snivels like a little bitch."

Roman nodded, aware of small hands gripping his forearm as Sidian stepped closer to him, their footsteps echoing off of the black and white tiled floors beneath them. Most of the Pits were monochrome, minimalist and standard issue because most of Ouroboros was composed of alphas. Only the Nests were outfitted with omega sensibilities in mind, created to be sanctuaries where they could rest and relax while relocation efforts were underway. But alphas needed no such creature comforts, and so they were not given them.

Not that Roman minded. The only comfort he needed was the lily-sweet omega at his side and the assurance that his mate was safe with him.

Hadeon beckoned them down a hallway that led to a solid steel door, hauling it open to reveal an industrial set of metal stairs coiling down into darkness; Sidian let out a little warning hiss as he clung to Roman's arm harder. But Hadeon said nothing as he thumped down the steps, throwing quick glances over his shoulder like he expected Sidian to lunge down the stairs and go for his throat. Truth be told, Sidian just might; Roman wasn't sure about every trace of trauma in his mate's past, and there might always be something he was missing.

Sidian's nails dug into his skin with each step. "Where the fuck are we going?"

"Basement," Hadeon answered from the front, waving a hand. "That's where we keep 'em until we get what we need. Then we feed their corpses into the incinerator."

"Incinerator? Never let 'em go, huh?" Sidian asked, sounding more excited.

"It's a security risk if we do. You never know who's stupid enough to open their mouths to rat us out to the authorities, and the boss lady would rather we didn't take the unnecessary risks to begin with." Hadeon paused at the foot of the stairs, his eyes drifting to Roman for a moment before they settled on Sidian once again. "Figured you'd know all about that if this is your snake, though. Killer Kane is what the Vipers call him, y'know? Because he doesn't leave anyone alive."

"Something like that," Roman murmured. It wasn't necessary to discuss it right then.

Hadeon's lips quirked up into an unfriendly smile as he spun on heel, opening another steel door that led through a dark hallway lit only by dim yellow bulbs hanging from the ceiling. "By all fucking means, kill him when you're done with him. I'd love to see what you and your mate got in person."

The beta was a middle-aged man, his short blond hair matted with blood, his right eye swollen with a purple bruise and his lip split open. He wore a typical white button-down and a pair of black slacks, though his shoes had been taken from him at some point. When the door clicked shut behind them, the beta lifted his head, peering up with his one good eye. The damage wasn't significant; just what was going through Hadeon's head these days that he lost patience?

Not my concern. Not my problem. Roman rolled his neck before he glanced down at Sidian, watching his omega's face for any telltale signs of excitement. "What are you thinking?"

"There are a couple of different ways we could go about it." Sidian glanced around the room, though the moment his eyes lit on the silver tray of tools set off to the side—untouched, as far as Roman could tell—he broke away to approach it, shrugging off his flannel as he did. "Are these free to use?"

Roman suppressed a smile as he leaned down to pick up the shirt, folding it over his arm before setting it aside to shed his own. Whatever they wore was likely going to be ruined, and he had no genuine desire to lose more clothing than was reasonable. "Of course, darling."

The implements were familiar enough to Roman; such kits had been handed out to everyone and were likely stocked at the Pit as need be, seeing as none of the instruments were special or noteworthy. Sidian picked up what looked like a scalpel and all but bounced over to the beta, who stared at him with a manic look in that one good eye. Roman kept his distance but walked a slow circle around the beta, noting that his wrists were zip-tied to the back legs of the chair he sat in, right beneath the stabilizing bar. That was good; it would be most unfortunate if the idiot tried to take a swing at Sidian because then Roman would be forced to kill him.

"Heard you keep some pretty nasty company," Sidian chirped, waving the blade in front of the beta's face with a little snicker. "Traffickers, huh? You know, I wasn't *trafficked* in the traditional sense, but all the fucked-up shit that happened to me resulted from people like you who think omegas are just toys you can sell to the highest bidder. So I'm not very sympathetic, so to speak."

Roman's jaw tightened. He hadn't considered how Sidian might feel about that topic, but he had to admit that his omega was correct. The breeding centers were much the same as the trafficking rings, if much easier to brute force and destroy. "What will you do to him?"

Sidian smiled, but he never took his eyes off of their target. "Every single day I was in that place, it felt like pieces of my soul were getting cut out of me. But I get that's not so easy to understand, so I'm gonna demonstrate how it felt, fucker. Roe, I want one of his hands."

"Wait," the beta said, squirming in his seat, though he did not even come close to squirming free. "Wait, wait, don't—"

Roman clapped a hand over his mouth, leaning over him to whisper in his ear. "Are you going to tell us what we want to know?"

He removed his hand, and the beta clamped his jaw shut so tight his chin trembled with the effort, his teeth all but grinding together. That was not surprising; people with powerful allies also made powerful enemies the moment they misspoke. Roman wondered if Hadeon might have convinced the beta he had a chance of survival if he spoke soon enough.

So be it, though. Everyone wanted to do things the hard way.

He snapped the zip tie with ease, his hand clamping down on the beta's elbow and wrist to keep him from flailing free. Without letting up so much as an ounce of pressure, he drew the beta's arm around in front of him, feeling the bones grinding together as the beta tried to free his vulnerable right hand. The odds of his being right-handed were good; he might take this a little more seriously if he knew his dominant hand was on the line. Or he might not. Roman never knew which way someone might lean until they were backed into a corner with no other option for escape.

It was easy to hold the weak beta in place, though. "Here you are, darling."

"Good dog." Sidian caught the beta's index finger before it could curl towards his palm, bending it back with an exaggerated slowness until the beta's quivering lips parted around shrill, panicked noises. "Nah, quit sniveling. You wanted to do this the hard way, didn't you?"

He paused, then snapped the finger the rest of the way back, the crack of bone and the hoarse, pained shout of their target echoing off of the concrete walls. Roman allowed his eyes to drift shut for a moment, drinking in Sidian's joy, the way his pheromones spiked hot and mouthwatering as he let out a delighted little cackle. When the beta's pained sounds raised an octave, Roman opened his eyes, unwilling to miss so much as a moment of what his mate was capable of.

"You gotta see it from my perspective," Sidian said as he pressed the sharp edge of the blade to the beta's first knuckle, just enough force behind it to dent the skin. "You fuck around with guys like the sick fucks who ruined my life, then you get what's coming to you."

And then he began to saw through the beta's finger.

Chapter Twenty-One

There was euphoria that came when causing pain to another person.

Sidian had known this for most of his life. It wasn't just the rush of control but the joy he gained in someone else's suffering, in bringing another person down into the pits he'd been struggling in for most of his life. He didn't give a shit who it was; anyone who crossed him was good enough. But the man who would take money from people *worse* than Pack Kincaid deserved a special hell that he knew he couldn't inflict on just anyone. He had to make it count. He wanted to make it last.

Even once he and Roman had the information the Mambas wanted, Sidian knew he wouldn't be able to stop.

The flesh gave way beneath the blade of the scalpel, the scrape of metal against bone sending a bolt of pleasure straight to his clit that struck him so hard it punched the air out of his lungs. The beta wailed and squirmed in his seat, but Roman held his arms steady while Sidian set the scalpel down and went to retrieve another tool from the tray. He wasn't sure they would do the job at first glance, but it had been a long time since he'd seen tools like these. The compact bolt cutters were heavy in his hand, the tool solid metal, the rubber grips pristine. Never used before.

"Do you know what it feels like to have someone touch you without your consent?" he asked, keeping his tone light as he returned to position. Blood sluiced over the metal blades, dripping down the jaws. "You remember every single hand on your body. You remember every single finger. Can you even imagine what that's like?"

The beta jerked legs zip-tied to the stabilizer at the front of the chair he sat on, but he made no progress. His head whipped from side to side as he screamed, spittle bubbling in the corners of his mouth, but that did him no good. There was no escape; he would suffer and die, and the only respite he might receive for his transgressions was a quick death rather than prolonged torture.

If he had spoken to Hadeon, that was. Sidian waited until the beta looked up at him before he squeezed the handles of the cutters, the blades slicing through ligament and bone.

The anguished howl made slick flood his underwear so fast he was dizzy.

Sidian braced himself, bent over, hands on his knees as he sucked in a deep breath. The beta's severed finger thumped onto the floor, the small pink tip of it resting in its own miniature pool of blood. Groaning, Sidian pressed a hand between his legs, rocking the heel of his hand against his clit until he felt a semblance of control. And then he picked the scalpel back up.

He sliced into the white flesh of the beta's finger, relishing his choked cries as he cut his way through to the second knuckle. "I know you can't. Pigs like you don't get it. You don't know what it's like to be used and abused and then forced to wait for the monsters who did it to come back and do it again."

He picked up the bolt cutters, the thick steel sliding into weeping flesh to settle against bone. The second chunk of flesh tumbled to the floor below, the small stump left behind jettisoning blood. It was a good look, and it was exciting to know there were *nine* more fingers to go before Sidian was content.

He would cut off every single one just to prove that he could.

"Who paid you?" Roman asked, the velvety richness of his deep voice brushing down Sidian's spine like the touch of a lover.

The beta bit down on his lower lip so hard that blood beaded up around his teeth, but he said nothing.

That was fine. With the second *crack* of another finger breaking and the rich scent of copper once again filling the room, Sidian imagined it was one of the Kincaid alphas tied to the chair while he worked them over. Tied up, helpless and begging, reeking of blood and piss and sweat, but he would have no mercy for them. For all the pain they'd inflicted on him over the years, for all the suffering they put him through, he would reward them with nothing more than disdain. He would treat them like shit under his shoes because that's what they were and always would be.

He would cut them into pieces until he felt whole again.

The beta fell silent after losing his thumb until Roman backhanded him across the face hard enough to slap his head to the side. "Wake up. We aren't done with you yet."

"Not gonna be able to jerk off anymore, are you?" Sidian asked, snickering when the beta sobbed up at him. "That's too bad. Might as well just cut your dick off at that point so you won't have anything to miss. But I think *that* would kill you, and we don't have what we want yet."

He wanted to cut up the other hand, but he also didn't want to waste his opportunity to be as creative as possible. So he backed off a little, looking the man over, wondering what would hurt the most. There were so many nerves in the human body, and though he knew where most of them were located, he didn't want to cut the guy's dick off just yet. He would, he would, but that was enough blood loss to be fatal or near enough to it, and they did promise they'd get the information for the Mambas.

And once the Mambas had what they wanted, Sidian would get what he wanted. He and Roman would track down their own targets, and he'd get to find out how easy it was to make an alpha squeal with pain.

Roman would love that. They could fuck each other covered in Dax Kincaid's blood.

"Let's see, let's see…" He set the scalpel down and reached for one of the man's ankles, looking up at Roman and pouting his lips. "Hold his leg for me, will you? I want to cut his foot open."

"Please stop," the beta gasped out, half-gagging as he struggled to breathe. "I can't… I c-can't tell you who paid me. I have a wife and k-kids. He'll kill them if I tell you his name."

Roman crouched down and snapped the zip tie around the beta's right ankle with such ease that Sidian considered pushing him over and riding his face just for the fun of it all. What right did Roman have to be so powerful and so sexy without even trying? That all of that strength was confined to Sidian's command made him hotter. As near perfect as an alpha could be.

"I'm gonna fuck your face after this," he said, and Roman's lips twitched.

"Looking forward to it." He seized the beta's knee and ankle, straightening his leg just like he had his arm, his own muscles flexing as he kept the man from struggling free of his hold.

One of the sickest things Sidian had ever heard of growing up was that some alphas mutilated their omegas' feet to keep them from running away. Plenty of omegas all over the country didn't have anyone to rely on or lean on; no one would come looking for them or rescue them once they were bitten in an alpha pack. It was the height of privilege to most people to have a pack, something that put male omegas in danger even more than female omegas. The world didn't want them; shouldn't they be grateful that anyone at all did?

"You should be lucky a worthless whore like you was deemed worthy of my seed."

"You're running away from your problems," Sidian quipped, pushing Dax's voice out of his head as he jammed the tip of the scalpel into the side of the beta's heel just to hear him squeal like a pig. "So let's put a stop to that and see if you feel differently when you can't even walk away from them."

He dragged the blade along the side of the beta's foot, watching in glee as the flesh parted, blood slicking the floor. The glistening pink interior of the flesh with splashes of color as blood vessels were revealed was fascinating to him; he would never cut Roman this deep no matter how the temptation grew. The likelihood of doing irreparable damage was not as sexy as scarring him, anyway.

The beta threw back his head and screamed, his body jerking and jittering in the chair, though Roman's hold never wavered. Never weakened.

"Think of it like this," Sidian said when he reached the beta's pinky toe, pulling the blade free and scooting over so he could cut open the other side of the beta's foot. "I'm doing you a favor. Do you think your wife and kids are gonna be safe if you don't come home? If your criminal sugary daddy is as scary as you make him out to be, then he'll figure out what it means that you're missing."

He slipped his little finger into the raw wound just to feel the wet warmth of it, remembering how it felt to touch his own pussy, and shuddered. His scent bloomed thick and hot in the room, and Roman's head swiveled in his direction, his eyes dark with hunger. Fuck's sake, this was not supposed to be about them getting it on, though Sidian had every intention of taking that knot as soon as they were done with the target. They had business to attend to, and he wanted Pack Kincaid's address.

That was the most important part. There was far too much riding on it.

He rocked back on his heels, staring up at the beta's ashen, swollen face, his eyes bulging out of their sockets and his lower lip bloody as if he'd bitten it repeatedly. "You tell us who paid you, or maybe I'll ask our host what your name is and hunt your family down myself."

The beta shook his head, his sweaty hair smacking against his glistening temples. "Please," he rasped out. "Please, they're innocent. They have nothing to do with this."

"Do the omegas that your buddy traffics like cattle have something to do with it, then?" Sidian placed the blade of the scalpel at the back of the beta's heel, aligning it with the torn edges of flesh he'd already scoured. "Are they no longer innocent once your buddies have had their fill of them?"

Tears streaked down the beta's cheeks. "I'm not involved. I just—"

"Just what?" Sidian asked, pausing his movements. "Tell me what it is you do, and maybe we can work something out here. I mean, let's be honest. The lives of a bunch of omegas are worth more to me than your family's lives, so I won't hesitate to make good on that promise."

He watched the beta's bruised and flushed features contort into various ugly expressions as he no doubt tried to figure out what the best outcome for him could be. There was no good outcome; Sidian doubted the Mambas cared much about the family of someone assisting a trafficker, and if the trafficker in question was dangerous like the beta thought, then it was likely his family was already dead. The moment they realized he had vanished, they might have taken preventative measures.

Hard to know what people like that were capable of.

When the beta did not answer him, Sidian got to work slicing through as much of the flesh in the middle of the man's foot as he could get the blade through.

The hellish screams that filled the air were like music to him, soothing an ache in his blood that always seemed to go unfulfilled. Truth be told, he didn't know when it would be enough or when he would be satisfied; it might have been when Pack Kincaid was dead and he had Amey in his arms again. Until he saw her, until he confirmed for himself that she was alive and well, he'd be hungry for blood.

Amethyst and his son were the only bright spots in the blackness of his suffering and anguish. He'd kill the alphas who took his daughter away from him, the alphas who'd hurt him, and then maybe he'd be at peace.

The beta passed out again just as Sidian reached the downturn of his arch, but Roman smacked him awake once more, the beta weeping. Blood coated Sidian's hands, thick and sticky, the piece of flesh quivering and wet in the harsh light of the room. The scent of copper was a fucking aphrodisiac for how wet he got for it, how turned on he was knowing what pain he could inflict.

If he ever did this again, maybe he'd have Roman fuck him right before and right after.

"Ready to talk yet?" he asked, glancing up at the beta, who drooled from one corner of his mouth.

He managed to choke out a faint, weak sound. "I'll tell you his name."

Excellent.

And now the real fun could begin.

Chapter Twenty-Two

There was something so erotic about watching Sidian take his pleasure from inflicting pain.

Roman was hard as he twisted the beta's limbs into place as Sidian requested, watching with bated breath as his mate sliced and sawed pieces off of the beta long after they'd gotten the information Hadeon requested. In his element, Sidian hummed what sounded like a lullaby to himself as he dug the blade into the beta's flesh again and again, then used the pliers to peel chunks of skin away from the muscle beneath. There was an almost artistic pattern to the way he worked, the pink tip of his tongue caught between the white of his teeth.

The beta gurgled and wept, his head lolling from side to side as the inevitability of his fate seemed to settle on his shoulders. There would be no escaping this, no freedom, no light at the end of the tunnel. If the Mambas cared about his family, they might step in to shield his children, but Sidian had a point; the person who paid off their scummy little target might have already moved in on the beta's family the moment there was a wind of him missing.

It didn't matter. Roman only cared about Sidian. Everything else fell by the wayside.

Sidian seemed to reach the end of his patience, placing the tip of the much larger knife he'd retrieved from the tray when his scalpel broke against bone between the beta's collarbones, settled into the shadowy hollow of his throat... And dragged it straight down.

Fish-belly white flesh parted around the blade, blood dribbling from the open wound as Sidian drew it down, down, down. To the beta's waistband where he tossed it aside and reached into the wound with his hands, gripping the edges of the beta's gut to pull it open.

Slippery wet intestines spilled onto the floor in a heap, and Sidian *giggled* with delight, stepping back to admire the sight as they settled into messy, steaming coils. Roman whistled low in his throat while the beta gagged a few more times before falling silent, his head tilted back and his one good eye pointed toward the ceiling. What he saw in his last moments was of no interest to Roman.

The sort of bastard who would assist an omega trafficker deserved a slow and painful death.

"Fuck yeah." Sidian sprang to his feet, almost bouncing, his entire body trembling with what smelled like euphoria as he gazed up at Roman with wide, wild eyes. "You didn't wanna join in?"

Roman chuckled. "You looked like you were having fun."

"I was. Goddess, yeah, I was. I'm so turned on it fucking hurts, but that was the most fun I've had in a long time." Sidian's fervent gaze made Roman's cock pulse, his alpha straining at his self-control to get closer to his excited, trembling mate. "Cunt feels like it's going to burn up from how bad I want it. You gonna give it to me, alpha?"

"Tell me what you need from me." Roman drifted away from the corpse, no longer interested in it, his eyes for Sidian and Sidian alone.

Without hesitation, Sidian tugged his shirt up and over his head, the pale perfection of his flesh smeared with blood that had soaked through the fabric. The air of the room was cool, hardening his pink nipples, and Roman wanted little more than to suck on them until they were swollen and red from the attention. He rumbled at the sight of his mate, desperate to sink to his knees and cover Sidian's body in as many kisses as possible.

Would it ever become bearable, or would it always feel so overwhelming?

Roman waited until Sidian's hands dropped to the buckle of his belt, the sleek black leather catching the light well. "Can I put this around your neck and choke you with it?"

"It may be dangerous," Roman pointed out, relishing the adorable pout he received for the words. This was the playful, sweet side of his mate that belonged to him and only to him. "But I would be honored."

He dropped to his knees without hesitation as Sidian approached him, holding as still as possible while the leather was looped around his throat, the tongue fed through the buckle to give Sidian a good grip on him. The leather pressed into Roman's throat from all sides as the buckle dug into his Adam's apple, his dick jumping at the sensation. Fortunately, he was just as wired for violence and danger as Sidian was, and he ached to prove it to his omega.

"I love the way you look at me." Sidian stroked down the side of his face with bloody fingers, and Roman rumbled in response, his eyelids growing heavy at the touch. "Like I'm an actual person."

That set off a snarl, but Roman choked it down. *Not right now.* "You're my person."

"You're no better than a dog. That's my favorite thing about you, y'know. Obedient fucker." Sidian caught a handful of his curls and pushed him down, and Roman took the hint, spreading his knees to better accommodate the difference between their heights.

He could smell the slick leaking through Sidian's underwear without having to try. Slick absorbent underwear handled the average amounts of wetness, but there was nothing much that could be done for an omega as turned on as Sidian was. Roman watched, mouth watering, as Sidian unfastened his jeans and pushed the denim down his hips, revealing the growing patch of wetness between his thighs.

"Please," Roman choked out, and Sidian laughed at him, then yanked the belt hard enough to squeeze, drawing him closer.

That was all the encouragement Roman needed.

He shifted forward on his knees and pressed his face against Sidian's cunt, tongue tracing that damp patch of fabric before he sucked it into his mouth. Even through the soft cotton, his omega's slick was the sweetest thing he'd ever tasted, and his cock pulsed in jealousy. His tongue found the swell of Sidian's clit through the underwear, and he sucked it, laving it with slow, wet licks until Sidian moaned and bucked against his face. He was so close, so fucking delicious, but Roman took his time so he could pay his omega the proper attention he deserved.

Pleasing Sidian was the only thing that Roman cared about.

"You've got such a pretty fucking face for an alpha." Sidian ground against him, the friction of the fabric rough and almost painful. "Get your mouth on my cunt and get me off."

Roman dragged the underwear down Sidian's thighs and left them tangled around his knees; he didn't need them any lower than that. His tongue slicked a hot path between flushed folds before he buried his face in Sidian's cunt, groaning deep in his throat as his eyes slid shut. It was his favorite place in the world to be, and Sidian knew that, rutting into every lick and sucking kiss with a gorgeous, perfect moan.

The broad swell of his clit slipped between Roman's lips, and he sucked greedily, tongue lashing over it as Sidian's fingers tightened in his hair, keeping him pinned in place. The ache in his scalp was well worth how beautiful Sidian sounded when he neared the edge of bliss, so worked up from his hack job that it only took another quick flick of the tongue for him to come undone. Slick gushed down Roman's chin, and he rumbled in response, letting himself be pulled off of oversensitive flesh just so he could shove his tongue as deep into Sidian's cunt as he could.

"On your back," Sidian snarled, and Roman forced himself back, eager to obey his mate. He stretched out on his back while he watched Sidian kick off his jeans and ruined underwear.

Roman's eyes raked over Sidian's body, rumble deepening down in his chest as he offered a hand to help his omega straddle him. His fingers brushed over the smooth, fair curve of Sidian's hip, his eyes crinkling as he basked in how perfect the moment was. As soon as they ended Pack Kincaid, Roman would devote himself to worshipping this omega the way he had always deserved to be praised.

"You were this hard the whole time?" Sidian asked as he unfastened Roman's jeans, yanking them open just enough to free his cock. "Just fucking with you, Roe. I could smell how bad you wanted me the whole time I cut that fucker up. You want me to cut you up like that?"

It would kill him, but Roman's pulse still jumped at the thought. "If you want to."

"Maybe I should cut you open right down the middle like him." Sidian shoved Roman's shirt up to trace down the center of his chest with blood-stained fingers, and then he raked his nails straight down to Roman's aching cock. "I could rip your ribcage open and crawl inside. We'd be one for real, then, wouldn't we?"

Pre-come wet the tip of Roman's dick at the image. "Get a knife and do it."

It was a bluff, and they both knew it, but Sidian still stood to retrieve one of the clean knives from the tray before he settled back down across Roman's hips. The slim blade was beautiful in the bright light as he set it at the tip of Roman's sternum, letting it rest there while he rocked his hips down, his pussy stroking the length of Roman's cock. Every movement spread those puffy folds around Roman's shaft, his knot brushing against Sidian's twitching, empty hole. When Sidian rolled his hips, slick coated both of them, the slick noises echoing off of the surrounding walls.

Sidian pressed down on the blade until it broke the skin, blood bubbling up beneath the blade and oozing through the wound as he dragged it down. It was barely deep at all, just enough to split the flesh, but Roman groaned through the pain, head straining against the floor. Fingers danced along the wound before wrapping around his cock, smearing him in his own blood as Sidian gripped his cock and then rose on his knees, sinking down with a throaty moan.

The blending of pain and pleasure was a heady sensation. Roman's head lolled back as Sidian drew the blade further down his chest, the burning sensation offset by the wet squeeze of Sidian's slick channel. His omega was soaked, so perfect. Tight, little noises catching in Sidian's throat as his head tipped forward. And the blade still continued its slow descent until it reached Roman's stomach, then dug in just a little deeper.

Just enough for him to feel the pain blossom into something hotter.

"What if I did it to you?" Sidian asked, planting a hand right over the wound on Roman's sternum, pressing down on it as he fucked himself on Roman's cock in slow, languid rolls of his hips. "Just stab the knife all the way in and rip your guts out? Maybe they'd make a prettier collar than the belt."

He yanked the leather, the bite of the buckle sharp, pushing the air from Roman's throat before he could brace for it. "I'd let you do it. I'd thank you."

Sidian laughed, face flushed a lovely shade of pink as he arched his back, and Roman wanted so badly to touch him, knowing damn well he didn't have the permission to do so. That knife would dig in deeper to warn him away, but it was exquisite torture. To watch Sidian pleasure himself, his skin damp with sweat, the roll of sinuous muscle beneath soft flesh begging to be traced and kissed. Every single inch of him was divine perfection, and Roman was content to bleed at his altar, letting Sidian use him for his pleasure as if he were nothing more than a toy to be discarded.

Beneath Sidian was the only place Roman had ever wanted to be.

A high-pitched whine echoed through the room as Sidian sank himself down on Roman's knot, the sudden pressure pushing Roman over the edge. He felt Sidian's cunt tense up and squeeze, the clenching grip making his eyes roll back in his head, and when Sidian jerked the belt tighter, it was better, somehow. Unable to breathe, unable to think, caught somewhere in the sudden pleasure of orgasm and the sharp bite of the knife, Roman felt like he was home.

He would never let the world rip Sidian Vey from his arms again.

Chapter Twenty-Three

"Am I right in assuming that you're the outsider we were forced to outsource interrogation to this evening?"

Sidian's head whipped toward the sound of the unfamiliar voice, hackles rising and a snarl on his lips as he took in the sight of the masked woman leaning against the doorway opposite him. The entire Pit already felt odd to him, the excess of black and white combined with concrete and sharp angles digging into his hindbrain in a way that he was unprepared for. He chalked it up to the pregnancy; he'd never been an omega who needed softness and color before, and he wasn't now. It was just another aspect of himself he had little to no control over while his body and instincts waged war against him.

The woman stared at him through the slit eyeholes of her mask, tall and lean in a black turtleneck and matching black jeans, an abundance of golden curls spilling wildly to her slim waist. Her eyes were such a pale shade of grey they looked silver, but beyond that, he could make out no details about her. From the top of her forehead to the curve of her chin, she was anonymous behind a white cat mask. It was polished, and it almost reminded him of porcelain, though the lack of color was disconcerting.

Roman must have been with the medic; Sidian had done enough of a number on him to warrant professional care, though he knew Roman would heal just fine. But that was where Roman had to be because even in a place surrounded by apparent allies, he never would have allowed an alpha to draw this close to Sidian.

"Who the fuck are you?" he asked, combing his fingers through his damp hair. As soon as Hadeon had the name and information he wanted, and as soon as Roman's knot went down, all Sidian wanted was a hot shower. Luckily, the Mambas had communal showers in their main building, and someone had been kind enough to retrieve their bags from the Ultima so Sidian had a fresh change of clothes.

The Mambas, like the Vipers, were all alphas. Made sense they were happy to get his stuff for him.

"No one important. I heard Hadeon talking about you, and I wanted to see you for myself." The alpha eyed him up and down, but there was none of the usual heat there, and no feeling of debasement followed. It felt more like being looked up and down like a predator, which was better as far as Sidian was concerned. "I don't understand *why* you could interrogate him instead of me. He was my target. I could have done the job myself without outside help."

The last thing he wanted on his hands was a pissed-off alpha. "I don't know what you're talking about."

"Of course not." Her scent—a sort of wildflower garden, sweet for an alpha—spiked thick and artificial, a nauseating perfume that made bile rise in his throat. It was *awful*.

Before he could say anything, a familiar voice called out. "Kitten, what are you doing here?"

The alpha, Kitten, stepped back out of the doorway just as Hadeon appeared, his face twisted into an ugly expression as his eyes met hers. The two of them held each other's gazes before she huffed and spun on heel, her boots thumping down the corridor until they were just out of earshot. Hadeon watched her go the entire way, his shoulders squared and his jaw set like he expected a fight of some kind. If the two of them were allies, why would that be?

Then he deflated, heaving a sigh and scrubbing both hands over his face. "Sorry about that. I knew she was skulking around, but I didn't know where she was."

In a different lifetime, Sidian might have almost thought of Hadeon as handsome. A rather pretty face softened the sharp cut of his jaw, and though pale blue eyes tended toward glacial, his were warm as he met Sidian's gaze. His black hair was long and messy, tumbling down to his shoulders, alternating between soft waves and a few wild, wing-like pieces that were still growing into their natural texture. Because he was ghostly pale, the dark circles under his eyes were on prominent display. Just how hard did Ouroboros work its alphas? Weren't they supposed to be in top shape?

Sidian shrugged it off, though he was more comfortable in Hadeon's presence than he had been in Kitten's. *The devil you know,* he guessed. "What was her deal? She wasn't super pissed off or anything, but she didn't look like she was happy with me, either."

Hadeon dropped his hands, tucking them into the pockets of his jeans. "She's pissed about the interrogation not being handed to her. She was the one who brought the guy in, but the captain pulled her off the mission as soon as she managed it. She's not been in a great headspace semi-recently."

"I get that." Sidian eyed the doorway, as if he expected Kitten to appear again. "Something happen?"

Hadeon pressed his lips together as if debating whether he even wanted to discuss it. Or maybe he couldn't? Either way. "Why don't I walk you to the dorms? Roman's gonna be a bit and still needs to shower. The dorms are at least a little cozier than this place. For an omega, at least."

"Sure." Sidian would choose not to take offense at that. "Lead the way, I guess."

The dorm building of the Pit was much the same as every other from the outside, but the inside was indeed slightly cozier than the main building had been. The floors were glossy hardwood instead of tile, and the lighting was warmer and dimmer, not bright and hospital-like. A few voices echoed down the long hallway of private bedrooms, but nobody came out to the common area with its living room of plush couches, its dining room, and the kitchen that Hadeon immediately hit up for snacks.

"It's been a long day," he said in a voice that sounded almost like an apology, tossing a bag of chips onto the counter as he rifled through a cabinet. "You want anything? It's yours."

"Nah, I'm not hungry." Sidian probably would be in the morning, but for the moment, he was calm and oddly centered. For the first time since his escape from the center, he didn't feel that frenetic buzzing under his skin like he was seconds away from being re-captured. "So, what was with, uh, Kitten?"

The corner of Hadeon's mouth quirked up slightly. "Yeah, that's her name. You get used to it after a while of knowing her, but it always throws people for a loop. She's got a sister named Puppy."

Right. Entirely normal-sounding names, then, though *Obsidian* was admittedly hardly common. "Does her sister have something to do with why she's been in such a shit mood?"

"Perceptive." Hadeon crammed three bags of chips under one arm and snagged a soda from the fridge, and Sidian was more than happy to take one of those when it was offered to him. It wasn't *that* much caffeine and sugar, and he'd used a lot of energy on that interrogation. "She's been missing for the past year, and our trail has almost gone cold. We were hoping that beta might have been a lead."

"Was he?" Sidian asked, though he feared he knew the answer without having to be told.

"One of the other Mambas is looking into it right now. There's only so much we can do with a name depending on how connected these people are." Hadeon shrugged, leading Sidian to the sitting area and dropping down on a couch. "Guy had a laptop on him when we picked him up, and we just got the report on his hard drive back. Nasty shit on there. Stuff with kids. You did a good job in hindsight."

It should not have been a surprise to hear that in retrospect, but it turned Sidian's stomach just the same and would have had a similar effect on anyone who heard it. *Kids?* It wasn't that surprising, though. Some of the omegas at the breeding centers were underage, brought in right after their first heat to serve as the breeding stock for the alphas most capable of paying for the services the center provided. So many people just did not care; alphas would look the other way if it meant they had the opportunity to take advantage of an omega's heat cycle and walk away from it with a baby and no mate to worry about.

Hadeon cleared his throat, popping a chip into his mouth. "Sorry if that freaks you out, but he's not exactly the first pedophile we've picked up. You see a lot of them in trafficking circles. What we didn't find was any connection to us, which means he's probably a dead end as far as Puppy goes."

"You said she's been missing. Do you think somebody took her?" As soon as he asked that question, Sidian rolled his eyes at himself. Of course, someone fucking took her. She was a mercenary.

"I don't know," Hadeon admitted quietly. His eyes darted toward the elevator that had led from the ground floor up to the dorms, then ate another chip and shrugged. "Can't say it around Kitten, but after two or three days, most missing person cases turn up bodies, not people."

"I get why she wouldn't want to accept that." His throat tightened slightly; it had occurred to him since Amey was taken from him that she might not still be alive. Pack Kincaid might have deemed her useless as an omega and spirited her elsewhere to do Goddess knows what to her. If they had, what would Sidian even do next? "I feel kind of bad for stepping on her toes, then."

Hadeon raised a shoulder. "Don't bother. We'll find her, or we won't. It's got nothing to do with you and Kane."

Sidian didn't argue the point as he sipped his soda, wondering what kind of person someone would have to be to capture a mercenary. He'd only been with Roman for a matter of days, but Roman was hyper vigilant to the point of being outright paranoid, constantly scanning his surroundings and keeping an eye on the nearest exit as if he expected something to burst through the door at any moment. Someone with that kind of senses would not be easy to capture. Or at least Sidian *assumed* they would not be easy to capture, so how in the hell had someone pulled it off?

Alphas were also generally very aware of their surroundings from an instinctual level, though he didn't know what training in Ouroboros had done to their instincts. Honed them to keep them sharp, or dampened them to ensure they wouldn't interfere with the mission? Hard to say, and though he could have asked, he wasn't sure if either answer would do anything more than piss him off. Because whatever they did to every alpha in the organization, they did to Roman.

Hadeon cleared his throat. "So, Pack Kincaid. You've got business with them?"

"You could say that. I'm looking to kill them, though I've heard that might inconvenience you. Too fucking bad." Sidian tossed the empty can toward what looked like a trashcan next to the TV, the metallic clang making his shoulders jerk slightly. "They found me at the breeding center, and I'm sure you can imagine how that went for me. I want to make sure they know how much I *appreciated* that."

"Did they breed you?" Hadeon asked, and Sidian's face twisted at the question.

But he couldn't answer it. Not truthfully. If he wasn't willing to tell Roman what happened in its entirety, no fucking way was he telling a stranger. "No. Dunno if they just didn't want to knock me up or if the stress of the place got to me, but they never pulled it off. I'm happy about that."

"Can't say I know what goes through the minds of sick fucks like that." Hadeon nudged a bag of chips toward him, and Sidian grabbed it. Maybe he should eat something. "Dax Kincaid is a piece of work."

"You know about him?" Might not be a bad idea to get a little information if possible.

"Spoiled rich brat like you'd expect. Don't know when he got involved with the trafficking scene, but his pack popped up on our radar about a year and a half ago. They're all mostly the same." Hadeon tilted his hand back and forth, then curled his fingers into a fist. "Sadistic pieces of shit. Get their kicks out of hurting people. They're allowed to sample the merchandise within reason, though we have no way of knowing whether their omega has any idea what's going on."

Their *what?* "What do you mean, their omega? They actually have a mate at home?"

"They do," Hadeon confirmed, then jumped to his feet. "Come on. I'll show you the files we have."

Sidian followed him without a word, shoving his hands into the pocket of his hoodie as they headed back toward the elevator. He wasn't sure where they were going, but at just that moment, he no longer cared. No longer cared that Hadeon was a stranger and that he was skulking around a place he didn't know without Roman at his side. If the Mambas had information on Pack Kincaid they were willing to share, then Sidian would do anything to get his hands on it. He needed to know everything he could.

And if they had an omega waiting at home, an omega who was probably *raising his daughter,* then he needed to know if he was about to add another person to his hit list.

It wasn't personal.

Chapter Twenty-Four

The main building of each Pit contained both an office for the leader of that branch of Ouroboros and an office that belonged to the captain. Roman had been in Jagger's office only once, so it felt odd to lower himself into a chair across from the desk belonging to Captain Noel Nightingale, who oversaw the Mambas. Office visits were often aligned with punishment; Jagger rarely had to speak to any of the Vipers unless they had done something he wanted to rip them a new asshole for.

Nightingale was nothing like Jagger, bulky and sharp. The Mamba captain was slim and almost gangly, his near-black eyes shadowed by the soft chestnut waves that tumbled down to his shoulders. There was a solemnity that cloaked him, which made Roman uneasy, though he couldn't have explained how even if asked to. Admittedly, it was hard to believe someone like this captained someone like Hadeon, but the same could be said about Jagger and Locke and Keay.

"I'm sorry to keep you away from your mate," Nightingale said, hands folded atop a manila folder. "He's with Hadeon, if you were concerned. They went off toward the dorms."

Roman hummed. "I'd be more concerned about Hadeon if I were you."

Nightingale did not smile. "You jest. I don't. I wanted to speak to you in private because I was reviewing the footage from the interrogation, and I have questions for you."

An interrogation following an interrogation? Perhaps just a debrief, then. Roman could handle that, though he wasn't part of the debriefing back in the Vipers' Pit. That honor belonged to Ghost and Mal. "Sure. What questions do you have for me?"

"Have you always been submissive where Sidian Vey is concerned, or is that something that's only sprung up between the two of you following his stay in the breeding center?"

Roman's mouth dried. "I don't think it's appropriate to talk about our personal lives."

"I would agree with you. However, in the current circumstances, I do not." Nightingale flipped open the folder and extracted a photograph from it, sliding it across the desk to Roman. It was of himself, a close-up of Sidian's name carved into his chest. "Is he the one who did this?"

So they were going there no matter what. "He did. It was something I consented to."

"I see." Nightingale studied him for a moment. "Have you tried to command him even once?"

"The Vipers are forbidden from using alpha commands during missions because we're in proximity to traumatized omegas. Sidian, unfortunately, is one such omega. So, no, I haven't." There was no need to explain; he never would. It was implicit, tied up in everything he said and did for Sidian.

"And has he tried to use a command on you?" Nightingale spoke with such a flat, toneless voice, but the question sent a series of chills down Roman's spine.

How could he have known that? "If there's something you're trying to get at, just say it. I don't enjoy games. I work with people who are upfront when they want to know something."

Nightingale studied him for a long moment before removing another photo from the folder and laying it out: a close-up of the lily carved into Roman's chest. "I imagine this would have taken serious time and caused you excruciating pain even with an alpha's pain tolerance. And you allowed it."

"We have a complex relationship. That's all." And he didn't see what the carvings had to do with the command. Whatever the connection between them, Roman couldn't see it.

It made him antsy, though. There *was* something in the fact Sidian could command him, though Roman didn't understand how or why that should have worked. Though he could have written it off as tied to the fact he liked to hand Sidian control without a second thought, he knew that wasn't all of it. *Couldn't* be all of it, as much as he would have been happy not to put any serious thought into it. Alphas and omegas had deep, instinctive, biological ties to one another, and Roman had never heard of an omega being able to do what Sidian did with flawless ease. There had to be more to it, and Nightingale saw that.

"You have a complex relationship if your mate can command you despite his omega status. It is not something an omega can do." Nightingale pursed his lips, ruminating before he leaned back in his chair. "I contacted your captain, and when dissatisfied with his answers, I went up one more link in the chain of command. What has Lorcan Devereaux told you about yourself?"

The boss's name felt like a weight that dropped into Roman's stomach. "What do you mean?"

"Did he tell you why he chose you?" Nightingale asked. "I mean the real reason. I would presume not, or you'd likely already know the answers to the questions I'm asking you."

What the fuck was that supposed to mean? "I don't speak to him very often. He's a busy man, and the Vipers are a busy group. What was it he told you?"

"According to the police report..." Nightingale removed a sheaf of papers from his folder, and Roman saw his own mugshot on one of them as the captain flipped through the documents with an empty expression. "You killed two betas and one alpha during your presentation at nineteen."

"That's correct." The records were supposed to be sealed, but of course Ouroboros had copies.

Nightingale fanned out several sheets of paper, including print-outs of the crime scene, the gore cataloged in vivid color that somehow seemed distant and sterile at the same time. If Roman hadn't been at the scene himself, if he weren't the cause of it, it might have seemed unreal to him. From a distant vantage point, the brutality of the crime surprised even him. His memories of that afternoon were still limited, pieces flickering through every so often, though it seemed his mind had decided long ago that it was better for him not to remember every chilling detail of the moment his life changed for good.

"This is unusual even for a very protective alpha," Nightingale explained, tucking a stray lock of hair behind one ear as his eyes swept across the photos. "Devereaux confirmed to me that was true."

So they were talking about him behind his back. Fantastic. "What did he say?"

"He is a very... Eccentric man, though you've met him, and I'm sure you are aware of that." Nightingale met Roman's eyes, and something about his gaze was all-consuming. It was impossible to look away for even a moment. "And dangerous. Very dangerous. He likes dangerous people."

"That still isn't an answer to my question, Captain."

"I had the distinct sense that while he understood the conversation was likely always coming, he didn't want to discuss it. Hard to tell with him. And here I would have suspected him to be excited to disclose the acquisition of such an effective killer." Nightingale said nothing for several moments, the tension between them stretching taut enough to tighten Roman's chest.

"But he did admit the truth to me. You're a prime alpha, Roman Kane. I would assume you didn't know that."

A prime alpha? "Are you implying that Sidian is—?"

"I'm not implying that he's a prime omega. I'm stating it outright." Nightingale shrugged when Roman only stared at him, not sure how to take the information as his brain struggled to process the possibility. "It would explain why he could command you. *Can* you command him?"

"I haven't tried. I wouldn't do that to him." Just the thought of it was alien, unusual, borderline very upsetting. Not all alpha commands were bad, but it still made Roman sick down to his soul.

Nightingale, meanwhile, looked pleased by that. "Because you *can't*," he stressed, stabbing one finger into the center of a crime scene photo. "But you can do this to protect him because prime omegas are so much more vulnerable than the average omega. You and I both know it to be true."

That was putting it lightly. Prime alphas and prime omegas were both vanishingly rare mutations of the alpha and omega designations, though there were far fewer prime omegas than prime alphas. Prime alphas were a step higher in the food chain, occupying a hierarchy that allowed them to shrug off an alpha's command with ease while demanding submission and respect from the alphas within their own packs. If those alphas refused, they were cast out or killed depending on how their prime took it.

But a prime omega was at the bottom of the hierarchy of designations, susceptible to alpha commands to a much more frightening degree than the average omega. Alphas took advantage of that; there were implications that there may be more prime omegas than society recognized, but alpha packs snapped them up before they could be registered as what they were. Locked away from the world, they would be at the mercy of their mates until the day they died.

And that difference was the root of what made prime alphas stand out from average alphas. A prime alpha could not command a prime omega, and therefore could not force them into anything. There was an almost guardian-like quality ascribed to them; they existed to protect their counterparts and had developed the ability to make alphas bow to them as part of it.

"I could be wrong, but I rarely am," Nightingale continued while Roman sorted through every memory he had of Sidian, trying to match up the pieces to see if that even made sense to him. "Your scent is harsher than any of my Mambas' scents. We know your reputation and what you do on missions, and of course, there's your past. So I called Devereaux to confirm because if I suspected you to be a prime, then I knew he would have suspected it first. He had you tested after you were taken in."

"Why didn't he tell me that?" No wonder Roman barely got along with the other Vipers, and no wonder it was only Mal—his sparring partner, someone who constantly lost to him—who could reach him on any personal level.

Nightingale hummed. "That, I couldn't tell you because I didn't care to ask. Your personal issues are your own. But for the next step of your mission, it was important that I know the truth."

"You mean Pack Kincaid?" But what *else* could Nightingale mean?

"Sidian will be susceptible to their alpha commands to a much higher degree than he would be if he were an average omega. This is important as they can, and likely will, try to use him against you as much as possible." Nightingale removed something from a desk drawer, setting it in front of Roman. It looked like a small plastic case, nothing special. "These earplugs should block just enough of their voices to protect him from that, but should one fall out, or should they notice him using them, he will be made vulnerable."

Of course he would be. If everything Sidian had both said and alluded to was true, then Pack Kincaid would do just as Nightingale said. "I suppose that's why he never ended up pregnant."

"Pardon?" Nightingale furrowed dark brows at him, a frown tugging at his mouth.

"It was a *breeding* center," Roman reminded him, and he let out a little ahh of understanding. "I thought it was odd he'd be there for two years and conceive no children, but prime omegas are prone to higher levels of stress. That might have been why it never worked out."

"Likely so," Nightingale agreed, rising to his feet. "Thank you for having this discussion with me. I wanted to make sure that you and your mate were well-prepared for what came next. You have an advantage, Kane. As a prime, you'll have an edge on them you do not want to waste. Be careful to keep it from being revealed until the proper moment. You are dismissed."

Roman pocketed the earplugs with a quick, curt nod of thanks and exited the office. He needed to find Sidian as quickly as possible.

They had a long, serious conversation ahead of them.

Chapter Twenty-Five

"There are eight registered alphas in Pack Kincaid," Hadeon said, dropping a thick manila folder onto the rickety plastic table. "But I'm sure you've met all of them by this point."

"I have." Just the same, Sidian scanned the list of names on the front page of the stack of documents, the first sheet of paper resting atop the stack. *Dax, Slate, Nash, Axel, Jett, Knox, Talon, Ford.* Every single alpha had been present for both of Sidian's heats, and every single one of them had taught him he didn't know the definition of true suffering. Not yet. Not until they were done with him. "They have such stupid fucking names. Stupid fucking names for stupid fucking alphas."

Hadeon snorted, then tapped the last name on the list: *Lilac.* "This is their omega. We've looked into him. They registered him out of nowhere. No courtship, no nothing. Weird for a pack of their status, but I've seen weirder, so I didn't think too much about it."

"Is there anything I need to know about him?" Sidian asked, already flipping through thick stacks of paper to find anything the Mambas might have had on the omega.

He couldn't tell Hadeon that he already suspected the *real* reason Lilac Kincaid had been chosen for the pack; if the time-lines matched up, they might have needed someone to watch Amey when they were away from the house. That was of course presuming they kept her. Might they have traded away an infant omega girl for a male omega? The thought made him faint. They'd better not have—

"I don't think he's with them willingly," Hadeon said, tapping the picture.

The male omega peered up at the camera through long dark lashes, his expression guarded and his eyes empty, almost lifeless. Lank black hair hung dull and frizzy around a pale, oval-shaped face. Sidian had seen his own reflection at the center once before they had opted to remove all reflective surfaces from his immediate vicinity, but he recognized the expression on that face all too well. That hopelessness. That certainty that life would never get better, but it could always get worse.

What turned Sidian's stomach the most though was the color of those eyes. Lilac's eyes matched his name, a delicate shade of violet with a warm, almost pinkish tone. But they were purple, like Sidian's own, and he could almost feel Dax's lips pressed up against his ear during that first heat.

"Your eyes are marvelous. Perhaps I'll keep them in a jar on my bedside table."

"He was seventeen when he was registered as their pack omega, though it's not like the law much gives a shit once the mating bond is in place." Hadeon's finger traced down the omega's face to the side of his throat; the bite still looked new, a bruising violence against fair skin. "His family wasn't notable either. We found no evidence of them trying to get him back, though."

Sidian nodded, swallowing the bile that burned up the back of his throat. "I'll keep all that in mind. Do you guys even know if he's still alive? Maybe they just... Killed him."

"We try not to get too close to them," Hadeon admitted after a moment. "The Vipers are lucky; they get in, kill everyone, get out. Traffickers are primed to pay close attention to anyone or anything suspicious, so we have to work from the darkest shadows we can find."

"I don't get something," Sidian said, flipping through the files, his eyes scanning each page. Much of it was just basic information that he didn't need. "Why bother me if they had an omega?"

Hadeon tugged the file closer and flipped back to Lilac's profile, carding through a couple of pages before pointing out a bold word near the top of the page: **Infertile.** "If I had to guess, that would be why. Guess they thought they'd get a kid or two out of you since their omega couldn't have any."

"Too bad for them," Sidian muttered, his chest tightening when he felt the telltale flutter of slight movement inside of him. The baby had been quiet, but he seemed to sense the moment his mother started thinking about him again. "I don't know what to do about their omega. If he gets in our way, there's nothing we *can* do about it. We can't risk their catching us. They'd kill Roe in a heartbeat."

"And do worse to you," Hadeon said, and Sidian felt goosebumps break out even beneath the layers he wore. "If you have to kill him, it's not like anyone will be there to judge you for it."

But Sidian would remember doing it for the rest of his life, no matter what his reasoning was. "What do we do if we don't have to kill him? Do we call you? How do we handle any of this?"

"The captain doesn't want us involved any more than we already are," Hadeon said, and Sidian nodded even as the unease slinking below his flesh prickled the hairs on the nape of his neck.

He understood that. Of course, he did. If the Mambas needed to creep about with as little influence as possible to avoid their targets growing suspicious, then getting involved was out of the question. Pack Kincaid was tied to the trafficking rings, even if only through a minor role, but it made sense that the Mambas didn't want to risk even that much. It was only fair.

And they weren't the Mambas' problem to deal with. They were Sidian's. Sidian's alone.

"We can supply you with weapons. They won't be traced back to us, but it's gonna depend on how you want to do this." Hadeon shut the file and slid it over to Sidian, who scooped it up into his arms and cradled it against his chest. "You know the best chance you've got is to walk in there and shoot 'em."

Of course, it was. "I know that, but they didn't let me off easy. They made me fucking suffer, and I want them to know what that felt like. They'll never get it, but still."

"I thought as much." Hadeon combed a hand through his face, his expression torn. "Kane will tell you he wants to case the place before you go in. You need to listen to him. You need to use a strategy."

That was fine, but the thought of Roman noticing Amethyst through a window or something sent Sidian's heart up into his throat. Though maybe... Maybe he could pass her off as Lilac's daughter or something until he could tell Roman the truth. "I'll do that. I want them dead, but I don't want both of us dead. Kinda defeats the purpose of everything."

"Good deal." Hadeon looked uncomfortable. "Are you like... Okay, dude?"

No, Sidian wasn't okay. He wouldn't be okay until Pack Kincaid was dead, until Roman knew the truth about Amethyst and the baby still inside of him, until all of this was over and they could decide to do what they *wanted* to do with their lives. Then, and only then, would he allow himself the chance to breathe, to think about what it might look like to heal on the other side of all of this.

He was holding it together because he had to. His daughter was in the hands of the most brutal men he knew, and the only way to retrieve her from them was to kill them. That was more important than just getting revenge; if Sidian didn't kill them, they could always come back. They could drag him into court where he would be no one and have nothing to show that he could care for Amey, and they would take her away from him all over again because they could.

But how could he explain that to someone like Hadeon? "I will be."

Hadeon escorted him back upstairs to the dorm floor where Roman was waiting, pacing back and forth between the dining room, living room, and kitchen with his arms folded over his chest. In nothing but a tank top with his hair still damp from his shower, he looked intense, and Sidian bit the inside of his cheek. His alpha was upset about something, which did not bode well. Was he angry that Sidian wasn't waiting somewhere for him? Because that shit would not fly.

"Sorry for stealing your mate away," Hadeon said in a bored voice, and Roman spun toward them. "I was just giving him the information he wanted. All our shit's downstairs."

Roman's face softened, though the tightness around his mouth did not ease. "That's fine. Sid, do you want to stay here tonight, or do you want to find a motel?"

"Here's fine. We need weapons anyway. We'd just have to drive back." And there was no use in going to find a place to stay when the Pit had nice, cozy beds already close at hand.

"Puppy's room is empty," Hadeon said. "You can sleep there for the night. Kitten might not be thrilled about it, but she'll keep her mouth shut until you're gone, so you don't have to worry about her. Get some sleep, omega. You're going to need it."

There was something endearingly sweet about the way Roman furrowed his brow, his eyes narrowing in Hadeon's direction while Sidian just scoffed at them both. "Sure thing. Thanks for the files. Hope you guys still find whatever you need to find without Pack Kincaid to stalk."

"I'm sure we will." Hadeon offered him a brief smile, though it seemed strained.

Roman slipped an arm around Sidian's shoulders and led him down the hall of dorm doors to one that stood cracked open, slipping past him to turn on a dim lamp that set on an empty nightstand. Only a digital clock and what looked like the snaking cord of a phone charger sat atop the smooth white surface, though it looked as though it had been chipped in places. There was no scent in the air despite this room belonging to someone, and there were no personal effects. Sidian supposed they might have kept minimalist quarters, but it seemed like the Mambas had already decided their missing alpha was dead.

He sank down on the edge of the mattress, the softness a comfort as he watched Roman shut and lock the door. There was a tension in his broad shoulders that set Sidian's teeth on edge, his shoulders hunching before he made himself sit up straight. Looking at Pack Kincaid's familiar faces just had him rattled; there was nothing to be afraid of with Roman. He was the gentlest alpha Sidian had ever known, and that had to count for something.

Roman turned to look at him, and though his face was devoid of emotion, there was a soft relief in his eyes. He *had* been worried then. "Can I see what Hadeon gave you? I think the Ultima has a GPS tracker, but I don't want to use it if I can avoid it. I'd rather follow paper directions."

Did using a built-in GPS have some danger associated with it? Sidian didn't know, and he decided he didn't care as he handed the folder over. Roman knew what he was doing. It was best to follow his lead. "This is them. I'd recognize their faces anywhere. There's just... A slight development."

"What kind of development?" Roman asked, flipping open the folder. "None of these names are familiar to me, but fair enough considering they live here in Jersey."

Sidian swallowed. "They have an omega. So that's an additional problem."

"That is an issue to contend with, though if we're lucky, that omega won't be treated well and won't want to stay with them. We might have an ally to consider." Roman flipped a few pages, studying the text, before snapping the folder shut. "But before we get into this, there's something else we need to talk about. I have a development of my own we need to discuss."

That was not what Sidian had wanted to hear. "What happened while you were with the medic? I didn't even think your wounds were bad enough to need it. I went easy on you."

The corner of Roman's mouth twitched as he came to join Sidian on the bed, the folder resting on one knee. "I don't disagree with you, but Captain Nightingale wanted to meet with me in person to discuss something he noticed in the footage. He called my boss to confirm whether or not it was true."

Sidian tensed. "Stop sounding so fucking ominous. What is it?"

"Lorcan Devereaux brought me into the Vipers because he suspected I was a prime alpha, and he was right." Roman glanced over at him, but Sidian could only blink at him, his head buzzing with electricity. "And Nightingale believes you might be a prime omega."

And just like that, everything was fucked.

Chapter Twenty-Six

Dax Kincaid was the second oldest son of Sterling Kincaid and the twin brother of Baxter Kincaid. Raised in a wealthy household and given everything necessary for a young alpha to succeed in life, he graduated college with honors, though he declined the ownership of his father's business when his father passed away. Roman imagined that likely went to the twin brother and wondered if Dax regretted not forging a more typical life, or if he preferred the power his position granted him.

He was unremarkable beyond his wealth and his status. Intelligent because money would have given him access to private tutors if necessary, powerful because of his family name, with a clean criminal record because nothing ever stuck to the upper echelons of society. He was uninteresting and unimportant, and Roman doubted he would have ever bothered to learn the man's name if not for what he and his pack had done to Sidian. He was older than both of them, in his mid-twenties, and there were no legal business dealings under his name that could be found.

He was likely making most of his money from the jobs he and his pack took alongside his own family inheritance. Why would he need to work a normal job if he had all of that going for him?

Roman glanced up at his mate as he read from his position on the edge of the mattress; Sidian had retreated to the far corner of the room and sat on the floor, his knees pulled to his slender chest. His eyes were wide and haunted, and he was still reeling from the information Roman had given him. A DNA test would be more conclusive than assumed evidence, but Sidian rejected that outright.

It went unsaid between them it was unnecessary. The shape of their own relationship belied certain things, sure, but there was an entire lifetime of experience Sidian was probably sorting through in his head, realizations coming to light about behavior he might have written off and was now forced to confront. Roman wanted to comfort him, but Sidian would come to him when he wanted that.

Being a prime alpha changed Roman's life not at all. It made a certain amount of sense to him, and it explained the utter carnage of his presentation. When that alpha tried to take Sidian away from him, it only made sense for Roman to lash out as violently as possible to protect the mate his instincts saw as especially in need of protection and care. It was easy to abandon the mission at the breeding center to protect the omega who needed it most. Even now, though it would be dangerous, he wanted to give Sidian the chance for the kills he needed to live in peace because he wouldn't be whole without them.

Sidian combed a hand through his hair at long last, his scent wilted as he drew in a slow, deep breath. "That fucks everything up. That's going to ruin this for both of us. We can't just... It's not safe."

It wouldn't be safe, but it could be made safe. "I have earplugs you can wear."

"They got in my head back at the center. I tried to push back, but it was... Fuck, Roe, it was bad." Sidian cradled his head in his hands, and a soft whine left his lips; Roman had to set the folder aside before he risked scattering the papers to get to his omega quicker. "Don't you dare fucking come near me. Don't you even think about it. I swear to Goddess I'll kill you."

Roman sank back down. Sidian wouldn't hurt him, but going against his words was difficult even without the explicit command woven through them. "Talk to me, darling. Tell me what you're thinking."

"What I'm thinking?" Sidian laughed, but the sound was thin, pained, and his eyes were heavy with something Roman *didn't* understand. Maybe he couldn't understand. "It makes too much sense. The way they treated me, the way I just *let them* after a while. I wanted to fight back but couldn't do it, and that's fucking terrifying. As soon as Dax got in my head, he had me right where he wanted me."

"Which won't happen again," Roman said. "You won't be alone. Not this time."

"No," Sidian agreed. "Instead, I'm dragging you in there with me so you can see just how bad it's gonna be when they get me on my knees. For fuck's sake, what did I do to deserve this?"

Roman slipped off the mattress and crept closer to Sidian, and when his omega didn't snap at him again, lowered himself on the floor as close as he dared. "They won't do that to you."

"They've already done it more times than I want to think about." Sidian rocked back and forth, his hands gripping his shins so tightly his knuckles bled white. A far cry from the omega who only hours ago had tortured a man to death, a testament to how much Pack Kincaid had hurt him. "You don't get it, and I don't blame you for it. How could you ever understand it?"

"Sid." Roman touched his cheek, and Sidian flinched. "You're okay. You're safe here."

"I don't feel safe. I'm not gonna feel safe until those fuckers are dead. And then we have to go somewhere far away from other alphas." Sidian smacked his hand away, and Roman let him. "How is this fair? What did I do wrong, Roe? Tell me that. What did I do wrong?"

He did nothing wrong, though Roman didn't know how to convince him of that. Sidian was a troubled teenager when they met, but that hadn't been his fault; his sick fuck of a father could have kept his hands to himself, and everything would be fine. None of this was his fault, and Roman would not sit by and let Sidian stew in the belief that he could ever deserve all the sorrow his life had put him through. There couldn't be anyone who deserved something like that.

He softened his approach, lowering his voice. "Sid, darling, please look at me?"

Wide violet eyes snapped to him, the scent of sour lilies pouring off of Sidian, a desperation laced through his scent. *Help me. Protect me.* "I am freaking the fuck out."

"I know that. I understand why." This time, Roman set one of his hands on top of Sidian's, which quivered beneath his touch. "No one is ever going to hurt you again."

"You can't promise me that. You can say it as much as you want to, but no one can promise me that. The kind of freak I am, I can't even protect myself." Sidian laughed, short and sharp and desperate, and something in Roman's chest tightened at the sound. He was so... Afraid.

You're the alpha, he reminded himself. *Do your job and comfort him.*

He cleared his throat. "I won't let a single alpha get close enough to you to so much as try it."

"But you can't stop them all," Sidian babbled on, rocking faster. "You can't just—"

An alpha command was impossible, though it would have been out of the question even if it *were* possible. Instead, Roman shifted close enough that he could draw Sidian's hand up to his own chest, a soothing rumble vibrating up to the omega's light touch. He was terrified out of his mind, and Roman wanted to help him as best he could, but he couldn't reach him with words because Sidian wasn't listening to him. And if his human mind was too entrenched in terror to understand, then Roman would speak to the part of him that would always understand on some animalistic, instinctive level.

Sidian fell quiet as the tension drained from his muscles, his body stilling before he slumped. It was a comforting sight compared to how he had been panicking just a moment ago.

He waited just the same, thumb stroking over Sidian's knuckles until a soft omega purr answered his rumble and Sidian looked up at him again. There was still a haunted look in his eyes, but his scent was easing into something sweet and soft once again. That was good.

"I can't promise you those things. You're right. Maybe it's wrong of me to even try when I don't understand why you're so afraid. It isn't something that can happen to me." He softened his voice, and Sidian's purr picked up just. "But I can promise you I'll be right beside you the entire time, and I will do every-thing in my power to keep you safe. You want retribution, and I want to give it to you. And I will lay my life on the line long before I let Dax Kincaid get anywhere near you again."

Sidian exhaled, his fingers digging into Roman's chest a little. "He's a monster."

"I've gathered that much." And Roman would be glad to see him dead. "He won't touch you. No one is going to touch you. And once this is over, you won't have to think about it again."

He knew that wasn't true; Sidian was traumatized but did a good job at hiding it from time to time. He was good at bravado, good at putting on the face of someone who was more than capable of handling what it would take to bring down eight alphas, but Roman, in the back of his mind, had known better. Seeing it in front of him did nothing more than confirm the concerns he'd been carrying with him since Sidian made it clear what he needed.

And if he were any other omega, Roman would tell him no. To stay behind. To let him handle the worst of it because he *could,* granted the ability and the power to face alphas like the Kincaids with relative ease where Sidian couldn't. But he knew Sidian wouldn't stay behind, and Roman wouldn't make him.

This meant so much to him. He needed this.

"Are you hearing me?" he asked, giving Sidian's hand a light squeeze.

Sidian nodded, then scooted across the carpet, unfolding his body so he could drag himself into Roman's lap. "I'm tired. I'm so fucking tired of all of this. I just want it to be over."

Roman tucked his chin down on top of Sidian's head. "It will be. I promise."

They sat on the floor together until Roman's back protested and Sidian's purrs softened into slow, easy breathing. Only when he was sure his mate was asleep did Roman stand, carrying Sidian to bed and tucking him in so he could get some much-needed rest. There would be no early morning for either of them; Roman wanted to case Dax Kincaid's pack house at night when it would be safer and they would be less likely to be seen. Sidian could sleep as long as his body allowed it.

And Roman would be there to watch over him until he woke.

He stretched out on his side of the mattress, paging through the documents to commit as much of it to memory as possible. Axel Kincaid had needed knee surgery on his left knee, which would ensure it was at least a slight weakness of his. Knox

Kincaid was blind in one eye, which meant his peripheral vision would be damaged. Others might have found it distasteful to target such areas, but Roman was not in the business of being courteous. He would use everything he could against the pack who had harmed his mate, and he would feel nothing in the process of doing so.

And then his attention was once again drawn to Lilac Kincaid, the violet-eyed omega with the ugly bond mark on the side of his throat. That wasn't typical placement but that might have been the point. Tormenting an omega with a half-assed bond would hurt them.

There was precious little information available on Lilac, but Roman didn't need there to be. He doubted the omega would be much trouble. It was just disconcerting to him.

There was no coincidence at play. Pack Kincaid had fixated on two black-haired, violet-eyed omegas likely on purpose, because that was their preferred aesthetic or because one of them served as a copy of the other. There was a pattern, though Roman wasn't sure what it was.

It didn't matter. What mattered was delivering a thorough punishment, so he returned to scanning the profiles of the alphas until his eyes protested, dry and exhausted.

They would have one evening to examine the home that Pack Kincaid called their own, and from there, Roman would devise the proper strategy to infiltrate that home and take all of them down. He knew he could command them and they couldn't do it to him; that was useful information.

All he had to do was ensure that Sidian was safe, and the earplugs would do just that. Protecting him was easy, given Roman had done it once before.

He would do it again. This time, there would be no one left to hurt his darling.

Chapter Twenty-Seven

Sidian didn't know if the Mambas had sworn a pact with each other to stay out of the dorm's communal shower as long as he was in there, but as he sat with his back against the tiles, letting the hot water soak the exhaustion from his muscles, no one walked in or knocked. He kept expecting it, kept waiting for someone to poke their head in to ask if he was all right, but no one came.

He wasn't sure if that was a blessing or a curse. He wasn't sure he wanted someone to check on him.

Though he'd asked Roman to give him some space this morning, he was cursing himself for doing it. What he wanted was for his alpha to come to him, comfort him, push through his boundaries and take care of him... At least, it was a pretty thought to have in the moment. He'd probably hate it happening.

Was that his prime omega side so desperate for affection and love after a lifetime of pain? Was it his human side that pushed back against needing that sort of care with everything he had?

In the shower's privacy, Sidian pressed both of his hands to his stomach, sure he could detect the slightest hint of a curve taking shape beneath his skin. It had taken him significant time to show with Amethyst, too, as if his body refused to carry more than the most minimal amount of weight necessary in order to keep his child alive and well. That Amey had been born a healthy eight pounds and five ounces was something he reminded himself of often. Despite how much of a fucking failure he was at being an omega, he'd still birthed a healthy baby girl. That was worth something.

And he could do it again. Would do it again to give her the little brother she deserved to have.

You can't stay in here all day, he reminded himself, his eyes fluttering shut as he pressed his head against the wall behind him, focusing on the pulse of the water through the showerhead, the rivulets that dripped over his bare skin. *Roman will worry even if he doesn't come check on you, and you need to get your shit together if you're going to go with him tonight.*

He had to go. Sidian refused to back down now that he was so close to getting his much-deserved revenge and to saving his daughter. Amey was so close he could almost delude himself into imagining her weight in his arms, leaning against his chest, soft and just oh-so-faintly floral like him.

Would Roman love her? Or would he decide Sidian's lies were too much for him?

What about the omega who had been raising her? What if she had bonded with him? It wasn't something Sidian wanted to think about because he knew he wouldn't be able to make peace with it. *He* was Amethyst's mother. He wanted her back too much to let her go to anyone else.

He needed her in his life. To care for her and provide for her in the way his parents never could and never would for him. To ensure she grew up healthy, happy, and safe.

Sidian dragged himself off the floor of the shower and shut the water off. A hook on the outside of the stall held the towel and robe Roman had given him, and he took his time drying off as thoroughly as possible before slipping the robe on. It was much larger than he was, but then, most of the clothing in the

Pit was likely sized for the alphas who lived there, not for a scrawny omega that none of them had asked to be responsible for. A bitter laugh rose in his throat, but he choked it down as he combed his hair back out of his face, hoping Roman was somewhere nearby. It was sickening how codependent he was becoming.

To his relief, Roman waited in the living room. A spiral notebook and the folder about the Kincaids were spread out on the coffee table while Roman sat on the floor, one hand over his mouth and the other scribbling notes as he muttered to himself.

It was so much like the boy who used to pore over his homework while waiting for Sidian to come down to the common room to see him it made Sidian's heart ache.

Before he could sink any further into his own guilt, Roman turned to look at him, green-silver eyes flicking up and down before he beckoned Sidian closer. Sidian went to him, crawling into his lap so he could get a better look at the notes Roman was working on. He didn't want to talk about what was wrong. Frankly, he didn't even want to think about it anymore.

And Roman seemed to sense it because he wrapped an arm around Sidian's waist, his hand settling on Sidian's stomach in a way that made Sidian tense up. *All he has to do is miss the pregnancy for a little while longer, and then he'll miss it for good.* "None of them have backgrounds in combat that would concern me. There's no evidence they have any personal trainers. If they're a bunch of gym rats, that's preferable. They'll be slower than I am, which should give me an advantage."

"That's good to hear." Sidian noted that Lilac's profile, slimmer than the others, had been set on the far corner of the table. "What are we going to do about their omega?"

Roman sighed, then pressed a kiss to Sidian's hair right over the nape of his neck, which made him tense just. No, it was fine.

Roman wouldn't bite him without permission. "I don't know. If he's on our side, we shouldn't have to do anything whatsoever. If he's on their side... I mean, the obvious is that we'd have to kill him, which I would do for our purposes there."

Sidian's stomach twisted at the thought. "I don't want to kill him. He wouldn't choose them if he could; you can see it in his eyes. Can you command him to stay out of our way?"

"I should be able to," Roman admitted after a moment, with a detectable amount of strain in his voice. "We have strict rules about not using alpha commands during missions, though."

"This isn't a standard mission, and if it keeps Lilac alive, then you'll do it whether or not you want to. I don't want him to get hurt for no reason." It was just too hard to believe he was dangerous at a glance, and Sidian knew firsthand just how much damage Pack Kincaid was capable of.

He wouldn't see another victim turned into a monster if he could avoid it.

"Okay," Roman conceded. "I'll do what I can to ensure he lives. When night falls, we're going to drive out there. I have a map, though their house is very remote."

"Old money packs often have countryside houses." It was almost the norm.

"Which is good and bad. Means it's less likely that a neighbor is going to overhear and call the police, but also more likely they'll know the terrain far better than we do." Roman flipped through his notes, then spread the notebook out again, slipping his other arm around Sidian's waist and giving him a brief squeeze. "They may also have cameras, but I should be able to hear them once we get so close. We should conceal our appearances as much as possible in case we're caught, anyway."

That was an upsetting thought to consider. "They might come after us."

"I doubt it," Roman murmured. "The risk is high if they're not sure who we are."

That was fair, though Sidian didn't want to risk it just the same. "If you think you hear cameras, we stay back as far as possible. There are eight alphas in that pack. There are no guarantees."

"Okay. I'll keep us back as far as we can." Roman kissed the back of his head this time, and against his will, Sidian melted into him with a relieved little sigh.

"You're too good at doing that," he muttered, settling his hands on top of Roman's.

"I try." Roman chuckled, then sobered. "Is there anything about them you know?"

Sidian knew plenty about Pack Kincaid, but not anything he thought would be useful to use against them in a fight. What he knew was that they were cruel, and that an omega in pain was not a deterrent to any of their actions. He wondered if they knew he was a prime omega, if they'd seen that somewhere in his private files and wanted him for that and that alone. Maybe Lilac was, too. Rich alphas could have anything they wanted, after all.

Roman nipped his ear. "You don't have to talk about them. It's okay."

"I feel like I'm not useful enough for this. I can fight, I think, but I'm not smart like you are." And he never had been. Would have flunked out of high school if he'd gotten to finish it.

It seemed so fucking stupid to think about the fact he didn't get the chance to.

A squeak tripped over his lips as Roman stood, pivoting to set Sidian down on the couch before sinking to his knees. He rested his chin on Sidian's lap like a dog, his expression almost wounded, and it was difficult to look him in the eye. Roman was *good*; Sidian knew that. There were things he couldn't tell him and things he might *never* talk to him about, but that didn't make Roman less of a good man, of a good alpha. The person who cared about his mate's well-being even in the face of something that could destroy them both.

"Don't talk about yourself like that," he said, and, Goddess, he sounded *sad*.

Sidian sighed, giving Roman's curls a gentle ruffle. "I know, I know, it's not doing me any good. I just feel like I don't know what the fuck I'm even doing here right now."

"Sid." Roman tilted his head so he could kiss the inside of Sidian's wrist. "You survived something that would have killed another omega. Do you understand that?"

"I do. I understand that. It's just not enough to kill them, and that's what I'm worried about." And worried that the earplugs would fail, and he'd be on his knees in front of Dax Kincaid, in front of *Roman,* and that his mate would see just how far he'd fallen because of those bastards.

Roman wrapped his arms around Sidian's legs, hugging him tight. "You are more than enough," he insisted, and Sidian's heart throbbed. "You came this far, and we'll get the rest of the way there together. I'll make it happen for you. All you have to do is trust me."

Trust. Did he trust Roman? Fuck, he wasn't sure. He knew Roman trusted him, knew he *had* to because otherwise why allow any of the things Sidian had done to him? Why allow the bleeding, the cutting, the collaring, the muzzling, the choking? Roman trusted Sidian more than anyone else ever had, but Sidian wasn't sure if that trust went both ways. Did he trust Roman like that?

You won't even tell him about the baby, he reminded himself, petting Roman's hair. *You won't tell him about Amey. You don't trust him to have your back if he knows the truth. You don't trust him.*

"I've got you." Roman kissed his forearm this time before letting Sidian go, and Sidian bit down on the inside of his cheek until the skin broke and he tasted blood. "Once we get a good look at the house, I should be able to figure out what we need to do to get in."

"And if you can't?" Sidian pressed, because they needed to be ready for disappointment.

As much as he hated to think about it, the possibility of failure refused to stop rearing its ugly head.

"Then we use guns." Roman shrugged, returning to his notebook. "The Mambas have sniper rifles. I'll pick them off through the windows until all eight of them are dead."

That wasn't what Sidian wanted, but he would deal with it if it meant every member of Pack Kincaid was dead and cold and he had his daughter back. He wanted them to suffer, but if he had to choose between their pain and Amey, he would choose Amey every single time.

He just hoped that when it came time, Roman would do the same.

"You should get something to eat." Roman threw the words over his shoulder, half-bent over his work again. "We'll start driving when the sun sets so we get there when it's dark. Make sure you wear all black too for the camo."

Sidian slid off of the couch without a word. He needed to eat for the baby, anyway.

Chapter Twenty-Eight

The house that belonged to Pack Kincaid looked abandoned.

It was the first thought Roman had when he and Sidian crested the hill on foot, staying close to the shadows of the trees despite the distinct lack of any faint camera buzz. The edge of the pack's property was still a few yards or so inward from where they stood, cloaked in all-black to make use of the moonless night, but Roman knew how paranoid the traffickings packs were. If the Kincaids made their money standing guard during omega auctions, then it would be as natural as breathing for them to mount cameras in trees they had no legal ownership of.

There were no telltale flashes of tiny red pinpricks amongst the leaves, no signs of vehicles or recent tracks in the dirt path winding around the large Victorian mansion. The siding was chipped in places and sloughing off in others, revealing the bare wall beneath. Pieces of the porch railing were broken off and tumbled down into the grass below, which was long, tangled, and unkempt. A few of the windows bore spiderweb cracks that stretched to the edges of the frames, though two of them on the ground floor had been shattered, the curtains swaying in the cool breeze.

What the fuck was going on?

Sidian made a small noise of confusion at Roman's side, lifting a pair of binoculars up to his eyes for a better look. Roman could see just fine from where he stood, but the moment Sidian lowered the lenses, Roman held out a hand for them so he could get a better look. This wasn't right.

There was a hole in the roof. The chimney must have collapsed with stray, broken bricks scattered close enough to the hole to let him know what made the impact.

And there were no signs of life anywhere.

They stood stock-still. Words came and went, fading on Roman's tongue; he wasn't sure what to say. The information the Mambas gave them was supposed to be correct, and when he checked the binoculars one more time, he could see the faded golden numbers on the side of the smashed mailbox that lay on the edge of the yard. The address was correct.

So where the fuck was Pack Kincaid, and what happened to their house?

The likelihood of that information being wrong is almost impossible, he reminded himself amidst the rising panic, eyes darting around the clearing where the Victorian stood. There was no sign of any other buildings in the area, though that didn't mean there wasn't one just because he couldn't see it from the hilltop. The safest thing to do would be to scout the area around the perimeter of the property to see if this was a ruse of some kind.

A hidden base wasn't unusual for criminal packs. For all they knew, it might be underground, which was a problem—

Sidian broke away from Roman before he could think of anything to say, walking straight toward the house. "Come on."

"Sid!" Roman snatched the back of Sidian's shirt and reeled him into the shadows, wrapping his arms around his omega as he watched the Victorian. "Don't go wandering off. They could see us from anywhere."

Violet eyes met his through the shadows, Sidian's jaw tightening the longer he stared up at Roman. "You have to be fucking stupid if you think they're here."

"This is their address. They have to be here." Pack Kincaid should have returned home. They had plenty of time to step off the plane, step into whatever cars were waiting for them, and return to their residence. There were no other home ownership records under their names; the Mambas had checked.

But the house was so old, so decrepit. Reality stared Roman straight in the face, but he refused to accept it. The Mambas *dealt* in information. Would they have lied about something like this?

Sidian wrenched himself out of Roman's arms and started walking toward the house again, stepping into a patch of grass unprotected by shadow. "Come *on*, Roman."

The command in Sidian's voice had Roman's feet moving before he could stop himself, and he swore under his breath as he jogged up behind his mate. It was the prime omega magic he knew Sidian possessed and now understood, and while no other alpha could ever bring Roman to heel, Sidian didn't even have to try to pull it off. Roman wondered if their status as mates had anything to do with it. If they got out of here in one piece, he might look into it one day.

As soon as Sidian reached the mailbox, he gave it one swift kick and sent it skittering across the grass.

Old yellowed envelopes spilled forth, their edges crinkled with age. Some of them were stained with various shades of brown.

Sidian loosed a shuddering breath, scrubbing his hands over his face. "So they're not here."

"They have to be here." Where else would they feel safe if not in their pack house? They had an omega they did not take with them to their auctions, so they had to have somewhere to leave them. None of their profiles had mentioned close family beyond Dax Kincaid's twin brother.

How could the Mambas have been wrong? They'd been *watching* the Kincaids, hadn't they?

Sidian rounded on Roman, his hands slamming into Roman's chest with surprising force and sending him stumbling back. "Are you fucking blind? They *aren't* here!"

"I... I can see that." But it made little sense. It made no sense.

Up close, there was no denying the level of disrepair the house was in. Cracked and broken windows, the porch steps sagging, missing boards on the porch itself, along the siding, chunks of railing and frame missing. There were cobwebs thick across the ceiling of the porch as well, dusty with age. Unless Roman was blind, there was even moss growing on the porch in a couple of places.

But it was Pack Kincaid's house. Legally, they owned it and the property attached to it. "This is the only house that was found under any of their names. Where else could they be?"

Sidian laughed and spun away from Roman, throwing his arms wide. "Do you hear that, guys? Why don't you come out of hiding? Roe says you gotta be here, and his stupid fucking friends couldn't have made a mistake, so where the fuck are you?"

The shrill tone of his voice set goosebumps rolling down Roman's spine, his hindbrain insisting he needed to calm his omega down. But when he reached out to touch him, Sidian slapped his hand away harder than he'd ever struck Roman before. His slim chest heaved with a harsh breath, his eyes as hard as amethyst stones, sharp enough to cut.

"Don't you fucking *dare* touch me," he hissed. "You promised me. You *promised* me we'd find them, Roman."

Roman did, and they would, but... Fuck. *Fuck.* Pack Kincaid was supposed to be there. The plan was to get as much intel about their house as possible, note their cars, and scope out just enough to get an idea of the safest way to infiltrate. It was always going to be risky; the breeding center missions were a breeze in comparison. Centers did not employ alphas, and betas had no sway over alphas, no ability to posture or command that might cause the Vipers any problems. In contrast, Pack Kincaid was much more dangerous, but Roman knew he could do this. He would do it because Sidian needed him to.

How could this be happening? Where the fuck *were* they?

Sidian all but jumped up the breaking steps to the porch, opening the storm door before kicking the front door in. The wood split under the force, and he shouldered his way through the gap with a snarl of irritation that made Roman's gut churn. Even if the pack wasn't here, Sidian needed to be careful. A house falling apart to that degree was dangerous, and Roman wanted nothing to happen to his omega. Enough already had.

He followed more cautiously and found Sidian standing in what looked like a living room. The couch, loveseat, and two armchairs were overturned, the fabric moth-eaten and rotting, the entire room smelling of decay. And Sidian stood in the center, his arms hanging by his sides, his sweet lily scent fading into the rot and ruin all around them.

He let out a slow, ragged breath. "She's not here."

"She?" The moment Roman's fingers brushed his omega's shoulder, Sidian growled at him, and he dropped his hand. "Sid, who are you—?"

A sharp cackle of laughter ripped the words from Roman's mouth before he could finish the thought. "Who am I talking about? That's what you're gonna ask, right, Roman? I'm talking about..." Sidian trailed off, his hands clenching into tight fists. "Those fucking monsters aren't here, and they have... They've got my..."

A little wheezing breath left Sidian's lips before he crumpled inward, wrapping his arms around himself. The sharp, keening cry he made echoed through the empty house; something fluttered high above them. Bats in the attic, maybe, disturbed by the mourning sounds spilling from Sidian's lips.

"I want my baby," he rasped, swaying on his feet as Roman's blood iced over. "I want my daughter."

Sidian didn't want Roman to touch him, but Roman couldn't stop himself from reaching out. What was going on? What baby? What daughter? What was Sidian talking about? Roman had to touch him, had to help him. Sidian was his mate, his omega, and no matter what happened, he had to take care of Sidian. And Goddess, those noises... The last time he heard Sidian cry like that was—

Sidian darted away from his touch, turning to face him in the dusty, molded living room. "Don't touch me. Don't you fucking... You said they were here. You *said*."

"They're supposed to be here. This was the address on their profiles. On all of them." The address on the mailbox was the same. It was their small town. "If the information is wrong, it's wrong, but we aren't at the wrong house. Sidian, what were you saying about a daughter?"

Sidian laughed and raked his hands through his hair, his cheeks damp with falling tears as he paced in tight, frantic circles. "I should have known. Should have fucking known it'd blow up in my face. Why would I trust you? Why would I believe in *you* of all people? If you'd just controlled yourself, I wouldn't even *be* in this place."

The words struck something deep in Roman's chest, flaying it open. His lips parted, but no words came to mind. Just shock. Numb, uncertain, disbelieving shock.

And then the cruel, curling flare of guilt that had never left him. *Even he knows this is your fault. You were supposed to protect him. You promised.*

"Sidian," Roman tried, but Sidian cut him off again.

"You're the reason I ended up in that place. Ended up in that..." He broke off, choking on a sob now, gripping his own arms as he paced faster and faster. "You're the one who killed my father *and* yours, and you got to spend the last two years of your life free while I was locked up in that fucking place. Do you know what they did to me? Do you know what they *did* to me?"

Roman didn't know what to say. He couldn't speak. The weight of Sidian's misery threatened to choke him, phantom fingers around his neck far stronger than his own hands were.

When he took a step forward, Sidian growled at him. "Get the fuck *down*."

The wooden floor buckled under the impact of Roman's knees, but it held. For the moment, it held.

Sidian stopped, trembling hands pressed to his face, his voice breaking on every word as his chest hitched and shuddered. "They took everything from me. They took everything I had left, and then they took Amethyst. They just..."

Amethyst. His daughter. They took his fucking daughter. Roman wanted to speak, wanted to say anything, do anything, but Sidian's command and the horror of it all gripped him too tight.

"I want my fucking daughter back!"

Sidian screamed, the sound ripping itself out of his chest like something alive and desperate for escape. He sank to his knees, his hands, limbs shaking with the effort of holding him upright as he screamed dend screamed and screamed, the noises cutting Roman open like so many knives. Every sound of anguish tore at his soul, sinking claws and teeth into him until his vision blurred, until everything ceased to exist but Sidian. His omega, his mate, who wouldn't let him help.

Sidian fell quiet after a moment, still sobbing, face hovering over the floor. Though it almost physically hurt to move, to push back against Sidian's word, Roman dragged himself over to his omega until he could draw Sidian into his arms, letting him flail, letting Sidian elbow him in the gut, wincing as his face was shoved away. After a minute or two, Sidian sagged against Roman's chest, broken noises shuddering from his lips.

"I hate you," he whispered even as his fingers tangled in Roman's shirt, twisting so that Roman couldn't pry him off even if he wanted to. "I hate you so fucking much."

"I'm sorry." What else was there to say?

But Sidian just closed his eyes, resting his cheek against Roman's chest as he hiccuped and whined. Try as he might, Roman couldn't quite force a rumble to soothe his omega, but he wrapped his arms around Sidian and rocked him back and forth, hoping it would do something for him. Anything for him.

Pack Kincaid had Sidian's daughter, and Roman did not know where they were.

What was he supposed to do?

Chapter Twenty-Nine

The drive to the motel was deadly silent. The only sounds that permeated the quiet were the tires crunching over asphalt and the dual sounds of breathing. Roman's remained steady and slow while Sidian's hitched and trembled, not quite recovered from his breakdown in the house despite it having been a good half an hour ago.

His chest hurt. The weight of failure draped itself over his shoulders, bearing him down to the earth like nothing ever had before, threatening another round of tears as if there was anything left in him. Maybe vomit. He'd felt the burn of bile multiple times but told himself to swallow it back, to keep whatever he could down for the sake of the baby still inside him. He couldn't risk his son too if he would never get Amethyst back after all.

White-hot rage coiled in his chest, demanding he lash out at Roman again for the sake of being able to do it. Instead, he forced himself to sit, trying to take deep breaths. Screaming at his alpha would not change anything. He could grab the wheel and jerk them off the road and into a ditch, and it still wouldn't change a fucking thing.

He wanted to. Fuck did he want to. Anything would be better than living with the crushing agony in his chest, the realization that he'd failed his daughter, and he'd never see her sweet face again. How big had she grown? How many milestones had he missed because of the psychopaths that used him like a fleshlight and left him in the center to bleed?

He would never see Amey again.

The car came to a stop on the cracked pavement of the parking lot, and Roman cut the engine. He stepped out of the car without a word and returned moments later with a key dangling from one finger, waiting on the sidewalk that stretched just far enough to give the motel a walkway. He hadn't said a single word on the entire drive, though he had to have questions. Sidian wondered what was going on in his alpha's head. If he was still *in* there.

Maybe he was angry, and silence was the only way to hold on to that anger, to keep it at bay instead of turning it on Sidian like he damn well knew he should.

Sidian dragged himself out of his seat, still aching to his gut as he followed Roman into the motel room. They'd been so hopeful about what information they might gather at Pack Kincaid's home that leaving empty-handed made Sidian feel a deep, simmering shame he didn't know how to handle. It was too much. All of it was too much. At least the Mambas couldn't see how much they'd failed, right?

What did he do to deserve it? Was it somehow punishment for what he did to his father? But that bastard wanted to break him, bleed him, use him, and abuse him just like Pack Kincaid. How can trying to protect himself have been wrong?

A desperate whine rose in his throat again, but he choked it back down and reached for the anger instead. It burned hotter, choked him, but it was so much easier to process than the pain. Horrible, agonizing fucking *failure* that threatened to eat him up from the inside out like a parasite.

Roman took a seat at the rickety table next to the window, dropping his head into his hands. "I'll make contact in the morning and see what the Mambas make of this."

"Why?" Sidian kicked his shoes off and dropped on the edge of the bed, his hands balling up into fists. Deep breaths, but he didn't want to breathe when every lungful of air hurt. "They don't know what the fuck they're doing. All that money just for them to be too fucking stupid to get us one address. I asked for so little."

Roman swallowed so hard that Sidian heard his throat click. "I know, Sidian. I'm sorry."

"You're sorry?" That wasn't good enough, and Roman knew that. It would never be good enough. "You should have thought of that when you turned into a psychopath. You should have thought about that when they hauled me off. I didn't get any peace before *they* showed up. Did you know that?"

Roman didn't look at him. Couldn't look at him. "Yes."

He was so calm, so controlled, that it pissed Sidian off. Why wouldn't Roman fight with him? Why wouldn't he yell back? Why did he let Sidian push him around, shove him, smack him? Sidian had seen with his own eyes what Roman was capable of, the level of violence that made him picture perfect in the eyes of Lorcan fucking Devereaux. Perfect enough to be spirited off to fight injustice or whatever bullshit while Sidian suffered and bled and begged for the mate he barely knew to come rescue him because he couldn't save himself.

And in the end, he couldn't save himself. He would have died of exposure out in the woods, alone and pregnant. And he couldn't even save his daughter from her monster fathers.

What fucking good was he if he couldn't do anything?

The tears came again, burning his already dry eyes, but he dashed them away and pushed himself to his feet, storming over to Roman and shoving him so hard his hands fell. His head snapped up, his eyes wide and uncertain, like he didn't know what to make of Sidian. Like he was looking at an animal, some kind of beast that was just out of his control. Coming upon a furious mountain lion, or maybe a bear.

Sidian wished he could be that, be *like* that. More like a rabid deer, useless and dying, and just as frightened and pathetic.

"What good are you as an alpha?" he asked Roman, and Roman winced but didn't speak. Didn't move. "Couldn't find me, couldn't save me, can't find my daughter. What can you do? Fuck me? That's not special. *They* could do that. *They* did that—"

Roman's jaw clenched, the first and only sign of anger Sidian had seen in him so far. "I'm nothing like them."

"I wish you were. That would make this so much easier." Sidian wouldn't have to feel anything at all. Roman would shove him down and take what he wanted, and it'd hurt, but Sidian would know the score. Roman would never have promised Sidian a future, never would have promised him a family, and maybe that would have been better. At least then, Sidian would have understood it.

He wanted Roman to hurt him, maybe. Wanted him to do something, anything, that made this simple for both of them. Bend him, break him, bleed him just like Pack Kincaid so Sidian could stop believing in the stupid fairy tale mate bullshit between them.

"Hit me," he said, and the color drained from Roman's stupid, pretty face. "Come on, big boy. You're the alpha. Don't you get tired of me pushing you around?"

Roman shook his head, the uneasy expression returning. "I will not hit you."

"Don't you get tired of being my bitch?" Sidian's hands found the collar of Roman's shirt and fisted it, dragging him closer, over the table until he knew the edge of it had to be pressing into Roman's chest. It had to hurt. "Show me who's in charge, Roman. Put me in my place. You gonna let me treat you like this? Huh?"

Without breaking Sidian's hold on his shirt, Roman all but melted out of the chair, his knees sinking into the dark carpet beneath them. The sight made Sidian's breath hitch, his omega whining for him to *stop*. It was one thing when Roman knelt for Sidian because he wanted to, because he enjoyed it, but it didn't feel like that at the moment. It didn't feel right.

Everything was spiraling out of control. Sidian couldn't take it.

"I fucking hate you." He tightened his grip on Roman's collar and stood over him, spitting the words into his face. *Yell at me. Fight me. Hit me. Do something.* "When we were in the woods that night, I thought about ramming that scalpel into your neck, and I should have done it."

Roman said nothing, hands resting on his thighs, his scent giving away nothing but the same soothing, calming, warm pheromones as always.

Always trying to take care of Sidian even when Sidian couldn't take care of himself.

His resolve cracked in the face of that silence, that steadiness, Roman's refusal to rise to any of his taunts. The tightness in his throat grew until it was too much, his hands falling from Roman's shirt. There was an angry red rash across his skin from the abrasion of the fabric, and Sidian's omega whimpered a soft apology at the sight. When Roman let Sidian hurt him, when he enjoyed the pain, that was one thing. And this wasn't that. This was...

What the fuck was wrong with him?

Apologize, he told himself, but the words never came. *For fuck's sake, apologize to the only person who ever gave a damn about you.*

"Sid." Roman inhaled, a hand rising to rub the front of his throat, but there was no hiding what Sidian had done to him. "It's okay. It's fine. Just take a deep breath."

None of it was okay. How could he not understand that? How stupid *was* he? "A deep breath isn't going to fix any of this shit. They took my fucking daughter. I know you don't care about that because she's not *yours*, but she matters to me. And now I don't know where she is."

Sidian had to stop. He knew that. Lashing out at Roman was only going to make this worse and was going to cost him the only ally he had, the only person who loved him. The last two years of his life had been torment with only one light at the end of the darkness, and he'd come. Roman had saved him, and now what? Sidian was going to rip his head off his shoulders for something he couldn't control? Because of someone else's mistake?

Roman was too forgiving. Too understanding of a monster like Sidian.

"Your daughter," Roman tried, his expression softening. "Goddess, I didn't even... Why didn't you tell me? Why wouldn't you tell me they'd taken something so precious from you?"

Sidian's jaw tightened, and he whirled away from his alpha, ripping at his own hair again as a furious growl rumbled up his chest. Why bother? It wouldn't have changed anything, and Roman couldn't understand. He could pretend to be forgiving, but he would never understand what Sidian was going through. Would never understand why he was so afraid.

Prime alphas didn't have to be afraid of anything. They were above it all.

"I hate this," he snapped, and because it was close, Sidian yanked one of the two chairs out from beneath the table and flung it at the door, the cheap wood splintering against the scuffed steel. "You don't get to *judge* me for not telling you! She's my daughter. What if you didn't want her?"

Roman's face crumpled. "What makes you think I wouldn't want her?"

Sidian sank down onto the mattress, nails scrabbling at his own scalp as he tried to suck in air, his lungs so tight that it hurt. Everything hurt. Amey was *gone,* and there was nothing they could do about it, if even the people who were supposed to know where she was had no idea. He'd never get to see her again. He'd never get to hold his daughter, to promise her she'd never be taken again.

He'd failed her. He'd failed her so completely. What if he failed his son, too?

A hand on his shoulder was slapped away, the floor beneath his feet shaky as he pushed himself away from the bed, away from Roman. Comfort from his alpha should have felt natural. It was all he wanted, all he needed, and yet the thought of letting Roman touch him sent a wave of unease through his entire body. *Don't touch me. Don't touch me, don't look at me, don't speak—*

"Sidian." Roman's voice was low, soft, though there was an urgency in his tone he couldn't disguise as he raised his hands, palms out, trying and failing to look harmless. How could an alpha of his size ever be harmless? Did he know what he was? "Talk to me. Let it out. Bottling it up will hurt you."

"Fuck off. Stop pretending you understand. You don't." Every word trembled on Sidian's tongue, and he hated it. Hated his own weakness, his own uselessness even in the face of the one person he wasn't supposed to be afraid of. How was any of this *fair?*

Roman tried again, voice even softer now. "You're right. I don't. But I know that holding it inside is bad for you. Just let it out. I don't care if you yell or break things. Just let it out."

He tried to take a step forward, and Sidian snarled at him in warning, hackles rising.

He didn't want Roman anywhere near him, something that startled him because Roman was the only person he'd ever wanted at his side. The two of them fit together; Roman was the only person in the world who ever made him feel like he might be worth something. The only alpha who treated him with respect and consideration, who put his wants and needs first. Always over his own.

What makes you think I wouldn't want her? He didn't know Amey. Had never seen her or held her and would not know how he felt until he did. Sidian *had* to lie to him; Roman couldn't have known how he would have felt if Sidian had told him the truth. He couldn't understand how important Amethyst was, how precious, how perfect, and how badly she needed Sidian to come and save her from her sorry excuses for fathers.

Roman didn't even understand just how evil Pack Kincaid was.

"Get out." The words tore themselves from Sidian's chest, and his omega whined in protest, but he silenced it as he had so many times before, his hands clenching into fists to steady himself. "Get the fuck away from me until you can tell me how your buddies fucked this up. Until you know where my daughter is, I don't want to look at you."

"All right." Roman lowered his hands, his expression blank as he took a step back. "I'll go. Take a shower, get some rest. By morning, I'll have an answer for you."

The moment the motel room door clicked shut, Sidian pressed his back against the wall and slid down, curling into the smallest ball he could as his shoulders shook with silent sobs.

What was the point of it if he never got to see Amethyst again?

Chapter Thirty

Cold air stung his face and hands as Roman lowered himself onto a fallen log just behind the motel, the darkness encroaching on his senses as he took a slow, deep breath to settle himself. His alpha was in turmoil inside of him, raging against his ribcage, clawing at his heart, doing everything possible to escape his useless flesh and get back to their omega who needed comfort so desperately. Seeing Sidian fall apart at the seams like that had shaken Roman in ways he never had been before, and he wasn't even entirely sure he could keep his promise to make things right.

The Mambas were the branch of Ouroboros whose information was most vital to their operations; even the Cobras could rely on the Internet and tabloids for juicy details about their political rivals. If the Mambas suspected Pack Kincaid were traffickers, they would *know* where they lived.

How could they have gotten it so wrong? Roman had to tell them. If that information was flawed, just how much of the rest of their data was wrong in some way?

He knew Hadeon's phone number only from memory and dialed it with shaky fingers, raising the device to his ear and listening to the comforting dial tone. Together, they could get to the bottom of this. Hadeon was smart, and there had to be more data within the Pit that he had access to. Something perhaps had been misfiled. Maybe that house was a former auction site, and the addresses were mixed up.

A cool breeze stung Roman's eyes, and he blinked away a few droplets of water as something cold and metallic pressed against the back of his skull. "Hang up the phone, Roman Kane."

Roman stared directly into the trees as he allowed the phone to drift away from his ear, picking up the tinny sound of Hadeon's voice before he snapped the flip phone shut. Someone yanked the device out of his hand a moment later and, more on reflex than anything else, he lifted his hands like he had for Sidian. It hadn't worked then, and he supposed it wouldn't work now.

You're upwind, he told himself, letting his eyes flutter shut for just a moment. *But how the fuck could the police have snuck up on you like this?*

The gun prodded the back of his head as someone sighed behind him. "Put your hands behind your back. If you make any sudden movements to escape, I'm going to shoot you."

He did as he was told, unsure what to say. Did the police know that Sidian was inside? Would any of this be held against him? It shouldn't be; Sidian had nothing to do with any of it and was as innocent as possible. "My mate had nothing to do with any of this."

Someone barked a sharp, unsettling laugh behind him as someone looped what felt like several zip ties around his wrists, tightening them painfully. "Oh, is that so?" It was a new voice, slimy compared to the original gruff one. Pigs. Go fucking fig-ure—

Something cut off his vision for a breath of a second before something cool pressed up against the front of his throat. Before Roman could react, a soft *click* filled the air, the sound alerting him that something was wrong. The police used zip ties on occasion instead of handcuffs, even though neither was particularly effective against someone of Roman's size, but he'd never known them to use collars of any kind. His hands flexed against the ties, reflex all but demanding he examine what they'd put on him.

The bolt of electricity shot through his system, white-hot pain that took his breath away.

Hyena-like laughter echoed through the air as Roman convulsed, his mouth open but no sound coming out as his limbs jerked and spasmed against the agony. Even when it cut, his muscles twitched, his body coiling in on itself in an attempt to get away from whatever that was. The skin beneath the metal of the collar burned as he panted harshly, sensitive where Sidian had given him a friction burn yanking on his shirt. That was fine, that was fine, he wasn't angry with Sidian at *all*.

"Tell the alpha that he was wrong," someone said, voice flat as someone rammed a steel-toed boot directly into Roman's ribs. "This one is going quietly after all. What a surprise!"

It hurt to move, but Roman forced his head back, squinting through the shadows so he got a clear look at his attackers. Something was wrong with his vision, fuzzy around the corners, but he couldn't think about that right now. He needed to know who had come for him. *What* had come for him.

What he saw sent a wave of nausea rolling over him, the panicky grip of fear wrapping long fingers around his throat and squeezing. *No, please no, anyone but them. No no no.*

The alpha closest to him knelt down, one hand sliding through Roman's curls before gripping them firmly, giving his head a shake. The eyes—one milky white, one icy blue—stared directly into his soul. Knox Kincaid. "Looks like he's still conscious. Now that's a surprise."

A bigger alpha crouched down next to him, a long twisting scar along his neck marking him as Nash Kincaid. "That shit is genuinely impressive. Maybe the alpha will want to keep him around."

"Too big and bulky for my taste, but he's got a pretty face on him." The alpha wearing the steel-toed boots did not lower himself to the ground, but then, Axel Kincaid had a bad knee, didn't he? So, getting on the ground might not have been the best of ideas for him. "Maybe we can have some fun with him. Not like you can spoil a male alpha the way you can a male omega."

Knox clicked his tongue against the roof of his mouth, his grip in Roman's hair tightening. "Maybe so. What are the risks if we give him another injection? He looks like he's out of it, but I don't want to take any unnecessary risks during transport. We've got an hour's drive."

An hour? Where the fuck are they taking me? But Roman knew, didn't he? The Victorian was only half an hour away, and it wasn't their actual house. *So the address was wrong after all.*

A snarling shriek split the air before breaking on a whimper, and Roman strained against the zip ties. *Sidian.*

"Fuck it." Axel kicked Roman in the gut this time, knocking the air out of him, his body crumpling inward from the impact. A sharp *sting* on his shoulder made him hiss. How hadn't he felt it before? When did they even do it? "So what if he's a little loopy? His buyer might appreciate that."

"No permanent damage, gentlemen," Nash said with a tsk-ing noise as he rose to his feet and Roman's vision grew hazier, shades of gray slowly layering themselves over his eyes. "Enjoy your nap, Kane."

He couldn't. He couldn't fall asleep; he couldn't let this happen. He had to get up, but no part of his body would respond, no muscle would answer him, his arms couldn't strain enough and—

Everything faded away, and Roman's eyes slipped shut.

The first scent Roman noticed was the buttery scent of leather. *The muzzle?*

His eyes fluttered open, his head pounding as he peered through the darkness that seemed to surround him on all sides. Wherever he was, it was warm, though the stiffness beneath him made his joints ache and throb. He tried to wet his lips, but his mouth was dry, and though he willed his head to move in any direction so he could get a sense of where he was or what was going on, it didn't listen to him. All he could do was stare at a hazy shape that formed itself into a person.

And what struck him in that moment, what had never occurred to him before, was how familiar the alpha looked. How the lines of Dax Kincaid's face, for one blurry moment, looked like someone else's.

The alpha who purchased Sidian that fateful afternoon was tall, handsome, with short white hair just long enough to slick back out of his face. He was sharper and more angular than Dax, and his eyes were a different color, but there were similarities if one knew where to look. The shape of the nose, the almost smirking curve of the mouth, the fine-boned hands. Dax held a tablet, stylus pressed against his lower lip, his eyes narrowed as he studied the screen before him.

When his eyes flicked toward Roman, it seemed to happen in slow motion. Dax's lips curved into a proper smirk, and he lowered the tablet so the screen highlighted him from below. *Creepy fucker.*

"I gave them strict instructions to inject you only once," he mused, his voice low, his tone smooth yet somehow *wrong*, like velvet stretched over a molding frame. "Looks like they didn't break you after all."

Roman opened his mouth to say something, anything—an insult if he could think of one—but the nausea that rolled through his gut had him flinching instead, his teeth clamping shut against it.

Dax waved his stylus as if in warning. "If you throw up, you'll lie in it until we get home."

It took a moment for Roman to gather control of himself, but he managed it. He glanced up through his lashes, taking measure of the man who sat across from him, from the rotting driftwood scent that seemed to roll off of him like a toxic cloud. If his scent was this nasty, something was wrong with him.

But unless it was fatal, it would not help him or Sidian to know that.

Dax studied him for a long moment, then set the tablet aside and shifted onto his knees. "You know, now that I have you, I think I want a closer look. The boys said you were *pretty*."

Roman tried to lean back, but Dax was on him before he could, shoving his back against the floor of what Roman realized was a van at the same moment he realized his arms were still tied behind his back. The plastic of the zip ties refused to give, but the moment he tried to tug at them regardless, something plastic thumped into his forehead. A remote, he realized, that he watched Dax drop into the front pocket of his neat button-down like it was nothing, that he carried it on his person.

He forced himself to lie still as Dax got comfortable on top of him, straddling Roman's waist. Long fingers looped through the metal bars of the muzzle, holding Roman's head in place as Dax leaned over him, staring down at him like he was nothing more than a butterfly beneath a pin, moments away from being snapped into a frame. His hands ached and his shoulders protested, but his head swam every single time Dax jerked it from side to side, leaving him nauseous and dizzy.

Dax laughed, the sound unsettling, needles pricking Roman's skin. "My, my, you *are* pretty."

The hand dropped from the muzzle to curl around the front of Roman's throat, and he remembered how Sidian's hand felt there—sweaty and trembling with excitement yet careful. It was nothing compared to the firm grip of Dax's fingers digging in too tight, cutting off Roman's air supply as another hand slid under the front of his shirt, fingers dragging over his bare skin.

Being touched like that was revolting, but when he squirmed, Dax tightened his grip.

"Your attitude and your insolence leave a lot to be desired, but we can always break you of that should we need to do so." Dax leaned closer to him, over him, his lips brushing against Roman's ear and making him shudder in disgust. "My men were right, though. You have potential. If you survive what we have planned for you, I'll break you at my feet just like I will that stupid little omega bitch."

Instinct told Roman to do something, *say* something, but he clamped his jaw and refused to rise to the challenge. Sidian was somewhere, likely not in the vehicle with him based on the lack of his sweet lily scent, but Pack Kincaid would have him. Roman had to get to him.

He would not cost himself that opportunity by letting Dax Kincaid hiss in his ear and piss him off. He'd hold out for the perfect chance to strike when he knew it wouldn't be a wasted chance.

Dax slid away, scooping his tablet back up. "This is going to be such a *fun* night."

Chapter Thirty-One

Within minutes of all but demanding Roman leave the room, Sidian felt like shit.

He pushed himself up from the floor, wiping his damp, sore cheeks with the long sleeves of his shirt as he studied the broken chair on the floor. Sighing, he bent down to pick the pieces up, tossing the smaller ones in the trashcan and setting the broken legs and the cracked back on top of the table. They would have to pay for that on their way out, and it didn't even make him feel better. All it did was make him feel worse than he already did, having to confront the sign of destroying something in his rage.

Better to break a chair than hurtling any more insulting words at his mate. Fuck, what was *wrong* with him? It had been months since he'd last seen Amey. Why did he take that out on Roman?

A soft knock at the door stirred him from his thoughts, and he scraped at his cheeks again as he rounded the table. It was either the motel manager, and Sidian hoped being an omega would give him an edge on apologizing, or it was Roman who hustled out and forgot the room key. Either way, Sidian owed both of them an apology, and if it was Roman, he was going to drag him to bed, tuck him in as best he could, and smother him with affection and touch until he knew how valued he was.

As soon as Sidian unlocked the door, someone shoved it open from the other side.

He stumbled backward over his own feet and would have fallen if a hand hadn't darted out to grasp him by the front of his shirt, keeping him standing if unsteady. It took him a second to process the familiar face in front of him, his brain refusing to let him see the reality of his situation as the floor vanished beneath his feet and his heart dropped straight into his gut. He knew the eyes that gazed into his own, the slight smirk that always set at the edges of Dax Kincaid's lips.

No, Sidian thought as Dax stepped further into the room, his grip on Sidian's shirt pushing him back. *No, no, no. This is a nightmare. It's not happening. He can't be here. That wasn't his house!*

"It's been a long time since we've spoken to one another, hasn't it?" Dax asked before he shoved Sidian onto the bed, letting him scrabble over the comforter so he could drop on the other side of it. "Look at you. You haven't forgotten how to cower when I show up."

"What the fuck are you doing here?" How could he have found them? Did he know they'd gone looking for him? Did he know where they'd gone? How did the Mambas have the wrong address, and how the fuck did all of it lead Dax right to Sidian's door?

Dax combed a hand through his hair as he rounded the bed, and Sidian pressed himself back against the wall, knocking over the lamp as he dragged himself up onto the nightstand. He felt so small, trapped, his heart thumping against his ribcage as more alphas spilled into the room. Talon and Ford guarded the door from the inside, and Sidian might have been wrong, but he could have sworn he saw Jett standing just outside the door. Guarding the room from the outside.

Half of the pack had come for him. There would be no escape. He couldn't take them all on by himself. "Get away from me. Get the fuck away from me!"

Dax caught him by one swatting hand and threw him onto the bed with far too much ease.

This time, though, Sidian barely dragged himself across it before a pale hand closed over his own, something digging into the mattress next to his hip. "*Stop moving,* omega."

Sidian's entire body jerked to a stop, his breath coming in rapid little gasps although his body refused to obey him. Tears burned in the corners of his eyes as frustration gnawed at him, the stress and fatigue of the night banding together with his own stupid prime omega hindbrain to leave him helpless and terrified beneath the weight of Dax Kincaid. Right where Dax wanted him.

"This is where you belong, little omega," Dax crooned in his ear, jarring another broken cry from Sidian's chewed, bleeding lips with a thrust that threatened to rip him open again. "The only place you could ever belong. Now just lie there and accept it."

"Please stop," Sidian wheezed, but he knew the alpha wouldn't. None of them ever stopped.

All his pleas earned him was a throaty laugh as Dax fucked into him again, the jeers of the rest of the pack echoing off the walls. "But your needy little cunt doesn't want me to stop."

Sidian shuddered as he felt Dax's fingers slip beneath his hair, drawing it away from the nape of his neck to bare the skin there. There was no mating mark; Sidian knew that was likely what he was looking for. Did they know about Roman? Did Dax know there was another alpha in the picture, that he was the *right* alpha, the only alpha Sidian had ever cared for? Did he know how fucked he was going to be when Roman found out what they were doing to Sidian?

Because he would kill them. He was one of the few people who could do that.

"I was worried Kane might have marked you," Dax mused, and Sidian's heart beat faster. He *knew* Roman's name? "Putting his teeth into what belongs to me would be a death sentence."

Like fuck Sidian would ever belong to him. "Get your hands off me," he growled, but the lack of any commanding weight to his voice made his words all but meaningless.

Dax chuckled in his ear and let his chest press against Sidian's back, a hand sliding beneath Sidian, finding the edge of his shirt and slipping beneath it. The sensation of another alpha's fingers on his bare skin had Sidian growling, his hindbrain demanding no other alpha *ever* touch him if they weren't his mate—Until the moment Dax's fingers pressed into the barely there taut stretch of his stomach. The only proof he would have had that Sidian was pregnant.

He knew. Of course he knew. The center probably told him as soon as the test came back positive, and how stupid could Sidian be? Of *course*, Dax knew. He'd come looking for Sidian because he knew his unborn child was out there, and he wanted it back. Just like with Amey, Dax wanted the children he'd forced into Sidian's body. Another baby to tear from his arms.

"You are *so* fertile." The praise landed horribly; Sidian squeezed his eyes shut, his hands trembling as he gripped the edge of the mattress. "Even under all that stress, you breed so well."

Ford whistled from where he stood next to the door. "Now that's a good little bitch."

"He always has been. Haven't you, Obsidian?" Dax peeled him off of the mattress, forcing Sidian to kneel on the bed with him, the pressure of a half-hard erection against his ass making

Sidian wretch. "It's all right. Boys, get their bags. It's time we took our naughty little omega home."

Sidian tried to flail free, but Dax's arms snapped shut around him, pinning his own arms to his sides. He tried to slam his head back but missed Dax's face and only froze when he felt the telltale scrape of teeth on the side of his neck. The others jeered while Dax knelt, the threat of a mating bond teetering on the edge of reality while Sidian whimpered out a pathetic noise in apology. *Don't bite me, don't bite me, please don't fucking bite me.*

"If you keep being bad," Dax whispered, "then I'll pack you up. It's fine either way, but I think you don't want that. Are you going to stop fighting?"

Before Sidian could reply, Jett poked his head into the room, his expression bored as he stifled a yawn against the palm of his hand. "The others have the alpha," he said, and Sidian's heart shattered at the words. "Got him in the Jeep. You said you wanted to ride with him, alpha?"

"Only one of us can keep him under control, so yes, I will be." Dax settled his hand low on Sidian's stomach. "Are you going to go now, little omega?"

Sidian didn't want to. He wanted to kick and bite and thrash, but the promise of a bond kept him still. "Yes," he whispered, and Dax crooned in approval in his ear.

"Such a good little bitch when you need to be." He backed off, and Sidian allowed himself to take a breath. "Take him to the car and get him situated. I want one of you on either side of him."

He felt like a doll when Ford gripped him by the shoulder and hauled him off the bed, propelling him through the room and out into the cool night. Though he had never seen the vehicles that Pack Kincaid drove when they went anywhere as a group, the sleek black van and the massive Jeep stuck out as far too nice and expensive to be parked outside of this motel. Sidian whimpered but didn't put up a fight as the back door of the van slid open and he was forced inside.

He cast his eyes toward the Jeep. Was that where they had Roman?

And if they'd caught Roman, what hope was there that anything could be done?

Jett pulled himself into the van behind Sidian and dropped into the seat next to him, one broad hand settling on Sidian's thigh and squeezing. "You wouldn't be thinking about doing something stupid, would you be, pet?"

That nickname sickened him, but Sidian forced himself to stare straight ahead, his hands sweating as he stuffed them under his thighs. "No, alpha. I'm just exhausted."

"Did you enjoy our little distraction?" Jett's fingers dug into his leg, and Sidian forced himself to listen. He didn't know what they had done to Roman; if he was going to get out of this, he was going to rely on himself. "The house belonged to Dax's great-grandfather. We set it as our addresses because he got a little paranoid, but it looks like he was right to be. How'd *you* know where to look?"

Sidian would relay that to the Mambas, but shouldn't they have known? Had they ever seen the house? "I don't know what you're talking about."

"That's all right. You don't have to answer to me because I'm not the one in charge." Jett gripped Sidian by the jaw, teeth catching at his earlobe while Sidian tried not to react. "But Dax will get it out of you. You always did *scream* for him, after all."

Axel joined them in the back a moment later, slinging an arm around Sidian's shoulders, one hand dropping close to his tits, though at least Axel didn't grope him. Still, being pinned between two of the alphas who'd spent hours torturing him while he sobbed and bled and begged for it all to stop succeeded only in making Sidian feel sick, his stomach churning as he forced himself to stare at the windshield. He had to get over it. He had to get his shit together.

They had his alpha, and they had him. They also had his daughter and an omega he knew nothing about but presumed he was about to meet. What happened next was important; he had to pay attention. He had to keep his head screwed on straight. Panicking wouldn't save any of them.

Talon and Ford climbed into the driver's seat and passenger seat, which meant the other four were in the same vehicle with Roman. That was important; they saw him as a threat, and they were right to. What they'd done to stop him from being one wasn't something Sidian wanted to think about.

Axel sighed and jostled him. "Welcome back, omega. Hope the alpha lets us break you back in the way you deserve. Your pussy's too good to go to waste."

Jett laughed, letting his head fall back against the seat. "He smells even better than I remember."

Sidian would kill them both, save his daughter and save his mate. He had to.

If he had no one else to rely on but himself, then what else was there to do?

Chapter Thirty-Two

R oman slipped in and out of consciousness until the van slowed to a stop.

He stared at the ceiling of the vehicle, only aware of the hatch opening and rough hands seizing his ankles, dragging him out and into the frosty night air once again. Two alphas gripped him by the elbows and kept him on his feet while Dax climbed out, tablet tucked under his arm.

"Take this inside," he said, offering the device to one of his pack brothers, who took it without complaint. "And retrieve Axel. I want him to bring the dog to the backyard."

"Yes, alpha." The man dipped his head and darted out of sight, and then Roman was being forced around the back of what turned out to be a Jeep, his hazy vision picking up what looked like a massive house silhouetted against a dark sky, a handful of the windows glowing golden from within.

"Take it easy on him," someone yelled, and another one of those hyena laughs split the air. "The alpha thinks we might keep him after all. Would be such a shame to ruin that body before any of us have time to break him from the inside out."

The house that belonged to Pack Kincaid was far more elaborate than the first one they'd visited, and Roman made a mental note of it as he was dragged past it and into what looked like a lush backyard of wild grasses and flowers. The pair who restrained him carried him all the way to the treeline where they dropped him in a heap, though stood guard over him. Although he was muzzled and bound, they still knew better than to leave him unoccupied.

Dax joined them a moment later with three more alphas trailing behind him. Roman knew Axel would be missing, but it seemed like Jett was missing as well. Not a good sign.

"Axel will be just a moment," Dax said, his tone apologetic. "The dog gives him some trouble. When you see her, I'm sure you'll understand why."

So they were bringing some kind of trained attack dog into the yard? Roman remained silent. He didn't know what they were plotting, but he already knew to be wary.

And then Axel Kincaid stepped from the shadows, dragging a chain leash behind him with each step.

The dog was not a dog. The *dog* was a young female alpha who snarled and growled with every forced step she took, her hands wrapped tight around the steel links as she tried in vain to dig her heels into the dirt. A leather collar was wrapped snug around her throat, fastened tight enough that Roman wondered how she could even breathe around it. She wore what looked like a tattered dress that was stained so badly he didn't know what its original color was, her bare skin streaked with dirt and grime. Her long hair was matted and tangled, but it was her bright crimson eyes that drew his attention. So bright they almost burned like twin flames in the darkness.

The Kincaids' dog was a feral alpha. The pine note of her scent was sick with rot, while the softer vanilla tone was rancid. Roman had never smelled an alpha scent like it before.

Dax sighed as Axel wrestled the girl to the ground, gripping her by a handful of her dirty hair and kicking her knees out from under her when she tried to stand. "Puppy. *Down.*"

Alpha commands did not always work from one alpha to another, but the woman settled on her knees even as her slender body vibrated with fury. Her teeth seemed almost permanently bared, a low rattling snarl filling the air as her eyes darted from alpha to alpha.

Then they landed on Roman, and she stilled, a flicker of human confusion splitting her gaze before pure animal fury reclaimed her, her growling getting louder by the second.

Dax turned his attention to Roman with a polite smile. "What do you think of her?"

Roman didn't have an answer for him. Feral alphas were few; most did not survive going feral the first time and never came back to their human senses. Roman himself had slipped only once, pure feral bloodlust staining everything around him, but Sidian had brought him back from the brink. He doubted this alpha had anyone who could do that for her.

Dax stretched out a hand, patting the top of her head, though she refused to take her eyes off of Roman as she squirmed in place. "Puppy has been a bit of a work in progress, you see. My brother worked very hard to tame her... Some might say *too hard,* for that matter. We've struggled to get her to obey, but she has one talent, and that's taking out my trash for me."

Puppy tugged on the leash, her hands still clinging to her collar as she scratched at her own neck.

"You are a pretty specimen, I'll give you that," Dax continued on, and Roman just stared at him. "But you are dangerous, very much so, and I don't know if we can trust you. You care *so much* for our little breeder that it makes you stupid, and I can't have stupid men in my pack."

Roman remained silent, his eyes fixed on the woman. *Puppy.* It was taking his drug-addled mind too long to connect the dots, but Puppy was Kitten's sister. He *knew* her.

"This will be an excellent litmus test to see if you're worthy of keeping," Dax continued, snapping his fingers in front of Puppy's face until her gaze jerked to his. "We'll give you a head start, Kane. I would suggest running as far as you can. She's quite vicious once she catches up with you."

Axel grunted as she started fighting against his hold again. "Get him up and let him go. I can't hold on to this bitch forever, and it's been way too long since the last time we let her out to play. She might not come back this time."

Dax snorted. "She'll come back. She always does. Nash, get him up."

Nash hauled Roman to his feet, steadying him against the trunk of the tree at his back while Roman tried to shake himself the rest of the way to awareness. Being caught in the middle of the woods by a feral alpha would not end well for him, and he knew that better than most. He *knew* what they were capable of, what he had once been capable of, and if he didn't focus, Puppy would catch him. She'd kill him. She wouldn't even remember doing it once it was done.

"There are no paths out here, so best of luck." Nash shot Roman an acidic smile before shoving him toward the trees, and Roman forced himself to move, his vision adjusting to the darkness and his pace picking up as he tried to account for every stone, every stick, every divot in the dirt.

"Five minutes, Kane," Dax called out. "I hope you don't disappoint your little omega."

As soon as he was out of sight of the treeline, Roman strained against the zip ties binding his wrists until he felt the pieces of plastic snap one by one. They dug into his skin, and he felt it break in places, blood slicking his fingers, but the pain was nothing. Pain meant nothing to him.

They had Sidian. The bastards had Sidian. Roman couldn't afford to die out in the woods.

He would make it back to the Kincaids, and he would kill every single one of them.

As soon as his hands were free, he took off into the woods, always aware of the clock ticking down. He breathed out the seconds as he fled into the darkness, trying to figure out what to do about Puppy. Feral alphas were as dangerous as they were fragile, hopped up on adrenaline that might send them into heart failure at any moment. How long had they had her? Since she went missing?

He could kill her, he knew that, but she didn't deserve to die just because of them.

Something crashed through the underbrush in the distance, a sharp howl cutting through the air and sending a flock of birds sailing up into the dark sky, wings fluttering.

His five minutes were up. Roman swore and started sprinting, trying not to run faster than his eyes could make out the surrounding details. A snapped ankle would get him killed.

He didn't know the woods as well as he wished he did; everything looked the same to him, and all he could do was aim straight forward as he listened to the sounds that spilled through the air behind him. Puppy was trailing him, but he couldn't tell how fast or how well she knew the terrain. Better than he did, he presumed, but was her feral mind keeping track of the details for her, or did she just break through everything in her path to get to her targets?

Was there anything left of her in there, or was she nothing more than a beast?

They have Kitten's sister. The Mambas have the wrong address. There has to be a leak. There was nothing Roman could do about it, but just the same, he made himself remember the details. *They have Sidian. They have his daughter. They have another omega. There are eight of them.*

And they had Puppy, someone that Roman didn't have a plan for at all.

He could try to force the muzzle onto her, but he was certain it was too big for her face, and he might lose a couple of fingers in the meantime. There had to be a way to stop her without hurting her, a way to get her under control if only so he could try to see if *she* was still there. If she wasn't, then he would kill her, but it was a last resort. If he could avoid it, he would.

The forest fell silent, and Roman glanced over his shoulder, his steps slowing as he tried to make sense of the lack of sound. Not even the frantic footsteps or snapping branches filled the air.

Had she stopped running? Why would she have stopped running?

She might be scenting the air, he thought, letting his back rest up against a trunk as he sucked in a lungful of air. It was cold out, but the exertion had him sweating as he dragged his forearm across his face above the muzzle. *Might be looking for me, and my scent isn't natural enough to fade into the forest like hers is. But I need to know where she is. I need to keep track of her.*

If she got the jump on him, he wasn't sure they would both survive it.

She was smaller than he was. He was stronger than she was. But she might not be *herself* anymore.

His eyes scanned the shadows as he waited for the sound of her approach, knowing she had to be somewhere out there in the darkness. Maybe she needed to take a break. Even feral, she was still human, and she had limits on her body whether or not she liked it. Or maybe the exertion on her heart had caught up to her, and on the way back to the house, he would find her body.

He didn't want that. He didn't want to take Kitten her sister's corpse, on top of confirming for the Mambas that they had problems that would be difficult to fix. If they had someone leaking information *and* giving them false information, then they needed to clean house.

Roman didn't know where he was. If he walked straight back, he would reach the house, but he needed a plan before he did *that*, too. Would Pack Kincaid wait, or would they go back inside for the night? It would be better if they were inside. He could case the house from the outside, and then—

And then what? He didn't know. Pack Kincaid had eight alphas at their disposal who were not stronger than him, not better fighters than him, unless they were and their entire profiles could be discarded. Maybe it would be best to do that considering the fact that some of the information was wrong; all of it might be useless to him. So, start from the ground up. They were strong, but they had nothing to fight for, and Roman would do anything to save Sidian and Amethyst. Goddess, *Amethyst.*

Sidian had a daughter, and Roman still didn't know how to process that information.

No, it was unimportant. She needed to be rescued, as did Pack Kincaid's omega in the likeliest scenario. He could process who she was and why she was important later.

Get back to the house. Infiltrate. Kill them. It didn't matter how or what it took; it didn't even matter if Roman died. Sidian would be fine without him. As long as he had his daughter, as long as the two of them were reunited, *that* was all Sidian needed. Roman would uphold his promise to ensure his mate would be safe even if it cost him everything. There was no price too high to pay.

But first, he needed to figure out where the fuck Puppy was.

A twig snapped to his right, and Roman's head whipped to the side just in time to catch the pair of luminous crimson eyes that watched him from mere feet away.

Puppy had gotten the jump on him after all.

With a delighted, snarling cry, she pounced, and Roman's arms swung up to catch her.

Chapter Thirty-Three

Jett gripped Sidian by the nape of the neck and dragged him into the house like a misbehaving dog.

In another lifetime, he would have liked to live in a house as nice as Pack Kincaid's. Lavish, expensive furniture decorated every room, with all the color palettes matching in deep, dark colors. It was too minimalist—not enough pillows or blankets for an omega's comfort—but Sidian knew the pack didn't care about omegas. All they cared about was exerting their power and dominance over those they considered being weak and inferior, and in that regard, Sidian had been one of their favorite targets.

Jett dragged him upstairs with no regard for his feet slipping and sliding on the hardwood steps, throwing him down on the landing like he was trash. Before Sidian could get his hands and knees beneath him, the alpha's foot came to rest in the small of his back, the slightest exertion of pressure more than enough to keep Sidian still. *My baby, my baby, please don't hurt my baby.*

"Dax always had a soft spot for you," Jett said, his voice low and thoughtful, "though I don't get it. Pussy is pussy. But I gotta say, your thinking you're tough enough to fight back gets me hard."

Sidian bit down on his tongue to keep himself quiet. *Do not rise to the bait. Never rise to the bait.*

"Maybe if your dog survives ours, we'll let him watch us fuck you." Jett chuckled, the sound dark, heavy in his throat. "Teach him how to give you what you need."

Sidian was saved from having to speak by the sound of a door creaking down the hallway, his eyes rising off the floor to see what was going on. The upstairs was dark save for a few dim nightlights, but the figure of the omega who stepped out of what was likely the master bedroom was easy to make out, especially since Sidian knew to expect him here.

"Jett?" Lilac Kincaid's voice was soft, uncertain. "What's—What are you doing? Who is that? Is that the omega from the center?"

Lilac knew who he was. Sidian didn't know if that was good or bad.

Jett grunted. "Dax wants him washed up. Get him changed into something pretty, too."

"Yes, alpha." Lilac scurried forward like a small animal frightened of being struck, and Jett shifted his foot away from Sidian's back just in time for Lilac to take his hands. "Come along now. The master bathroom is through the bedroom. I'll find you something to wear."

Behind them, Jett's heavy footsteps started downstairs. "Show him what it means to be a good bitch."

Lilac helped Sidian to his feet and wrapped an arm around his shoulders, hustling him down the hallway to the bedroom and pushing the door shut behind them. The bedroom itself was dark, the only light spilling from the dim screen of a tablet sitting on the bed and a couple of ambient lights set into the ceiling. It was a comfort, though, because it smelled of omega.

"I'm so sorry." The arm around Sidian's shoulders squeezed as he was turned, nudged toward a closed door. "I didn't think they could find you."

Sidian didn't know what to say about that. "Where's my daughter? Do you have Amey?"

"Amey?" Lilac cocked his head as he flicked on the bathroom light, and Sidian hissed at the harsh white lighting. "Oh. That's a nickname for Amethyst, isn't it?"

Sidian's heart pounded as he nodded, his nails biting into his palms as his hands flexed, curling into fists, nerves making him feel sick. The bathroom had pot-pourri in it, and the sickly sweet scent made him dizzy; he wanted to burrow into the darkness of the bedroom and find somewhere to hide.

Lilac's face softened. "Come on. Let's get you cleaned up, and then you can go see her, I think."

The sweet relief that poured through Sidian's veins threatened to bring him to his knees, but he allowed himself to be led to a glass shower stall in the corner on shaky legs. Lilac left him to wash himself, and though he loathed the thought of undressing anywhere in the house, he didn't know what else to do. So he focused on scrubbing himself clean as fast as possible, opting for the scentless soap because he didn't want to remove a single trace of Roman's scent from his skin.

He might lose him forever. Yet again, Sidian had put Roman in harm's way because of his own selfishness, and if he couldn't save him, he'd carry him for as long as he could.

Lilac had left clothes on the sink counter without Sidian noticing him coming and going, which made the hairs on the nape of his neck prickle. The sight of the black satin nightie made his gorge rise, and he set it back on the sink, pressing his hands over his face and taking a deep breath. His father had tried to force him into feminine clothing ever since he had come out. It was part of the reason Sidian lost control.

Get through it, he told himself, sucking in a harsh breath through his teeth. He made himself look at his reflection, at the manic light behind his eyes. *It's just a piece of clothing. It doesn't matter. After tonight, you're never going to wear it again.*

Because after tonight, either the Kincaids would be dead, or Sidian would be. He couldn't survive in this house; he would go down with a fight, or he would win. It was as simple as that.

Lilac waited for him on the edge of the mattress, fiddling with the cover on the tablet as he rose on his own weak legs. He looked much as he did in the photograph Sidian had seen, though his hair was longer and just a touch messier. His eyes were almost hollowed out, and he was thinner than an omega should have been, his complexion too sallow. While Sidian had suffered at his pack's hands during his heats, Lilac bore their abuse daily, and it showed in him. For just a moment, Sidian had hoped this was going to go the way he needed it to go.

"It wasn't so bad, was it?" Lilac offered him a trembling smile. "Would you like to see her now?"

"Can I?" What he wanted to ask was if the pack would be angry at Lilac for allowing it, but Sidian didn't want to ask it. He was afraid that if he did, Lilac would realize that the offer might be dangerous and rescind it. Sidian *had* to see Amey. If she was in the house, he *had* to.

"I don't see why not." Lilac took him by the hand, and Sidian let him.

The hallway was still dark, and the lack of voices in the house set Sidian on edge. Were all the alphas outside? He could make a run for it, but without knowing where he was or where to go, all he would do was get lost and die of exposure. It was just like being back in the center except, at the very least, he could see his daughter again.

Lilac pushed open a door about halfway down the hallway, revealing soft pastel walls and racks of toys and children's books, a dresser and a changing table pushed up against the wall. At the very least, it looked like someone had done the bare minimum for Amethyst, and Sidian was grateful for that. She could have died. She could have died out there, and he never would have known.

The crib was smooth white wood, and the sheet was a soft, floral pattern. An infant slept on top of it in a cute sleep set that was a pale pastel purple, one tiny hand resting on her chest and the other half-curled into a fist next to her cheek. Her dark hair was thick and lush already, the same glossy black as Sidian's own, her cheeks chubby and her lips parted just enough that he could hear her tiny inhales and exhales. Amethyst was relaxed in her crib, fast asleep and dreaming sweet dreams, and the sight of her brought tears to Sidian's eyes as a tiny whimper broke from his lips.

"She's yours, isn't she?" Lilac murmured, and Sidian nodded as he reached down to touch her small hand, his chest aching when her fingers curled around one of his. "They brought her to me and told me to take care of her. I didn't know where she came from."

Sidian swallowed. "She was born at a breeding center."

She shouldn't have been. She should have been in a normal omega clinic, surrounded by soft ambient lighting and only people who would love her and care for her. She should have been left in his arms so that he could hold her and bond with her, so that he could nurse her and kiss her and sing her to sleep. Instead, she'd been taken so far away. All the way across the country. She was so *small*.

"I'm sorry," Lilac said. "I did the best I could. She's healthy, and she's so sweet."

"I wanted her back more than anything." Sidian brushed this thumb over her tiny knuckles. "I wanted her so much I got myself caught. They have my fucking alpha."

Lilac bit the corner of his mouth. "He's probably out in the woods with Puppy."

"What?" Sidian's head jerked up. *Puppy?* But that was Kitten's missing sister. So the Kincaids had her after all, which meant the leak in the Mambas was far worse than they likely already imagined. "What's going to happen to him? Is he going to be okay?"

"I don't know." Lilac shook his head as Amey shifted in her sleep, letting out a tiny coo. "Puppy's feral most of the time. Sometimes I'd sneak out to check on her, but I don't think she's been herself for a long time. She's only an alpha, but other alphas rile her up."

Feral. Sidian could have laughed. "How do we get out of here, Lilac?"

"I don't know," Lilac responded. "If I had known how, I would have left with your baby."

That wasn't good enough; they had to get out. If it were possible to leave without Pack Kincaid catching up, then Sidian would, but he knew better. So if escape was impossible, then what he needed to do was anything it took to make it happen.

"Well, well, well," Dax purred from behind them, "I see we're having a family reunion."

Sidian's heart leaped into his throat as he looked over his shoulder, not sure what to say or what to do. He watched as Dax's eyes skimmed him up and down, a familiar hunger flickering through his gaze for just a moment before he collected himself. It showed up in his scent, though, a salty tang that made Sidian flinch. There had never been an alpha he wanted less than he wanted Dax, and there would be no way to hide that no matter what he tried.

Lilac tried to smile at him. "Hi, alpha. He said he wanted to see the baby. Is it all right?"

"I didn't give you the express command *not* to let him see her, I suppose." Dax sauntered into the room, right up to both of them. "How nice to have both of my bitches in the same room together."

An arm slid around Sidian's waist and pulled him back, and he shuddered as Dax's hand smoothed over the nightie to settle on his stomach. The knowledge that Dax *knew,* that there was no hiding the pregnancy from him, was terrifying. He knew Sidian's body too well, and if he got his teeth into Sidian's neck, there would never be a way to hide from him ever again.

"You see, Lilac," Dax said conversationally, "Sidian's made for breeding. You'll help raise every child he births, and that will be your role alongside satisfying us during our ruts."

Lilac dipped his head, the picture of submission. "Yes, alpha."

"And that seems to be where the real trouble lies, doesn't it?" Dax tipped his head back, his expression thoughtful before he wrapped a hand around Lilac's neck. "Come. We'll put on a demonstration. Sidian is very disobedient. You'll assist me in teaching him what it means to be a good, submissive bitch."

Sidian's mouth dried when Lilac only nodded, resignation settling on his features as they were led out of the room, Dax pushing both of them out into the hallway before closing the door. Outside, a sudden rumble of thunder made Sidian jump, his eyes darting toward the wall that faced the forest.

Roman...

"Oh, Puppy loves thunderstorms," Dax mused before his hand closed around Lilac's throat once again. "Let's go to bed, omegas. I've been expecting this night for a long time."

Sidian didn't know where the other alphas were, but as he followed obediently behind Dax, he realized his opening was right in front of him.

He could only hope that Roman was holding his own.

Chapter Thirty-Four

Sharp teeth dug into Roman's bicep as he squashed Puppy against his chest, the two of them rolling through the leaf litter until his back slammed into the wide trunk of another tree.

The impact pushed the air from his lungs, but he refused to weaken his hold on her, crushing her into his chest as he rolled on top of her. Her teeth dug deeper into his skin as she all but screamed against him, kicking her legs as hard as she could in an effort to get away. Her hands scrabbled at his sides, nails digging into his shirt and trying to slice through the flesh beneath. The noises that spilled from her throat were purely animal, completely alien to him. She didn't sound like a human.

She reeled back to slam her forehead into his chin, and his vision shone with stars before she darted forward to try to take a bite out of his throat that forced him to dodge, her teeth cutting into his shoulder.

Her scent was rot and ruin and sickness, and he wanted to help her, wanted to get her back to herself. The pain was nothing; her sharp little canines hurt, but Roman had been hurt worse before. By Sidian's hands, Sidian's blades, Sidian being ripped from his life, Sidian saying he *hated* him—

He doesn't have to love me, Roman thought, getting a hand in Puppy's hair so he could drag her off of him. *I love him. I've always loved him. That's what matters most to me.*

She let out an indignant wail as Roman pinned her head to the earth, her mouth open against the grass as she hissed and snarled and drooled, blood smeared across her teeth. Her wild eyes met his, her pupils glossy and black, irises flaring crimson against her sickly white skin.

What had they done to her? Why do this to a person? What was it about Pack Kincaid that made them turn others into shells of their former selves? What kind of fucking monsters had their parents raised? What kind of demons were they, protected by a system designed to benefit them?

She arched her back off of the ground, sheer power overwhelming him slightly despite her small stature. She wiggled a leg between them and kicked him in the chest, shoving him off of her as she scrabbled to her feet. Her dress had torn up the side all the way to her hip, and a nasty cut oozed blood along her thigh. As he watched, she wiped at her messy face, but she never took her eyes off of him. Instead, she coiled herself, every lean muscle in her body preparing to launch her at him again. He knew her, had met her in the past, but she didn't remember him.

There was nothing behind those eyes. She wasn't there anymore.

He was going to have to kill her.

No, he thought, taking a step back, hands raised, ready to defend himself as need be. *Avoid it at all costs. There has to be a way to reach her.*

"You have an advantage, Kane. As a prime, you'll have an edge on them that you do not want to waste."

Puppy sprinted forward so quickly that she almost blurred around the edges, letting out a shriek that made Roman think of a mountain lion as she charged him. She threw her shoulder into his midsection but only succeeded in knocking him back, her nails digging into his back as she tried to force him down.

Fury intermingled with her scent, a righteous anger as Roman peeled her off of him, uncaring of the damage she did to his back. A roll of thunder made both of them twitch, and she took advantage, twisting her head to bite him on the forearm while one bare foot slammed into his thigh.

He'd never done it before. At the Pit, Jagger had told him precisely how it was performed and demonstrated it on the others, but Roman had been told not to do it, and so he never had. The urge to command an omega had never risen, and he didn't need to command alphas.

But he needed to this time. Just this once. *"Puppy, stop."*

He felt the dominance intermingle with his words, his voice deepening into something that was distinctly unfamiliar to his ears. Puppy jerked to a halt, her small body still vibrating with far too much energy, her teeth lodged in his skin, but her eyes swiveled toward him as something flashed behind her gaze. She let out a disgruntled noise but bit him no deeper, her panting harsh and hot against his torn skin. When he gripped her by the back of the neck and squeezed, her mouth opened and she coughed, spluttering, smacking at her face with her still-shaking hands.

She was all adrenaline, all frenetic energy bound into a body too small for it. He shifted so he could press his thumb under her jaw and felt the frantic thrum of her pulse, desperate and quick as the wingbeats of a hummingbird. She growled up at him and tried to twist out of his hold, but all he had to do was exhale a short, harsh hiss and she fell still once again, though she never stopped baring her teeth.

"Easy," he whispered, and her eyes narrowed as if she didn't trust him. Her hands gripped him firmly even as he started to pull her back down toward the earth, never easing his grip for a moment. "We're going to sit down. *Sit.* I know you don't want to, but you don't have a choice."

The command brought her down slowly; he felt her go dead weight but refused to let her fall as he lowered her to the earth, kneeling in front of her.

A few fat raindrops smacked him on the cheeks, and then the heavens above opened up.

Puppy shivered as the downpour soaked both of them within moments, blinking furiously up at him as Roman settled himself cross-legged on the ground. He didn't have time for what he was doing, but he had to make time, dragging her into his lap like an ill-behaved child and wrapping his arms tight around her, keeping her bundled up against his chest. She was too hot, almost feverish in her feral state.

The comedown had been hell. He remembered that part, shaking apart in the back of the cop car.

"Easy," he whispered again when she hissed at him, gripping the front of his shirt in one hand. "Easy, Puppy, it's just me. I know it's been a while, but I know you remember who I am."

Her hand stilled as her head tilted, her brows furrowing as her jaw finally started to relax, her face smoothing into an expression of pure confusion.

Roman was not a dominant alpha. He was not a forceful person. He might have been for the right person, if they had ever come along, but that wasn't who he was at heart. That was who *Sidian* was, who he had always been, and the two of them clicked because of that. Made for each other.

He exhaled and brushed Puppy's hair back out of her face, trying to be as gentle with her as possible. She was, if he remembered correctly, just a few years older than he was. In her mid-twenties and having her life ripped away from her by the same monsters who had hurt his mate. Having had her days chipped away one at a time in a haze of animal instinct that slowly ate away at her humanity, she had been strong, too. She had to be in there. She had to be in there, because he didn't know what to do if she wasn't.

"It's okay," he tried to reassure her, and her eyes narrowed further, a fury of mistrust tangling in her bloody gaze. "I know it hurts, I know you're confused and angry with me, but it's okay. Just shh. Just calm down for a second, just breathe. You're so hot. Doesn't the rain feel nice?"

He tilted his head back, aware of just how dangerous a move it was to do so, and let his eyes flutter shut as he basked in the cool rain that showered his skin. It would have been pleasant if the night was warmer, but he could suck it up. He could deal with it.

When he opened his eyes, he saw Puppy looking up at the sky herself, her lips pursed. Slowly, she closed her eyes, and a bit of the dirt was slowly washed from her pallid skin.

She looked so sick. She probably needed to see a doctor, but Roman didn't have one on hand.

All he had was himself, and for now, that would have to be enough.

With a careful touch, Roman brushed some of her damp hair back from her face, using his thumb to rub some of the dirt off of her cheeks. She blinked at him as he did so, her eyelashes wet with water, her face twisting again. Puppy didn't understand what he was doing or why, but she wasn't reading it as something inherently dangerous, and that was a start.

"Puppy?" Roman tried again, and when she just stared at him, he sighed. What the fuck was he even doing out there? His mate needed him. If he couldn't bring Puppy back, he didn't know what chance he stood of saving Sidian. "I don't know what to do. I don't know how to help you."

She simply stared at him, blinking raindrops out of her eyes.

He risked it, then. He risked shifting closer to her, and though he felt her tense up in his arms, he rested his forehead against hers and closed his eyes, trying to keep himself calm.

An alpha's rumble was meant to soothe an omega or a child in need of care, and rarely did it work for anyone else. It certainly didn't work on other alphas, and nothing worked on betas, but Roman had little left to try. He could have commanded her out of her feral state to the best of his ability, but care was what he was good at. Not dominance. Not bossing people around. Not forcing them into subservience.

If that didn't work, he had no other ideas. No other options. She would stay like that, and he would have to kill her to get back to his mate.

Delicate hands settled on his shoulders a moment before a quiet rumble joined his own.

Puppy's rumble was choppy, broken up in her chest like she didn't know how to make the noise anymore, but it *was* an alpha rumble just the same. She drew closer to him of her own accord, then wrapped her arms around his shoulders and pressed her cheek against his, smoothing her hands down his back. Roman wasn't used to affection from another alpha, but he returned it, giving her a gentle squeeze as the rain continued to drench both of them and thunder rumbled overhead. When he felt her hands wander up to the back of his head, he thought nothing of it until the straps of the muzzle gave free, and he tilted his head to shake it off, letting it thud into the grass below.

She leaned back first, and though her movements were clumsy and uncertain, she smoothed her own wet hair back out of her face, then tugged the tangles in front of herself and stared at them. Her eyes were still red, but they lacked that almost preternatural glow. Instead, she just looked sad.

"Are you back?" Roman asked her, relieved when she merely nodded her head, pressing her hands to her face with a low, hollow sound. "Hey, it's all right. It was bad, but you survived it. You're back now. Deep breaths. It's okay. It's going to be okay now."

She peeked at him through her fingers as if to ask, *Do you promise?*

"I promise." He gently took her by the wrists. "Come on. We have to get up."

Despite her speed and fluid grace, Puppy stood haltingly like a baby deer trying to remember how to walk on its own. She glanced around the forest and loosed a small whine, then wrapped her arms around herself. How much of the place did she remember? Roman wasn't sure, and given she didn't seem like she wanted to talk, he didn't think he would get an answer if he asked.

They could and would talk about it later if she wanted. For now, though... "Puppy, I need your help. Dax Kincaid has my mate. I need to save him, the other omega, and his daughter."

She glanced at him, her brows furrowed as if she didn't understand.

Patience. He had to have patience. She'd just come out of Goddess knew how long of a feral state, so he could be patient with her. "I need to kill them. First, I need to get into the house. Can you help me?"

Her face smoothed out then, expression solemn. And she gave him a single curt nod.

The speed with which she whipped off into the trees startled him, but Roman tore after her without a second thought. He hoped the storm would disguise their arrival back at the house for as long as possible, that the Kincaids would have no idea they were coming as thunder rumbled and lightning flashed.

Two against eight. Two once-feral alphas against eight id-iots. He liked those odds.

Chapter Thirty-Five

"Since we're going to teach you how to behave like a proper omega once and for all, I believe we can start with what should be the simplest of lessons, and that is acts of service." Dax pointed toward the bed, and Lilac went obediently, those cold eyes settling on Sidian where he stood just past the doorway. "Help me undress. You never were very good at it back at the center."

Sidian swallowed, his hands shaking. "Sure. I can do that."

It took far too much effort to close the narrow space between them, his fingers locating the smooth white buttons on Dax's shirt as he slid each of them from their respective holes. Ripping off Roman's clothes had been wild and exciting, and Sidian had ached to see every inch of olive skin laid bare, but the thought of so much as brushing Dax's pale flesh left Sidian shuddering in distaste. The longer he took, however, the longer it took for Dax to touch Lilac.

Maybe it was stupid to care so much about an omega he didn't know, but Sidian knew one thing: he saw himself when he looked into Lilac's eyes. There had been no one there to help him when he was alone with Pack Kincaid, but if he could spare someone else even a moment of that anguish, he would do it no matter how it made him feel.

Dax sighed. "This is nice, isn't it? Acting civilized."

What a remark to come from *him*. "I was in heat when you came to see me."

He chuckled and wrapped his hands around Sidian's wrists, stilling his movements as Dax leaned in close enough that his warm breath curled against Sidian's cheek. "But you looked so lovely in heat. Sweet, desperate little bitch. It's a shame it'll be such a long time until I can have you like that again, but in order to join you to our pack, I have one special surprise in mind."

What the fuck was he talking about? "I don't know what you mean."

"That's for me to worry about. You just focus your pretty little head on the task at hand." Dax shrugged his shirt off, and when Sidian tried to step back, he was jerked forward, his hands laid over Dax's belt. "Go ahead, omega. You're intimately familiar with this part, aren't you?"

He was. The memory threatened to leave him sick and shaking, but Sidian made himself unbuckle the belt as the warmth drained from his fingertips. A numbness threatened to settle over him to blanket him from the rest of the situation, taking his mind somewhere where he wouldn't have to acknowledge the situation he was in. Where he wouldn't have to worry so much that Dax was moments away from raping someone just to teach Sidian a lesson.

"There you go," Dax cooed. "See? Not so hopeless after all. How quaint."

The heat that rolled off of the flesh between his legs made Sidian's stomach roil, his guts churning at how close he was to something that had hurt him. "If you say so."

Dax's pants dropped around his ankles, and he stepped out of them in one fluid motion, leaving him in just a pair of boxers. "Now take my clothing to the laundry basket in the corner of the room. You and Lilac can handle the washing tomorrow. I'm sure he'll be amenable to showing you how the machine works since I doubt you've ever had to do such a thing for yourself."

Of course, he had. Who the fuck else was supposed to do laundry back home? "I know how to wash clothes. I'm not fucking stupid."

"I never said you were." But Dax smiled as if they were sharing a private joke.

Sidian hated him. He'd hated Dax from the moment he realized what the alpha intended to do to him, but he hated him more for every assumption he'd made, every conclusion he'd drawn. Dax did not even see him as a person; who the fuck was he to decide what Sidian was and was not capable of? Who was he to think he knew anything about Sidian at all?

He chuckled as he stepped forward, hand rising to cup Sidian's jaw, forcing their eyes to meet. "Your scent is so interesting when you're angry, little pet," he murmured, voice husky with lust; Sidian knew that tone. He'd heard it before. "I always enjoyed seeing you get angry."

"Fuck you," Sidian hissed. He couldn't help himself.

"Such a naughty little creature. Never able to hold that tongue of yours, hmm? But I know how many uses it has." Dax squeezed his jaw tighter, drawing him closer. "I knew you would be bad if you got a chance. That's why I had to have the tracker implanted the day Amethyst was born. The moment you lost consciousness, I knew what had to be done."

Wait... What? What the fuck did he just say?

Dax laughed as Sidian stared at him, his brain refusing to process the words the alpha had just spoken. What tracker? What was he talking about? No, Sidian would have *known* if something like that had been done to him. The thought that Dax had violated his body in ways he didn't even know about made him sick. He had to get out of there. He had to kill the son of a bitch.

"What are you talking about?" he demanded, though his voice came out whisper-soft.

"When the breeding center told me you were a prime omega, I knew we had something special on our hands, and I didn't want to see anything bad happen to you. I didn't want someone to claim what belonged to us." Dax thumbed over Sidian's lower lip, his gaze distant as if trying to figure out *what* he wanted Sidian to do with his mouth. "Did you think I would ever let you go? I mean, if you'd been a regular omega, I might have. I wasn't close to my father, so, contrary to popular belief, I felt nothing when your stupid little alpha dog killed him."

"The alpha who tried to buy me was your father?" Sidian asked, his heart beating faster.

"Sterling Kincaid was his name. A businessman by trade. I forget what he owns in Washington. That's my brother's area, not mine." Dax trailed the backs of his knuckles along Sidian's throat, and Sidian shuddered at the touch. "My entire pack was more than happy to rape you when I told them what happened, though. And then you were *far* too precious to let go of."

Sidian didn't know what to say. What to think. His brain fuzzed over, static crackling between his ears so much so that he almost didn't feel it when Dax turned him around and gave him a light swat on the ass, pushing him toward the laundry basket in the corner as he turned his attention to Lilac.

Sidian almost wanted to laugh. The son of the man Roman had killed... It explained so much. *Too* much. His skin itched as he tried to figure out where the tracker could have been placed, his guts churning as tears stung his eyes. Dax had always known where he was. He had never escaped.

All that shared time with Roman, and they had been *watching* in their sick little way.

No wonder they hadn't acted sooner. Dax had watched whatever device he used for the tracker and saw that Sidian was making his way across the country right to Dax's doorstep. When Sidian had been screaming himself to pieces on the floor of that dilapidated house, Dax laughed. There had never been a moment in which Sidian had any freedom whatsoever.

It would only come when Dax was dead. Sidian understood it in its totality now.

There was wanting him dead because he could not come back from the grave; there was needing him dead for the security it would provide, but none of that compared to the simple truth: Dax would never stop, and Sidian had proof now. If he didn't kill the alpha who had tormented him for years, then he could never raise his children. Never live happily alongside his mate.

He balled up the fabric in his hands, and something hard pressed against his palm.

He threw a quick glance over his shoulder to see Dax nudging Lilac up toward the pillows, his attention focused on the other omega. It gave Sidian just enough time to realize he was feeling something inside the pocket of Dax's pants, sliding the piece of metal out.

It was a pair of brass knuckles with just a little blood flecked on the steel.

Sidian stared at them for a moment before curling his hand tight around them, gripping them as he dumped the clothes in the hamper. Before Dax could look up, he slipped the weapon under the nightie and into the side of the embarrassing panties he'd been given to wear, the tight satin pinning the metal in place against Sidian's hip. It bit in just enough to feel secure.

Dax glanced up just as Sidian returned to the mattress, his eyes looking him up and down as he seemed to consider something. "Maybe this would be a nicer affair in the nest. What do you think, Lilac?"

"No." Lilac said it so quickly that it caught Sidian's attention, his brow furrowing as his eyes flicked toward what he assumed was the nest in the corner of the room. What was wrong with it that Lilac didn't want to go in there? "No, alpha, please, the bed is more than comfortable enough—"

But Dax rose to his feet, taking Sidian by the wrist and dragging him around the bed to lead him toward the double doors on the far side of the room. "Come here. It'll be *your* nest soon, too."

"What is it?" Sidian glanced back at Lilac, who only stared at him with wide, horrified eyes as he pressed his back into the pillows. "What's wrong? What did you do?"

"I wanted to decorate it nice and special for our pack omega while he was settling in, and I thought, you know, he should get to know you as best he can." Dax pushed the doors open and reached inside to flick on a light that was far too blinding for an omega's nest. "Come here. Tell me what you think."

He didn't give Sidian a chance before shoving him into the room.

An omega's nest was supposed to be a dark space tucked away from the world, small and secure, soft and comforting. Having such harsh light defeated the purpose of it all together, and Sidian blinked until his eyes adjusted to the light. The nest itself was far too neat; Lilac wasn't nesting. Big surprise.

Sidian glanced around the room, not sure what he was looking for until his eyes settled on the wall that faced the nest. Settled on the myriad photographs pinned to the pale plaster.

"No," he said, the word a dying gasp on his lips.

Dax's chest pressed up against his back. "Oh, yes, Obsidian. What do you think?"

He didn't remember most of his heats beyond the pain and the blood, and evidently, Sidian didn't remember cameras being shoved in his face. His mind refused to let him process a single photo, but the longer he stared at them, the more they took shape and form. Photos of his naked body in every position possible. Photos of the blood and semen smeared into his skin, the bruises that marred his flesh. Photos of his tear-stained face, his pupils shot wide from his heat, his lips bruised from sharp kisses. And far, far too many close-ups of every intimate part of him that was never meant for Pack Kincaid.

The horror of it washed over him, and he felt lightheaded. He knew they were evil, knew they had no limits in what they would do to him beyond what the center put in place, but it was too much. The grotesque array of images was too fucking much.

A sharp prick on his arm made him whine, hugging it close to his chest. "What did you do that for?"

"Just a little something to make sure you're in the mood. A true heat would cause you to miscarry, and while I'm certain I can breed your fertile womb with ease, I wouldn't want to lose a potential alpha son just the same. That injection will send you into a pseudo-heat, and you'll look just as lovely as you do in these photographs." Dax's hand found his stomach once again, pressing down enough to feel the shape of Sidian's womb, taut with the growth of his child as he tossed what looked like a slender syringe into the center of Lilac's nest. "I wonder what your children will think of you when they're old enough to see their mother for what he is, hmm?"

The reminder of his children was all Sidian needed to act.

He ripped himself away from Dax's touch, a snarl twisting his lips as he stared up at the alpha who had ruined so much of his life. The rage that washed over him was familiar, an old friend that he knew how to work with. Fear and pain and grief did nothing for him, but rage was something Sidian knew far too well. And no one had ever taken it from him.

The flicker of amusement in Dax's eyes only fanned the flames higher. "What are you going to do, little bitch? Do you think you can stand up to me?"

Sidian lunged at him. Even if it killed him, that alpha would die tonight.

Chapter Thirty-Six

Seven of the eight alphas of Pack Kincaid loitered on the wide back porch, talking amongst themselves, smoking, and passing around what looked like a bottle of gin.

That was not what Roman wanted to see. He had been of the belief that the pack would likely wait inside with perhaps one of them standing guard over the yard to see who would emerge victorious from the trees first. On the one hand, he didn't have to worry about sneaking into the house if they were all outside, but it meant he and Puppy had to be careful in engaging with the enemy. They were at a supreme disadvantage like that.

Puppy huffed in irritation and stamped one bare foot into the dirt, squinting through the leaves before turning a questioning glance toward Roman. She didn't know what to do.

A distraction was necessary. Roman weighed the odds of what he thought they might get away with, though he doubted they would get more than one alpha out into the woods with them. Killing one would alert the entire pack to what was going on.

So it had to count. "Walk further down. Cry like you're hurt. Don't make any other sounds."

Puppy stared at him for a moment before grunting and slinking through the trees, her footsteps eerily quiet as she avoided stepping on twigs and leaves. She disappeared from his sight after a moment, and Roman could only hope that she would do as she was told, gripping a branch above his head and giving it a sudden, harsh shake. The wind had died down mostly, and a few curious heads tilted toward the sudden rustling noise.

No one stepped off the porch, though. Not until a high-pitched whine split the night, sharp and brittle over the cascading rain. An alpha had good hearing, and every single member of Pack Kincaid looked toward the forest, each of them clocking the noise. Would one of them come to see what was the matter, or would they leave an injured female alpha in the woods to die?

"Shit," Axel Kincaid swore from the porch. "Was that Puppy crying?"

Knox cocked his head, his eyes sweeping the forest, though Roman knew it would be hard to see through the foliage. The grass was long and thick and lush, and the lack of moonlight or even starlight made the night darker. "She sounds like she's hurt. You think Kane fucked her up that bad?"

"The alpha is going to be *pissed* if she's hurt," Nash groaned, taking a drag on his cigarette. "Axe, you go get her. You're the only one who can handle her when she's jumpy."

Axel heaved a put-upon sigh. "Fine. Fucker. Next time, deal with her *yourself.*"

He stepped off the porch and cursed under the rainfall, jerking the hood of his jacket up as if that would do anything to protect him. Roman crouched low to the ground, never taking his eyes off of his target, his tongue sliding over his teeth in preparation.

On every single mission he had been on with the Vipers, he could kill one staff member of each breeding center. All of them had been betas, and while Roman had delighted in their deaths, they weren't proper challenges to him. A beta could never stand up to him, and now that he knew what he was, he realized just how pitiful they were as prey compared to what he *could* have.

Killing an alpha would be easy. Pitifully easy. Especially when it was an alpha who stood between him and his darling, who had done nothing but aided in Sidian's suffering. For that choice, for that mistake, Roman would pay back the agony tenfold.

After all, hadn't he been trained to do just that?

He nearly jumped a foot in the air when he felt a pair of small hands around his neck, fingers curling under the metal of the shock collar that still rested against his throat.

He glanced up to see Puppy looking down at him, with a meaningful expression in her eyes as she gave her wrists one quick twist. Whatever the latching mechanism on the collar was, it broke, emitting a tiny electric whine that was drowned out by a rumble of thunder. She slipped the metal between her teeth and crept back into the shadows with it, though Roman didn't know why she wanted it.

He watched her go before turning his attention back to the yard, his blood rushing in his ears as Axel stepped through the trees and entered the darkness of the forest.

"I don't know where the fuck you are, but I know you're in here," he shouted, all bravado whether or not he knew it. "Puppy, where are you, you misbehaving little bitch?"

Roman edged just behind a trunk so he would be out of Axel's direct line of sight, his lips parting as he inhaled the alpha's scent. It was rancid—they all were—and he took some comfort in knowing it would never torment Sidian again. *Just a little closer. You're almost there.*

Axel's head twisted off toward the right when something rustled in the bushes, his shoulders tensing and his eyes narrowing. But he was looking the wrong way, and it was easy for

Roman to slink around the trunk of the tree and take him down from the left side.

"Fuck!" Axel thrashed like a child, punches and kicks thrown wild as Roman wrapped an arm around his waist and slammed him into the ground. "Get the fuck off of me, you damned mutt!"

"Wrong dog," Roman murmured before he slammed his fist into Axel's throat.

The wet crunch made him giggle, the sound alien to his ears as Axel's hands fumbled with the front of his throat. Trachea collapse was simple under Roman's precise strike; he'd been sparring with a trained fighter for the last two years of his life and pleasure surged through him at how effective the hit had been. It wasn't suffering to the depth he would have preferred, but there was something satisfying about watching someone wheeze as they suffocated to death.

He sank to his knees in the mud, watching as Axel's face reddened. "Hurts, right?"

Axel stared at him with wide and disbelieving eyes, trying to draw in breath through a throat that no longer worked. For just a moment, Roman considered ripping his throat open to give him one last gasp before he gurgled his last, but he didn't possess the quality of mercy.

Those alphas bled it out of him the moment they laid hands on his mate.

"You're going to die soon," he said, relishing the way Axel's eyes widened up at him, blinking to clear away the rain that fell into them every few seconds. "There is no saving you. I want you to know that. You are going to die, and you are going to die because you touched my omega."

Sidian, sharp and prickly and yet sweet when he wanted to be. Sidian, who once said all he wanted to do was disappear into the woods and live like a cryptid or something equivalent.

Sidian, who trusted Roman enough to open up to him, who accepted the hand Roman offered him, who wanted nothing more than to be *seen*, to be *respected*, to be treated with kindness that did not come with conditions attached. Sidian, who was so, so afraid of everyone around him, and yet sought connection with a desperation that made Roman feel sick to his stomach.

His tormented, beautiful mate, who only deserved the best things in life.

"I am going to kill your entire pack," Roman promised as Axel's body bucked, instinct kicking in as he pissed himself, as the fear took hold of him. "So don't get too lonely down in hell. I'll send your brothers to you as soon as I get done with them."

He held Axel's gaze with his own until the alpha stopped moving, his body slumping against the earth as the last of the life drained out of him. Blue-tinted lips stopped smacking, hanging half-open as a thin line of drool trailed down from the corner of his mouth. The front of his throat looked almost comical, dented in as deeply as it was. Roman had done a good job with it.

He wished he had his phone. It took shitty pictures, but it would have been a trip to show Mal what he had pulled off.

Shouts echoed through the trees, and he lifted his head to see the Kincaids spilling off the porch.

When an alpha bonded into a pack died, the entire pack would feel it. That none of them had noticed Axel's desperate attempts at survival said something about how sick their bond was, but Roman didn't care about that. It was a relief that they hadn't been able to stop him.

He wondered about their omega just as Jett Kincaid fell to his knees.

"No," Nash said, shaking his head as he raked his hands through his hair. "No, no, no, that's not possible, is it? There's no way that just happened."

They could feel the absence within the bond, which was more than enough for them to know something horrible must have happened. Roman chuckled as he leaned back, taking in a deep breath of the fresh night air, of the blood and piss and shit of the corpse beneath him.

He wasn't able to give the doctor at the breeding center enough time or attention, but he would rectify that now. He would send everyone who had hurt his mate straight into the fire.

"Axel!" Knox shouted into the trees. "This isn't funny. Where the fuck are you?"

Denial is such an addictive drug. Roman blew a breath and rose to his feet, rolling his shoulders to work the slight tension out of them.

Puppy was nowhere to be seen, but now that he knew she was there, he could almost feel her like a phantom limb. Could almost imagine her silent pacing back and forth as she waited to see what would happen next. She would know Axel was dead; Roman wondered if she would be disappointed she didn't get to do it herself, but he supposed it didn't matter too much to her.

All of them had a hand in hurting her, after all. Just like all of them had hurt Sidian.

"Why isn't he answering?" Jett's voice was low, careful, controlled, but Roman could see the way his hands shook before he shoved them into the pockets of his jeans. So much weakness on open display; they must have relied on numbers to get by this long. "Where the hell is he, Knox? There's... There's no way, is there? There's no way they could have..."

He trailed off, unwilling to admit the truth, but Knox did not answer. He stared into the trees instead, alert and hoping the impossible would come true.

Roman watched him for a moment before his gaze dropped back to the corpse at his feet. If the Kincaids were unwilling to admit the truth, then it was up to Roman to ensure that they understood the gravity of their situation. He doubted they would rise to the occasion, but the least he could do was give them a chance to brace themselves.

Sidian did not have that chance. He did not have the luxury of being given an opportunity to prepare himself for what Pack Kincaid had done to him. But he had survived, and Roman would ensure that the Kincaid alphas did not.

He owed it to his mate, and he would deliver no matter what it took.

Chapter Thirty-Seven

Dax grunted as Sidian slammed him into the wall of the nest as hard as he could, plaster cracking all the way up to the ceiling from the force of the blow. Several of the photographs fluttered to the ground as their fragile adhesive was disturbed, the sight of them drawing a snarl from Sidian's lips. How dare he? How fucking dare he ever think he could do something like *that?*

"You stupid bitch!" Dax backhanded him across the face and Sidian stumbled back, his cheek throbbing from the impact. "Don't ruin what little progress you've made. You'll regret it."

A sharp laugh tore from Sidian's throat as he pressed a hand to his face, looking up at Dax through vision that was starting to blur just slightly around the edges. His vision seemed almost tinted red, his nose picking up a faint whiff of copper. "You're a monster. You're a fucking *demon.*"

"You are an omega who is good for nothing but spreading your legs." Dax caught him by the throat, squeezing roughly. "Now *get down on your knees* like the good little breeder you are."

The command choked with a vicious pressure that no hand could ever match.

It was agony to push back against it, claws digging into Sidian's mind in an effort to force him down into the position Dax demanded of him. The alpha's dominance surrounded him on all sides and threatened to devour him whole if he did not submit, but he couldn't. He *couldn't.*

No alpha had ever earned his submission. Pack Kincaid ripped it from his body and his mind again and again in a desperate attempt to force him into what they wanted him to be, but Sidian wasn't that. Could never be that. It wasn't in his nature to submit, to give in, to let others dominate him when he ached for some semblance of control over his whirlwind life. His omega whined, terrified of the ramifications of not obeying the alpha, but Sidian only powered through the pain that lanced through his mind. It ripped a shout from him, his knees nearly buckling before he forced them straight.

Every single part of him ached, but he spat in Dax Kincaid's face. "Go fuck yourself."

It was eerie the way Dax's face smoothed into a perfectly neutral position as he wiped the saliva off of his cheek. "I'm going to make you wish I were a merciful alpha."

He moved faster than Sidian was prepared for, a punch catching him in the jaw and sending him stumbling into the wall. When Dax came at him again, he slid down and around the alpha's feet, cackling when Dax's hand broke through the plaster instead. The cold of the brass knuckles against his hip reminded him of the weapon's existence, and Sidian slid them onto his fingers as he darted toward the nest door.

A hand caught him by the hair and dragged him back. "No, you don't, you disobedient little slut. You're not leaving this room until I'm satisfied I've broken you in like you *need* to be."

"What if I break you in instead?" The movement yanked at his scalp, but Sidian twisted around and threw a punch directly at that insolent, smarmy, smug little smile.

Dax wheeled back, his hand slipping from Sidian's hair as it flew to his mouth instead. The impact shuddered up Sidian's arm, his fingers stinging, small wounds swelling with a few droplets of blood as he fled into the bedroom. A glance back revealed Dax's mouth smeared with claret that he spat onto the hardwood, his eyes blazing with a hatred Sidian had never seen before.

Lilac cowered against the headboard, his eyes wide and disbelieving as Sidian weighed what options he had. Running for the hallway was the safest bet only if none of the others were in the house. If they were, it was a numbers game, and Sidian would lose. He didn't have any real training and only one weapon, and he didn't think it would do him much good against the rest of the pack. That they weren't already thundering up the stairs was a miracle in and of itself.

"Don't do this," Dax said, his voice low, threatening, sending shivers down Sidian's spine. "If you thought I hurt you before, you would be surprised at what I can do to you."

"What's surprising about it?" Sidian demanded, his fingers curling in against the brass knuckles. *Don't let them go. No matter what you do, don't let them go.* "You're just a psycho alpha rapist like your entire fucking designation. It's not a surprise when you act the way you've always been."

There were lamps on the nightstands, and Sidian edged toward the closest one, which put the bed between him and Dax. It also put him against the wall and what was probably the closet, which wasn't ideal. The further he was away from the door, the harder it would be to run, but he needed a weapon. On speed alone, he might not win, and it was Dax's house. He knew the layout perfectly.

Dax coughed wetly, and Sidian hoped beyond hope that he'd lost at least a tooth or two from that punch. "Oh, little omega, you have no idea what horrors I could visit upon that little body. I wonder what you'd do if I dressed you up and paraded you around like the useless *female* that you are."

Sidian flinched despite himself. He almost hated how easy it was to hurt him with those words. "You won't get a chance, asshole. I promise you that."

He dove for one of the lamps, and Dax flew at him, sliding across the slick comforter and drawing a soft, startled scream from Lilac's lips. Sidian's hands closed around the metal base just as Dax slammed into him, sending them both rolling across the hardwood as something shattered.

Was it the light bulb? Sidian didn't know. He didn't care.

"And what will you have gained when you fail?" Dax demanded, pinning Sidian down onto his stomach, flattening him against the floor. Tiny shards of glass were scattered across the wood, but it was the cord that Dax wrapped his fist around. "Honestly, maybe you *like* it when I'm cruel to you."

"Go to hell!" Sidian tried to kick him off, but Dax was so much *bigger* than he was.

The cord was cold as it looped around his neck, digging into his skin and choking a rasping whine from his throat. Sidian scrabbled at it with one hand while he clung to the lamp with the other, unwilling to relinquish the only weapon he had on hand. The tension of the cord made it impossible to swing no matter how much he thrashed and struggled, every gasping breath weaker than the last.

Dax dug a knee into the small of Sidian's back and yanked the cord tighter, and Sidian's hindbrain set off alarm bells in his head. *His baby, his baby, not his baby*. The pain in his stomach sent him screeching and clawing and kicking, broken glass digging into his hands until he gripped a fistful of it. Though he couldn't see, he could *feel* Dax behind him and slapped him as best he could with the glass.

The alpha bellowed, and the cord loosened, and Sidian yanked it from around his neck as he choked air into his straining lungs. Then he threw himself at the lamp, gripping the metal base with one hand and swinging it at Dax's head with all the strength he had.

It wasn't much because he was scrawny, an underfed runt of an omega who could barely take care of himself, but the clang of metal against bone still made his heart race.

He darted for the door, intent on putting as much distance between himself and Dax as possible. This was too much for him. He wasn't cut out for physical brutality of this level, for hand-to-hand combat, for fighting off an alpha twice his size. When a hand caught him by the ankle and jerked him to the floor, he barely had time to cover his head with his arms to keep himself from smacking his face off the hardwood.

"I'm so tired of you thinking you're *worth* something." Dax jerked Sidian closer, rolling him onto his back, his knees pinning Sidian's thighs apart and shoving the nightie up around his hips. *No no no.*

But Sidian *was* worth something. He knew that now. No one as special as Roman Kane would give him the time of day if he weren't worth at least a little.

Rough hands gripped his wrists and pinned them over his head as Dax leered down at him, the heat of his erection pressed up against Sidian through the thin fabric of the panties. "And now you're right back where I want you. How much more adrenaline can you take before the drug kicks in? How loud are you going to whine for my knot this time?"

His hold tightened suddenly, impossibly, the crushing strength making Sidian cry out as he squirmed and struggled. Dax's entire body went rigged, his eyes wide, his mouth falling open to reveal a couple of his teeth were missing, bloody holes left in his gums.

It was the least he deserved for everything he'd done.

His hands went slack, and Sidian broke his hold, dragging himself across the floor to the doorway to grip the frame tightly in his hands. He watched as Dax's body jerked and shuddered, a single tear trailing down his cheek. What the fuck was going on with him? Was he having a heart attack or a stroke or something? Fuck, that would be such a godsend right now.

"Axel," Dax breathed, scrubbing his hands over his face, then wincing and dropping them. He stared at nothing in particular before his gaze settled on Sidian again, staring up at him with an expression that Sidian didn't know how to describe. Was he upset? "What the fuck did your alpha do to my pack brother, Obsidian? What the fuck have you *done?*"

Sidian scrambled backward toward the hallway as Dax caught him by the shoulders and slammed him into the bedroom door, his entire body twitching from the pain as the sharp woodcuts dug into his skin.

"You stupid fucking *bitch,*" he snapped, spittle flying into Sidian's face. "My brother is dead. What the fuck did your stupid mutt *do to Axel?*"

Dax let go of him and let out a scream that sent goosebumps crawling along Sidian's bare skin, his muscles going slack as he slid down the door, coughing weakly.

Every single part of his body ached, and he drew his knees up to his chest as Dax screamed again, raking his hands through white hair that stained a rusty color where the blood soaked into the pale strands. What the fuck was he talking about? What was wrong with him? Sidian had spent precious little time around alphas and had never seen one act like that before.

Mutt. *Roman.* Had Roman done something? Was he safe? Was he alive?

He had to be. He had to be alive because Sidian couldn't save them both, but he could kill the monster in front of him to get back to his mate. As long as Roman survived, they would reunite, and they would find somewhere safe and quiet and raise their children together and maybe have more. How beautiful would a baby be with Roman's eyes and Roman's smile and Roman's good, pure heart?

Sidian was only vaguely aware he was weeping silently, the panic and pain tangling up in his chest until it was harder to breathe than it had been with the lamp cord across his throat. He was going to have a panic attack, and then Dax was going to kill him in that moment of weakness.

I can't do it I can't do it I can't do it I CAN'T FUCKING DO IT—

Dax jerked himself upright, sucking in great lungfuls of breath before his gaze settled on Sidian once again. He took one jerking, halting step closer, then growled and forced another step. Something was wrong with him. Something was very wrong with him. How could anyone turn out like him?

"I'm going to fuck you like you *deserve*," Dax sneered, "and then I'm going to make you watch as I cut that worthless fucking thing out of you once and for all."

And just like that, something in Sidian's mind *snapped*.

It was almost gratifying to see the look of surprise on Dax's face as Sidian shot toward him, the alpha's throat flexing with a harsh swallow as Sidian prepared to sink his teeth in deep.

No one threatens my children.

Chapter Thirty-Eight

The natural strength of an alpha permitted them to shield and protect their mates and children from harm, as well as to visit brutality upon those who deserved it. Roman considered it both as he wrapped a hand around Axel's jaw, gripping him by the chin while the other hand slid into his hair. The satisfying *crack* of bone was lovely, but not as satisfying as the wet squelch of ripping flesh.

He watched as the bronze flesh split open, blood cascading down Axel's chest as his limbs jerked and twitched with muscle spasms. The scent of copper filled the air, and Roman greeted it like an old friend as he gave another vicious yank, severing the spine so that the heavy body beneath crumpled to the ground. Axel's head was still warm as Roman lifted it until their eyes met through the shadows.

"Ugly motherfucker," he muttered to no one in particular before he shifted his attention back to the yard. Several of the Kincaids were standing closer to the trees now; they were all so desperate to believe there might still be some saving their pack brother. "Here, guys. Catch."

He had never been good at sports. Therefore, it pleased him far too much when Axel's head arced through the air and landed in the hands that Talon stretched toward the sky.

A beat passed as the alphas in the yard all stared at their pack brother's still and paling face, the bloody stump that jutted from his torn neck. Talon dropped it and stumbled back several steps. "What the fuck?" he rasped. "What the fuck, what the fuck, *what the fuck!*"

"I'm gonna be sick," Nash proclaimed right before bending at the waist, bracing his hands on his knees as he vomited into the grass. The wet retching noises brought a smile to Roman's face.

"Puppy wouldn't have done that." Knox looked toward the forest again, but his eyes never settled on any spot. "Kane is in there somewhere. Get in there and find him!"

But nobody dared take the first step across the tree line, and Roman realized they were *afraid.*

Jagger told him just once that the boss's status as a feral earned him far more fear and intimidation than his designation as an epsilon. An epsilon's violent tendencies could be controlled, and the boss worked hard to ensure alphas would be safe in his presence. But a feral's pheromones never quite felt the same after that first shift into bloodlust, and Roman wondered if that was why they were afraid of him.

That wasn't a good enough reason. He would have to give them a better one.

Slate squared his shoulders and stepped toward the woods, his jaw set, his eyes narrowing the closer he drew to the trees. "Fucking pussies have to sneak attack us, huh? Well, I'm not afraid of you stupid fucking dogs. I'm gonna make you regret putting your hands on one of your alphas!"

Roman bit back a snort; he *had* no alphas, and he never would. The only person in the world who mattered in his eyes was locked up in that house, and he would raze the entire thing to the ground in order to get Sidian back. They couldn't keep him away from his omega, and now that they had tried, he'd pay them back in kind. He'd rip them to pieces one by one just because he could.

He eased back into the shadows as quietly as possible, leaving Axel's decapitated corpse to bleed into the earth, waiting for the precise moment when Slate would notice it.

Because of course he did. The ricochet of anguish and loss through the bond drew him to the spot where his pack brother lay, the gaping wound at his neck almost black in the darkness. Slate moaned at the sight, reaching down to press a hand to Axel's still, lifeless chest.

It was beneficial that the worthless scum seemed to care about each other.

Roman didn't bother sneaking around. He charged him headlong and slammed into him, pinning Slate up against the tree at his back and wrapping his arms tight around him. Just like he had Puppy, he pinned Slate's arms to his sides, crushing him, squeezing him, the edges of his vision bleeding just like they had on that afternoon when Dax Kincaid's father stepped into his home.

"You piece of shit!" Slate tried to struggle free and only slammed his head back into the trunk, stunning himself for just a moment.

Soft scurrying in the underbrush revealed Puppy coming to join him, her teeth bared and her eyes hard. Without missing a beat, Roman swung Slate around, and Puppy jumped on his back, her slender arms winding tight around his throat as she dug her teeth into the side of his face. *That* woke him up, and he caterwauled as she craned her neck back, his cheek tearing open and spilling a fountain of blood.

Roman admired how the wound exposed his teeth and squirming tongue.

Footsteps rushing through the grass had him dropping Slate, who was dragged to the ground by Puppy's weight. She dug her fingers into his eyes, and the wet *pops* that followed would remain in Roman's dreams forever, he was certain. Slate screeched and jerked and then went still, and Puppy dragged her fingers from his eye sockets with a satisfied huff.

"The remote's not picking up a fucking signal!" Knox shouted as he broke through the trees, his head swinging from side to side as Roman and Puppy both darted out of sight in different directions. "There's no way our bitch's stupid dog got that collar off."

Jett tripped over Slate's leg and turned to see what had caught him, scrambling back on his ass with a shout of terror at the sight. The other alphas hurried to reach him, all of them struck suddenly silent no doubt at the sight of what Puppy had done to their brother. Though Roman was not sure what it was that had killed him, it was possible to reach the brain through the eyes.

Knox knelt on the forest floor and reached out to touch Slate's undamaged cheek before he shot straight up, paler as he sucked in air through his teeth. "Canvas the woods," he snarled at the others, who all stared at him in disbelief. "Dead or alive, I want them found. They killed two of our brothers. You shouldn't need me to tell you to do what's right!"

Nash gagged, pressing a hand against the nearest tree. "What the fuck is happening?"

"*Go!*" Knox shouted, a command laced through his voice.

Roman flexed his knuckles as he eased through the trees, intent on not being caught before the time was right. He watched where the others headed, ducking down as low as he could, off to the side and out of sight. The advantage of being trained to kill was that he could stay calm when the situation demanded it; the remaining Kincaids were frantic with anxiety, scents tangy with the rich scent of fear.

If Knox were in a position of power, then Roman would remove him from it.

Cut the head off a chicken and watch its bloody corpse continue to run as if it could still escape.

Knox spun toward him at the last second just as Roman reached him, the two of them colliding in a pile of limbs and teeth and snarls. Something sharp and plastic cracked Roman on the side of the head, and he *felt* the pain in the same way he knew the night was cold and his skin was soaked from rain. He *felt* it and then discarded it, shaking it off before he slammed his fist into Knox Kincaid's face.

His nose snapped, and he spat out a mouthful of blood. "Get the fuck *off of me!*"

The sound would call his brothers, but Roman didn't care. He would kill them all. It was even almost *kind* of Knox to draw the others back to their location.

Sudden rustling movement in the trees preceded a surprised cry that degraded into a howling anguish that made Roman's eyebrows twitch up in surprise. Knox's face twisted with shock, and he made the mistake of trying to look to the source of his brother's pain.

That day at the house, Roman had ripped open the throat of Sidian's father like it was as natural to him as drawing in his next breath, as stretching a stiff muscle, as turning his face up toward the sun. His memories of the afternoon were spotty at best, but he still remembered the give of tender flesh and the way blood had geysered from the wound, soaking him in crimson heat. It would be the quickest, most efficient way to chase away the cold of the night air.

Knox swung his head back around just in time for Roman to grab a handful of his hair, yanking his head back and forcing his throat to arch. The pale skin stretched, the beautiful blue tracery of veins beneath the surface begging to be ripped open. His pulse beat beneath his jaw.

"Wait," he rasped, kicking his feet, trying to drive his knees into Roman's back where he sat straddling the other alpha. "Wait, wait, you don't have to do this. You just want the omega, right? That's your primary concern. You just want your omega back."

One of his hands patted his pocket; Roman snagged it with his free hand and pinned it next to Knox's head, leaning forward to brace his weight against the earth. "He's *my* omega."

"It was a mistake," Knox said, trying to look at him, his lips parted with frantic breaths that plumed white in the cool air. "We didn't know he belonged to someone."

Roman almost wanted to laugh. "Do you think that makes a difference to me?"

The cries of pain fell silent, and the forest slipped into a stillness that told Roman that the living members of Pack Kincaid were terrified. They knew another of their number was dead and that Knox was at least subdued, and that did not bode well for the remaining three. Would they try to find Roman and Puppy, or would they sprint back to the house like the cowards they were?

Maybe they were afraid to move. Maybe they were afraid to reveal their locations hoping remaining quiet would throw Roman and Puppy off of their trails.

Knox gulped air, his hand opening and closing. "Kane, listen—"

"I don't want to. I don't like you." Roman stared down into his eyes, and Knox's mouth snapped shut, the scent of piss once again heavy in the air. "And I don't think you benefit me by being alive."

He lunged forward, his teeth finding Knox's throat, pale and thin and vulnerable, sinking into the flesh while Knox loosed a scream that sent shivers down Roman's spine. Skin split beneath the grip of his mouth, and blood spilled across his tongue, the coppery sweetness overwhelming his senses. There was nothing for a moment except the jets of blood and the wet gurgling that issued from Knox's twitching mouth.

It was far, far more glorious than Roman remembered it being.

He dug his teeth in deep and gave his head a shake, feeling the flesh tear until it gave, a piece coming loose in his mouth. He spat it onto the grass, his eyes closing as blood coated his face. He was right; it was far hotter than the rain, and for a moment, he felt warm.

Knox jerked and spasmed on the earth beneath him, and Roman opened his eyes so he could watch the alpha die. There was something about watching the life leave someone's gaze, the moment their body went limp even as their limbs still gave the occasional spasm. Blood still dribbled from the gaping wound in Knox's throat, and Roman watched as rain pooled in the tear. It looked like a wild animal had torn him apart, and in a way, one had.

After all, was Roman not an apex predator among their kind?

He sat back on his knees and tilted his head up toward the rain, allowing the chilly droplets to rinse his face as he cast his gaze around the forest. Three more. He wasn't sure who Puppy had killed, but in the end, he supposed it didn't matter. They were all the same. Useless for nothing more than sating his bloodlust and dying like the pathetic little men they were.

Roman rose to his feet, rolling his neck until it cracked. He heard the soft scurrying once again and turned to find Puppy had come to join him, her dress stained with fresh blood.

She glanced at Knox, then up at him, her eyes gleaming. Oh, she wanted more. So much more.

"Let's go," he said, tilting his head toward the trees. "Let's get them, and then we'll go back to the house to finish off Dax. How does that sound to you?"

Puppy whooped and flew off into the trees, and Roman gave chase with a delighted yell of his own.

Chapter Thirty-Nine

Pain shot through Sidian's body as a console table shattered beneath his weight, the impact leaving a hole in the wall as he hit the floor with a grunt.

Blood-slicked palms grabbed him by the shoulders and hauled him up, slamming him into the wall, the back of his head catching a picture frame as Dax leered into his face. "Look at you struggle. Look at you fight. Useless little bitch. When will you learn what you're good for?"

Sidian hissed and slammed his forehead into Dax's nose to shatter it, and the alpha released him with a wail of pain, hands smothering the blood that gushed down his chin.

The headbutt was a calculated risk given the fact Sidian's head now spun, but he didn't care. Instead, he bent down to grab the broken leg of the console table, fingers brushing over the splintered end of it before he rammed it as hard as he could into Dax's gut.

Flesh gave way beneath the impact, bloody lines opening in Dax's skin as Sidian shoved him back into the wall. The alpha yanked the leg out of his hold, and Sidian ducked before it could be used against him, well aware of how much more dangerous the hallway was. Longer than the bedroom but narrower, which meant close quarters. He couldn't afford to get too close to Dax, who had the reach advantage to begin with.

"I'm going to enjoy breaking you," Dax said, his voice quivering with an anticipation that made Sidian gag. "I'm going to fuck you until you bleed all over my bed."

He stumbled back a moment later, his hands flying to his head, his eyes wide and disbelieving. They darted past Sidian toward the stairs, his mouth falling open on a wheeze. What was it? This was the second time he'd done it, and Sidian didn't understand what was happening, but he knew an opportunity when he saw it and pounced on the alpha without a second thought.

Weapons weren't necessary when he had his nails and teeth and sheer determination.

His knee dug into the wound at Dax's gut, the solid muscle beneath making him snarl in frustration. "I'll rip your dick off if you ever bring it anywhere near me again, you disgusting fuck."

Dax threw a wide punch that Sidian dodged, his eyes wide and vacant as if he was somewhere else. And again, Sidian took advantage, twisting his head to sink his teeth as deep into the alpha's forearm as he could. *Off the artery. Not gonna bleed him enough. I've gotta make it count.*

He dug his teeth as deep in as he could, wishing they were as sharp as an alpha's could be, and shook his head back and forth as furiously as a Pitbull.

Dax screamed beneath him, bucking his hips in an effort to dislodge Sidian's teeth. Blood flowed thick and freely, and Sidian had to let go to breathe, coughing out a mouthful of flesh as he dodged another haymaker thrown at his face. Something was wrong. Dax was dealing with something that Sidian couldn't see and did not care to. All that mattered was staying in control, staying out of the line of his hits, because every punch made Sidian's vision that much blurrier at the edges.

And if he lost consciousness, the injection would take effect, and there would be no one to step in to protect him from the monster before him.

He rolled off of the alpha before he ended up getting hit by accident, the stairs so close. Where were the others? They had to feel Dax's pain and rage through the pack bond, and yet they had not come. There was no explanation that Sidian could think of.

Barring one. His eyes darted toward the end of the hall where Lilac stood in the bedroom doorway.

There were risks with bonding an omega into a pack; they were considered pack centers for a reason, able to control the ebb and flow of the bond in order to keep it balanced. Only strong omegas would have been able to handle the many alphas of Pack Kincaid, but what was Lilac if not strong? What was he if not incredible for withstanding the might of their violence and rage and dominance while also bearing the mental weight of their emotions?

Lilac leaned against the doorframe, panting as he gripped it. His hands were shaking, and there were tears streaking down his cheeks, but Sidian didn't think he was crying. Not really. Something was wrong, very wrong with the pack, and Lilac felt it just as keenly as Dax did. But he was stronger than Dax, holding himself together enough to take a stumbling step into the hallway, his feet soundless on the slick wood.

But Dax saw him just the same. "Lilac! *Stop him.*"

The command made Sidian's omega whimper even though it was not aimed at him, his head stinging from the force of resisting words intended for another. He watched as Lilac faltered, one hand scrabbling for purchase against the wall as he let out a desperate cry.

His back bowed, the strain of fighting off those words painful, and Sidian saw the way Lilac had to grit his teeth to resist it. "No, alpha, I *won't*."

Dax laughed, harsh and short, as he dragged himself to his feet, panting, his eyes rolling as something manic slipped into his gaze. "You want me to retrain you, little omega?"

An acrid tang stole through Lilac's floral scent, and he whined before he shook his head, screaming as he smacked his hand into the wall. The impact seemed to jar all the way through him, and Sidian watched, torn between wanting to help him and wanting to kill Dax.

The sound of a soft, muffled cry made all three of them freeze.

Sidian's hindbrain came to life in the way it only did when his son moved inside of him, shrieking at him to get up, to get to his daughter, to protect her from the monster in the house. He stumbled to his feet just as Lilac dove for the nursery doorway and Dax, so much faster despite the blood slicking down his skin, gripped Lilac's hair and threw him backwards into the wall.

"She's not your daughter," he snapped as Lilac slid down the plaster, blinking rapidly. "Let *me* get her, why don't you? Stay here and *rest* since you're feeling so out of sorts."

No. No, Dax couldn't be allowed to get anywhere near Amey. He'd hurt her. He'd hurt her, and Sidian could never undo it. He could never fix it.

He dove at Dax's legs, and the alpha landed on top of him, the weight knocking the air out of him for just a moment. He didn't *need* to breathe as he rolled them over, slashing Dax across the face, his nails digging in until bright, bloody furrows opened in one of his cheeks. Dax growled and caught him by the throat, but Sidian just dug his fingers into the open wound until Dax shrieked and let him go.

Not Amey. Anything but her. Anyone but her. She was half of his world. Dax *couldn't touch her.*

"All of this over some stupid omega brat," Dax spat, catching Sidian by the hair and slamming his head into the wall. "*Get on your knees* where you belong, *omega.*"

The command ricocheted through Sidian's throbbing head, and he almost, *almost* obeyed, his wounded body dragging itself off of the floor. But the moment he had his knees under him, he scrambled back to his feet, putting himself between Dax and the nursery doorway. A cursory glance over his shoulder revealed Lilac climbing to his feet, still looking dazed.

"Protect my daughter," he managed, and Lilac looked at him, wide-eyed and uncertain. "Please. Protect my daughter, and I swear he won't get to you."

Dax laughed as he sat up on the floor, his face twisted into a mask of manic glee that made Sidian's stomach wobble. What the fuck was wrong with him? "Don't make promises you can't keep. I'll make you watch while I punish him for disobeying me."

Amethyst wailed from inside the nursery, and Sidian's entire body bowed in response. Fighting off his urge to submit, fighting off his urge to run to his daughter... It was too much. It was more pain than Pack Kincaid had ever put him through, more anguish than he knew what to do with. If he went to Amethyst, then they'd all die. Lilac wasn't strong enough to fight Dax, and Sidian wouldn't ask him to. That he had taken care of Amey was enough. That he was here now to help her was enough.

Dax was Sidian's worst nightmare given flesh and form, and it was his job to kill him. To send him right back into the depths of the hellhole he'd crawled from and to make sure he could never, ever crawl out of it again. No matter what it demanded of him.

He had to do it for Amey. And he had to do it for Roman.

"I've got her," Lilac said, and Sidian glanced over his shoulder only long enough to watch the other omega race into the nursery, the door slamming shut behind him. A metallic *click* echoed through the hallway, louder than Sidian's panting breaths and Dax's damp wheezing.

"He'll regret it." Dax rose to his feet, oozing blood and dominance, his self-assurance, his *cockiness* setting Sidian's teeth on edge. "But he won't regret it as much as you will. Taking her away from you wasn't enough to break you. I'll make you watch as I snap her little neck. She's a worthless omega just like you, so what do I even need her for?"

The stairs were behind him. They were wide but wooden, all sharp edges that bent in the middle to jut out to the left. If Dax hit the railing hard enough, he might break straight through it and hit the floor below, and maybe that would slow him down. Maybe it would even kill him.

It was an option. Sidian weighed his chances, digging his heels into the floor as he stood upright. Every single muscle ached. His joints protested just in standing up.

He wasn't built for this. Omegas were not built to be fighters, and he was so small, so fucking fragile compared to an alpha like Dax.

He thought of Amethyst, of her tiny face scrunched up and pink a moment before her eyes opened, wide and dark and almost in disbelief as they met his own. For just a moment, Sidian thought she knew him. He thought she knew she was looking up at the mother who had loved her despite everything. Despite the circumstances of her conception, despite the knowledge that her biological father was one of his rapists. He'd looked forward to meeting her every day she was inside him.

And he wanted to meet the child inside of him, too. What he was going to do was risky, too *risky*, but he wasn't a fighter and he was running out of options.

Dax took a deep breath, coughing before he cleared his throat. "Sidian," he purred, "be a good little bitch and, for the last fucking time, *get on your—*"

Sidian ran at him, and the moment Dax's feet left the floor, it almost felt like flying.

He wasn't heavy, but Dax was injured and unsteady on his feet, whether from repeated head trauma or blood loss or both, or whatever the fuck had him twitching and screaming in the bedroom. Either way, his feet slipped out from under him, and then the two of them were airborne.

The stairs bit into Sidian's back when he hit them, and he whined in pain.

He'd fallen down the stairs at the psych ward just once as a kid, and it had hurt then, and fuck, it hurt *worse* the second time. Dax slammed into him as they rolled down the steps, and Sidian slid across the landing, watching as Dax slammed into the railing right next to his face.

The wood splintered as it gave way, the alpha disappearing over the edge with a shout.

The sickening thud of a body below echoed through the quiet house. Sidian panted where he lay on the stairs, his hands moving down to his stomach as a sharp pain ripped through him. He moaned in discomfort, fear ratcheting through his body as something soaked the gusset of his panties.

Far below him and out of sight, a mighty crash of shattering glass broke the quiet.

And the delectable scent of a funeral pyre blasted through the house like a mushroom cloud.

Chapter Forty

Chasing down the three surviving alphas in the woods treated Roman to a view of Nash's body when he and Puppy raced past it. He whistled low at the sight of his slashed abdomen, organs strewn across the dirt and still steaming in the air, the metallic wink of the broken collar jutting from his flesh and telling Roman precisely what Puppy wanted the collar for. It reminded him of Sidian and the beta he'd watched his omega torture, and it only propelled him forward faster. The sooner they finished killing the alphas, the sooner he could return to Sidian's side.

He didn't know if Sidian was okay, but Roman trusted him to survive. As long as Sidian was alive, Roman would do everything in his power to return to him.

And if anything had happened to him, Roman would ensure that Dax Kincaid paid the price. He would pay it repeatedly until Roman was satisfied he had learned his lesson, determined to ensure that his omega's pain would be avenged.

Puppy skidded to a stop and twisted her head around, sniffing the air before she darted toward the right, Roman on her tail. She was faster than he was, but he kept up just the same, ignoring the burn of lactic acid in his muscles and his body's insistence he slowed down. Limits be damned, pain be damned, all that mattered was revenge and getting back to his mate as fast as possible.

A shot rang through the night. A chunk of tree trunk burst into pieces just ahead of Puppy, showering her in splinters that had her hissing in utter rage.

Roman caught her around the waist and tackled her to the ground as another shot rang out, his head already turning in the direction it came from as heavy footsteps thudded into the darkness.

Knox had been armed back at the motel, but where his gun had been when he needed it most, Roman did not know. But another of them was armed. That only had to be tricky if they allowed it; he left Puppy on the ground to collect herself and cut a wide berth around the sound of running steps, his eyes narrowing as his vision sharpened. Jett Kincaid, he thought, and ran wider still, determined to cut him off when he would least expect it. If he were a bad shot or shaky, then it would be easy to catch him off-guard and kill him.

Being shot was not fatal if the bullet missed any important internal organs. If Roman needed to take a hit to get close, he would do that.

Just don't bleed out in the middle of the woods, he told himself, his nose twitching as he picked up the acidic burn of Jett's gin and lime scent. His footsteps were growing closer once again. He was going to run right into Roman, and he didn't know it. That was how it had to be.

Something crashed through the trees after him, and Jett swore, half-stumbling over his own feet, and Roman realized it was Puppy. Whether she was chasing him for the thrill of it or running him into where Roman stood, he didn't know. He also didn't care.

He waited until the last possible second, watching as Jett spun on heel and aimed into the darkness. The moment his back was turned, Roman darted up behind him and caught him around the neck.

"Fuck!" Jett fired high and off-center as Roman drew his forearm tight against the other alpha's throat, cutting off his air supply before he could get out another word. No cries for help, no pleas for mercy.

He watched as Puppy reached them, her eyes glinting before she turned and took off in another direction. Either she didn't want the easy kill or she trusted him to get the job done; either way, Roman was flattered as he gave Jett a vicious toss into the nearest tree trunk.

The gun slipped from his hand, and Roman retrieved it as he watched Jett try to crawl away from him.

The steel was heavy and familiar in Roman's hands; he put the safety back on and slipped it into the back of his jeans, tucking his shirt down over it in case he needed it later. Then he followed at a leisurely pace, watching as Jett crawled through the mud and leaves, his hands grasping for anything to hold on to as he gulped in much-needed air. How hard they fought to live moments before the end came; Roman had to admit to himself that the Kincaids put on a hell of a show.

He watched as Jett's hands grasped a jagged rock jutting out of the ground, his hands sliding over its slippery surface as he crawled over it.

And the moment his face drew level with the stone, Roman made his move, one effortless leap into the air that ended with the sole of his boot meeting the back of Jett's head.

Mal had done it just once to Ghost before Jagger tore both of them off the sparring mats and ripped them new assholes for daring to push each other so far during training. On a flat surface, a curb stomp was dangerous enough; Mal was wound up, and Ghost had a way of getting under his skin, but he'd also known what to expect and took the blow well enough to avoid having his face busted open.

Jett Kincaid did not know to expect until the full weight of an alpha came down on his neck.

His face slammed into the rock with a wet crunch, the sound sending a shiver of pleasure down Roman's spine. But he bore down harder, lifting his boot up just to slam it back down, driving Jett's bloodied face into the stone until his skull cracked open from the pressure.

Gray matter gushed onto the forest floor. Roman watched it ooze from between pieces of skull, glistening and wet and white enough that it almost made him think of flower petals. He didn't have to check if Jett was dead before turning to find his way back into the fray.

Five down. Two to go. And then straight back to the house for Sidian.

Someone ran past him, and he turned to see Ford powering through the trees as fast as he could, his face as white as a sheet. Talon followed a moment later, his breaths coming out in harsh whining cries that were not befitting of the status of an alpha. When Puppy came through the brush a moment later, Roman understood what they were running from.

She pointed after them, and the two of them gave chase once again.

Axel had been the bulkiest of the alphas, but Ford and Talon were close behind, and that made them slower and clumsier on their feet in their panic. Roman could scent the fear thick and metallic on the air, and it fed into his bloodlust, predatory instinct demanding he run faster, catch up with them, take them down to the ground and rip them apart piece by piece. He ached, and his muscles burned, and his skin was numb from the cold and itching from dried blood, and still he wanted more.

It would never be enough to sate his desire for vengeance, but it would be enough for Sidian, and that mattered more. That had to come first.

Puppy leaped, almost flying to land on Ford's back. She slammed into him so hard he hit the dirt, and Talon half-turned as if to help before he ran again, stumbling when Puppy sank her teeth into Ford's shoulder and he screamed in pain. As Roman passed them, he watched her jerk her head back, tearing through fabric to rip off a chunk of skin that was red and raw beneath, glistening as the rain cascaded down onto it.

He gave her credit where credit was due and focused his attention on Talon as they broke through the trees and into the backyard, long grass dragging against his ruined jeans. The alpha aimed for the sliding glass door that led inside, but Roman would not let him get that far.

He didn't even need to worry about it. Talon tripped over his own damned feet and fell headlong in the grass halfway to the back porch.

Roman allowed himself to slow at the sight, pulling the gun without a second thought and cocking it when Talon made to stand up. "Get back on the *fucking ground*," he growled, the command lacing itself through his words and flattening Talon back to the grass. "You get up and I blow out your knees. You can drag yourself to the porch without them."

When he stepped closer, he realized Talon was crying. The wet, panicky breaths had morphed into desperate little hitching sobs, his eyes wide and round as he looked back at Roman. That frightened gaze never left him, not even as Roman circled the big man so he could put himself between Talon and the house.

None of the Kincaids would get back inside. Roman would be the only alpha to cross that threshold. His mate was in there, and he had already done so much to keep Sidian safe. What was one more body stacked on top of all the others? What was a little more blood spilled, even if it was his?

"Listen, man, listen," Talon blubbered, his hands fisting in the grass, "we didn't even know he was someone's mate. I wouldn't have fucking touched him if I had known. I'm sorry, okay?"

Roman stopped and stared at Talon, his lips parting around a surprised breath.

Without taking his eyes off the alpha, he threw back his head and *laughed*. It felt *good* to laugh, good to let it out, the tension unhitching itself from his body until he felt an eerie calm coil through his nerves. He rolled his shoulders and cracked his neck again, and he supposed the sound of his laugh must have come out for Talon to be looking up at him with such horror.

"You're sorry," Roman echoed. "Do you think that means anything? Do you think that changes anything?"

Talon opened his mouth and closed it, face straining like he was trying to think of anything that might somehow save him from getting his brains blown across the grass. "What do you want, dude? You want money? You want status? We got it. It's yours. You can have it. You want the kid back? She's yours. It was Dax's idea to take her in the first place!"

Roman nodded, absorbing the words. "How did you know how to find us?"

"Tracker," Talon gasped out. "In the omega's arm. Dax told the center he wanted it installed the moment he passed out after the birth. Didn't want him to go missing. Said he was too valuable."

"I see." They would have to remove that, though Roman was not sure how . That depended on what Sidian wanted to do and where he wanted to go next. "The address we were given of your house was an incorrect address. That address came from the Mambas mercenary group. How did they get the wrong address in the first place, and who would have given it to them?"

Talon whimpered. "If I tell you, will you let me go?"

"I'll consider it. But you'd better give me worthwhile answers. I'm exhausted. It's been a long night, and my mate still needs me." And Roman would do nothing to betray Sidian.

Talon wet his lips, pushing himself up just a little, though a sharp growl flattened him once again. "Okay, okay! Dax got paranoid after Baxter grabbed the alpha girl because he knew the snakes would be trailing us to figure out where she was. The house belonged to a relative of his, and he inherited it when his father died. All he did was go in and change the address."

"Changing the address would have done nothing to change the official information that the Mambas kept about your pack. I want to know who had access to that information that your pack would have been in contact with." It had to be someone on the inside. It had to be someone who would have lied about checking the house to keep the others off the trail for as long as possible.

It wouldn't have been Kitten, who hadn't been allowed to interrogate her own target.

And Roman knew Hadeon. He wasn't that kind of alpha.

"I don't know," Talon wheezed out. "I wasn't in charge of the contact. Dax was. You'd have to ask him. All I know is that it's one of the snakes and that Dax has been paying them to keep the rest of their team off of our backs. If he hadn't, they probably would have found the girl."

Of that, Roman had no doubt. "Did you hurt my mate out of vengeance for what I did to Dax Kincaid's father, or were there other reasons at play I don't know about?"

"It was revenge at first, but Dax found out the omega was a prime and wanted to keep him." Talon peeked up, his eyes wide and begging. "That's all I know. Can I go now, man?"

Roman pretended to consider the option, allowing the gun to lower one centimeter before raising it back up, enjoying that sudden look of pure, animal fear in Talon's eyes. "Feel free. Join your brothers."

The back of Talon's head exploded from the impact, his forehead denting in from the impact of the bullet as blood trickled from the wound just above the bridge of his nose. He slumped forward, brains leaking from the ragged tear in his skull, and Roman lowered the gun with a satisfied sigh.

Then he walked up the handful of steps to the sliding glass door and slammed his boot through the glass.

Chapter Forty-One

Roman strode into the living room dripping with blood and rainwater, his hair plastered to his face and his t-shirt framing every single muscle in his broad chest.

Sidian's omega purred at the sight of him as he gripped the edge of the landing, pulling himself closer so he could peer down into the room below. Dax lay in a heap, his eyes wide and disbelieving, his chest rising and falling with labored breaths despite the state of his body. He was still alive, the *fucker*.

Another cramp ripped a noise from Sidian's throat. He drew his knees up to relieve the pressure, aware of the needy throb between his thighs as his eyes were once again drawn to his mate. Roman was alive and well and in one piece, and though Sidian could see what looked like visible bite marks, he walked as if he felt no pain at all. His stroll was relaxed as he rounded the couch, his head tilting back as his bright forest eyes met Sidian's from below. The corner of his mouth twitched, a small sign of relief that had Sidian smiling down at him.

They were both alive. They were going to get out of this in one piece, weren't they?

"Evening, darling," Roman murmured, and Sidian's smile widened. "Are you all right?"

He was about to shake apart at the seams if Roman did not get up the stairs and *fuck him,* and it was a miracle nothing was broken, but Sidian nodded anyway. "Yeah. I'm good. Sore, but good."

Roman's nostrils flared, and his pupils dilated. "Are you sure you're all right?"

"I need you to fuck me as soon as you're done with him," Sidian said, and from the way Roman's scent coiled thick and heady around him, he assumed the message was clear.

He stayed curled at the edge of the landing, peering down as he watched Roman turn his attention to where Dax lay. There was an odd resignation on the alpha's face as Roman stepped over him and then pivoted to kneel, his knees bracketing Dax's hips as one big hand came to rest on the center of Dax's chest. In any other situation, it might have seemed almost intimate, but there was a dangerous, rolling grace to every movement. It was like watching a wolf play with its food before ripping out its throat.

"I killed your worthless excuse of a pack," Roman said, his hand sliding up to grip Dax by the front of his throat. "I killed your disgusting freak of a father. And now, I'm being granted the opportunity to kill you. You should have kept your hands off my omega, Kincaid."

My omega. Sidian bit back a moan at the words, sliding a hand down to press on his clit.

His alpha stood, and Roman's eyes met Sidian's once again for a moment before he turned his attention back to Dax. The muscles in one powerful thigh tensed before Roman placed the sole of his boot where his hand had been just a moment before; the sight of him pinning Dax to the ground was satisfying. That was how it should be, the inferior alpha put in his place. It was an aphrodisiac unlike anything Sidian had ever witnessed, his omega whining for his mate's attention.

"Rich alphas are all the same," Roman mused, pressing down just enough to make Dax grunt, his head tilting when

Dax let out a shaky little laugh. "Tell your father I said hello when you see him in hell."

He raised his boot just high enough to stomp down with crushing force, the sound of bones snapping and crackling sending another rivulet of slick spilling down Sidian's thighs.

Dax's chest caved inward from the pressure, and he let out a short, sharp scream that cut, his hands flying to where Roman's boot remained pressed into his chest. Something was wrong, and as Sidian watched, the alpha of his nightmares panicked. Pink spittle frothed at the corners of his mouth as he bucked under Roman's boot, but he failed to dislodge him. One sharp cough sent a shower of bloody droplets spraying into the air above his battered face.

And Roman remained where he was, pressing down harder when Dax squirmed and gurgled, the wet choking noises among the most beautiful sounds Sidian had ever heard. His hips bucked against the pressure of his own fingers as he watched more froth bubble out of Dax's lips, his eyes widening as the front of his boxers grew wet. Watching the bastard drown in his own blood was the sweetest gift Roman could have offered, and oh, did he offer it in style?

He stepped back only when Dax let out one final, rattling wheeze and then went still.

"Alpha," Sidian rasped, and Roman's head jerked in his direction, their eyes meeting, the connection between them sizzling like an exposed live wire. "Roe, please, fuck, I'm going to die if you don't fuck me. I need your knot now."

It only annoyed *a little* him that Roman smiled, leaving Dax's body on the ground as he rounded the bottom of the stairs. "When have I ever told you *no*, omega?"

There was a moment of sudden, sharp fear that stung Sidian like the injection had. Roman had never seen him like *that*, the black nightie feminine and *wrong* on Sidian's body. The first time they met each other, he'd been wearing jeans and layers to hide as much of himself from view as possible, and the thought that Roman might look at him and not see *him* choked him.

Roman was the only person who had ever seen him for who he was.

And Roman didn't even blink at him, hauling Sidian off of the ground and into his arms with a deep alpha rumble that eased Sidian's cramps. "I've got you, darling. I'm here."

He carried Sidian back downstairs, making a show out of stepping on Dax's body to get to the plush couch stretched out in front of the TV. As soon as he dropped Sidian onto the cushions, Sidian ripped the nightie off, snarling as he tore through the thin satin. It fell into glossy shreds on the floor, and he trilled in satisfaction before leaning back, getting situated, spreading his thighs wide and bracing his heels on the edge of the cushions to present the fabric that clung to his slick, needy cunt.

Roman dropped to his knees, the good boy he'd always been, and pressed a kiss to the inside of Sidian's thigh. "Tell me what you need from me."

"I need your fucking mouth to take the edge off, and then I need your dick." A wave of pain made him groan in discomfort, and Roman's low, concerned growl buzzed beneath his skin. "Shot me up with some pseudo-heat inducer shit. I need you to fuck me through it."

"Gladly." Roman's hands were so hot when they found Sidian's hips, thick fingers sliding beneath the waistband before one quick twist had both seams splitting open so Roman could rip them off.

Sidian had the five seconds necessary to process how fucking hot that was before Roman's mouth was on his cunt, nose bumping up against his clit while licking a hot path over his throbbing hole and then *inside,* his toes curling against the cushions. His head fell back as he whined, hands sinking into Roman's curls, twisting the wet strands around his fingers and *yanking* as hard as he could, grinding his cunt against Roman's face to get what he needed.

It was so fucking good, the way Roman ate him out. There was no hesitation, no uncertainty, no pause to see if he was doing it right. No, Roman knew what he was doing as he folded his upper lip over Sidian's clit and messily sucked, his tongue as deep as he could get it. The *noise* was almost disgusting, but it made Sidian burn even hotter, his hips spasming as his eyes squeezed shut. His alpha was right where Sidian wanted him, doing what Sidian wanted, obedient to a fault.

Roman was perfect. So fucking beyond perfect it was dizzying.

Mossy birch eyes met Sidian's from between his thighs, pupils blown wide and staring straight through him as Roman pressed a kiss to his swollen, twitching clit. Then he sucked it between his lips and closed his eyes, moaning into Sidian's flesh as his tongue flicked over the far too sensitive nerves. It was too much too fast, and Sidian arched toward his mouth, chasing the burn that threatened to immolate him.

The orgasm almost hurt. Every sore muscle twitched and spasmed with the force of it as Sidian wailed, his thighs snapping shut around Roman's head as he fucked himself against his alpha's face. Slick soaked them both, but Roman only lapped it up, growling into Sidian's flesh, the noise vibrating against his clit and sending another riotous wave of pleasure coiling through his body.

And Roman knew not to stop. Instead, he wrapped his arms around Sidian's thighs and dragged him down, holding him aloft like it was nothing as Roman licked and kissed at Sidian's soaking wet cunt.

His head spun as he pulled Roman's hair, shuddering when all Roman did was grunt and lick his clit harder, fast and punishing flicks of his tongue. "Fuck, fuck, just like that, *fuck!*"

Roman didn't come up for air. Didn't stop. Didn't slow. He just ate at Sidian like he couldn't stop, come to claim the prize the blood smeared across his skin demanded. He reeked of death and dominance and, for the first time in his life, Sidian *liked* that scent laced through with Roman's fiery, fragrant perfection. It appealed to his needy omega side, soothing the fire in his gut.

The moment Sidian went limp against the couch, Roman leaned back to breathe. His face was shiny with slick from the nose down, diluting some of the blood, and Sidian realized there were rusty scarlet trails of it along the insides of his thighs. He purred at the sight and reached for his alpha, and Roman came up to meet him, their lips crashing together, all tongue and teeth.

"I need you," Sidian told him between kisses, groaning when Roman kissed down to his throat, tongue rasping over his swollen scent gland. "I need your cock so fucking bad, alpha."

"Anything you want." Roman kissed him again and hauled Sidian down into his lap, caging him against the couch, and Sidian could feel the telltale swell of his erection through the wet denim of his jeans, the fabric cool and unpleasant and yet Sidian still rubbed himself against it like the bitch in heat he was. "Talk to me. Tell me what you need. Tell me what you want."

Sidian wanted so many things. He wanted Roman's knot lodged so deep inside of him he forgot where he ended and Roman began. He wanted assurance that nothing could tear them apart.

But most of all, as he looked up at Roman, wreathed in violence and blood and death, he wanted Roman's teeth. He wanted the bond that had only ever been a threat, a promise of forever, a scarred pattern of Roman's affection for him because Roman belonged to him. They belonged to each other.

For hours, Sidian didn't know whether Roman was dead or alive. Didn't know if he was hurt. He didn't know if he was *okay,* and he never wanted that to happen again. If any force on the earth ever parted them, then he wanted the assurance, the tangible proof Roman was all right.

"I'm sorry," he said, and when Roman frowned down at him, Sidian leaned up to kiss the pout of his mouth, licking the taste of copper off of his lips. "All that shit I said to you. I'm sorry, Roe. It wasn't your fault. None of this was your fault. You did nothing wrong. You *never* did."

Roman's face softened, and he curled himself around Sidian, warm and protective, shielding him, and Sidian didn't need to be protected from anything or anyone, but he was more than happy to have Roman more than willing to keep him safe. "It wasn't your fault either. And you don't have to apologize. You never have to apologize to me. I know you, Sid. I'll always know you."

It hurt hearing those words. Hurt because it was all Sidian had ever wanted from the only person he ever wanted it from and he didn't know what to do with it, the swell of emotion in his chest. So he leaned up and kissed his mate again, twining his fingers in Roman's hair, gentle instead of rough. He purred and dragged his cheeks over Roman's, intent on scenting him, intent on ensuring that wherever one of them went, the other would always be present even if only in the wind's ghost.

"I love you." Words he had never spoken before, not to anyone. Words he never thought he *would* speak. Not in his lifetime. Not in the next. "I love you so fucking much, Roe."

Roman shuddered in his arms and squeezed him tighter, burying his face in Sidian's hair, and Sidian almost thought he was about to cry when he heard a small, soft laugh muffled against the top of his head. "I love you, too. I think I've been in love with you since the day I first met you."

"It's an enormous commitment, loving my fucked-up ass. I want you to know that." Sidian laughed when Roman scowled at him, then leaned back, schooling his features. "I have a daughter. Dunno about the other one, but I'm sort of hoping for a boy so I can have one of each."

There was something so sweetly comical about the way Roman's brows furrowed before his eyes widened, his mouth falling open on a little almost squeak of a sound that did not fit him at all. "You're pregnant?" he rasped, his eyes falling to Sidian's stomach as pure wonder filled his face.

It had been stupid to hide it from him after all. "You ready to be a daddy?"

"Yes." No hesitation. No second guessing. Roman lifted Sidian off the floor and back onto the couch, pulling his blood-stained shirt up and over his head, muscles flexing with the movement. "In fact, do me the honor of letting me prove it to you."

Chapter Forty-Two

R oman only came to the ward when he was too restless to bear the long bus ride that seemed to wind through every single suburb before it deigned to reach his home.

He was never allowed further than the common room, but that suited him just fine as he slunk through the doorway, pressing his back up against the smooth, sterile plaster as he inhaled through his mouth. Still unpresented, he picked up the surrounding scents just the same, the edges of pheromones that he would have to contend with when he was a mature alpha. It wasn't something he was looking forward to, though he spoke to his father about it. Dad was kind, but he didn't understand.

Betas never did.

One patient twisted around to face him, lithe body curled up in the couch's corner, knees tucked up against a lean chest and raven hair framing a delicate face. It was only because the patient looked at him that Roman looked back, almost swallowing his tongue when a pair of the most vivid violet eyes he'd ever seen locked with his. Tangled lashes and dark circles had never looked lovelier than they did on the face of the omega who looked him up and down, then sneered at him.

"What the fuck are you looking at?" he demanded, the sharp tone of his voice pulling at Roman's gut in a way nothing ever had before. He looked petite, all delicate limbs and sharp cheekbones, the full pout of his mouth the only sign of softness anywhere on his person.

But he was beautiful, and Roman's hands were sweaty as he tucked them behind his back, pressing them against the wall to ground himself. The soft floral scent that tickled his nose made his chest tingle with warmth, though he thought little of it. He was too busy staring into the mean omega's eyes, separating the shades of amethyst in wonder. He'd seen green and blue and golden eyes before, but never such a vibrant shade of purple. Like royalty. Like gemstones.

It took him far too long to find his own voice. "You have beautiful eyes."

"What?" The omega's eyes widened, a flicker of shock before his face settled into a scowl once again. "I'm a fucking mental patient, asshole. You're not getting anything from me."

Roman shook his head, his face hot as embarrassment flooded him. "I'm just waiting for my dad," he said, and the omega's face softened. Just enough for him to notice. "I'm Roman, uh, Roman Kane. Doctor Kane is my father. I'm sure you've met him."

What a stupid fucking thing to say. Everyone in the ward had met him.

"Obsidian Vey." The omega's voice was halting, slow, and it did not occur to Roman right away that it was a name at all, that it was the first token offered to him, something he would cherish for the rest of his life. "But you can call me Sidian. Most people do."

"It's nice to meet you, Sidian."

He would think about the sharp-tongued omega until sleep claimed him late in the evening, and when his eyes finally fell shut, he would dream of those violet eyes.

Sidian rolled onto his hands and knees before Roman could process what he was doing, dropping to his elbows, his back arching in that position. "Fuck me like this. Mount me."

"Are you sure?" It took everything Roman had in him not to lose his mind at the sight of *Obsidian Vey* presenting for him, offering his heat-flushed pussy like a true omega would.

Sidian laughed and dropped his head onto the cushions, his eyes crinkling at the corners as Roman unbuckled his belt and unfastened his jeans, shoving it all down as fast as he could. "Dunno. Never done it before, but it must feel pretty good if every heated-up omega ends up on their knees. I trust you, Roe. Besides, don't you want a *real* reward for all the bodies you stacked up?"

His alpha swelled with pride as Roman wrapped a hand around his aching cock, sinking to his knees on the cushions. "Only if you allow me to have it."

"It's yours." Sidian reached down between his thighs; Roman watched as slender fingers parted his already spread folds even wider, revealing the slick throb of his opening. "Just for tonight, it's yours."

Roman groaned at the thought, stroking his cock before pressing the tip against Sidian's clit just so he could feel it twitch against where he was most sensitive. There was no sweeter place in the world than between Sidian's thighs, and his alpha strained to get closer, driven wild by the pheromones rolling off of Sidian's skin. Even if he wasn't in proper heat, it didn't seem to matter; Roman wanted to fuck him and knot him and bite him and tell him what a good omega he was, how perfect, how lucky Roman was to have such a gorgeous, powerful, loving mate in his life.

He wet his cock with Sidian's slick before dragging his head against the twitching muscles of Sidian's entrance, watching with rapt attention as pink flesh stretched around him. Sidian moaned and clawed at the cushion beneath him, the arch in his back deepening as he sought to take Roman inside faster, but Roman slowed him. He wanted to savor the moment, a shudder of pure bliss leaving goosebumps in its wake as Sidian's pussy drew him deep inside those hot, velvet walls.

Nothing had ever felt better. Nothing would ever feel better than that.

Roman leaned over his omega and covered Sidian with his body as best he could, his hand settling on top of Sidian's own as he trailed kisses across trembling shoulders. "You're so beautiful," he whispered, and Sidian whined up at him, his hips giving an impatient little wiggle until Roman thrust deep inside of him, drawing a cry from his kiss-swollen lips. "I'm so lucky to have you, Sid."

Sidian laughed, spreading his fingers to twine them with Roman's. "I'm the lucky one."

He wasn't. Roman wouldn't argue the point because it would go nowhere, burying his face in Sidian's hair as he filled up the trembling omega beneath him. Every thrust and roll of his hips dragged his cock along that slick channel, parting Sidian wider, urging him to take it all.

And he took it, his head falling into the cushions, his hair splayed around him, his eyes closed and his lips parted. Angelic. The most beautiful omega Roman had ever seen.

His chest tightened as he wrapped himself around Sidian, an arm sliding beneath him just to hold him, just to touch him, fingers splaying over his stomach. He wasn't showing, but Roman could feel the tautness of his skin, the proof of Sidian's second pregnancy, and he pressed his cheek against Sidian's and rumbled. His strong little mate, who had survived so much and was still with him.

"I love you," he whispered, and Sidian whined up at him. "Gorgeous boy, I love you so much."

Sidian purred in response and leaned up for a kiss that Roman gave him, smiling into it when he felt the telltale squirming beneath him. He sheathed his cock up to the knot and drew out, luxuriating in how perfectly wet Sidian was, how hot inside, the tight grip of his pussy giving them both just enough sensation. When he slid his hand down, fingers brushing over Sidian's clit, Sidian moaned into his mouth, the sound sweet as Roman licked it off of his omega's tongue.

"More," Sidian urged him, biting at his lower lip. "Roe, I need *more*."

"Faster? Harder?" Roman could guess, but he waited for Sidian's brief nod before he laid him back down on the cushions, digging his knees into the upholstery. One hand wrapped around the back of the couch to brace himself. If he broke it, he supposed it wouldn't matter. No one was going to use it and making Sidian come until he cried was likely the best use it had ever seen.

The first rough thrust jarred Sidian's entire body, and Sidian wailed with the pleasure of it.

Roman groaned at the sound of his mate's pleasure, gripping the couch tighter as he focused. Fast, hard, *deep*, his cock rubbed up against every sensitive nerve while his fingers teased Sidian's clit. He kept up the tight little circles, watching his cock vanish with every pump of his hips, his knot bumping up against flushed folds and teasing Sidian's pussy. The temptation to fuck his knot into that waiting heat was powerful, but Roman held out. It wasn't time. Not yet. *Not yet.*

Not until Sidian came apart for him one last time. Not until one last orgasm.

He watched Sidian's face, watched his nose crinkle, his lips part, listened to the beautiful litany of his whines as Roman refused to let himself so much as slow. His entire body ached, but he didn't care, the pain second to the pleasure that tensed

Sidian's limbs and made the muscles in his inner thighs twitch, his clit pulsing under Roman's fingers as he gripped Roman's cock tighter. There, he was there, he was right *there*, and Roman could taste the coming orgasm in his scent.

Sidian's lily scent thickened, honey-like and sappy, thick and sticky on Roman's tongue, and he moaned at the indulgence of it.

"Your dick's so fucking good," Sidian slurred, his hips bucking as if he didn't know whether to chase the touch of Roman's fingers or the stroke of his cock, his head lolling back as he whimpered. "Fuck, Roe, so close, so close, I'm so close. Make me come again, I wanna come on your cock."

Roman leaned over him, nuzzling into his dark hair. "You still want my bite?"

"Yes, yes, yes." Sidian chanted the words as he clawed at his own hair, pushing it off of the back of his neck, and Roman pressed a kiss to the skin there, tongue rolling over the gland to draw another pretty whine from Sidian's lips. "I need it. I need you. Don't leave me. Never leave me."

As if that were possible. "I love you, Sid. I'll never leave you. I promise."

And he wouldn't. They were made to be together, their souls, dark and stained and broken as they were, jagged at just the right edges to fit together. Maybe they were broken because they were always meant to complete each other. Roman didn't know. He didn't think he cared.

All that mattered was that he would never let go of Sidian again.

He felt the moment Sidian's cunt pulsed around him, tightening up with the beginnings of his orgasm, and Sidian cried out as his entire body stiffened. The peak of it sent a gush of fluid over Roman's knot, and he rumbled deep in his chest as he gripped Sidian's hip, pulling the omega back in one sharp movement to sink his knot deep into that waiting, welcoming heat. And Sidian clamped down on him, grasping so tight around his knot that grinding inside of him was almost impossible.

But Roman did, swearing as he felt Sidian come again, thrashing underneath him from the force of it. Then, and only then, lost in the throes of pleasure, his voice breaking in shouts and cries, was Sidian ready for the bite. Roman would not hurt him. He refused.

His teeth found thin, tender flesh, and he bit down, sinking his bite in deep until skin broke and blood flowed over his tongue, the coppery richness of it making his alpha crow in triumph.

The bond between them bloomed as sweet as Sidian's lily scent, washing over Roman in warm waves of satisfaction that made his own climax roar through him with that much more ferocity. A pure, relieved, relaxed happiness coiled through his mind, foreign at first before melding into his own thoughts, his own emotions, his own satisfaction at finally being able to call this omega his. Sidian *was* his. His mate, his life, his light, everything he had ever wanted.

"Fuck yeah." Sidian laughed a little, the sound breezy and sweet, and Roman felt a hand pat him on the cheek. "Good dog. Knew you had it in you."

He couldn't help himself; Roman grinned against his mate's neck, releasing his hold on him to lick over the edges of the bite. "I'll always give you what you want."

"Know you will. That's why you're the only alpha I want." Sidian settled into the cushions, and as Roman tended to his neck, licking up the blood and urging the wound to clot, he picked up the sweet, faint sounds of sleepy purrs vibrating up Sidian's throat. "Keep me warm until your knot goes down."

"I will. Both of you." Roman smoothed his hand over Sidian's stomach, and he knew he wasn't imagining it when Sidian purred a little harder at the touch.

Sidian blinked up at him as Roman eased them both down on their sides, wrapping his arms around Sidian to keep him warm and close. "Amey's upstairs," he murmured, and Roman's heart climbed into his throat. "When we, uh... Get cleaned up, I guess, you can meet her."

"I'm looking forward to it." And he was. He was ready to be a father.

Roman would be whatever Sidian needed him to be, and the pleased smile on Sidian's face only reassured him he was choosing the right path. Everything else fell by the wayside; all he cared about was making Sidian happy, and if he wanted a family, then he would get one.

Roman would figure it out like he had everything else between them.

Chapter Forty-Three

I t took hours and all the hot water in the house to scrub off the blood and slick and come.

Lilac was a good sport and assisted Puppy in washing her matted hair, his hands slick with copious amounts of conditioner while she muttered under her breath, little noises that did not quite shape themselves into words. When Roman had explained the state she was in prior to his intervention, Sidian felt a familiar spike of fear in his gut. Not for her; she was harmless enough, it seemed, content to allow herself to be washed, never so much as growling when Lilac had to tug at the knots in her hair. It was fear of what Roman might have become if Sidian hadn't been there to bring him out of it.

He allowed himself to be seated, letting Roman examine his hands to pick a few pieces of slivered glass from his skin, examining the bruises already beginning to mottle his flesh with a severe frown. As gently as he could, Sidian sanitized and bandaged the bite marks Puppy had left in Roman's flesh, then laid kisses over the rough, reddened skin of Roman's throat until his alpha rumbled for him.

As soon as the two of them were cleaned and wrapped in stolen towels, Roman hunted through the house for their suitcases. He found them stored in a hall closet, and Sidian breathed a sigh of relief, diving into the layers and yanking a shirt out of Roman's suitcase as well. He *needed* it.

The nape of his neck ached, a tingling sensation spreading through his limbs every time he felt a flicker of amusement or happiness from Roman's side of the bond. Just like in real life, he was muted, but Sidian could *feel* him now, and that was all he cared about.

As soon as he was dressed, he left Roman to finish with his own clothes and danced upstairs to the nursery. The once-locked door now stood open, and when he stepped into the room, he found Amey awake, gumming one of her hands and cooing up at the ceiling. Lilac hadn't been able to lull her back to sleep, but that was fine. She had to meet her daddy, after all.

"Hey, sweetheart." Sidian dared to reach out to touch her, stroking his knuckle against her tiny round cheek. "You think you wanna get up for a little while?"

She babbled up at him, one of her feet giving a kick before she giggled.

Fuck, she was precious. He crooned as he lowered the side of the crib to retrieve her, the warm, solid weight of her in his arms like a dream come true. He buried his face in her hair and inhaled, his heart thudding as he cuddled her close. He rubbed his cheek against the top of her head as gently as possible, intent on making sure she smelled like him, that she knew his scent, that she would take comfort in it and come to him when she needed him.

Amethyst caught a lock of his hair in her small hand and held it, blinking up at him with wide, violet eyes the precise shade of his own. Oh, Roman would love that. He would fall in love with her at first sight; Sidian was sure of it. There had been nothing to worry about.

"I missed you." He took her tiny hand in his and kissed her fingers, nuzzling into her tiny palm and chuckling when she made a soft *oooh* noise up at him. "I've thought about you so much. About how big you'd gotten, about how far you'd come. But it's okay now, sweetheart. Momma's here, and I'm never going to let you go. I'm going to take good care of you. I promise."

He kissed her forehead, her cheeks, the tip of her tiny nose, and Amey burst into giggles, the sound healing a hairline fracture deep in his soul that had been present since the moment he lost her.

Sidian wanted to take her to a nest, safe and secure, and just hold her until he forgot the rest of the world existed. Instead, he took a deep breath and picked up the blanket from the rocking chair, wrapping her up in it since the sliding glass door was in pieces. He didn't want her to catch a chill.

"We're going to go see Daddy now," he told her, and she hummed up at him, grabbing the collar of Roman's shirt as Sidian carried her out into the hallway. "He's been waiting a long time to get to see you, too, but don't worry. He only looks big and scary. He's so nice."

He cradled Amethyst against his chest, holding onto her as tightly as he dared while he navigated the stairs, skirting the splinters still littering the landing. Dax Kincaid's cooling corpse remained where Roman had left it, and while the alpha had been terrifying in life, he seemed like nothing more than a deflated Halloween decoration, cheap and ineffective. Sidian sniffed at the sight of him and hurried to the couch where Roman was still going through their bags.

He'd only reached the end of the couch when Roman looked up at him, then down at Amey.

She was so beautiful. She was tiny and porcelain perfect, but Lilac had reassured Sidian that she was in a healthy percentile for her age. Just six months old; Roman would freak the fuck out as soon as he realized Sidian had gone into heat only a few months after giving birth, but he'd worry about that later. The past was the past, and there was no changing it.

Roman knocked a throw pillow aside so Sidian could sit down next to him, turning until Amey's wandering eyes landed on Roman. She linked up at him a few times before babbling while Roman stared at her like she was a miracle come to life, one hand rising to touch her. She pressed her tiny hand into his palm like it was what she wanted, and Sidian saw the brief sheen of tears in Roman's eyes before he blinked them away.

"She's beautiful," he whispered, his voice wrecked as Amey patted her hand against his, babbling up at him. "Goddess, she has your eyes. She's an omega, isn't she? Her scent isn't developed at all, but I can still tell."

Sidian nodded, his throat tightening. "We're going to protect her. The world sucks, and she's too sweet to let it destroy her."

"I'd burn it all down to keep her safe." Roman seemed to marvel as Amey clasped one of his fingers in hers, and she looked up at Sidian like she expected him to do something about it. When all he did was croon in response, her little face lit up. "Can I hold her? I know you just got her back and it'll only be for a moment, but... I just want to hold her."

"Of course you can. She's your daughter." But just the same, it took a mighty effort to relinquish her when all Sidian wanted to do was cling to her, to the undeniable proof she was real and alive and in front of him. He had her back. It almost didn't seem real.

He showed Roman how to hold her and then leaned back to give him space, his heart clenching at the sight of his mate cradling their daughter in his arms. She looked so small in his embrace but so comfortable, patting his arms as she gazed around the living room. When a cool breeze filtered into the room and ruffled her hair, she perked up and patted Roman's arm, babbling louder at him as if to tell him about the wind. And the way he smiled at her, eyes glittering and crinkling at the corners... Goddess, he *loved* her. He loved her.

"Amethyst is the perfect name for her," he said, stroking her dark hair before he laid a kiss on her tiny forehead. "I promise you on my life that nothing will ever happen to her. And when our second child is born, I'll swear the same. No matter what, Sid, this is our family. *Ours.* And I will do everything to take care of all three of you."

"I know you will," Sidian reassured him, and Amey cooed in agreement.

For just a moment, it was nice to lean back against the couch and just be. Roman gave Amethyst back to him, and Sidian sighed in relief, then cackled when his alpha dragged *both* of them into his lap, his arms bracketing them with strength and warmth. Though he'd never wanted to be an omega, Sidian indulged his instincts and let his alpha cradle him and his daughter, secure in his mate's embrace.

"Thank you for letting me know." Captain Nightingale's voice was clipped. *"I'll talk to the boss and figure out where she wants to go from here. We'll need to investigate. How's Puppy?"*

Sidian glanced over to where she was sitting on the coffee table, her legs folded beneath her, chewing at one of her nails with a blank expression. Better than he would have been, that was for certain, though the fact she still hadn't spoken did concern him.

Roman sighed into the phone. "She's all right. I think she's going to stay with us for a while."

"That would be acceptable." Nightingale paused. *"And the omega? Extraction will take him in if he needs somewhere to go. We've handled far more omegas than just one."*

Lilac glanced up from where he was still packing Amey's diaper bag. "Is that okay?"

"I think he would appreciate that. Place him somewhere where none of this can ever touch him if you can. He took care of my daughter. He deserves it." Roman wasn't looking at Lilac; he missed the soft blush as the omega dropped his head, bundling tiny socks together.

Sidian smiled and tickled Amey's stomach, grinning when she giggled. "He did a good job, too."

"Consider it done. Is there anything you need from us going forward?" Nightingale asked.

Roman rested his chin on Sidian's shoulder, and Sidian rubbed their cheeks together without thinking. It seemed the right thing to do, scenting his bonded mate. "No. We're going to go off grid for a while, I think. We'll let you know if we need anything, but I would appreciate if you would pass on a message to the captain for me. I don't know when I'll next speak to him."

Nightingale paused. *"What would you like me to tell him?"*

"That I appreciate everything, but as I have a family to take care of, I'll be retiring from the Vipers. It was an honor, though." Roman gave Sidian a gentle squeeze, not even wincing when Amethyst caught one of his damp curls and gave it a yank. "We'll take care of Puppy, you take care of Lilac, and I think we can call this even."

He cut the call off after, passing the phone back to Lilac, and kissed the side of Sidian's head.

"Where are you going to go?" Lilac glanced between them, his expression troubled.

He was a sweet omega. Sidian rather liked him. "We're just gonna go. It's supposed to be a nice day out and we could all use some actual fresh air. When we figure out what we wanna do, we'll do it. For now, I think we just want to be together for a little while."

Puppy hummed in agreement, and Amey hummed back at her, eliciting a small, genuine smile.

Yeah. They would figure it out together.

Chapter Forty-Four

Roman thought he might be a coward for not calling the Vipers himself.

It occurred to him it would have been the respectful thing to do, the *right* thing to do, to reassure them that all was fine, and he was where he wanted to be. He knew that disappearing into the trees was what he needed to do for himself, and his happy ending had materialized in front of him after years of separation, so how could he stop himself from pursuing it? But as he watched Sidian change Amey, the two of them vocalizing to each other as only omegas could, he didn't think he had it in him to make another call. He didn't have it in him to hold on to that life anymore.

But he did second-guess himself in the end. He made one more phone call standing at the broken sliding glass door, staring out at Talon's body and the crow that pecked at his broken skull.

Lorcan Devereaux picked up on the second ring. *"Hello, Roman."*

"You knew I was calling you, boss." It wasn't a question. It didn't need to be. They knew each other better than that.

"I expected a phone call after speaking with Noel. The moment he broached the subject of your designation, I knew it was a matter of time." Lorcan chuckled, the faint hiss underpinning his words. Wherever he was, he was masked, then. *"If you're expecting an*

apology, I wouldn't hold your breath. I don't regret the decision I made not to tell you."

Roman let himself digest that, though he didn't know what to do with the way he felt about it. "That's fine, I guess. Did you know about Sidian, or was that a miscalculation?"

Lorcan quieted on his end of the line. *"I suspected it , but I did not have enough evidence. Considering everything that has occurred, my current assumption is that Kincaid was informed about Vey's placement within the breeding center before I searched for him on your behalf."*

"Did Silver go through the files he recovered? If you think the center was blocking his information, that would be your proof."

"You're sharp," Lorcan praised. *"That's where my assumption comes from. Obsidian Vey is not registered as a patient within any of their internal files. Either they were not keeping files on him, or they were sent somewhere that we could not access."*

That figured. "We need a car to get out of here. You think you can send us one?"

"There is a gas station fifteen and three-quarters of a mile from the Kincaid residence. I have something waiting there for you. The plates will give you no trouble. ID is in the visor."

"You did know I would call." It was almost reassuring, in a way, how competent Lorcan could be in a situation like that.

He scoffed as if offended. *"I'm not ignorant, Roman. You're right not to take one of the Kincaid cars. It would look suspicious. Besides, there are external signals being broadcast somewhere that we're looking into. Someone has them bugged. I'm not sure why."*

"Kincaid had a tracker implanted in Sidian's body when he was unconscious from childbirth," Roman said, and it took serious effort not to crush the phone in his hand. He had to remind himself it belonged to Lilac. "Can you do anything about that?"

"I'll have Silver on it. We'll cut the signal if we can find it, though I must advise that you find a safe and reliable way to remove it as soon as possible. Just in case."

Roman would figure that one out on his own; it wasn't something his mate should have to worry about. Part of him wanted to do it in the house, then and there, but he didn't trust himself not to do something wrong, and he knew precious little about first aid. "I'm not coming back to the Vipers."

Lorcan sighed at him. *"I knew that the moment I was told you went missing."*

"Were you worried about me?"

"Worried about you?" Lorcan laughed into his ear, and Roman's lip twitched at the corner. *"No, Roman. I've never needed to worry about you, no matter the circumstance. Not because you are a prime alpha and not because you are forever a serpent of Ouroboros. You have been competent from the moment we took you in, so I assume this is a quality that belongs to you."*

"I owe you some gratitude. The mercenary training helped with the Kincaids. I don't know if I would have been able to handle them without it." He considered, eyes flicking toward the living room over his shoulder to where Puppy was rearranging her things once again. "And I wouldn't have known who Puppy was at all. I would have either killed her, or she would have killed me."

"Oh, she would have killed you," Lorcan reassured him.

Roman rolled his eyes. "Just the same. Thank you. I know what would have happened to me if you had left me in that jail cell, and you could have. You have plenty of talented people at your disposal. If you hadn't stepped in, I never would have been able to save Sidian."

"For that, you are welcome," Lorcan said, and Roman bit back a smile. Of course, he was welcome. *"I would like you to be careful, and to take care of yourself, your mate, and your child. Should you*

need anything, reach out. My resources are vast and limitless, and manipulating the stocks of the tech sector is proving to be lucrative these days."

"I'll keep that in mind. Thanks again." Roman exhaled, then hung up the phone, closing that chapter of his life once and for all.

Puppy trotted up to him, outfitted with the black leather bag and all the clothing Lilac had convinced her to take. She had changed from her torn dress into a pair of jeans and a long-sleeved shirt, with a sweatshirt tied around her waist in case she got cold. With her auburn hair washed and tamed and her face cleaned of dirt and grime, she looked normal. The only thing that set her apart was the crimson blaze of her eyes, but there was nothing they could do about that. It would be a part of her for the rest of her life, and she would do well to learn to live with it.

Roman gave her hair a light ruffle. "You ready to hit the road?"

She didn't answer with words, scowling at him as she swatted his hand before giving him a firm nod. She might never speak again, but he was hoping she found her words one day.

It was reckless to take off on foot, and he knew that as well as anyone else, but a few hours' walk to the gas station felt far safer than taking the Kincaid cars especially now that Lorcan confirmed they were bugged. Sidian's tracker would stop being a problem soon, and when they were somewhere safe, Roman would locate someone capable of removing it without hurting his mate more than was necessary. A hospital was an option, but Goddess only knew what information might turn up there.

They could have waited for the Mambas, but none of them wanted to. The itch to get out of the house was powerful, and now that Roman's little family had been reunited, he wanted to spirit them away from the blood and the gore as soon as possible, no matter what it took to do so.

Sidian tucked Amethyst's blanket back around her, eyeing Roman. "Are you sure about carrying her? I can do it if you don't think you can manage."

"I can manage." Roman tilted his head toward the car seat. "Strap her in. I've got her."

He hadn't said it out loud, not wanting to disturb the fragile peace in the house, but part of him feared the cars might have trackers of some kind. If the Kincaids had been working alongside traffickers, it was always possible. He didn't know how important they were or if anyone would come looking for them, so their plates could stay where they belonged for the time being. Goddess forbid they take one of the fancy pieces of shit just down the road only to trip a system Roman didn't know about and couldn't expect. He could handle anything that endangered Sidian, but also, he was tired. He needed a break, and it was a nice day out.

He and Sidian had gotten this far. They could keep going together.

"All right," Lilac said, zipping the bag shut and handing it to Sidian. "Got as much in there as I could. There's formula, but you should let her try to latch when she's hungry. With you being pregnant, your milk production would kick back in right away. Assuming you want to breastfeed."

Sidian tilted his head. "I'll keep that in mind. Thanks for your help."

"Take care of yourselves out there. I mean, I think you have more than enough protection." Lilac eyed Roman and Puppy, and Roman chuckled to himself. It was a compliment; he knew what he was capable of, and now he knew what Puppy was willing to do if need be. "Amey was a wonderful baby. I wasn't ready for a kid, so I did the best I could do, but, Goddess, she was a breath of fresh air in this place. I'm glad you're all together now. Just make sure you stay together."

They would. Roman would make sure of that.

He handed Lilac back his phone. "I dialed my former boss's number. He's a good man, and he takes care of omegas. If you need anything, I'm sure you can call him and he'd be more than happy to help."

Lilac clutched the phone and nodded. "Thanks. I'll call him if I ever need anything, I think."

Puppy gave Roman's sleeve a tug and nodded her head at the door, and he took the hint. She was ready to go. "All right, let's head out. Lorcan said he had a car for us at a gas station, but it's going to take us a few hours to get there on foot."

"No stealing this time?" Sidian asked, a hopeful note in his voice as he shouldered the duffel bag they'd stolen from the closet upstairs.

"No stealing this time. Probably for the best. If we hadn't been driving across state lines, I don't know how much longer we would have kept the Ultima." Hopefully, Lorcan had chosen something inconspicuous enough not to stand out, though Roman wouldn't be surprised to find a sleek black van that screamed *Someone who kills people drives this.*

They would have to make sure not to stray so far from the trees that it was difficult to duck into the foliage if need be during their walk. After all, the last thing they wanted to do was draw the attention of the police. None of them had any form of ID, which would not be explained easily. And cops made everything worse. What if they tried to take Amey?

Roman didn't want to kill a cop if he didn't have to. After all, it was always such a fucking mess.

"Sounds like a plan." Sidian pouted his lips, and Roman gave him the kiss he wanted before he picked up the car seat, letting himself get used to the weight of it. He'd switch it back and forth from hand to hand as needed. "Are you ready to go on a quick trip, Amey? We're going to find somewhere nice and pretty to settle down. Somewhere you can grow up big and strong and not afraid of anything."

Amethyst kicked her little feet and giggled with delight, and Roman felt a warmth swell in his chest that was unfamiliar to him. Fatherhood was going to be an adjustment, but he was glad for it.

Because she was Sidian's, and that made her more precious than anything in the world.

He ran through a mental checklist of everything they had as he shouldered the heaviest of the duffel bags, which held all of his and Sidian's clothes, as well as a few weapons secreted between the folds just in case. Sidian's duffel bag contained the food that Roman felt comfortable traveling with, and he refused to let Roman take the diaper bag, which was fine. If he tired of it, Roman would take it without a word, and they both knew it.

They had what they needed for the time being. On foot, they'd put some distance between themselves and the house. Get some fresh air, soak in some sunshine, enjoy the scent of rain drying on the damp asphalt. They would reach the gas station, pile into the car, choose a direction, and just drive for as long as it made sense to. They could decide where to stop when they were ready to rest.

And Puppy would tag along for as long as she wanted to. Roman didn't know why she wanted to stay with them, but as she turned curious eyes to Amethyst once again, he found he didn't care so much. As long as she kept his mate and child safe, she could stay as long as she wanted.

Lilac opened the front door for them, and Roman stepped out onto the porch, turning to offer his free arm to Sidian, who tucked up underneath it with a happy little trill. Though his hair hid his mating bond from view, Roman didn't mind; he knew it was there, and he delighted in it. And even without seeing it, he felt it; Sidian's happiness was like champagne, bubbly and sweet. Seeing him smile, *feeling* his joy, Roman was at peace for the first time in... Maybe ever.

Distantly, he wished his father could have witnessed it. Dad had done everything in his power to help Roman, and none of it had worked in the end. He'd tried to help Sidian, but all it had done was end in bloodshed. But that was the past. It was time to let it go once and for all.

It was time to let everything go but the present and the immediate future, to plan for what came next and to play everything where it lay. They could do that much.

"I'm thinking cottage in the woods," Sidian said, spreading his hands out in front of him as they walked down the long driveway toward the road. "Honeysuckle and wildflowers. What do you think?"

Roman considered the image. It seemed a little more storybook than he would have thought his mate wanted, but it had potential. "We could hang feeders outside the house. We might see hummingbirds in nicer weather. They're beautiful."

Sidian beamed up at him. "You've gotta take care of any wasp nests that show up."

"I think I can handle a few wasps now and then." They stung like motherfuckers, but Roman had been a young alpha once, and he still remembered just how many times he'd end up dealing with the stings every single spring and summer without fail. He never learned.

Puppy snorted into her hand and hurried around him to walk next to Sidian, peering at him out of the corner of her eye as if she thought Roman might have missed that.

He jabbed a finger at her, and she stuck her tongue out at him. It took him aback at the same time it relieved him; any small show of humanity was worth something, after all. "What was that? You think I can't handle a wasp? It's a *bug*. Anyone can handle a wasp."

She had the audacity to mutter at him, and Sidian smothered a laugh behind his hand.

Fuck, he had such a beautiful laugh. He was beautiful, snarky, and sweet, and Roman loved him so much he didn't know what to do with himself anymore.

He watched as Sidian tilted his head back toward the warm morning sunlight, his eyes closed, his lips parted as he sighed. The sun brought out the hints of purple that highlighted his black hair, and then he looked at Roman as if feeling the weight of his gaze. Their eyes met, and the gentle happiness in Roman's chest that was not his own glowed just a little brighter.

"Not to get sappy," Sidian said, "but I was thinking about what you said."

Roman arched an eyebrow at him. "What I said about what?"

"When you told me you thought you loved me the first time we met." Sidian nibbled on his bottom lip, and Roman felt the telltale urge to kiss him, complicated only because Amethyst's car seat swung between them, ensuring Sidian was as close to her as he could be. "I don't even know if I could love another person back then when I hated myself so much, but I still fucking adored you. You were too good for me, but I wanted you."

"No," Roman corrected him. "You were perfect for me. It's that simple."

He could have argued the point that Sidian was the better of the two of them, poised and graceful, strong and stubborn, embodying every aspect of survival. He'd come out the other side of something horrible, and he had everything in the world to show for it.

But he was very stubborn, and arguing never got Roman anywhere. "You are still perfect."

"Thank you." The serene acceptance made Roman's eyes widen a touch, and Sidian smiled like he was proud of himself, preening a little before he stretched his arms up and over his head. "You're pretty perfect yourself. I'm glad you're my mate. I wouldn't want anyone else."

Roman felt the same. When he'd been younger and they were just teenagers skirting the idea of what it might mean to be in love, he had once dreamed of giving Sidian a pack. Multiple mates to love him and cherish him, to show him how special he was, to protect him and nurture him, but they didn't need a pack. They had each other, and that was more than enough for both of them.

Amethyst squealed with excitement and pointed toward a cardinal as it swooped across the road, and Sidian grinned down at her. "You like the pretty bird, baby girl?"

The morning was warm, the breeze just cool enough to keep them from overheating as they walked along the curving stretch of asphalt. Roman listened to Sidian and Amethyst talk to each other, picking up the occasional mumble from Puppy as she kicked at gravel and sent it skittering across the pavement. They had everything they needed, the people who had hurt his mate were dead, and there were endless possibilities stretching out in every direction. They could go anywhere and do anything; as long as he had Sidian, Roman was content.

He had his darling, and he had his daughter. There was nothing else an alpha could want.

Epilogue I

The silence in the car smothered Jasper D'Arlowe as he slumped down as far as possible in the passenger seat, lower lip clamped between his teeth. He'd been chewing on it off and on since Val pulled out of the hospital's parking lot, and it was a miracle he hadn't bitten it off yet.

Val had attempted light conversation a few times during the drive, but Jasper wasn't having it. They had come for the bad news they knew they would receive, news that coiled through his chest like thorny vines, lodging into every part of him that was tender and vulnerable. Months of wasted time to force his failing body to accomplish the one thing it was supposed to do well, and it had all been for nothing. The final, desperate heat they coaxed out of him had gone nowhere, just as every single one that came before it.

Omegas were supposed to be breeders. What the fuck was wrong with him?

"I'm fine with it," Val insisted for the sixth time during their three-hour drive, his gaze focused on the dark road ahead. "I am. I mean, we can always look into fostering and adoption if we want to."

Jasper's eyes stung with unshed tears, and he swiped at them to keep himself under control. He wouldn't break down in the car. He wouldn't. "Just shut the fuck up, Val. I don't want to talk about it right now."

He felt like a piece of shit for snapping at his mate like that, but Val wasn't the one who was declared infertile. He wasn't an omega, and he couldn't understand it. Jasper wanted children, yes, and they could always foster or adopt, but he would not have the experience of being pregnant, of the doctor's visits, of the birth, of holding his child in his arms for the very first time and having that bonding experience. It was something he'd wanted since he was a teenager and realized it was something he could and was allowed, and even encouraged, to want.

It wasn't fair. An omega's value was not supposed to be tied to their ability to birth children, but Jasper *wanted* them. His irregular heats would slough off into nothing, and both of his alpha mates would have to deal with Goddess only knew what hormonal issues.

He didn't want it. He had never asked for it.

"You don't have to talk, but I'm going to talk to you," Val said, and Jasper rolled his eyes, resigning himself to dealing with Val's pep talk for the rest of the drive. He meant well, but it changed nothing. "You mean so much to me. I *chose* you, Jasper. You're the only omega I've ever wanted."

Jasper pinched the bridge of his nose. Deep breaths, in and out, just like his therapist had taught him. "We're never gonna be able to have kids. Never gonna be able to have a family. All those fucking dreams of buying a bigger house to cram all the kids into mean nothing now, Val. I'm broken. We know. Just... Let it go. Just let it go."

"I'll let it go when I believe you're feeling better. I can feel how miserable you are about it, and I get that, but let me in. Tell me what you need to feel better."

What a stupid request. "I need a uterus that functions the way it should function when it grew in my body. I want a baby. What's so hard to understand?"

They had been arguing for the past two weeks while they waited for their scheduled appointment, though Jasper swore up and down it wasn't necessary. Both Val and Brady—his other alpha mate—had regular ruts. Even Cass's periods were always on time. It felt like a cruel joke from the universe that Jasper's heat cycles were all over the place.

And he knew what that meant in the back of his head long before he became addicted to late nights scrolling forums of omegas all bemoaning their infertile status.

He was one of the lucky ones, at least. Most infertile omegas without mates or partners struggled to find alphas who were interested in them. None of his mates had so much as whispered an urge to find someone to replace him, and Jasper doubted they would, but he almost *wished* they would. They deserved to live their own dreams, too.

Val pursed his lips, his gaze fixed on the stretch of dark road ahead of them. "Well, that was just one opinion, right? Give me a few weeks to do some research, and maybe we can figure something else out. Maybe that doctor was just an idiot, who knows? Maybe we can still fix this."

"I love you," Jasper said, and Val's face softened, "but you and I both know there isn't any fixing this. It happens. It sucks, but it happens. We just have to make our peace with it."

The rest of the drive home was quiet, Val reaching out to turn on the radio but leaving it low. Jasper was fine with that; it broke up the awkward silence between them, and the occasional crackle through the speakers felt nostalgic as he settled his head against the cool glass of the window, his eyelids fluttering shut. Dad's car radio never picked up anything that wasn't laced with static, and those long night drives that served as nothing more than a waste of gas to calm Jasper down from whatever anxiety he was spiraling through at the moment had given the crackling sound a soothing effect.

He wasn't even aware he was dozing off until the car came to a stop and Val touched his shoulder. "Hey, baby, wake up. We're home now."

Jasper huffed and pushed himself into a sitting position, rubbing his eyes. "Thanks."

He wanted to crawl into his nest and scream into the pillows until the frustration ebbed enough for him to get some sleep. Even though his appointment was in the afternoon, he still spent most of last night wide awake, waiting for the inevitable diagnosis that he was fucked-up and unable to fix. Now that he knew that, maybe he could get a few solid hours of rest.

It would do nothing to soothe the ache in his heart. He thought nothing would. Maybe a few drinks, or maybe it was time to get involved in kickboxing once again to see if that went anywhere.

He dragged himself out of the car, stretching his arms over his head until his back popped, and paused when he noticed a faint golden light through the trees across the road.

His pack lived in the countryside for the peace, and though there was one other property within walking distance of their home, no one had lived there for as long as Jasper had known the place existed. Whether the price was too steep, the cottage undesirable, or something about the interior was bad, he did not know. He kept expecting to just see another car on the road one day, pulling off onto that twisting little dirt path that slithered through the trees.

"Did someone move in across the road?" he asked Val, nodding toward the light. The urge to cross the asphalt just to see if he might glimpse the cottage from the road was tempting, but Jasper knew that until the dead of winter, it was impossible to see anything without walking down that path.

Val frowned, cocking his head. "You know, I think I might have heard someone driving when I was getting out of the shower, but I didn't think too much about it. I mean... About time, I guess? I'm surprised nobody moved in sooner. It's nice out here."

Jasper could agree with that much . "Maybe we should go say hi tomorrow or something. Might not be a bad idea to have friends out here when the weather gets bad."

"Maybe," Val hedged. "Come on, let's get inside. Brady and Cass are waiting."

As petty as it was, they could *keep* waiting as long as Jasper was concerned. He would have to sit them down and tell them both that his body wasn't working right, that they wouldn't get to have the family they wanted to build together, that he was the wrong choice of a mate after all. The frisson of anxiety that threaded through his mind let him know Brady was indeed waiting for them, and not for the first time, he wished Cass was as tied up in their bond as everyone else.

While Val unlocked the door to let them into the house, Jasper turned to throw a glance toward the dirt road. It was a short walk; he would try to think of something nice to bake, maybe, so he'd have an excuse to go over. Maybe it was a pack with an omega. Couldn't hurt to try.

As he stepped into the house, though, he could have sworn he saw someone standing at the edge of the shadows spilling across the road, tucked just out of sight.

And it looked like they were facing him.

Epilogue II

Valentine D'Arlowe knew that the belief they had failed their omega would spread through the pack bond, tainting everything it touched until it brought their ruin unless he did something about it.

The house was quiet as he sat at the kitchen table, his head in his hands and his heart breaking piece by piece, chipping away until there was almost nothing left of him. Though he had suspected Jasper's diagnosis would be just as disappointing as he suspected it to be, he kept turning the details over in his head to find some sort of way to fix it. An omega becoming infertile at twenty-two just didn't seem fair to him, especially when Jasper wanted children more than he wanted anything else. There had been stay-at-home mom jokes when they were still teenagers.

That had served as the motivation for Val to ensure he had a good job. Good enough so that Jasper could stay home, take care of the house, and pretty it up however he pleased while they waited for one successful heat. In the end, there hadn't been one. His heats ranged from several hours to nearly a week; he'd had two awful heats in one month, then went six months without having another one. Such things were common enough that Val knew what to expect, but he still hadn't *wanted* it.

Jasper was the most important thing in his life. Of course, he wanted Jasper to have everything he had ever wanted. What alpha wouldn't?

He pushed himself away from the table and walked a slow circuit of the downstairs, aware of the settling of the house, the wind in the pines, the occasional snap of a twig as small animals scurried through the undergrowth. Winter would come soon enough, but Jasper was already freezing them out, and that was something Val had to stop as soon as possible. It would be devastating.

Bonds could rot straight through. They could fall apart. Mending them took serious time, dedication, and effort that would be hard for someone hurting as much as Jasper was. That meant Val needed to put a stop to the dissolution while he had the chance; Jasper needed the bond, and so did Brady. And even if Cass was barely an echo, Val didn't want to lose him, either.

He didn't want to lose anyone he cared about. Such was life as a pack alpha.

A soft crunching sound caught his attention, and he frowned, one foot in the kitchen and one foot in the living room. On another night when he was busier or already in bed, he might have missed the sound for how quiet it was, but it wasn't silent. There was a slow, steady rhythm to the crunches, muted but consistent. Footsteps. Was he hearing footsteps?

You don't know what people might have moved in across the road.

Fuck. *Fuck.* No, it was fine. It might have been a deer, a bear, or even a wolf that had come slinking out of the woods in search of food. Mostly, he could ignore the animals as they wouldn't try to break into the house, but that was assuming the sound *was* an animal. And he needed to verify that in case it wasn't.

It took the emergency services far too long to drive as far out as the house.

He flicked off the kitchen light, bathing the downstairs in darkness, and the footsteps stopped.

Val remained frozen, waiting for his vision to adjust, head cocked toward the noise as he held his breath. If someone was creeping around the house, then he would need to get the gun closest to him, and he would need to put a stop to it. Plenty of odd things happened out in the countryside where few people were around to witness it. And though he had never been paranoid about what might happen, he wasn't stupid enough to ignore something so obvious.

The nearest window was the bay window in the living room, and he crept up to it, his socked feet near-silent on the glossy hardwood floor. Why someone would be near the house was beyond him, but he didn't need to figure out the logistics of it all just yet. He needed to verify. That was all.

If there were a person walking around the front of the house, they might stare at the window searching for movement. That was a risk Val had to take.

He edged up as close to the curtain as he could, slipping a finger beneath the edge to tug it away from the wall. Though he had wanted blinds for the house, Jasper made it very clear he wanted curtains, and Val was not in the business of denying his omega anything he wanted. But as he eased the edge of the curtain aside so he could peer out into the night, he appreciated his mate's decision. It would have been much harder to sneak open the blinds.

At first, he saw nothing more than some pines next to the house and the edge of the car. Sighing, he almost dropped the curtain when movement caught his attention, his gaze honing in on something just visible next to the car. In the next breath, someone stepped into his line of view, though their back was to him, so he couldn't make out their face.

Fuck. Holy fuck. Someone *was* outside the house.

Good enough. Val smoothed the curtain back into place and made for the slim closet next to the door, popping it open so he could lay hands on the rifle tucked inside of it.

Though plenty of people would argue it wasn't the safest place to store a gun, he didn't care. Having quick and convenient access was more important out in the country, where anything might happen and wild animals could be a serious concern. The plan had been to move all the guns into more secure storage once they bred Jasper, but that wasn't happening.

A slight twinge in his chest made him wince.

He loaded shells into the gun as quietly as possible, then crept back toward the curtain to peer out into the darkness again. The person was hard to make out, tucked into the shadows of the house, but Val thought it might have been a woman. The lithe shape of the body and the long mane of curly hair seemed feminine to him, though without a proper look at their face, he couldn't be sure.

Were they an omega? They might have been looking for a safe place to stay.

He scoffed at himself. No omega went sneaking around someone's house if they needed help, but it was a wonderful insight into his mind. He was stupid enough to walk right into a trap if an omega was involved, but as far as he knew, that should have been the norm.

Alphas should always be willing to go out on a limb for the sake of an omega.

From his vantage point, he couldn't tell if the person was armed or not. If they had no weapons on their person, then the gun should be adequate intimidation even without pulling the trigger. If it wasn't, he wasn't afraid to put the gun to use. Anything to keep his pack safe. Especially his mate.

Val frowned when he saw the figure glance around. *What the hell are you doing?*

And then the mane shifted as the figure leaned back.

He frowned at the sight, unable to know what to make of it, though his pulse sped up as the person kept bending backward, and backward, and backward. The dark hair gave way to the pale expanse of a forehead, the curve of a dainty nose, a mouth pressed into a thin line.

And most disturbing of all, a pair of crimson eyes that cut straight through the shadows.

The woman stood on the gravel of the driveway, arms hanging at her sides, leaning back far enough that she should have toppled over. Instead, she remained in that position, her red eyes meeting Val's and holding his gaze while the wind stirred her curls. The arch of her back seemed alien, inhuman.

And then she twisted around, rolling her head grotesquely, so she never took her eyes off of him.

What the fuck? The shotgun didn't seem like quite enough to handle whatever the fuck that was. Red eyes meant feral, but feral alpha or feral omega? If she were a feral alpha, then he would need to shoot her, but where had she come from? Did she live in the house across the road?

Or had she turned up there when her bloodlust died out?

Val knew how much damage a feral alpha could do, and he was not about to let her get anywhere near the house. Instead, he stepped back out of her line of sight and took a deep breath, then headed for the door. He might frighten her off if she wasn't too deep in her instincts, but he couldn't depend on that working. He needed to be ready to do what needed to be done.

The locks *clicked* as he twisted them, and with one more deep breath, he swung the door open.

The feral woman stood on his doorstep, staring into his eyes.

Without thinking, Val raised the rifle.

Epilogue III

I t took three days for Puppy's curiosity to get the best of her.

Sidian swore as he shoved his hands into the pockets of the jacket he'd stolen from Roman, shivering in the chill that laced the air. Three days of settling in at what had once been a Mamba safe house so they could have an actual place to stay, a house where they could sleep each night and where Sidian could laze away the rest of his pregnancy. After a month of being out on the road, finding some of the most breathtakingly scenic views they could find throughout New Jersey and even up into New York, it was nice to have somewhere to settle down for a little while.

Didn't mean it was home. He wondered if he would ever feel at home anywhere in the world. Maybe it would just take time. Growing up in a trailer that seemed to stand only because of duct tape and poorly hammered nails did not give him a feeling of security, and it had been from there to the psych ward, then straight to the breeding center.

He could give himself time. Be patient or something. Whatever.

But he had to get Puppy back into the house before Roman woke up. He'd fallen asleep waiting for Sidian to get out of the shower with Amey stretched out on her back next to him on the king-sized mattress in the master bedroom. The house was a pretty average place with a lot of wood paneling and an overall cozy interior, three bedrooms—one of which would become a nursery over the next few months if Sidian had anything to say about it—and a nest off the master bedroom that Sidian still needed to poke around in.

Roman had muttered something under his breath the day they moved in about *Lorcan* and *money*. Sidian believed that meant they would get whatever they wanted when they asked for it.

Of course, Devereaux could not magically teleport across the country to drag the half-feral female alpha who accompanied them back into the house. She had been restless since the evening they pulled the Toyota into the detached garage, making muttering sounds under her breath or staring out at the dirt path that led to the main road. Out in the middle of nowhere, there was only one other house around for miles, and it was more or less across the street.

Given how she was, it wasn't a surprise she wanted to know more about their neighbors. Every time they stopped anywhere to eat, she wedged herself into the booth next to Sidian and radiated such tension and hostility that Roman tipped extra as an apology. If an alpha in public glanced over at them, Puppy would catch that alpha's gaze and hold it until they got spooked and broke it themself. More than a few freaked out as soon as they realized what eyes they were looking into.

She had been living in a feral state that, according to the Kincaids, was induced through purposeful trauma of some kind. Fresh out of that, she was in fight-or-flight mode. She just picked *fight* at every opportunity, and while that was endearing, it could be dangerous.

Puppy could flay open an asshole who tried to put his hands on Sidian or leered at Amey, but she sort of needed to leave their neighbors alone.

And what the fuck was she thinking, wandering over there in the middle of the night?

"Probably wasn't thinking fucking anything," Sidian muttered just as he reached the edge of the road that would let him see across the way to the other house. "Just wandered on over and... What the fuck is she *doing* over there?"

Unless Sidian was insane, it looked very much like Puppy had decided their neighbors' driveway was the perfect place to act out a horror film in the middle of the night.

He watched as she bent herself backward, hands outstretched to keep her balance because of course she was doing it on purpose. It was almost comical just how fast the poor person at the door all but slammed it shut when she twisted around; Sidian swore he could almost see the flicker of confusion that flashed in her eyes every time one of her disturbing actions disturbed someone. When she got around to talking again, he planned to ask her what was going through her head every time she acted like something straight out of a nightmare.

He jogged across the empty road, glancing both ways though he knew he would have heard any approaching cars long before he saw them, and hissed at her. "*Puppy*. The fuck are you doing?"

She ignored him and darted toward the front porch. Was she going to break into the house? Why do that? What was she doing? Did she think this was the way to introduce herself to someone they were living across from? If the person she'd freaked out started spreading rumors about some forest demon skulking around his house, it would be never-ending.

Sidian scrubbed his hands over his face as he walked up the driveway toward the porch. Fine. He could hopefully explain to their neighbor who Puppy was and why she was acting the way she was, and of course, he would have to lie and assure the person that she was harmless. Like fuck anyone would believe that after her contortionist stunt, but it was what had to be said.

If contacts for ferals were not illegal, he would have found something dark or neutral enough to cover up her eyes. Convincing anyone she was harmless was hard enough without having that used against her.

The door swung open again, and everything happened fast.

Puppy's hand flew up and hit something that flashed metallic a moment before an ear-splitting *crack* sounded through the night. The very edge of the porch roof exploded in a shower of splinters, and Sidian swore as he took a few steps back. Oh shit. They had a gun.

"Puppy!" He shouted her name then, and she looked at him, her expression serene as she darted past the open door to his side. "What the fuck are you doing out here?"

She cocked her head at him like that was a ridiculous question to ask.

The person at the door stepped out onto the porch and leveled a shotgun at them, holding it with steady hands. Looked like a guy from where Sidian was standing, not as built as Roman but damn was he close. "Who are you two, and what are you doing on my property?"

It was not surprising that someone living out in the woods had a gun and was not afraid to brandish it like that. But Sidian had been threatened with far worse, and as soon as the guy clocked Sidian was an omega, he'd see sense. "We just moved in across the road. Sorry about her. She's been through a lot, so she acts like a freak sometimes for no reason."

Puppy huffed at him, giving the side of his shoe a light kick.

"For no reason?" The man deadpanned, and Sidian bit back a chuckle. "She's a feral alpha. Somehow, I don't think it's for no reason."

"Her eyes are fucked up, but she's back to normal. She was just feral for a long time, so it's going to take her a long time to recover. And she wasn't living around *people* when she was feral." For obvious reasons, he did not count Pack Kincaid as people.

The man lowered the gun slightly. "So she's not dangerous? Why's she creeping around then?"

"I don't know," Sidian said, and the man just stared at him. "I'm serious. I don't know. She was feral for a long time, so she doesn't speak so much as she makes noises we approximate. I didn't even realize she'd left the house until I went to tell her goodnight before going to bed."

"She pack?" the man asked, lowering the gun further.

"In a platonic sense. She's not part of my mate pack." At least, Sidian hoped she considered herself pack if for no reason other than he didn't want her to argue with him in front of this stranger.

"I see." The gun lowered the rest of the way, and the man sighed, combing a hand through the soft-looking fluff of his short black hair. "You, uh, should put a bell on her or something. I heard her creeping around the house and almost had a heart attack. I thought someone was trying to break in."

Out of the corner of his eye, Sidian thought he saw Puppy roll both of hers. "She wouldn't do something like that, and she's *sorry* for the record. Hell of a way to meet your new neighbors, huh?"

"Seems like it." After a moment, the man set the shotgun on the porch, leaning it against the wall next to the door before he cleared his throat a little and took a couple of steps toward them. His gaze was nervous as it shifted to Puppy, but she relaxed her body for his comfort. "I'm Valentine D'Arlowe. Val's fine, though. My entire pack lives here."

He offered a hand to shake when he reached them, but another chilly breeze scattered the dead leaves across the gravel driveway and carried a scent to Sidian's nose that nearly brought him to his knees.

When he'd been a child and still thought his family life might better itself one day, he used to fantasize about family trips to the beach. His and Roman's hometown wasn't too far from the coast, and had his parents given a damn, they would have been able to make the drive. If they had gone early, it could have been a day trip, and they would have been home by nightfall. Instead, he'd never gotten to see the ocean or feel the sand between his toes. The closest he came were the beach-scented candles that always smelled more like soap than he imagined the ocean would.

Val's scent burned in the way Sidian used to imagine that sand would beneath bare feet when the sun was high in a cloudless blue sky. There was a delicious salty quality to his scent, a briny sting that made Sidian's mouth water for a taste, overlaid atop a woody, earthy scent that he thought might have been driftwood. Val smelled like Sidian used to dream the ocean would, and it made his omega sit up and take notice when that should not have been a thing that was possible.

Puppy tilted her head and made a noise at him, a question in her current attempt at language.

"Holy shit." Sidian fanned a hand in front of his face, though that did little to quell the heat that raged in his gut. The last time he'd responded to a scent like that, it had been…

It had been Roman's scent.

Fuck. That's a problem.

Val took a step closer before his body went rigid, his lips parted just as a sound of faint confusion rasped its way out of his throat. No doubt he was close enough to pick up Sidian's scent as well, which meant that if Sidian was correct in what he assumed was happening... Then he was in trouble, and so was Val, and there was not supposed to be anymore trouble.

This was supposed to be the start of the actual happy ending that Sidian deserved with his *mate,* the one who was sleeping next to their daughter. Not a complete stranger, whose name he had just learned and who had nearly shot his brand new pack sister.

Before he could think of something intelligent to say, soft footsteps caught his attention, and a tousled-looking man stepped out onto the front porch, smothering a yawn against the palm of his hand. "Val? What the fuck are you doing out here? Are there *people* here?"

A faint flicker of emotion caught Sidian's attention, uncertainty that twisted its way into concern; he sighed and pinched the bridge of his nose, squeezing his eyes shut.

How would Roman handle Sidian having a *second* alpha mate?

Acknowledgements

Thank you to Church and Angel, my two cats. None of this would ever be possible without you, and every night when I go to work, I long to be at home with you or to bring you with me.

Thank you to my best friend, Amanda, who suffered the process of what this novel became and who was there for me every step of the way.

Thank you to my editor, Tabitha, for putting up with me and the deadline shifting.

Thank you to my ARC readers, as always, for offering support and excitement before this novel releases.

And the biggest thank you to Evan Jennings, whose work inspired Obsidian Vey.

About Acacia Lockwood

Acacia Lockwood is an omegaverse romance fiction author whose work is inspired by [redacted].

Further information about them has been classified as a cognitohazard and requires a higher level of clearance.

If you are interested in applying for a higher level of clearance, consider signing up for their newsletter: